LISA
JACKSON

THE NIGHT BEFORE

HODDER

First published in 2003 by Kensington Books Corp.
First published in 2013 by Hodder & Stoughton
An Hachette UK company

First published in paperback in 2013 by Hodder & Stoughton

1

A CIP catalogue record for this title is available from the British Library

ISBN 978 1 444 78023 9
E-book ISBN 978 1 444 78025 3

Printed and bound by CPI Group (UK) Ltd, Croydon, CR0 4YY

Hodder & Stoughton policy is to use papers that are natural, renewable and
recyclable products and made from wood grown in sustainable forests. The
logging and manufacturing processes are expected to conform to the
environmental regulations of the country of origin.

Prologue

Help me!

His head was thick, his mind muddled.

His eyes swam.

He couldn't move.

His thoughts were disjointed and jumbled. Out of sync.

Something was wrong . . . horribly wrong.

If only he could think. If only he could concentrate beyond the pain slicing like razors in his brain.

I'm dying. Please, someone help me.

He tried to force the words, but his tongue wouldn't work and he couldn't make more than a hideous mewling sound as he lay slumped over his desk . . . at least he thought it was his desk. Blinking with difficulty, he tried to focus, but there was little light and the darkened images were blurry, as if he were looking at the world through a foggy wide-angle lens.

How had he gotten here?

He couldn't remember, but he sensed that he'd just woken up. . . .

No . . . that wasn't right . . . he'd come in here to do some paperwork . . . yes . . . and then . . . *and then what?*

Caitlyn. This was about Caitlyn and the divorce! But why couldn't he move his hand? Or his leg? Or . . . or any damned part of him? Panic surged through him. He tried harder. Not one muscle budged. *Jesus H. Christ, what was happening?*

Music was playing. Soft classical. Baroque. Something he didn't recognize oozing through the hidden speakers surrounding the room.

What the hell was going on?

Concentrate. Pull yourself together. Don't panic. You're in the den at your house in Savannah . . . at the desk and the phone is on the corner of the desk where it always is . . .

So why the hell can't I fucking move?

Alarm tore through him and yet he felt a great lethargy, as if he might succumb to the darkness playing at the edges of his eyesight. Sweat beaded on his brow, but he couldn't lift a hand to wipe the drops away. Behind him, he heard a footstep . . . or thought he did. Good. Someone was here to help him.

Or . . . not.

The hairs on the back of his neck rose. Adrenalin pumped wildly through his bloodstream.

Try as he might, he couldn't turn his head. Why? Was he sick? Drugged? Dreaming? Nausea gripped his stomach. How did he get this way? What had he done? Who the hell was behind him?

No one. There's no one there. No one evil, *for Christ's sake. You're freaking out. Get ahold of yourself!* The phone! If he could just reach the telephone and dial 911 . . . But his arm wouldn't move. His muscles were heavy . . . unresponsive.

"Josh?"

His heart jolted but his body didn't move.

The voice was hushed. Disguised? Or was that his imagination?

Again he strained to turn his head.

Again he failed.

"Josh? Can you hear me?" Soft. Seductive. And deadly.

Someone was calling to him. Maybe someone had come

to help, to rescue him. But his hopes died instantly. If someone was going to help him, they would have rushed over. The whole situation was too damned weird. If someone truly was with him and not a figment of his imagination, then it was an enemy who had found him.

God help me.

Cool fingers touched his wrist. Inwardly he jumped. Outwardly he didn't move.

Who the hell was touching him, rubbing the inside of his arm? Checking for his pulse? Did he look dead? He couldn't turn his head, couldn't raise it off the desk to twist his neck and see who was tending to him just out of focus in his peripheral vision. A doctor? Oh, please, God.

Suddenly an intense light was flashed into his eyes, as if someone was examining him, checking for dilation. Desperately he attempted to make out an image, to see around the brilliance burning its way into his brain, hoping to catch a glimpse of whoever was holding the penlight. But there was no visage, just a foggy image of fingers encased in examination gloves and the faint tinge of cigarette smoke.

For God's sake, quit creeping me out and get me to the hospital!

The penlight clicked off. Darkness surrounded him, and his vision was worse than ever. Bright rings of illumination still seared through his brain. He slumped lower on the top of the desk and an empty glass toppled, falling onto its side and rolling off the desk to land on the carpet with a soft thud. The cool fingers massaging his wrist didn't stop, but he could barely feel them, hardly stay awake.

I'm alive, you idiot, can't you see that? Get me to a hospital! But the words were lodged in his throat; he couldn't force them out, couldn't make his tongue work. The only sounds were the ticking of the clock in the foyer, the whisper of the wind blowing through the French doors he'd left ajar and the beating of his heart. But instead of wild and frantic, his heart was as sluggish as his head, not jackhammering in fear as he would have expected. Maybe this was a dream after all. It was all so surreal. As if in slow motion.

He noticed that his shirt sleeve was being pushed up his forearm by those gloved fingers. Higher the linen rode, exposing more of his arm. What the hell? Rolling his eyes backward, he hoped to make out whoever was with him, but he saw only shadows and movement, a dark figure and . . . a glint of something. Steel.

Oh, God.

The blades were razor thin. Two of them. Scissors. *Surgical scissors?* But . . . but . . . Fear jetted through his bloodstream. Desperately he tried to move his arm. His feet. Any damned part of him, but he couldn't wriggle away, was forced to lie with his head on the desk to await his doom.

And doom came in the form of a shadowy figure with scissors.

This was crazy. Who was this person? What was with the scissors? Nothing good.

He heard a clip and saw a button fly off his cuff.

He nearly soiled himself.

His shirt sleeve was pushed higher, exposing his arm, his bare arm. He saw his white flesh, caught the glint of the blade.

Snip!

His heart nearly gave out.

The scissors neatly clipped a single hair from his forearm.

He jumped. But only on the inside. His nerves were flashing, but not connecting. He couldn't pull his arm away, could only watch as the scissors moved closer to the veins and arteries that webbed just beneath the skin. A part of him didn't care. Another part of him was silently screaming in panic.

"You know who I am, don't you?"

The voice was so familiar. Obscenely provocative.

He couldn't speak.

"You can think of me as Atropos."

Atropos? What the hell?

"Oh. That's right. You probably don't know about the three fates, do you? In mythology, there were three women who determined your fate. The daughters of Zeus were called the Moirai. Three sisters who determined a man's destiny.''

Mythology? What the hell? The scissors winked in the light from the desk lamp. He shivered inside.

''There's Klotho, of course. She's the youngest and she spins the thread of life while the middle sister Lachesis is the measurer. She selects one's lot in life and determines how long that life will be.''

The scissors came closer, their sharp point touching the skin beneath his eye.

He tried to flinch but remained as if cemented to the desk.

''Then there is Atropos. The strongest. Who actually ends the life by snipping that precious thread.'' She clicked the scissors. ''The name I chose.''

What? No!

Snip!

The scissors bit at the flesh of his cheek, touching his eyelashes.

He felt nothing. No pain.

She held up his bare wrist.

Clip!

The first welling drops of red blood rose to the surface.

Oh, God, no! Desperately he tried to jerk away. Succeeded only in grunting. Couldn't even cringe as the evil weapon took another nasty little bite, blood smearing the blade, fear jolting through him as he realized that the person he couldn't see was determined to slowly and methodically kill him.

This couldn't be happening! It had to be a dream. A nightmare. What demented person would do this? Oh, God . . . blood was flowing freely now, down his wrist and into his palm, running down his fingers to pool on the desk. *Stop! For God's sake, stop!*

Maybe this was just to scare him, maybe he wasn't going to die. Maybe someone was just making a cruel point. God knew there were enough people in this town who wanted him dead.

But a gunshot to the head would have done the trick.

Or a pill slipped into his drink.

Or a knife in his damned heart.

Unless his would-be killer was enjoying this . . . that it wasn't so much his death as his dying that mattered. Unless the sick bitch got off on the knowledge that he was helpless as he watched his own lifeblood trickle and spurt from his body. Gasping, realizing that he would slowly bleed to death, Josh moved his eyes to the glass humidor located on one corner of his desk. In the smooth, curved surface he saw his own pale reflection and just the hint of a figure, grotesque in the distorted glass, leaning over him.

For a second, his eyes locked with those of his attacker. He saw the face of his killer. A suggestion of a smile, the hint of satisfaction curved his murderer's lips.

All hope fled.

He recognized the warped face, and he realized with heart-stopping clarity that he was condemned to watch himself slowly bleed to death.

One

Pain thundered through her head. As if a thousand horses were stampeding through her brain. Her tongue was thick and a bad taste lingered in her mouth and there was something more . . . something bad, a sensation of oppression that seemed to pin her to her bed. Her heart was pounding wildly, her skin soaked in sweat, faint images of her dream . . . of Josh . . . of walking up the brick path to his house cut through her consciousness.

Her shoes crunched against dry leaves. The wind rattled through the branches of the oaks, billowing the Spanish moss. Somewhere nearby a dog barked and the smell of cigar smoke hung in the air. *You shouldn't be here. Go, run!* Up the steps to the brick house that used to be her home. The door was cracked. A slice of light spilled onto the front porch. An invitation in a dark, sultry night. *Don't do it. Don't go inside!*

Dear God, what did I do last night? Caitlyn opened one bleary eye just a slit. She was so thirsty . . . and her entire body ached. Too much alcohol . . . Way too much. She was in her bedroom. The ceiling fan whirred overhead as dawn began to filter past the curtains. Images of the night before were hazy and out of sequence. She'd gone out to meet her sister . . . yes, that was it because . . . she needed to get out, to unwind.

Yesterday was Jamie's birthday.

Eerily, as if a dozen children were singing off key, she heard,

"Happy birthday to you
Happy birthday to you
Happy birthday dear Ja-mie—"

Caitlyn's heart squeezed. Her daughter would have been five.

If she had lived.

She closed her eyes again as raw pain tore through her. *Jamie. Precious, precious baby.* Snatched away when she was barely three—a cherub-faced toddler. Oh, Lord, Caitlyn missed her child. So bad that at times she found it impossible to move forward, go on with her life. Now, on the bed, squeezing her eyes against the truth, she felt the familiar ache of the loss, so deep it scratched at her soul.

"It was your fault, Caitlyn. If you'd been half a mother, this never would have happened!"

Josh's accusations tore through her brain bringing the guilt, the ever-present sense that she should have done more, that if she'd tried harder she would have somehow saved her child.

Don't even think about it. Don't listen to him, and for God's sake don't believe his poison! You know you did all you could to save her.

She let out her breath slowly, breathed deeply again, remembered what Dr. Wade had said about letting go of the negative energy, of finding herself, her new purpose. Slowly the grief subsided to a small, dark ache that lay just beneath her headache.

Man, it was a monster. She must've really tied one on.

Another sharp image sizzled through her brain.

Josh was in his den, but he wasn't moving. No. He was slumped over his desk, his arms at his sides, his neck twisted so that he faced the door. Blood had oozed from his arms, staining the carpet. His mouth gaping open, his skin pale, his eyes unblinking as they stared at her.

She sat bolt upright. God, what kind of a dream was that? Her heart slammed against her chest. Pieces of the nightmare slid through her brain only to disappear.

"Oh, God, oh, God, oh, God!"

Slow down, Caitlyn. Breathe deep. It was only a dream. Don't fall apart!

Desperately she gulped air. Remembered all the techniques she'd learned in therapy, forced herself to rein in her galloping emotions. "Never again," she vowed. Whatever it was she'd drunk last night, she would never take as much as one sip again . . . but what was it? She blinked. Tried to remember. But nothing came except the brittle, jagged pieces of the nightmare.

"Jesus," she whispered. Once again, she'd lost track of time, hours of her life missing. She didn't even remember how she'd gotten home. An inkling that something was very, very wrong slithered through her consciousness. She couldn't name it, but the sensation was strong enough to cause her skin to prickle.

You had a bad dream. That's all. Get over it. She drew in another long breath. She was in her own bed. Home. Safe.

With a mother of a migraine. Her head throbbed. Her throat ached, and she smelled smoke in her hair from sitting too many hours in the bar. Oh, God, she'd really overdone it last night. She winced against the first rays of the new morning as dawn crept through the open window. A jasmine-scented breeze carried with it the sounds of fresh rainwater gurgling in the gutters. The French doors were slightly ajar, and the lacy curtains lifted and fluttered, shadowed in places, darkened and stained.

Why was the door open? Had she opened it last night before crawling into bed because of the heat? Images of the nightmare stabbed into her consciousness, mingling with blurred memories from the night before. She'd had a few drinks at a bar . . . somewhere on the waterfront. Or was that part of the disjointed dream, too? She remembered the noise of the band, and she could still smell the cloud of old cigarette smoke that had hung over the crowd. She'd drunk a little too much—well, a lot too much, but she'd managed to get home. Somehow. But that part was blank.

The headache no amount of Excedrin would be able to quell throbbed behind one eye and she felt groggy, disconnected, as she glanced at the clock. Red digital numbers flashed. Twelve o'clock. Midnight? Noon? No way. Birds were just beginning to warble. It had to be early. Five or six. A god-awful time to wake up. The power must've been interrupted. It was the dream that had awoken her, the ragged, disjointed scenes screaming through her brain.

Her mouth tasted bad. Dry as cotton. Her stomach felt empty, as if she'd lost its contents sometime during the night. Swiping a hand over her sweaty forehead, she brushed back a clump of damp curls and felt something crusty. Her fingers were dirty or . . . or . . . What the devil was that smell? For a second she thought she might have thrown up, but the odor was metallic rather than sour and . . . and . . . oh, God . . . She held her hand in front of her face and saw the stains that had run down her arm. Dark purple. Thick and crusty, having seeped from the slices on the wrists.

What?

Blinking hard, she pushed herself up in the bed, higher against the pillows. Panic swelled. She fumbled for the light switch. *Click.* In a blinding burst of light, she saw the blood.

Pooled on the sheets.

Scraped across the headboard.

Wiped on the curtains.

Smeared on the walls.

*Every*where.

"No . . . oh, God, no!" Caitlyn bolted from the bed, her legs tangled in her nightgown and she fell face first on the apricot-colored carpet now stained red. "Jesus!" Dear God, what *was* this? She scuttled like a crab over the crusty carpet. It looked as if someone, or something, had been slaughtered in this fifteen by twelve-foot room. *And you slept through it!*

Her heart froze as she saw a handprint on the door casing, another wiped on the panels. She had to fight the nausea that climbed up her throat. Scared out of her wits, she scrambled to the bathroom.

Whose blood is this?

Yours. Look at you!

Her gaze landed on the mirror over the sink. Red stains smudged her face where her hands had swiped her skin, and her nostrils were caked with blood. Her hair was matted and wild. Had she just had a horrid nosebleed, like the ones she'd had as a child and somehow managed to sleep through? No . . . that wouldn't explain the nicks on her wrists. Nor the blood smeared everywhere in the room.

She remembered the open door . . . Had someone done this to her? Fear knotted her stomach. Oh, God . . . but why? *Who?* She was beginning to hyperventilate but forced herself to calm down. The blood wasn't all hers. It couldn't be. She was alive. Anyone who had lost this much would certainly be dead. No one could have survived such a massacre.

She leaned against the sink and tried to think. She *did* feel woozy, lightheaded, her migraine eating away at her brain.

Oh, God, what if the person who did this is still in the house?

No, that didn't make sense. If someone had tried to kill her, he would have finished the job. The blood in her hair, on the walls, in the shower had dried. Time had gone by. So he was either scared off or took off.

Or you did it and left the door open.

No . . . But she couldn't remember, didn't know.

If the blood isn't yours, whose is it?

"I don't know," she whispered.

Maybe the victim is still in the house.

She glanced at the shower; the frosted glass was cracked, a bloody handprint visible.

God help me.

Steeling herself, she placed her hand on the glass. She half expected to find a dead body, eyes rolled to the ceiling, tongue lolling, red stains running into the drain. Nervously, she pushed the door open.

No one jumped out at her.

No half-dead body was sprawled over the shower floor.

Dried blood was splattered and ran down the tiles in ragged rivulets. She felt her stomach turn. What had happened here? What? Her whole body was shaking as she raised her hand and found that it was the same size as the print on the shower door.

"Mother of God," she whispered. *Think, Caitlyn, think. Don't panic.*

She caught a glimpse of herself in the mirror again.

How had this happened? Where had she been? Whose blood was smeared everywhere? Her knees gave way. She caught herself on the edge of the sink and leaned forward to splash cold water over her face to keep herself from passing out.

Maybe you're not alone. Maybe even now there's someone with you, someone downstairs. Someone waiting. She looked up quickly at her reflection. White skin, wild hair sticking up at odd angles, panic in her hazel eyes. *The door to the verandah was left open and you don't remember doing it.* Her gaze moved and in the mirror she saw an image of the door ajar, the curtains billowing and stained. She thought she might be sick.

Had some killer come in and she, suffering one of her black-out headaches, not heard him invade her home? But— there was no body. Nothing but her own hacked wrists and bloody nose . . . no one would come here to slice up someone and take away the body . . . no. Her head was pounding, leaping with wild ideas.

If someone else had even stepped into the house, why hadn't the alarm gone off?

The door to the verandah isn't latched, you idiot. Obviously the alarm wasn't set.

She leaned a hip against the counter and closed her eyes. This made no sense. None. And it scared the hell out of her.

Maybe you invited someone in. But who? And why? And

if it was an intruder . . . why hadn't Oscar barked so loudly the entire neighborhood had woken up?

Oscar!

Where was he?

Scared to death, she took another horrified look at the stains on the floor. Not the dog . . . not Oscar! Swallowing back her fear, she mopped her face with the sleeve of her stained nightgown and started for the staircase. She gave a low whistle.

Nothing.

Her throat tightened.

You'd better grab a weapon. Just in case.

She didn't keep a gun in the house, didn't believe in it. Biting her lip, she grabbed a small dumbbell, one she used when working out while watching television, then inched into the hallway.

Ears straining over the frantic beat of her heart, she listened as she moved. The house was still. Quiet. As if all were safe.

Pull yourself together. Do it, Caitlyn. Don't let fear paralyze you! Her fingers tightened over her weapon as she peered into the hall bath. It was empty.

Nervous sweat slick on her body, she slowly eased open the door to one of the other bedrooms and her heart tugged as it always did as she looked into the space that had been her daughter's. Jamie's favorite stuffed animal, a droopy-eared bunny was propped against the pillows of a double bed covered with a quilt hand-stitched in soft pastels. Luminescent stars and clouds that she had painted for Jamie still covered the ceiling. But the room was empty and, she thought sadly, was starting to smell musty and stale, reminding her that her baby was gone.

"Happy birthday dear Ja-mie . . ." The discordant children's voices blared in her head.

Don't go there. Not now.

Her sweaty fingers tightened around the weight. Nervously she eased into her den with its drafting table and computer desk, just as she'd left it. Her desk, drafting table, computer all stood silent, the desk slightly cluttered. But no one was hiding in the corners or behind the closet doors. Turning, she spied a figure in the darkness. No! She gasped, before realizing it was her own reflection staring back at her from the full-length mirror she'd hung on the door.

She nearly collapsed.

Come on, Caitlyn. Toughen up!

Silently she edged down the stairs, the fingers of her left hand trailing along the banister, her right fist coiled tightly over the weight. But no dark figure wielding a knife or gun leaped out of the dining alcove at her as she stepped onto the second riser. No gunshot blasted through the house. No—

She heard a quick, loud scrape.

The sole of a leather boot on hardwood?

She froze.

Over the mad drumming of her heart, she heard the hum of the refrigerator, the ticking of the hall clock. She wanted to call out to the dog, but decided to wait. But she forced herself to inch forward, her gaze sweeping the rooms. The living room was just as she'd left it, still smelling of the roses she'd cut and placed in the vase on the coffee table. No trace of blood.

She began to calm. The house felt empty. She checked the laundry room and kitchen, where morning light was beginning to filter through the windows, and the dining alcove with its view of the back courtyard. Everything was in its place.

Eerily so.

Except it looks like Charles Manson held a party in your bedroom while you were sleeping.

She heard a sharp bark.

Oscar!

She saw him through the bay window, a scruffy mutt scratching at the back door. She nearly collapsed in relief. "How did you get out here?" Caitlyn scolded kindly as the scrappy terrier-mix stood on his hind legs and pawed frantically at the glass. The sound she'd heard. She unlatched the door and he flew into her arms. Ruffling his coarse mottled fur, she wondered if she'd left him out by mistake. Had she come home, let the dog out, then, because she'd had one or two too many Cosmopolitans, wandered upstairs and forgotten him?

Why would you do that? Just so you could hack away at your wrists and suffer the worst nosebleed you've had in five years? You know, Caitlyn, Kelly might be right. You might just be losing it. Big time.

"What happened last night?" she asked the little dog as she set him on the floor, then opened a can of dog food and scraped the contents into his bowl while he turned in quick tight circles. "You're not half as glad to see me as I am to see you," she assured him as she set his bowl on the floor. Tail whipping frantically, he plunged his nose into the dish and ignored the fact that she patted him on his head. He'd been Jamie's dog, named after her favorite *Sesame Street* character, Oscar the Grouch, for his rumpled fur. "See . . . we're okay," she said, but had trouble believing it herself.

The smell of the dog food made her stomach quiver. She rocked back on her heels. What the hell had she done last night? Where had all the blood come from? Her bedroom looked as if something or someone had been diced to ribbons there. But she remembered nothing after going to the bar— what was the name of it? The Swamp. Yeah, The Swamp. She'd sat in a booth for a long time waiting for her twin sister, Kelly, to show up.

She'd noticed the bartender staring at her from time to time. Probably because he thought it odd that she'd ordered two drinks—a Cosmo for her and a dry martini for Kelly, which, if she remembered correctly, she'd swilled down when Kelly had pulled one of her usual disappearing acts.

But aside from tackling both stemmed glasses and sucking the pimento out of three olives before chewing them, she remembered very little. Too little.

It had been noisy . . . loud hip-hop music at odds with the conversation and laughter and . . .

Like a razor slicing through flesh, a quicksilver image

passed through her mind. She was in the foyer of the house she'd decorated—the paintings of thoroughbreds adorned the walls, the grandfather clock stood guard at the foot of the stairs. The heels of her shoes tapped across the marble as she crossed to the open door of the den. The sound of classical music lured her to open the door and find her estranged husband looking up at her with sightless eyes, blood pooling beneath his desk chair.

Caitlyn gasped. Why would she think of Josh now? The image of his white, lifeless face flashed in front of her eyes again. Why would she envision him dead?

Because it was your daughter's birthday yesterday.

Because the bastard was divorcing you.

And because he was going to sue you for wrongful death. Of your child. Your baby. "Stop it!" She'd had a dream. No big deal. No harm done. She grabbed a bottle of water from the refrigerator, twisted it open and drank half of it down only to feel it coming back up again. Fast. She doubled over the sink.

She threw up. Over and over. Until the dry heaves took over and she was wringing wet with sweat.

You should call your shrink. You're losing it!

But she couldn't. Dr. Wade had moved recently. So Caitlyn was fresh out of psychiatric help. Great. She hadn't bothered trying to find another therapist. Didn't want one.

Until now.

Then the police. Call them.

Why? Because I had a nosebleed? Because I might have . . . in my drunken state . . . tried to slash my wrists?

Again. You might have tried again, that nagging voice in her brain reminded her.

If I call the cops, they'll haul me away. To the psych ward.

Maybe that's where you belong.

"No!" She glanced down at her arms and frowned. That other incident was a long time ago.

That "other incident" nearly cost you your life.

She didn't want to think of that. Not now.

First things first. She had to pull herself together. Calm down. Get a major grip. She needed to make sure the house was locked, then clean herself up and tackle the mess upstairs. But first she'd call Kelly. Find out what had happened.

Maybe the blood upstairs is hers.

A new fear gripped Caitlyn, and she frantically punched out the numbers to Kelly's cabin at the river, her "hideaway," as she called it. The phone rang. Once. Twice. "Come on, come on. Pick up!" The phone jangled a third time. Caitlyn leaned against the counter and willed her twin to answer. A fourth ring and then a distinctive click. "Hi–you reached me, but I'm not here. Leave your number!" She heard a flat beep as the recorder clicked on.

"Kelly? Kelly? Are you there? If you are, pick up. Now ... it's Caitlyn ... I need to talk to you. I mean, I really need to talk to you ... about last night. Please, call me back ASAP." She hung up slowly and tried not to panic. With a trembling hand, she pushed the hair from her eyes. Was Kelly going out of town again? She had a business trip planned, but when?

Caitlyn's heart was racing. Faster and faster. *Think, Caitlyn, think!*

Kelly's cell phone! She dialed, then waited, silently counting the rings as she prayed her sister would pick up. One. Two. Three. Oh, no. "Please answer." Voice mail picked up. "You've reached Kelly's cell. Leave a message."

Great!

Just calm down. The answering machine beeped. "Kelly, it's Caitlyn. Give me a call. It's important." She hung up and considered driving out to her sister's cabin. But what good would that do? What good at all? If Kelly was around, she'd call back.

Or would she?

Sometimes Caitlyn wasn't sure.

Two

"Who the hell is Josh Bandeaux?" Pierce Reed asked.

Sylvie Morrisette, his partner, was speeding along East Bay Street as if they were in the Grand-damned-Prix. "You mean besides being a major prick?" Her eyes hidden behind wrap-around shades, Morrisette slid a glance his way.

"Yeah, besides that."

She sighed through her nose. "Sometimes I forget what a greenhorn you really are. Cute, but a greenhorn." With her spiked blond hair, athletic body and sharp tongue, Sylvie was as tough as her snakeskin boots and as prickly as a saguaro cactus. From the moment Reed had been paired up with her, he'd won looks of condolence from the other men in the department. "Lived your life in a goddamned vacuum," she added in her West Texas drawl. A transplant from El Paso, she had fifteen years on the Savannah police force. To his six months. Aside from a short stint here twelve years earlier, Reed had spent most of his adult life on the West Coast, most recently San Francisco. He'd left San Francisco on bad terms, but managed to land a senior detective position here. If Sylvie resented his status, she had the good sense not to show it.

Lights flashing, tires squealing, she took a corner too fast and nearly swung into the oncoming lane.

"Hey, let's get there in one piece."

"We will." She managed to keep the cruiser on the pavement as the driver of a new pickup passed and looked about to flip them off when he realized he was dealing with cops and kept his middle finger from springing to attention.

"So fill me in."

"He's just one of the wealthiest son of a bitches in the city, maybe even the state. Grew up with a silver spoon wedged between his gorgeous Georgian teeth and married into more money. Big-time gambler. Made and lost fortunes but always came out of each thorny deal smelling like a damned rose."

"Until last night," Reed reminded her.

"Yeah. Last night I guess his luck ran out." She blasted her way through a red light. "Dead at forty-two. Possible suicide." She couldn't keep the sarcasm from her voice.

"But you don't buy it."

"No way, José. I had the misfortune to meet the prick a couple of times. He donated money to the department. Any charity we hosted, he was certain to show up in an Armani suit with a big check in hand." Her lips twisted downward. "Then he'd have a few drinks and the next thing you knew he'd be pinching some cutie's ass. A real charmer, our Josh." She smiled without a hint of humor and floored it through the next yellow light. "The fact that he was married didn't stop him from making a pass at anything in a skirt."

"The wife find his body?"

"No, they're separated. Shit!" She braked hard, then swerved around a delivery truck double-parked. "Asshole!"

"So Bandeaux wasn't divorced?"

"Not quite. Now I guess he won't ever be." She cranked on the wheel and the cruiser flew down an alley, barely missing a Dumpster and sending papers that hadn't quite made it into the bin flying. With a bump they were on another side street and careening into the heart of the historic district. "Think of all the money Caitlyn Bandeaux will save on lawyer's fees. Not that she needs to worry."

"You said she was wealthy."

"Beyond wealthy. She's a Montgomery, as in Montgomery Bank and Trust, Montgomery Cotton, Montgomery Estates, Montgomery-every-damned thing. Some distant descendent from a Civil War hero, I think. At least that's what her granddaddy, Old Benedict Montgomery, claimed before he died."

"Shit." Even he'd heard of *those* Montgomerys.

"Exactly."

Reed made a quick mental note as the cruiser tore through the city streets. Estranged wives were always suspects. Even wealthy ones. "She live nearby?"

"Not far."

Convenient.

"Any kids?" he asked.

"One. Dead. Died a couple of years back. Only three or four years old, I think. It was bad." Sylvie scowled as the police band crackled. "From what I hear, Caitlyn, that's Bandeaux's wife, nearly went around the bend when the kid died. Josh blamed her and maybe she did herself. I even heard a rumor that she tried to kill herself. Anyway, there's a whole lot of secrets in that family and a whole lot of hush money's been spent to hide 'em. Let me tell you." She snorted derisively.

"You know a lot about the Montgomerys."

"I suppose." Her jaw slid to the side and she checked the rearview mirror.

"A hobby of yours?"

"Not exactly. But I've done my share of research. Bandeaux was always skirting the law. I did a lot of looking into his professional and personal life because there were rumors that he had ties to the mob."

"Did he?"

"I couldn't find any, but I did find out a lot about him."

He waited. She pressed on the lighter and found a crumpled pack of Marlboro Lights on the dash. "You may as well figure this out and fast, Reed. Savannah might look like a big city, but she's a small town at her soul.'' He didn't respond. Had already learned that silence worked best with Morrisette, and he sensed there was more to the story.

He was right.

''Oh, hell, I suppose you're gonna find out anyway.'' With a steely, humorless grin, she said, ''My ex, Bart, worked for Bandeaux for a while.'' Reed had met Bart Yelkis, a tall, brooding man with some Native American in his blood.

Morrisette shook out a cigarette and passed a delivery van in one motion. ''The reason we got divorced?'' Sylvie hesitated a second as the lighter clicked. She cracked the window, then managed to light up, driving with one hand and never slowing for an instant. ''Well, there were tons of 'em. Tons. But the one that everyone believes is that I had an affair with Josh Bandeaux.'' She let out a jet of smoke. ''For the record, it's not true. My taste in men might be lousy, but it's not that lousy.''

Reed didn't comment. Didn't know what to believe. He wasn't good at reading a woman's mind—hell, who was?— but his gut instinct told him that Sylvie-tough-as-snakeskin-Morrisette was stretching the truth. How much he wasn't certain. But it gave him a bad feeling. A real bad feeling.

''Shit.'' Kelly clicked off the recorder after listening to Caitlyn's panicked message. What was it with Caitlyn? She was always getting herself into trouble. Big trouble. And always expecting Kelly to bail her out. God, what a basket case!

Angrily, Kelly hit the replay button and sank into her desk chair as Caitlyn's terrified voice repeated the message.

''Kelly? Kelly? Are you there? If you are pick up. Now . . . it's Caitlyn . . .

Damn it all to hell.

Sighing, Kelly hit the erase button.

I need to talk to you about last night.

''I bet,'' Kelly muttered under her breath. She wasn't

surprised. Nor did it take a brain surgeon to guess that left to her own devices, Caitlyn had gotten herself into another mess. So what else was new?

Suddenly she was cold to the bone, though the temperature was a sweltering ninety-plus. Kelly rubbed her arms as she stared out the window of her little cabin. Sooner or later Caitlyn would end up in the looney bin. Unfortunately, this time, it could be permanent. Kelly couldn't keep saving her. The trouble was, Caitlyn was falling apart. Again. Just like so many of the damned Montgomerys. Like it or not, Kelly realized that a lot of the members of her family weren't playing with full decks . . . not even by half.

The Montgomery curse.

Shoving her hair from her eyes, she walked barefoot across the living area of her cabin to the French doors, which opened to a small deck overlooking the river. Outside the air was hot, cloying, just the way she liked it. She watched an egret glide over the sluggish water near the dock and felt the late-morning sun on her face. Leaning against the railing, she thought about her sister. Her first instinct was to climb into the car and drive like a bat out of hell to Caitlyn's place, to placate her and soothe her as she always did when these situations occurred, but that wouldn't solve the problem. Far from it. What was the psychobabble word they used for it these days? Enabling. That was it. She could try to allay Caitlyn's fears, help her . . . but, truth to tell, she was sick to death of it.

Because Caitlyn was messed up. Always had been. Always would be. Not that Kelly blamed her, she thought, sliding her sunglasses onto her nose to watch a fishing boat move slowly upriver. Caitlyn had been through a lot. Even when they were kids . . . oh, the secrets Kelly knew about her twin. Even Caitlyn didn't realize that Kelly understood the root of her demons; probably better than Caitlyn did herself. Hadn't Kelly warned her about marrying Josh? Only about a million times. But had Caitlyn listened? Oh, noooooo. She'd been in love. So much in love. Trouble was, it had been with a snake.

And Caitlyn had been pregnant to boot.

For a while things had been okay. And then there was the baby. Kelly felt a familiar pang of regret as she conjured up Jamie's impish face. So sad. Leaning against the railing, she watched the egret take off in a spread of snowy wings.

God, Caitlyn had loved that child. Who could blame her? Jamie had been adorable. As beautiful as her mother and as charming as her dad. Kelly scowled down at the dark, slow water as it lapped at the pilings under the dock. She hated to admit it, but Josh could be as tempting as the very devil. And Caitlyn's hasty marriage had been all right for a while—if not perfect, at least tolerable. Even during the separation. Until Jamie had gotten sick . . . Poor baby. Kelly swallowed hard and her eyes burned as she fought tears. Hell, she'd loved that little girl. Almost as much as Caitlyn had. Almost as if the baby had been her own. Probably because she knew she'd never have any children. It just wasn't in the cards. She sniffed and walked back inside to scrounge through her purse looking for a cigarette. No luck. The pack was empty. She tossed it into the trash near her desk and saw a picture of her niece sitting near the phone. Big smile, twinkling blue eyes, chubby hands clasped in front of her as Jamie, at two and a half, sat in the shade of a magnolia tree. Kelly picked up the silver frame and her eyes filled with tears.

Caitlyn had never gotten over Jamie's death, not even with the help of that shrink, Rebecca What's-her-name—Wade, that was it. Dr. Rebecca Wade. Well, she wasn't the only one. Kelly frowned darkly and set the photo back in its resting place. Thinking about Dr. Wade reminded her that Caitlyn, soon after Jamie's death, had almost overdosed on sleeping pills.

On purpose?

With Caitlyn, who knew?

And now Caitlyn was all knotted up about the divorce. From Josh Bandeaux, the lowlife. The man couldn't keep his hands off women. He'd even had the nerve to come on to *her,* his wife's twin, for crying out loud! What was that all about? She and Caitlyn were identical, so what was the thrill in that? Well, the being identical was literally only skin deep. Their personalities were acutely dissimilar. Night to day. Caitlyn was more shy, more intellectual and Kelly the emotional firecracker, the ''party girl.'' Besides, Josh Bandeaux would bed anything that moved.

Kelly glanced at the telephone. Caitlyn had sounded desperate. Whether she wanted to or not, Kelly would have to go over to her twin's home and calm her down. She flopped onto her suede couch and stared at the open door. But she couldn't face it right now. She knew what Caitlyn wanted to discuss. For the moment, she'd let Caitlyn chill. What was there to say about last night? Caitlyn had downed one too many Cosmopolitans—maybe more than one too many.

End of story.

Well, not quite.

But as much as anyone needed to know.

Morrisette crushed out her cigarette and stood on the brakes. The cruiser slid to a stop inches from the police barricade surrounding Bandeaux's house. Several police cars and the crime scene team's van were already parked at odd angles on the street and in the alley. A wrought-iron fence and lush shrubbery encircled a tall brick house with long windows, green shutters and a wide front porch. A couple of uniformed cops were posted outside, yellow crime scene tape roped off the area, and curious neighbors peeked from behind drawn curtains or more blatantly from their own front yards.

Reed was out of the cruiser before Sylvie cut the siren. The outside temperature was soaring, the humidity thick. Sweat prickled Reed's scalp as he pushed open the gate and flashed his badge. Morrisette caught up with him just as a van from one of the local television stations rolled up.

''Vultures at two o'clock,'' she warned.

''Keep 'em out,'' Reed growled to one of the cops as he hitched his chin at the reporter and cameraman spilling from the white vehicle splashed with WKOK's logo.

"You got it." The young cop crossed his arms over his chest, dark eyes severe as they focused on the reporters.

Reed walked through the open front door, eyeing the refurbished old manor. Careful to disturb nothing, he followed the sounds of voices across the marble floor of the foyer, where expensive rugs muffled his footsteps, paintings of ancient thoroughbreds adorned the walls and a sweeping staircase that split at a landing beckoned visitors upstairs. Through an open doorway he spied the den. Reed's gut clenched as he viewed the scene.

The victim, presumably Bandeaux, sat slumped over his desk, his hands dangling at his sides, blood pooled on the thick white carpet in a dark puddle. A gloved officer was gingerly picking up what appeared to be a pocketknife found directly under the victim's right hand. The blade was dark with dried blood.

"Jesus H. Christ," Morrisette whispered.

The criminologists had done a quick walk-through, taking notes while photographers and videographers had taken pictures, an artist had sketched the scene, preserving it for later examination and, if Bandeaux's death proved to be because of foul play, for use in court. Provided they caught the guy. Now the members of the team with their kits and tools were setting up for a more intense search and evidence gathering.

"He slit his wrists?" Reed asked. Using his pen, he carefully pushed Bandeaux's sleeve up his arm to reveal the ugly slashes on the inside of one arm.

Morrisette visibly paled.

"Looks that way to me, but I ain't the coroner," a photographer said. Reed glanced around the room, noting that the door to the verandah was open, the shades drawn, the carpet showing tracks from a recent vacuuming.

"You're still not buying the suicide?" Reed asked Morrisette, and she slowly shook her head. Her lips were rolled over her teeth and she clicked her tongue. "I just don't think it was Bandeaux's style," she said as the M.E. arrived.

Gerard St. Claire was brusque, short and balding. Pushing seventy, he was still fit and shaved what was left of his white hair about half an inch from his scalp, so that he had what Sylvie had referred to as the "high-fashion toothbrush look." He smelled faintly of cigarettes and formaldehyde and was all business. "Nothing's been disturbed?" he asked as he always did.

"Nothing. We were waitin' on you," Diane Moses responded automatically. The same words passed between them at every scene. Forced to work together, they kept things professional, but their personalities were oil and water. "We've just done the preliminary walk-through to get a feel for the scene. Once you do your thing, we'll tear the place apart." She was being sarcastic, as usual. As the lead crime scene investigator, she was in charge and she knew it. Black, bossy and smart as a whip, she didn't believe in handling anyone with kid gloves. Not even St. Claire. He glared at her through rimless glasses and she glared right back. "At first glance it looks like a suicide."

"No way." Sylvie still wasn't convinced, even with the evidence coagulating on the thick nap. She shoved her sunglasses onto her head, making the spikes even more pronounced.

"Maybe he had financial worries," Reed suggested. "We already know that his marriage was on the rocks."

"Bandeaux loved himself too much to slice and dice himself," Sylvie insisted as she threw the deceased a final glance. "I did research on this guy, remember? Handsome bastard, wasn't he?" She sighed as she took in Josh Bandeaux's strong chin, high forehead and sightless brown eyes. "A shame."

"So you think he was murdered?" Reed asked.

Morrisette nodded and her lips pinched together. "I'd bet on it. For one thing, there won't be too many people in town grievin' for our boy here." She lifted one slim shoulder. "Josh made himself more than his share of enemies, that's for sure."

"We got a suicide note," one of the cops who'd been called to Bandeaux's place offered up. "It's still in the computer printer, right here." He motioned toward the low filing cabinet situated behind the desk. Reed scanned the note without touching it.

No one can help.

"Oh, give me a break," Sylvie muttered under her breath. "As if he was at the end of his rope. No effin' way. Bandeaux wasn't one to overdramatize."

"Maybe he was depressed."

Sylvie rolled her eyes expressively. "Oh, sure, because life here sucks so bad. The guy only had one BMW. But he did have a Range Rover and a Corvette, some race horses, this little place and a house in St. Thomas on three lots with a private bay. Yeah, he was certainly a prime candidate for Prozac."

Diane swallowed a smile as the M.E. looked over what was left of good old Josh. Morrisette, shaking her head at the image of Josh Bandeaux offing himself, scanned the room with its cherry wood and leather furniture, state-of-the-art computer, expensive stereo equipment and a glass humidor filled with cigars that were probably worth more than a beat cop made in a week. "The 'poor me' routine is a little hard to swallow!"

Reed cocked an eyebrow. "Just how well did you know him?"

"I knew *of* him, okay? *Of* him. And well enough to guess that he wouldn't have wanted to mess up his Brooks Brothers shirts with a damned jackknife." She cast a disparaging look at the bloody weapon.

Reed did his own mental inventory. She had a point. From all outward appearances, Josh Bandeaux's life seemed enviable; but that didn't necessarily mean the guy hadn't killed himself. Reed was keeping all of his options open. "What do we know?" he asked one of the cops who'd been called to the scene.

"Not much. Bandeaux seemed to be working on this." He pointed to a legal document peeking out of a manila folder, then slowly, using a pencil, flipped the file open.

"What is it?"

"A wrongful death suit," Moses said, frowning as she

scanned the legalese. "Looks like Bandeaux was going to sue his wife for the death of their kid."

"Lovely." Morrisette rolled her eyes. "Now, *that* sounds more like Bandeaux."

"How'd the kid die?" Reed asked.

Diane lifted a shoulder, "Beats me."

Reed looked at Sylvie.

"Don't know," she admitted, her eyebrows drawing together as she tried to recall the incident.

"We'd better find out. Anything else?" Reed asked the cop.

"No forced entry—if we're lookin' at murder. The front and back door are locked, the windows shut, except for a couple upstairs, but the side doors, there"—he motioned at the open French doors in the office—"they lead to a veranda."

"Dust 'em," Reed said automatically.

"We will, Detective." Diane Moses was still bristly. "Along with everything else. I *know* how to do my job."

"Oops," Sylvie whispered as Diane walked around the desk. "Touchy, touchy. I believe some professional toes have been stepped on."

"I heard that, Morrisette," Moses muttered, but was too busy with the photographer to get into it.

"What else do you know?" Reed asked the officer.

"Just that the radio was playing, tuned to some classical station. We talked to the cleaning lady, Estelle Pontiac— yeah, I know, like the car—she called nine-one-one this morning after coming into the house and discovering the body. Was really freaked out. He was cold by the time the EMTs arrived, been dead since sometime last night. Officer Spencer talked to one neighbor"—he checked his notes—"Stanley Hubert, lives next door to the north. Hubert says he saw a white compact roll in around eleven and then take off half an hour or so later. Hubert didn't get the license plate, but he thinks he's seen the car here before. He claims it looks like the one Mrs. Bandeaux drives."

"The estranged wife?" Reed clarified.

"That's what he said. We've roped off the area and we'll check the vic's vehicles along with those of his acquaintances."

"And the wife?"

"Number one on the list."

Reed took a second look at Bandeaux's arms as the M.E. carefully rolled up the victim's sleeves. One of the buttons on the cuff of his dress shirt was missing, which seemed odd as hardly a hair on the man's head was out of place, few wrinkles showed on his clothes and his shoes were polished to a gloss. So why the missing button?

Reed studied Bandeaux's arms. The gashes on his wrists were at odd angles ... Shit, maybe Morrisette was right about the crime. Maybe someone got a little sloppy in making it look like Josh offed himself. If that was the case, there was a chance that they'd get lucky if the killer was careless and left evidence.

"Also, there were two wineglasses in the dishwasher. The maid had unloaded it before she left last night, so either Josh had company or he decided to dirty two goblets himself. We're already checking for prints. Looks like one has a lipstick smudge. We'll do a sample on it. See if the lab can figure out the manufacturer and product."

Reed stepped out of the room as the M.E. finished and the crime scene team was let loose to vacuum, dust for prints, measure blood splatter and generally sweep the room and the rest of the house for evidence. "Anything on the answering machine?"

"He's got voice mail. We're looking into it."

"What about e-mail?"

"As soon as the computer's dusted, we'll go into his computer files and desk files."

"Where does he work?"

"Self-employed," Morrisette said. "Investments. Consulting. Kind of a financial Jack of all trades. Been in trouble with the SEC. I think he's got an office on Abercorn, just off of Reynolds Square."

"You've been there?"

"Why would I have been there?" she asked.

"During your 'investigation.' "

" 'Unofficial' investigation," she corrected, her eyes narrowing defensively.

The cop said, "I've got the address here. Found it on some letterhead. Abercorn's right."

"You check it out," Reed said to Morrisette. "Talk to the staff. See if anything's out of place. If Josh was depressed. We'll need phone records and financial statements, interviews with his neighbors and family and friends."

"If he had any," Morrisette said. "And I don't need a lecture. I know the drill. I've been here a while, remember."

Long enough to know one helluva lot about Josh Bandeaux.

"I'll double-check with the neighbor, what was his name? Hubert? Maybe he can describe the driver of the white car."

"Let's hope," Morrisette said without much enthusiasm as Reed glanced down at the victim again.

Maybe he could jog the old guy's memory. Maybe they'd get lucky.

But he wasn't betting on it.

Three

Caitlyn felt ill, so ill that she'd taken a nap and now was hurrying to make up for lost time . . . lost time . . . forever a problem, she thought as she wrung out her sponge in the pail and noticed how red the sudsy water was, how much blood she'd managed to wipe off the walls, mirrors, headboard and carpet of her bedroom. She'd soaped down the tub and shower, mopped, scraped and scrubbed until her fingernails were broken, the skin on her hands red and stinging from the disinfectant and cleansers. She'd taken down the sheer curtains, and they were working their way through the rinse cycle of her washer. She'd even had to scold Oscar and lock him in the garage when he'd begun sniffing and licking the blood on the carpet.

She couldn't stand the mess. The reminder. It wasn't as if she was hiding evidence, she told herself. There was no crime. She'd had a bad nosebleed and even though she didn't feel as if she'd lost all the blood, she couldn't call the police.

What is it you're afraid of?

Ignoring the question, she poured the murky water down the drain in the shower and wiped down the tiles one last time.

A flash of memory sizzled through her brain.

Caitlyn froze.

Papers. Legal papers—a lawsuit—tucked in a corner of Josh's desk. And blood . . . thick red blood oozing from him as he stared up at her with those condemning, sightless eyes.

"Jesus!" she whispered, shaking. It was the dream. Last night's horrid dream. She hurried downstairs, stuffed the mop and pail into a closet off the garage, then in the bath off her office washed her hands for the dozenth time and checked the cuts that she'd dressed with surgical glue and butterfly bandages. The cuts hadn't been deep, just quick little slices. God, why couldn't she remember the self-mutilation?

That's what it is, isn't it? Some deep psychosis. Probably self-inflicted to assuage the guilt for Jamie. Isn't that what Dr. Wade would say?

If only she could speak to Dr. Wade. Tell her about last night. She would understand. She would try to help. She would . . .

But she's gone. She left you. Took off on a sabbatical and left you high and dry. To fight your ghosts and demons yourself.

"No!" she yelled, pounding her fist against the wall. From the garage, Oscar let out a sharp, worried bark.

Don't do this. Be strong. For God's sake, don't lose it now or you'll end up back in the psych ward for sure.

She took several deep breaths, then slowly, refusing to get upset, she applied lotion to her hands and stared at her reflection in the mirror mounted over the sink. She was pale. Her freckles showed up more distinctly on her skin. Her auburn hair was starting to curl with the sweat she'd worked up. She felt the pressure building in her head, the remainder of her migraine pounding behind her eye, and fought the same panicky feeling that was never far from her. She couldn't allow the anxiety that lurked just under the surface of her equanimity, couldn't let in the fear that she could be losing her mind. Hadn't she assured Dr. Wade she was able to face the world herself?

"Are you certain?" the psychologist had asked in their last session. A petite woman with thick red hair cropped short, she hadn't been able to cloud the doubt in her eyes. "I could call someone. I have several colleagues who would be glad to help you. Let me give you the number of a couple."

"I'll be fine. I really think it's time I handled my own life," Caitlyn had replied, and Dr. Wade had tried and failed to hide her skepticism.

"We all need help from time to time," she'd assured Caitlyn. "Even shrinks like me."

"Maybe I should go into psychology, give up graphic design and websites," Caitlyn had responded as Dr. Wade handed her a short list of names which Caitlyn had subsequently lost. And now she could use one of those damned head doctors. Badly.

Her mind wandered back to the night before.

How could she have lost track of time last night?

Why had she blacked out?

What had she done?

Where the hell was Kelly? Even if she was out of town, surely she would have called home to pick up her messages . . . right? Why hadn't she called back?

Because she doesn't want to talk to you. Figure it out, okay? Your sister's avoiding you. And do you blame her? Every time you call it's always a problem, always some new crisis, you're always in trouble.

The voice in her head seemed to scream at her from every corner of the bathroom. *Don't you get it? She's sick to death of hearing about all the things that are wrong in your life, sick of being your support, sick of you!*

No, that wasn't right. Kelly was her twin; her identical twin. They were closer than anyone in the world. Kelly was just busy, that was it . . . Sweating, ignoring the frantic beating of her heart, Caitlyn splashed cool water over her face.

"Get a grip," she said to her reflection as she blotted a

towel to her cheeks and forehead. "Pull yourself together. Right now. You don't have the luxury of falling apart."

Oscar whined and scratched in the garage.

"I'm coming," she called, tossing the towel aside and taking deep breaths as she made her way to the door. She had to get some help. *Had* to. Before she cracked up. She opened the garage door and Oscar shot in, turning in tight circles at her feet. "Come on, I'll take you for a walk, okay?" she said to the whirling dervish as he yipped and made a fool of himself. "Calm down a sec." She ruffled the hair on the back of his neck. "I've got a couple of things I've got to take care of. You can help."

With Oscar trotting behind, she hurried up the stairs to her office, flipped on her computer, located the phone number for Dr. Rebecca Wade and dialed quickly. On the desperate and off chance that her shrink had returned. Or had left a forwarding number. Or a recording referring patients to one of the colleagues.

Caitlyn's palms began to sweat as the phone rang. *Be there,* she silently prayed as a disembodied recorded voice advised her that the phone number had been disconnected and there was no new number. "Great." She set the cordless in its cradle and chewed on a fingernail. How long had Dr. Wade said she'd be gone? Three months? Six? Indefinitely? Wasn't the doctor heading west to L.A.? Or was it San Francisco? Why couldn't she remember?

She glanced at her calendar and frowned. When had she had her last appointment? None in June. She flipped back the page to May ... no ... or had she neglected to write the appointment down? Cradling her head in her hands, she tried to think. What were the names of the other shrinks Dr. Wade had given her, or even other doctors in the old house that had become an office building where Rebecca Wade had practiced? Wasn't there a Dr. Nash or Nichols or Newell, something like that, some other doctor she could call? But as she stared at the telephone, Caitlyn knew she couldn't just pick a name out of the air or run her finger down the Yellow Pages. She needed to meet and make eye contact with any potential psychologist or psychiatrist. She had to trust whoever it was completely before she told them about her life. Her *weird* life.

Oscar let out a soft yip, and she glanced out the window. Through the leafy branches of a sassafras tree, she spied a police cruiser turning into the alley next to her property. Her heart dropped. *Now what?* She hurried across the hallway to her room with its stripped bed, wet carpet and missing curtains. Oscar trotted after her and cocked his head as she peeked through the French doors to the verandah, where she watched the police car roll to a stop near her trash bins at the back of the house. This didn't bode well . . . not at all. Again she glanced at her bedroom. Would they want to see it? Had she destroyed evidence?

Of what?

She swallowed hard. Two officers climbed out of the vehicle. From the passenger side, a tall, lanky man with dark hair and an even darker expression emerged. The driver opened her door and stepped into the shaded parking strip, and for a second Caitlyn thought she knew the slim woman with spiked platinum hair and wraparound sunglasses. But that was nuts.

As the woman officer scanned the house, Caitlyn ducked behind the wall, not wanting to be caught staring. *Just like a criminal in an old film noir.* She was acting paranoid. As if she really did have something to hide. *Get over it.*

But she couldn't stop the hammering of her heart, and she noticed that she'd missed a smudge of blood on the door casing surrounding the closet. Great. Just . . . great. Oscar was growling and as Caitlyn reached down to pick him up, she noticed the bandages on her wrists with their hint of red soaking through the strips of gauze. Self-consciously she tugged at the long sleeves of her T-shirt, hiding her wounds, knowing instinctively that she didn't want the prying eyes of some cop to see the red marks or the tape at her wrists.

Not that she had anything to hide.

Except for the pints of blood that were smeared all over your bedroom.

So she'd bled a little. Or a lot. Suffered a nosebleed. Even tried to slice her wrists. So what? It wasn't a crime and this was her house, her private spot in the world.

Yeah, then why are you so paranoid?

Because of all the blood . . . so much . . . how did she do that and not know? Too much alcohol? Another one of her blackouts where time slipped past way too fast? Please, God, no. Not that. Whatever had happened. It was creepy. Damned creepy. And the possibility of self-mutilation was terrifying.

The officers had rounded the house, and as Caitlyn moved to her office she saw they were at the gate to her front courtyard. So much for hoping they were paying a visit to the neighbors.

You know better, don't you? They're here because of the mess in your bedroom. They're here because of something you did. Somehow they know what happened. And you don't.

Clenching her jaw and refusing to listen to her self-doubts, she slipped into a pair of flip-flops and hurried down the stairs. The doorbell chimed. Oscar, barking wildly, bounded to the entry hall. "Be good," Caitlyn warned, taking a deep breath and yanking the door open.

The officers were on the front porch, all right. The tall, rugged-looking man with his craggy face was holding up his badge. His partner, the tiny whip-thin woman with the near-white hair and shades, stood at his side. Grim-faced, she, too, was holding a wallet displaying her police ID.

Bad news. Bad, bad news.

"Mrs. Bandeaux?" the man asked.

"Yes." She nodded, her heart sinking, her broken fingernails digging into the edge of the door she was holding open. "I'm Caitlyn Bandeaux."

He offered a smile that didn't touch his eyes. "I'm Detective Reed, this is my partner, Detective Morrisette. Would you mind if we came in for a few minutes?"

The badges looked legit, the photographs unflattering but recognizable. She hesitated. Thought of the mess upstairs. The blood still on the closet. Somehow, she managed to pull herself together and open the door wider and had the distinct impression that the woman was sizing her up. "What's this about?" Caitlyn asked, but knew, deep in the marrow of her bones, that they were the bearers of horrible news.

She stood aside, allowing them to enter, and even though a blast of heat from the outside followed them in, she was so cold she nearly shivered.

"I'm afraid we have some bad news, Mrs. Bandeaux," the man said, motioning to a chair as Caitlyn, her legs numb, propped herself on the chair back.

"What?"

"It's about your husband."

"Josh?" she whispered and felt as if someone had wrapped ice-cold fingers around her neck, cutting off her oxygen. A sudden roar in her head, like the sea trapped inside a cave, was nearly deafening. She had a quick image of Josh lying pale and still upon his desk. "What about him?" She swallowed against a mouth that was as dry as the Sahara. Knew what was coming.

"I'm afraid he's dead," Detective Reed said as the roar increased and her knees weakened.

"But how . . .?"

"We're not sure what happened yet. We're exploring all possibilities and waiting for the coroner's report to come in."

"No!" She shook her head vehemently. "I don't believe it." But she did. She'd known. Somehow she'd known.

"I'm sorry," Reed said and the woman whispered some kind of condolences as well, but Caitlyn's brain wasn't processing their words. Her fingers curled around the upholstered back of the chair, but her legs were shaking so badly she could barely stand.

"I know this is hard," the woman was saying as if from a distance. Caitlyn barely heard. In her mind's eye a kaleidoscope of images flashed. Josh as a young man at the helm of his sailboat, in Naples where he'd proposed, at Jamie's birth, trying to hide his disappointment that the baby wasn't a boy, sneaking in late at night, claiming he was working, angry when his investment turned down, white-faced and shaken at their daughter's funeral.

"Did your husband have any enemies?" the female officer—what-was-her-name?—asked, and Caitlyn snapped to the present.

"I don't know . . . yes, I suppose so." But she couldn't think.

"I'll need their names."

"Of course . . . but . . . he . . . he was a businessman in town. Some of his deals went sour." Caitlyn's head was pounding painfully, as if her brain was suddenly too big for her skull.

"Was he depressed?"

"Josh? Depressed? I don't know. We . . . we were separated, oh . . . you must know that already since you're here. We've . . . we've been living apart for about three years." Numb from the inside out, Caitlyn tried to keep her wits about her. Impossible. She suddenly felt faint . . . sensed blackness picking at the corners of her consciousness.

"She needs to sit down. Mrs. Bandeaux?" a woman asked from far away, and she felt arms around her, steadying her, leading her into the living room. Her legs were like jelly.

"My husband . . . he, um, he was filing for divorce." If she could just hang on until the police left her alone, gave her time to sort this out. She felt herself being lowered onto the couch.

"And you?" the man asked.

"What about me?"

"Did you want the divorce?"

"I don't think she can answer right now," the female cop said quietly.

But Caitlyn wanted to answer. To get the interview over with. Now.

"I, um, I had thought we could get back together, but . . ." She felt the first tear slide from her eyes. Josh. Dead? Healthy, vibrant, take-life-by-the-balls Josh? No . . . she couldn't believe it. Josh couldn't be dead. The tears began in earnest and her shoulders shook. Someone, the woman, she thought, handed her a tissue and she held back her sobs, but the tears flowed wildly, streaming down her face.

"Was he having financial problems?"

"Not that I know of. Nothing specific." *But he was always short on money. Always dealing with a "temporary cash flow problem," always borrowing from you.*

"Was he involved with anyone else?"

She'd known this was coming and somehow the reminder of her husband's infidelity gave her strength and cleared her head. "Yes," she admitted and the pain still hurt. It was one thing for Josh to want a divorce, another to be flaunting another woman in her face. "Her name is Naomi Crisman."

"How did he know her?"

"I'm not sure, but I think they met at some kind of fund-raiser." She was pulling together now, the threatening blackness receding. " Josh is . . . was . . . involved in a lot of philanthropic causes." She caught the look between the two detectives and suddenly it struck her that they weren't just here to deliver the bad news, but that they were digging for information.

"Do you know her?"

"She was dating my husband, Detective," she said and sniffed back her tears for a husband who hadn't loved her. "That doesn't make for a buddy-buddy situation." Swiping at her eyes and feeling the bandages hidden beneath her sleeves, she added, "Thank you for coming by to tell me about my husband . . . I'll want to see him if that's possible . . . but you're asking me a lot of questions and you said this might be a homicide, right?"

"We're not certain yet."

"Am I a suspect?" The idea was unthinkable but as she stared at the unmoving expressions of the two cops, she knew that she was considered a possible killer. Which was ridiculous. Absurd. "How did my husband die?"

There was a slight hesitation.

"He was still my husband," she pointed out, angry and wanting to lash out at someone. Anyone. These people intruding into her home, giving her the horrid news, were as good a scapegoat as anyone. "I think I have the right to know."

Detective Morrisette nodded. "It's possible your husband took his own life, but, as I said, we still have a lot of unanswered questions about what happened to him. We found him in his den. His wrists had been slit."

She cringed. Saw the vision of him slumped over his desk in her mind's eye. How could she have known? "Suicide," Caitlyn whispered, disbelieving, then thinking of the cuts along the insides of her own arms. "No way. He wouldn't do that." She was shaking her head, trying to dispel the image of her husband bleeding to death. "He . . . he'd use his rifle, or fire up his Mercedes and let it idle in the garage or . . ." Her voice faded as she realized she had their rapt attention.

"Or what?" Reed asked.

"I don't know."

He didn't prod, but the look in his sober eyes said, *Sure you do. You lived with the man. You knew what made him tick. And you just might have killed him. He was divorcing you. He was after your money. He had another woman. He was threatening to sue you for the wrongful death of your child. And then there was all the blood in your bedroom. But the detectives don't know about that. At least not yet.* "Look, if you're finished, I think . . . I think I'd like to lie down."

"If you can bear with us, we only have a few more questions," Detective Morrisette insisted with the hint of a kind smile that Caitlyn was certain she practiced. "Then we'll get out of your hair." And she was true to her word. They asked some general questions about Josh, his family and business dealings, of which Caitlyn knew little, and then stood as if they were finally ready to leave.

"Just one more thing," Reed said. "Where were you last night?"

Every muscle in Caitlyn's body froze. "I was out."

He made a note. "All night?"

Oh, dear God. "I went out around eight-thirty or nine and was home sometime after midnight. I'm not sure of the exact time," she admitted, feeling Reed's unflinching gaze bore deep, searching for a lie.

"Did you visit your husband last night?"

She nearly wilted. "No. As I said, we were separated," she said, telling herself that what she'd seen was a dream, that was all. *Then why did it seem so real? Why are you getting flashes of Josh at his desk, his wrists covered in blood?* "Do I need a lawyer, Detective?" she demanded, suddenly stronger.

"I'm just trying to figure out what went on last night."

Me, too! "When you do, would you fill me in?" she said, feeling heat climb up the back of her neck.

"Of course," the woman, Morrisette, cut in. She shot her partner a warning glance. "Now, I would feel better if there was someone here with you," she said, touching her on the arm gently, inadvertently putting pressure on the wounds.

Caitlyn gritted her teeth against the pain. The last thing she wanted was to deal with anyone. Except Kelly. "I can call one of my sisters or my brother."

"Promise?"

"Yes. Please. I'll be fine." *Liar! You'll never be fine!*

Reed looked skeptical, but the woman cop bristled, sending him a silent message that warned him to hold back whatever protest he was about to voice.

Frowning hard, Reed snapped his notebook closed. "We could phone someone for you. One of the siblings you mentioned." He scratched his chin, seemed lost in thought as he glanced out the window to a spot where a bird feeder turned slowly as it hung from a limb of her magnolia tree. A cardinal balanced on a small perch and was busily pecking at the tiny seeds. "You'll need someone with you. Some reporters were already showing up at your husband's house as we left."

Her heart nearly stopped beating. "Reporters?"

"It won't be long before they put two and two together and show up here," he said matter-of-factly.

"Wonderful." Dealing with the police was tough enough; she couldn't imagine taking on the press. Not now.

"I wouldn't talk to them if I were you."

Don't worry.

Detective Morrisette nodded her agreement as she slid her dark glasses onto the bridge of her nose. "They can be nasty. Please let us call someone. A friend or a family member. You shouldn't be alone right now."

"No—I'll be all right . . ." A ridiculous statement. She would never be all right. Maybe never had been. Now Josh was dead and there was so much blood in her own bedroom and her dream . . . was it a dream? If only she could get through to Kelly and find out what the hell had happened last night. She forced a calm, humorless smile. "I'll call my brother, Troy. He works downtown at the bank." Both officers appeared skeptical as she walked them to the back door.

"It's Saturday," Reed pointed out. "Aren't the banks closed?"

"Not Montgomery Bank and Trust," she said, glancing at the clock. The bank was open a few hours in the middle of the day, an innovation her grandfather had incorporated years before. "I don't need anyone to call my brother. I'll be fine," she insisted, knowing that she was lying. "Just give me some time alone to pull myself together."

Reed looked as though he was about to say more but caught a quick shake of his partner's head and held his tongue. Caitlyn watched as they walked through her front yard. The old gate creaked as they passed through and Oscar, spying a neighbor's cat lurking in the branches of the sassa-fras tree, started barking insanely.

Before he could race outside, Caitlyn closed the door, and as it latched she leaned against the cool panels. Somehow, some way, she had to figure out what had happened last night.

Josh was dead. *Dead.*

Probably murdered.

And she couldn't even swear that she hadn't killed him.

Four

This morning the spirits were still restless.

Angry.

Hissing as they darted through the shadows.

Mocking.

As they had been all night long.

Their movements had kept Lucille from sleep, haunting her, touching her mind if she dared drop off even for a second. They'd started around midnight, sighing through the branches of the live oaks, causing the Spanish moss to sway. The wraiths grumbled by the old waterwheel that creaked as it turned in the stream flowing past the orchard, and they hid in the rafters of the third story of this grand old decaying manor where Lucille had tried and failed to sleep. She'd thought they would disappear into the shadows with the morning light. But she'd been wrong. They were still annoying her as she swept the wide porch of Oak Hill, the Montgomery plantation, poking her broom at a cottonlike nest of spiders in the corner.

"You all, jest git. Go away, leave me be," she muttered, her lips flattening over her teeth as she spied the gardener's boy clipping dying blooms off the roses. He didn't look up from beneath the bill of his cap, but she knew he'd heard her. She'd have to be careful.

Though some people thought she was a little touched in the head, that some of the Montgomery lunacy had somehow invaded her, Lucille was as sane as anyone she knew. Saner. She was just cursed with the ability to hear those who should have passed on, and she was certain the old three-storied home with its beveled windows, crystal chandeliers and pillared brick porch was haunted. She knew some of the ghosts' names, had read them time and time again on the crumbling gravestones. Some of the angry, bodyless beings had been slaves over a century before, some had been children, poor little souls who'd never had a chance to grow up, but what they had in common was that every last one of the angry souls had been born with at least one drop of Montgomery blood running through their veins.

She just wished they'd be silent. Slide back into their tombs where they belonged. But that was not to be because something vile and dark had happened last night; she just didn't know what. Yet.

Pausing to wipe her forehead with the hem of her apron, she glanced down the long drive, as if expecting the bearer of bad news, even Satan himself, to appear. But the late morning was deceptively quiet. Too still. Only the lapping of the creek and the buzz of a hornet searching for its nest were audible over the whispers of the ghosts.

Pushing her broom around terra-cotta planters bursting with petunias and marigolds, she kept a wary eye out for palmetto bugs and listened to the raspy voices. Lucille heard them and, she suspected, others did as well; they were too frightened to admit to the existence of the undead.

Caitlyn . . . now that poor child was cursed. Just like her grandma Evelyn . . . another tortured soul. Lucille made a quick sign of the cross over her bosom without breaking stride as she swept. She'd bet a month's wages that Caitlyn heard the voices, that the dead whispered through her head. As they had with Evelyn.

She paused again. To listen. The lawn mower growled as

the gardener cut the grass near the stables. A squirrel scolded from one of the live oak trees, and further away traffic rumbled on a distant highway. Yet, above it all, Lucille heard the sounds of the spirits—quiet, angry voices. She felt the ghosts moving, churning, causing a hot wind to brush against her cheeks. Evil seemed nearer somehow, though Lucille could not pinpoint it; didn't know its source.

It had started last night.

She'd gone to bed at eleven, as was her usual time, after giving Miss Berneda her final dose of medication and some warm milk with honey. Once Berneda had dozed off and begun to snore, Lucille had pulled the curtains around her bed and eased out of the room. She'd climbed the back staircase to the third floor, the arthritis in her knees complaining as she made her way up each narrowing riser, her breathing exaggerated with the effort. She was getting too old and fat for the hard work she did, and though she was compensated well and she loved the Montgomery family as if it were her own, she would have to retire soon, to Florida maybe to be with her sister, Mabel.

But not as long as Berneda Montgomery drew a breath. Lucille had promised Berneda's husband that she would take care of his wife for the rest of Berneda's years. With the good Lord's blessing, large doses of Extra Strength Excedrin, a shot of brandy each night and her own pacemaker keeping her tired heart beating regularly, Lucille intended to keep her vow to Cameron Montgomery even though he'd been a contemptible son of a bitch if ever there was one. Lord knew none of Berneda's children were capable of caring for their ailing mother. They all thought Berneda's pacemaker and nitroglycerine pills could ward off her heart problems, but Lucille knew better. Death was clamoring for Berneda Montgomery, and once he'd started calling, there was no stopping the bastard.

She snorted as she lifted the dustpan and glared at the hot sun inching its way across the clear sky. All those kids and not one worth his or her salt.

Then again, who was she to point fingers? It wasn't as if

her own daughter was much better. No, Marta, bless her thoughtless heart, was another one of this generation who did as she pleased, letting the chips fall where they may, "doing her own thing," leaving destruction in her wake and never once looking back. Even now. She was supposed to have visited, but never did, was supposedly dating some hotshot cop named Montoya in New Orleans, but that must've gone south, too, as he'd called looking for her. That was the trouble with Marta. She was a flake. But then that wasn't a surprise. Lucille had spent over thirty years questioning her own foolish decisions. Decisions she'd made before Marta had been conceived. Even now, Lucille felt sharp shards of guilt about her only child. She loved her daughter with all of her guilty heart and had been Marta's single support since the kid was five. Yet, sometimes it seemed the bad had outweighed the good.

But one would have thought, with all the children Berneda and Cameron Montgomery had brought into this world, one of them would have turned out decent enough. Lucille tossed the contents of the dustpan over the porch rail, the debris falling to a growing pile beneath a thick wisteria vine that twisted and turned as it curled around the eaves. What chance did any of the Montgomery progeny have with all the bad blood that trickled through their veins? None, that's what.

She checked on the sun tea she had brewing on the porch railing. Sunlight glinted against the glass jar. Like buoyant bodies on a tepid sea, the bags floated and danced in the amber liquid.

From inside the house, the phone jangled.

Lucille's old heart missed a beat.

No one had to tell her it was bad news.

"Let me get this straight," Troy said as he folded his suit jacket over the back of one of the chairs in Caitlyn's kitchen. "Josh is dead. It could be suicide or it might be homicide. The police are still trying to figure out which. Have I got that much right?"

"Yes." Caitlyn poured fresh water into Oscar's dish and hoped she didn't appear as ragged as she felt. She'd called her brother at Montgomery Bank and Trust as soon as Detectives Reed and Morrisette had driven away. Two hours later, after getting her message and calling her back, he'd arrived, made his way through the cluster of reporters hovering near the front gate and landed here, looking more pissed than sad that his brother-in-law was dead.

As Detective Reed had predicted, television crews and reporters for the local papers had shown up shortly after the police had left, knocked on her door, and when she'd refused to answer, taken up residence on the sidewalk in front of her house. She'd caught a glimpse of one slim woman in a smart purple dress and black scarf standing near her front gate while a cameraman filmed her. Caitlyn's stomach clenched. *Not again. No cameras. No reporters. No questions about the intimate details of my life.*

"Can't they tell whether someone did him in or he killed himself?" Troy asked, jarring her back to the here and now. Oh, God, she had to pull herself together; she couldn't let anyone, not even Troy, know about her own fears.

"Oh . . . yes, I mean . . . I'm sure they can. It just takes time."

Troy snorted his disgust and jingled his keys in the pocket of his slacks. "Savannah's finest. You didn't tell them anything, did you?" Hard blue eyes examined hers, looked for a crack, for the lie.

"I couldn't. I don't know anything." *Except that there was blood smeared upstairs. So damned much blood.* It wasn't Josh's lifeblood. It *couldn't* be! She slid into one of the chairs, exhausted and scared to death.

"But you've got to be one of their prime suspects," Troy said, frowning. His hair was as dark as hers, just the hint of gray visible at his temples. He stood arrow-straight, wide shoulders and slim hips, a man of thirty-three in excellent shape. "It's no big secret that he was having an affair and going to divorce you."

"Nice, Troy," she muttered. "No reason to sugarcoat things."

"Exactly. What you've got on your hands here is a crisis."

"Me?" she asked, then saw the white lines bracketing his lips. "What're you saying? That *I* killed Josh?"

"Of course not."

Still, she was burned. "You know, I could use a little support. It's been a helluva day and it's not over yet." Tears blistered her eyes, but she didn't swipe at them. Wouldn't give in. Oscar, sensing a fight, slunk to his favorite spot under the table.

Troy's keys jangled as he stared outside to the back garden. "I'm sorry. I . . . I'm not very good in the support department."

"No argument there."

"But you do have to face the fact that you're an obvious suspect." Plowing the fingers of both hands through his hair, he let out a world-weary sigh. As if being the only living Montgomery male was sometimes too much to bear. "Maybe you should move home for a while."

"This is my home."

"I know, I know, but it might be better if you got out of town, moved out to the country, stayed with Mom at Oak Hill."

"You mean 'lay low'?"

"I didn't say—"

"I'm not a criminal, Troy," she insisted, forcing herself to her feet and steadfastly shoving aside the doubts in her mind.

"Just a victim." His lips pursed in repressed anger. "Always a victim. Jesus!"

"I knew I shouldn't have called you," she spat.

"Why did you?"

She reached for a bottle of water in the refrigerator and twisted off the cap. "The police didn't want me to be left alone."

"So you called your brother?"

"You were the closest." Sometimes Troy was a royal

pain, but then weren't all of her siblings? She'd known it had been a mistake the minute she'd dialed his office. She took a long pull on the water. "Let's just get this straight. It wasn't because you're a male, okay?"

"Listen, Caitlyn—"

Her free hand flew up to the side of her head and she spread her fingers as if ready to ward off a blow. "Never mind, strike that. I wanted to call Kelly—"

"Kelly? Oh, for God's sake, Caitlyn. Let's not even go there!"

"But—" She knew she'd made a mistake the minute she'd brought up her twin.

"That would be just plain crazy and you know it!" His dark brows drew together. "Oh, I get it! You're already looking for an insanity defense. Kelly." He clucked his tongue.

"Stop it! I'm not guilty. I'm not insane. And . . . and . . . Josh is dead," she added, her voice cracking. "He was a bastard, okay, I know it, but . . . there was a time when I did love him." She felt her cheeks flame at her admission. "He was my husband. Jamie's father."

"Who only wanted you for your inheritance."

The words spilled over her like icy rain. As ugly as it was, it was the truth. Oscar let out a low whimper from his hiding spot. "Please, Troy, for my dignity's sake, leave me a few of my illusions, okay?"

To her surprise he crossed the room and placed a hand on her shoulder, but his touch was tentative, as if he were afraid that she might do something as foolish as turn to him and bury her face in his shoulder. There was hesitation in his eyes, a guardedness that never allowed her, or anyone else for that matter, too close. Two years younger than Caitlyn and Kelly, Troy, the only surviving son of their parents, had a huge burden to carry on his muscular shoulders. "It's not that easy, Caitlyn. Your illusions tend to get you into trouble. Today isn't the first time. It's just the most serious."

"You're right," she admitted and felt a sliver of regret

for her anger. "Look, Troy, thanks for coming today. I needed to talk to someone and I thought I could count on you. I suppose I could have called Amanda. Her office is nearby, but, well, as much of a workaholic as she is, she sometimes works at home on the weekends. Besides, she's always so busy."

"And I'm not?"

Caitlyn managed a smile, the remainder of her outrage dissipating. "You're the boss at the bank."

"All the more reason for me to be there. Even on a Saturday." But the fingers resting on her shoulder squeezed her gently, reminding her that they had a bond. "You know I'm here for you . . . I'm just not very good at the emotional support thing."

"That's all that macho-male posturing you've been doing since you were around twelve," she said. "You're like a porcupine, though. Bristly on the outside, soft in the middle."

"And Amanda's pure steel all the way through?" he asked, then checked his watch and scowled at the dial. "Look, I've really got to get back to the bank. I've got a client coming in soon."

"I know. I'll be okay."

He wasn't convinced. "Why don't you go stay with Mom for a few days, just until the police figure out what's going on and the vultures outside"—he hooked a thumb toward the front of the house to the windows visible past the foot of the stairs—"find other carrion to feed on."

"Nice analogy," she muttered, but followed his gaze nonetheless. Through the curtains and glass Caitlyn watched the newswoman in the purple dress walk toward the van. The cameraman was stowing his gear in zippered cases.

"Don't be fooled. The minute those guys leave, more will show up."

"I'll be all right."

"Will you?" he asked, and the question resonated through the house.

He didn't say what he really thought, what the entire

family had decided, that Caitlyn would never truly be healthy, that there would always be the past chasing her, that tragedy would forever be her companion. She'd seen her siblings exchange glances, detected their gazes staring at her only to slide furtively away when they sensed she'd caught them looking her way.

"Caitlyn?"

"What?"

"You're sure you'll be okay here?"

"I've got Oscar. He's a fabulous companion and security system and I can pay him in dog chow," she said lightly, but noticed the frown etching its way across her brother's smooth brow. She let out a sigh and turned more serious. "Really, Troy, don't worry."

"Yeah, right."

"I mean it." She jutted out her jaw. Tried to look tough.

Troy's eyebrows rose skeptically as he reached for his jacket. "It's impossible not to worry about you."

"Give it a shot, will ya?"

He managed a bit of a smile. "You know you can call me anytime."

"And you'll work me into your busy schedule?" she snapped.

"Ouch."

"The truth hurts."

"I came today, didn't I?"

"Yeah, you did," she admitted, with the barest trace of a smile. "And I appreciate it. Really."

"Just promise me one thing." His eyes narrowed on her as he slid his arms into the jacket's sleeves and shrugged the shoulders into place.

"Mmm?"

"If the police stop by again, don't talk to them. Not without your lawyer present."

Her good mood was shattered. The claustrophobic sensation she'd pushed aside was suddenly all over her and she felt as if she was being suffocated. She should never have trusted Troy. Knew better. "You think I killed him, don't you?'' she whispered, disbelieving. ''You think I killed my own husband.'' Inwardly she cringed. *And what do you think, Caitlyn?*

''It doesn't matter what I think, Caitlyn, but for the record, no. I don't think you're capable of murder. You have your problems—well, hell, we all do—but I don't think you're a cold-blooded murderer.''

''Thanks for the vote of confidence,'' she said, stung.

''I'm just warning you, that's all.'' He adjusted his tie. ''For Christ's sake, don't wig out on me.''

''Wouldn't dream of it.'' She folded her arms over her chest and walked him to the front door where, thank God, no reporters were camping out. But she knew that her empty front garden with its hummingbirds hovering near her feeder and a dragonfly skittering through the vines wouldn't be peaceful for long.

This was just the calm before the storm.

She glanced at the sky.

Clear and blue.

Deceptive.

As Troy climbed into his Range Rover, she waved and felt the burn and tightness in her wrists, the scratches that were healing . . . how in the world had they gotten there? All she had to go on were the horrifying flashes—sharp-edged bursts that sizzled through her brain like lightning bolts.

Disjointed pieces of a dream?

Some kind of ESP?

Coincidence?

Or horrific bits of a memory too terrible to remember?

Five

Adam Hunt picked the lock deftly. Anyone watching might have thought he owned the key to this thick wooden door because the latch sprang so easily. But he'd been careful. He was alone. No one was in the hallway of the hundred-and-fifty-year-old house that had been converted into an office building. Nobody had seen him enter silently, swinging the door closed behind him.

Inside, the room was hot. Cloying. Dust had settled on every surface; a potted palm was brittle and dead near the window, the soil surrounding its roots bone dry. He looked around the office as he cracked a window, and the smell of Old Savannah slipped into the tiny office with its worn wooden floors and haphazardly placed rugs.

A leather recliner, sofa and rocking chair were grouped together. Positioned catty-corner to the seating area was a tall armoire that held video equipment. Beneath the window a short, glass-fronted bookcase contained a small library on human psychoses, sexuality, morals, hypnosis and every human frailty or depravity known to man. Some of the books had belonged to him. So had the rocker. But no longer.

His jaw clenched as he crossed to the rolltop.

Her desk was locked.

Of course.

Not that it was a problem.

Her desk chair squeaked as he sat in it, and he noticed where its rollers had worn a path on the carpet, a small arc, so that she could turn to her computer or notes, then face her clients again. Jaw tightening, he quickly pried the desk open and rolled the top up. Inside, the cubicles and drawers of stamps, paper clips, envelopes and the like were neat. Tidy.

Just like the woman who had so recently sat in this scarred chair.

So where the hell are you, Rebecca? Absently he rubbed his knee. It was starting to bother him again, the result of a recent motorcycle accident.

He turned on the computer, tapped his fingers nervously on the arm of the chair and glared at the dusty screen as it clicked and hummed, the monitor glowing bright. He found her files, skimmed them, his lips flat over his teeth. Was it his imagination or did he smell a faint trace of her perfume lingering over the musty odor of the office?

Wishful thinking, nothing more.

Fingers moving skillfully, he scrolled through her patient files, getting quick peeks into the problems, heartbreaks and psychoses of patients he'd never met. Nothing caught his eye or made him think that this was the case that she was certain would change the course of her life.

He glanced at his watch. He'd been here nearly forty-five minutes and heard the sounds of shuffling feet and scraping chairs from an office down the hall. He checked to see that he'd locked the door, so that no one searching for an office or the rest room might burst in and see him; then he crossed to the windows. From the third-floor view, he caught a glimpse of the alley below and a neighboring house. An elderly lady wearing a straw hat and dressing gown was watering her geraniums. He slid out of her view before she looked up; didn't want to have to explain himself. At least not yet. Not until he had some answers himself.

He'd probably have to lie to get those answers.

So be it.

Adam believed that lies came in differing shades, hues and textures. There were black lies and white lies and a variety of shades of gray lying in between. Some were thick and sticky, others thin and gossamer, but as far as he could remember, there had never been a good lie. And yet, he decided as he slid a pick into the locked cabinet and, with a sensitive touch he would never admit to having, sprung the simple latch, sometimes a lie was necessary.

With a click the drawer opened.

If a lie was necessary to get to the truth . . . was it such a bad thing?

There is no such thing as a "white lie," his grandmother had preached often enough. "A lie is a lie and if you can't tell the truth, then there's something very wrong with you." She had looked at him with her unblinking hawklike eyes, searching for a glimmer of deceit in his gaze, and he had stared straight back at her, refusing to squirm even though they'd both known he was lying through his teeth.

Norma Hunt had been a fair woman. When she had been unable to prove that he wasn't telling the truth, she had been forced to pretend to believe him.

He wondered what she'd think of her only grandson now as he opened the top file drawer, flipping through the tabs, smelling the dry, musty odor of unused documents. His fingers riffled over the names; then he closed the drawer and opened the lower one . . . and there, taking up half the space, were the documents that might help him on his quest. Thick files. Packed with notations and information:

BANDEAUX, Caitlyn Montgomery.

How had he missed it on the computer? Quickly he turned to the flickering screen and sorted through the files again, but Caitlyn was definitely missing in action. He did a quick cross search and found all the other patients' records, but not one solitary entry on Caitlyn Bandeaux. A search didn't bring up any files. He even looked through the computer's "recycle bin," but nothing on Caitlyn had been recently deleted.

It was almost as if she'd never been an active client.

But the thick paper file in his lap argued the point. And Rebecca had mentioned the name Montgomery in one of their conversations.

He leaned back in Rebecca's chair. Why wouldn't the information in the paper files be transferred to the computer? He flipped through the pages and found a photograph, a snapshot of a striking woman of about thirty-five. Long red-brown hair was blowing over her eyes as she balanced a child on one hip. The little girl's head was thrown back in laughter, pink ribbons slipping out of curly brown hair and the woman, presumably Caitlyn Bandeaux, appeared care-free. Wearing an identical white sundress to the child's, the skirt billowing against her legs in the wind, Caitlyn stood upon the sweeping lawn of a grand antebellum house of white clapboard and brick. The sky was ominously dark with clouds, but mother and child didn't seem to feel the threat of the impending storm.

Adam stared at the image for a long time.

She was one more puzzle to figure out.

He slipped the photograph into his pocket.

"So tell me everything you know about Josh Bandeaux," Reed said as he dropped a slim file onto Sylvie Morrisette's desk at the police station. Chewing gum, she looked over her shoulder, ignoring the flickering computer monitor where some of the images of Josh Bandeaux's slumped, very dead body, were visible. "And you can leave out the part about him being a prick. I already got that."

"I was gonna mention that he was a smooth talker and con man. Just another example of Southern gentility gone bad." She fingered the manila folder, laying it open. "What's this?"

"Preliminary autopsy report. *Very* preliminary. Nothing in it we don't already know. Approximate time of death is midnight. From outward appearances it looks like he died of blood loss, maybe self-inflicted. We'll get more information once the autopsy is completed.'' He dropped into a battered side chair in her cubicle and noticed, not for the first time, how neat she kept her work space. Nothing out of place. Pictures of her family arranged on her desk, a potted fern in one corner, pens and pencils kept in an old mug with faded letters that read, ''If you don't like cops, next time you're in trouble, call a hippie.'' A denim jacket decorated with rhinestones hung from a hall tree; above it was perched a Braves baseball cap.

''I don't know that much about Bandeaux really.'' Spying the skepticism in his eyes, she added, ''*Really*. I *wasn't* involved with him, but I'd met him, okay? What I do know was that he was married a couple of times.''

Reed's ears pricked up. ''Caitlyn Montgomery wasn't his first wife?''

''Nah.'' Morrisette leaned back in her desk chair and twiddled a pencil between her fingers. ''The first one was named Maude. Maude Havenbrooke. Later, he hooked up with Caitlyn, who became wife number two. Then, I guess, he was gonna divorce her.''

''Because of a potential wife number three?''

She lifted a shoulder. ''That's the rumor. He had himself a live-in.''

''And you know this . . . how?''

''I checked up on him. Remember? For a friend who was interested.''

''And her name is?''

Morrisette hesitated.

''This is a potential homicide investigation,'' Reed reminded her and noticed her mouth tighten at the corners.

''Millie. Millicent Torme. And she's married, okay, so try to be discreet.''

''Discretion is my middle name.''

''My ass.''

''Do you know Maude Havenbrooke?''

''Never met her, not personally.''

"But she's still around?" he asked casually, thinking that Morrisette had taken a major interest in Josh Bandeaux and his personal life. Maybe she was telling the truth about her lack of interest in the deceased; then again, he wouldn't put it past her to stretch the truth a little if it meant keeping her reputation intact.

"Far as I know. She owns a bed-and-breakfast near Forsyth Park. Mockingbird Manor or something like that, one of those old showpiece homes filled with antiques and such. The kind where rich tourists stay when they're in town. Word has it that she makes croissants to die for. Drizzles them with a combo of honey and homemade raspberry jam."

Reed decided to have a chat with the first Mrs. Bandeaux. "Was she friendly with her ex?"

"Maude? Friendly with Bandeaux? I have no idea. But she remarried. A guy by the name of Springer, I think."

Reed made a mental note.

"She have any kids with Josh?"

"I'm not sure . . ." Morrisette said, then snapped her fingers and sat upright. "No, that's wrong. I don't think they had any kids between them, but Maude was a little older and had a kid by her first husband."

"Complicated."

"Families always are. Josh might have adopted the kid. I don't know. As I said, I wasn't involved." A slight flush darkened the tops of her cheeks. "And don't take that attitude with me. I just checked him out for Millie, who was split from her husband at the time."

"So Millie took up with him?"

"Not really took up with him, or if she did, it was a fling. She and her husband were separated for a while and Bandeaux was going through a divorce. I doubt that Millie, if she did get together with him, had what he was interested in. Bandeaux liked his women rich, beautiful and willing to go down on him whenever he got the urge."

Reed cleared his throat. "How would you know—?"

"I don't, okay. But he was a player. Big time. Hung out at the strip clubs. Threw money around. This I do know. Saw him there a couple of times when I worked vice and I was involved in the raids down at the Silk Tassel or Pussies In Booties, those kind of places. Anyway, Josh hooked up with Caitlyn Montgomery and within a couple of months or so, they weren't only an item, they were married, for Christ's sake! Millie returned to her husband and kept pretty quiet about it. I figured he dumped her and she was embarrassed, not that she considered herself in love with him or anything. From what I understand old Josh's charm rubbed off pretty fast once she got to know him. He and the new missus, they had a baby right away and the rest, as they say, is history."

Resting one ankle over his opposing knee, Reed said, "I did some checking on the missus. No priors."

"So *now* you think Bandeaux was murdered?"

"I don't know. I'm just keeping an open mind."

Morrisette chewed her gum a little more loudly. "You? Like hell."

"We'll see what the coroner says after the autopsy. I'm waiting for a report from the crime scene team about the evidence. All I've got so far is that the body doesn't appear to have been moved. He died right in his desk chair. The last person known to have seen him alive was the maid, Ms. Pontiac, when she left for the night, but after that he could have had himself a damned party."

"I think it was a private party because of the wineglasses in the dishwasher. Only two. Not forty," Morrisette mused aloud.

"So we know he had company. Ms. Pontiac insists she'd cleaned up everything and even emptied the dishwasher before she left."

"Any prints on the wineglasses?" Reed asked.

"Nope. Wiped clean, except for the lipstick smudge."

"Why would someone wipe for prints and ignore the lipstick?"

"Careless or believes no one will be able to trace the smudge to her. There was also what looks like a couple of drops of wine on the carpet in the den. Depending upon how old the stains are, it's possible that the wine was spilled and the glasses taken to the dishwasher.''

"A neat killer.''

"Or visitor. We're not sure he was murdered,'' she reminded him.

"Yeah, I know.'' Reed plucked a piece of lint from his dark sock. "But let's run with the murder idea for a sec. You have any ideas who might want to see him dead?''

"At least half of Savannah. To begin with, he went through women like toilet paper. That doesn't sit well with a lot of us. Then there's his business partner, Al Fitzgerald. I think Josh pulled a fast one and cut him out of his share of stock in the company. And that's not his first brush with the law. He'd been involved with some kind of securities scam before, but he lined enough pockets in Atlanta to keep himself out of serious trouble, so he was never prosecuted.'' Her eyes narrowed a bit and she chewed her gum more vigorously. "I'm sure the list of people who had Josh Bandeaux on their most-hated list is long and distinguished.''

"I'd like to see it. Maybe you could come up with a few names.''

"My pleasure.'' Leaning across the desk, narrowly missing her coffee cup with her elbows, Morrisette said, "Wanna hear what I learned about Caitlyn Bandeaux?''

Reed inclined his head and wondered if Morrisette's interest in Josh's not-quite-ex-wife was more than idle interest. "Shoot.''

"First of all, she's pretty unstable. She's got herself a nice long history of ending up in psych wards, ever since she was a kid. Off and on. I don't know what the diagnosis is, or if there is one. It could be anything from dealing with slight depression to being manic, or, what do they call it these days? Bipolar. Maybe she was traumatized as a kid or got into drugs; some of those can end up makin' ya effin' paranoid. But I have heard that mental illness runs in the family. Neuroses lurk like catfish on the bottom of the Montgomery gene pool.''

"So—has our estranged widow ever been violent?''

Morrisette lifted a slim shoulder as she spat her gum into a trash can near her desk. "Not to the point of getting arrested, obviously."

"Where do you get your information?"

"A friend of a friend."

"Gossip," he guessed, a little disappointed.

"Yeah, the kind of gossip we pay stoolies for every day of the week."

"Hearsay doesn't hold up in court."

"We aren't even sure we've got a homicide. I'm just giving you some information I gathered. I'll check it out and see what's what with the missus." She smiled, her faded lipstick darker around the edges of her lips. "In case we do go to court."

He glanced at her spiked hair and a few dark roots that deigned to show. "You didn't hear this at the local beauty shop?"

"Shit, no." One side of her mouth inched up. "I don't go to the 'beauty shop.' God, I hate that term. 'Salon' isn't a whole lot better. This"—she motioned to her stiff blond hair—"it may surprise you to know, *isn't* a professional job. Oh, you may think I paid forty, sixty or even a hundred dollars to some hairdresser with a name like Claude or Antoine, but hell, no. This here 'do' is compliments of good old Lady Clairol and a pair of shears I inherited from my grannie. I give myself a couple of hours every six weeks or so and voila, the piece of the damned resistance!"

"I think that's *piece de resistance,* you know, complete with French accent."

"Yeah, I *do* know." She motioned toward her head as she stood. "It's cheap, it's fast and it's state of the art!"

"If you say so."

"I do," she said, scrounging in her purse and coming up with a pack of Marlboro Lights. "Time to have myself a little break. Wanna come?" she asked as she shook out a cigarette.

"I'll take a rain check. I think I'd better do a little more checking on the friends and relatives of Josh Bandeaux since you seem to think he was so detested and unrespected."

Grinning, she motioned to the image of Josh Bandeaux visible on her computer monitor. "Some people even called him Josh 'The Bandit' Bandeaux."

"Cute."

"It fit. He was always taking something from someone. I think one of his ex-partners dubbed him with the name and the press loved it."

"They would."

"No love of the Fourth Estate, eh, Reed?"

"None," he growled.

She asked, "So you think I can sell this picture?" In the shot Josh Bandeaux was as they'd found him, slumped over his expensive desk, blood drizzling down his fingers to pool on the carpet. "Anyone who pays the price can put this little pinup on their own PC . . . you know as wallpaper or a screen saver or something."

"Funny," he said without a laugh.

"Thought you'd appreciate the humor." But any trace of a smile that had lingered on her thin lips had faded. Reed guessed Morrisette had been closer to "the prick" than she'd ever admit.

Which was par for the course. In Reed's estimation Sylvie Morrisette hadn't gotten over any of her ex-husbands or lovers. Brittle as she tried to appear, she wasn't as tough as she feigned. Just had bad taste in men. The way he'd heard it, she'd grown up without a father. Rumor suggested her old man had left her mother for a younger woman the day Morrisette had been brought home from the hospital. But that was just talk. Speculation by the local rednecks who couldn't handle Sylvie's tough-woman attitude.

Reed didn't know the truth and didn't care. Or at least he hadn't until now. "You wouldn't do anything to compromise the case, would you?" he asked.

"What?" she demanded, but he didn't really buy her innocence.

"You heard me."

"Blow it out your ass, Reed. You know what kind of cop I am."

"That's the problem," he said as he got to his feet and suffered a ball-shriveling glare from her. "You bend the rules more than I do."

She glanced at her watch and scowled. "I've got to get out of here. It is Saturday. I already missed my daughter's soccer game. Again."

"Cops don't have weekends."

"Just great pay, fabulous benefits and more glamor than a rock star," she quipped. "Madonna's been calling me and asking to trade places. I'm thinking it over. Told her I'd get back to her."

Reed laughed as her phone shrilled, then walked back to his office. He didn't want to think what a shrink would make of his partner.

Or Caitlyn Bandeaux, if Morrisette's information was correct. He tried to work around his gut feeling that Caitlyn Bandeaux was the prime suspect in the death of her husband. But he couldn't shake the feeling that she was involved.

He'd learned from Bandeaux's maid that Caitlyn, estranged or not, was a regular visitor to his house, had once lived there and probably still had a key since Bandeaux hadn't bothered to change his locks. A woman had been with Bandeaux that night if the glasses in the dishwasher were to be believed; the lipstick was a pink color that was similar to the one that she'd worn today, though without tests, the similarity could be coincidental. There were hundreds of shades of pink lipstick, possibly thousands. Most of all, she didn't have an alibi, at least one that would hold up it court. He'd thought during the interview this morning that she'd been shocked and bereaved, but also holding back, keeping a secret. He'd met enough liars in his years as an investigator with the San Francisco Police Department to spot one.

But this could be a suicide, don't discount that. Not yet. He snapped on his desk lamp. He'd bet a month's salary that Caitlyn Montgomery Bandeaux wouldn't pass a polygraph test if he administered one to her right now.

She was lying about last night; Reed was sure of it.

He just had to figure out why.

Six

The telephone jangled.

Caitlyn, thinking the caller might be her sister, dashed into the kitchen. Almost tripping over Oscar, she snagged the handset and noticed the lack of a name and number on Caller ID. "Hello?"

"Hi. Is this Caitlyn Bandeaux?" an unfamiliar female voice asked.

Caitlyn was instantly wary. Every muscle in her body tensed. "Yes."

"I'm glad I caught you." The voice was friendly. Had a "smile" to it. Which made Caitlyn all the more cautious. This wasn't the day for smiling, disembodied voices cozying up to her.

"My name's Nikki Gillette, and I'm with the *Savannah Sentinel*. I know you're going through a rough period right now, and I'd like to offer my condolences about your husband."

Oh, yeah, right. "Let me guess," Caitlyn said, trying to control her temper as she leaned a hip against the kitchen counter. "You'd like an interview. Maybe even an exclusive."

"I thought you'd like to tell your side of the story." Now there was an edge to Nikki's voice.

"I wasn't aware there were 'sides' and I'm not sure there is much of a story."

"Of course there is. Your husband was a very influential man, and the police seem to think he was either the victim of homicide or a suicide. I thought you'd like to set the record straight."

"My husband and I were separated," she said, then immediately wished she'd held her tongue. Her personal life wasn't anyone else's business.

"But you were still married."

Caitlyn didn't reply.

"Every marriage has its ups and downs," Nikki Gillette cajoled, using a tone usually reserved for women's confidences.

The ploy didn't work. Caitlyn's back was already up. "That's right and it's private, so let's stick with the 'no comment.'"

"But—"

It was time to end this. "Listen, Ms. Gillette. I have nothing more to say. Please, don't call again." Caitlyn slammed the receiver down before the woman could argue with her. The phone jangled instantly. "Damn it all." She picked up the receiver, hung up and then let the answering machine take any other messages. Even Kelly's. If her sister were to call, she'd leave a message or Caitlyn would recognize her cell number on Caller ID, or, if all else failed, Caitlyn would drive out to her place by the river and try to track her down. But she was getting desperate. *For God's sake, Kelly, call me.* She poured herself a glass of iced tea, took a sip then slid into a chair at the kitchen table and held her head in her hands. What had happened last night? How had she dreamed that Josh had been killed? How had all the blood gotten into her room? Her head throbbed, the ice melting in her barely touched glass. She remembered driving downtown and parking just off Emmet Park on River Street. Yes . . . she was certain of it. She closed her eyes, trying to relive the night before. Her headache thundered. Distorted images of the city at night spun crazily through her mind.

Neon lights.

Boats on the river.

A crush of people on the street.

Vaguely, in bits and disjointed pieces, she remembered crossing a street against the light as some taxi had careened around the corner and blared its horn. She'd ducked past the Cotton Exchange and down the cobblestone walk to the river. Wending her way through people on the crowded sidewalk, past shops, the smell of the slow-moving river ever present, she'd gone into a bar ... The Swamp, one she'd never been in before. Why had Kelly asked her to meet there, then not shown up? Or had she? Why couldn't she remember?

Had she somehow ended up at Josh's house?

Dear God, where had she been?

Her lower lip began to tremble, then slowly, bit by bit, her entire body followed suit. She felt the threat of tears and steadfastly pushed them back. What was Troy's comment, that she always played the victim? Well, no more. Never again. Her jaw clenched when she thought of her dead husband. "Damn it, Josh," she whispered. "What the hell happened?" She noticed a business card that Detective Reed had left on the coffee table. Maybe she should call him.

And tell him what, that you dreamed you were at Josh's house? Or that you don't remember if you were really there? That your memory is shot—you just have bits and pieces that don't make any sense. Or maybe you could explain that you're a fruitcake, just like Grandma Evelyn ... you remember her, don't you ... remember what happened at the lodge?

Caitlyn shivered, her mind reverberating with the questions Kelly would certainly throw at her if she ever found out that Caitlyn was considering confiding in the police. *You want to end up in the looney bin, again? That's what'll happen. And how the hell are you going to explain the blood? Jesus, Caitie-Did, one way or another, they'll lock you away for good this time! Prison or a psych hospital. Take your pick.*

"But I didn't do anything!" she said, pounding a fist on the table. Breathing hard, nearly gasping, she felt herself falling apart. But she wasn't out of her mind. No . . . hadn't Dr. Wade said as much? She willed her body to quit shaking, refused to feel sorry for herself. When she talked to Kelly, she would find out the truth. Whatever it was. *Oh, yeah? Well, paranoia runs in the family . . .*

She shot to her feet, knocking over her tea, scattering ice cubes across the table and feeling the scabs on her wrists pull tight. She couldn't think this way . . . couldn't let all her self-doubts get the better of her. Quickly grabbing a sponge from the sink, she began swabbing up the tea while tossing the skittering ice cubes into the sink. She was losing it. Really losing it. She threw the towel into the basin. She needed to get out of the house, to take Oscar for a walk or run through Forsyth Park until she was sweating and breathing rapidly, her heart pounding, her head finally clearing. Yes, that was it. She had to get out. Get away. Just as she had since she was a kid.

Life had been so much simpler then.

Or had it been?

Staring out the window to the walled garden, she remembered growing up in the old plantation house, running with Kelly and their friend Griffin through the woods and the squatty old slave quarters, chasing through the dilapidated rooms with hard dirt floors, crumbling walls and the musty smell of old sweat and wasted dreams. Wasps had droned in the rafters, and spider webs had clung to windowsills leaving the dried, desiccated corpses of insects littering the ledges.

Caitlyn and Kelly hadn't been ten years old yet, more like eight or nine, and Kelly had loved to play hide-and-seek in the interconnected rooms, disappearing into the shadows.

"You can't find me . . ." Kelly had taunted, and Griffin had always run toward the sound, not realizing that it bounced and ricocheted through the rotting timbers and broken doors. Some of the roofs had fallen in, and there were bird droppings flecked against the weathered walls.

Kelly had hidden in the most disturbing of places, old alcoves and dark niches that made Caitlyn's skin crawl. Places where rats and palmetto bugs and snakes could hide. Places that felt dark. Evil.

"Oh, you're just a fraidy cat," Kelly had teased, egging Caitlyn and Griffin into a crammed corner where a dark stain discolored a wall. "See here . . . this is where the old slave, Maryland—you remember the one Great-grannie told us about, she was named after the state where she was born—this is where Old Maryland squatted down and had herself that baby that died. Right here." Kelly had pointed to the floor beneath the stain and Caitlyn had shuddered.

Somehow Kelly had garnered all kinds of knowledge of the slaves and she'd sworn they practiced voodoo, killing chickens and heaven knew what else in a particular room or closet she found in the long row of houses. Her stories had never seemed to be the same, changing with the seasons or her whims, yet she'd insisted that every atrocity she spoke of was true. "If you don't believe me, ask Lucille, she'll tell you." Kelly's eyes had twinkled mischievously as sunlight danced through the leaves of a gnarled oak to dapple the ground in eerie, shifting shadows. It had been sticky-hot. Muggy. The temperature over a hundred degrees. But Caitlyn had felt a chill as cold as death.

"Maryland still haunts the house," Kelly had said. "I've seen her. She's looking for that dead baby."

"No way." Caitlyn had shaken her head vehemently. She'd always hated it when Kelly started telling her ghost stories.

"I have. Swear to God."

"I don't believe you," Caitlyn had lied, but Griffin, always gullible, had trembled and whispered, "I think it's the truth. I heard 'em one night, moanin' and cryin'."

"Why would I lie?" Kelly had asked with a smug smile. She'd known she'd gotten to them both.

Because you like to, Caitlyn had thought, but hadn't said it. Would never. Didn't want to chance a lashing from her twin's sharp tongue, or worse yet, her lapse into silence which could last days and require a hundred apologies from Caitlyn.

"It's the truth," Kelly had said more times than Caitlyn could remember. "Swear to God and if I lie, poke a thousand needles in my eye."

Just the image had made Caitlyn cringe, but Kelly had only giggled and darted off, her laughter trailing after her and fading like the music at the end of a movie scene. Caitlyn had turned on Griffin. "You never heard those slaves."

"Oh, yes, I have," Griffin had insisted, nodding his head, his brown hair flopping in his eyes, his skin pale even though it was summer.

"When?"

"Tons of times. It's . . . creepy."

Caitlyn had let the subject drop. Griffin, a neighbor boy whom Caitlyn and Kelly had been told to avoid, who was not allowed on the Montgomery property, had always sneaked over. He'd ridden his bike along an old deer trail through the woods and left it hidden in a thicket by the stream, until he had to go.

Two years younger than Caitlyn and Kelly, Griffin was gullible enough to believe anything Kelly said. Secretly, Caitlyn thought he was fascinated by her sister and afraid to disagree with Kelly. The truth of the matter was that Griffin wasn't any smarter than he was welcome at Oak Hill.

Caitlyn tried not to mention his name around the house, for when she did, her mother would get that pinched expression on her face, as if she was worried or mad. As if Griffin had done something Mother disapproved of. Amanda, their older sister, had always rolled her eyes expressively whenever Caitlyn slipped and talked about him. Lucille, forever hovering near Berneda and usually polishing some piece of already gleaming furniture, had, behind Berneda's back, pressed a thick finger to her lips, silently warning Caitlyn not to distress her sickly mother with talk of the boy. Caitlyn never understood why her mother disliked Griffin so, but assumed it was because of "bad blood," which was always the reason Berneda Pomeroy Montgomery snubbed a person.

But that had been years ago. Caitlyn didn't know why she'd thought of him now. She hadn't seen Griffin since they were kids; didn't know what had happened to him. Today, she had to concentrate on the problem at hand. She sent a dark look toward the telephone, desperate to hear from her twin. She looked for her cell phone, missing since yesterday. Not in her purse. Not in the car. Not in the bedroom . . . not anywhere. Maybe she'd left it with Kelly . . . or at Kelly's house. . . .

So why do you think Kelly will help you now? she asked herself as the walls seemed to close in on her. "Because she has to. She knows what happened!" she said so loudly that Oscar let out a bark. God, she was going out of her mind. Crazy. Just like Grandma Evelyn. In her mind's eye she saw an image of the old woman, skin pasty white, eyes staring glassily as she lay on the pillow, hands cold to the touch.

Caitlyn shivered, the image that had haunted her for nearly thirty years retreating into the shadows, but just barely. It was always there, ready to appear, mocking. Taunting. "You'll understand someday," the old woman had warned her.

Suddenly Caitlyn had to get out, to break free, to get away from these bloodstained walls.

"Come on, let's go for a walk," she said to the dog and took the stairs two at a time. Oscar bounded after her. Ignoring a stack of work on her desk in the den and the eerie sensation that assailed her when she stepped back into her bedroom, Caitlyn refused to notice the places on the walls where she'd scrubbed so hard she'd nearly rubbed the paint off. Nor would she think too hard about the absence of her sheer drapes which were still in the washer, or the discolored nap on the carpet where she'd washed the stained fibers with soap, water and every cleanser she'd found in her cupboard. To no avail. The spot was still visible.

So what? It's your blood, Caitlyn. Yours! No one else's. Certainly not Josh's. She had to believe that.

Had to.

The stains were just part of a huge optical illusion, that was all. It *seemed* like there was a lot more blood than had really been spilled.

So why then was the water in the pail where you rinsed the rags bright, deep red?

I just lost a lot of blood.

Because you sliced your own wrists and don't remember?

It doesn't matter. It only matters that the blood isn't Josh's.

How do you know?

I know—okay? So stop it! Just . . . stop! Her head was pounding, echoing with silent accusations and recriminations that gnawed at her guts, making her doubt anything she thought was real. "Hang on," she told herself. She just had to get out. Walk as far as she could to clear her mind. Get away from here and sweat. That was all. Then she'd be all right. Then she could think straight again. Oh, God, please . . . Her hands shook violently as she twisted her hair up onto her head. Trying in vain to turn off the questions pounding through her brain, she stripped out of her clothes to don jogging bra, long-sleeved T-shirt, shorts and running shoes. Then, on impulse, she walked into her den, ignored the stacks of work and checked her e-mail. Maybe Kelly had sent her a message . . . She was surprised she hadn't thought of it before. She clicked on her mailbox but saw nothing other than the usual offers of low-mortgage rates, discreet Viagra or a free peek at some porn site. Nothing from Kelly.

"Damn." She clicked off the computer and with Oscar at her heels, hurried downstairs, where she peeked out the front blinds and saw no trace of reporters on the street. Still, she'd be careful. She slapped a pair of sunglasses over her eyes and added a baseball cap to her disguise, as if she were some high-profile celebrity, for God's sake, then clicked on Oscar's leash. She pushed her way through the iron gate of the back courtyard and hit the street at a brisk pace.

Later, she'd deal with her family.
Later, she'd deal with the reporters.
Later, she'd deal with the police.
Later, she'd find out what the hell happened last night.

Adam checked his watch and frowned. He'd intended to stay only an hour and nearly three had passed. He didn't dare stay any longer. It wouldn't be long before the police had figured out that Rebecca was Caitlyn Montgomery Bandeaux's therapist. Which might be a good thing. Then they'd start looking for her, which, of course, would eventually lead them to him. He didn't have much time.

Carefully, he took the files he needed, stuffing them into a backpack he found in the closet. A backpack he recognized. One that had hung on a peg near the back door when he'd been in college. He'd thought she'd probably thrown it away, but there it hung, dusty, a few cobwebs clinging to it, empty except for an old parking receipt, a grocery list and a nearly empty tube of lipstick.

An image of her gulping the last of her coffee as she eyed the kitchen clock in their crummy upstairs apartment sliced through his mind. "Oh, God, I'm late. Dr. Connally will kill me!" She'd brushed a coffee-flavored kiss against his cheek, grabbed the backpack from its peg and flown out the door. "Don't forget to feed Rufus!" she'd called over her shoulder as the screen door slapped shut.

Rufus was their new kitten—snow white and big trouble. Cradling his cup, Adam had walked barefoot to the screen door, stared through the torn mesh and watched as she'd lithely thrown a leg over the seat of his mountain bike and pedaled into traffic. With no helmet, her red hair streaming behind her, she'd headed uphill toward campus while the new kitten had attacked his bare ankles and feet.

Now, in her abandoned office, his throat tightened as he remembered the girl she'd been nearly fifteen years ago. A lot of time had passed. Their lives had taken divergent paths.

The carefree twenty-two-year-old had grown up and matured into a woman he'd loved and hated; adored and despised.

It was funny how time had a way of tarnishing even the brightest futures.

So where the hell was she?

He glanced around the room one last time. Not that he wouldn't be back. He'd found a key ring in the top desk drawer and had pocketed it.

He didn't figure Rebecca would mind.

Seven

The walk helped.

Caitlyn's head was clearer than it had been when she'd woken up, but her memory was still fragmented and dull, the night before coming at her in shards of frosty glass, images in murky color and slow motion. In the kitchen she noticed that there were sixteen new messages on her answering machine, and she refused to listen to any of them. Most likely they were all reporters. She checked the numbers on Caller ID. Some were anonymous, others unfamiliar; none were from Kelly's little cabin on the river.

Upstairs, she threw on a sleeveless cotton dress that she covered with a lightweight but long-sleeved sweater, then walked across the hall to her den.

Snagging her keys from her desk, she figured her hair would dry on the way to Oak Hill. But she stopped when she saw the digital readout of her office clock. It was correct. Hadn't lost so much as a minute of time. Showed no sign of a power interruption.

Unlike the clock radio in her bedroom.

She looked at the other clocks in the house. All were

keeping perfect time. There was no sign of any interruption of electricity to them.

The hairs on the back of her neck rose.

If there hadn't been a power outage, then there had been some kind of power interrupt, as if the clock had been unplugged. But when she'd cleaned up earlier in the day, the plug had been firmly in the light socket. And it wasn't that particular socket because the lamp, attached to the same source, had been just fine.

Someone unplugged the clock either on purpose or by accident and then, in his hurry to leave, forgot to reset it.

Who? Why? And for God's sake, what did it have to do with the blood that had been spattered all over her bedroom?

A fleeting image burned behind her eyes.

The bar. Loud music. People laughing, talking, packed in so close you couldn't move. Caitlyn sat in a booth, two drinks in front of her, waiting, looking at her watch, noticing the bartender staring at her through the crowd, sipping one drink . . . then another . . . come on, Kelly. Come on. Where the hell are you?

The image shrank away as quickly as it had appeared, and Caitlyn was left knowing no more of what happened than before. But she couldn't dwell on it now. Her family was expecting her.

She double-checked that the doors were locked, then was out the door and on the road, driving east out of the city, glancing in her rearview mirror to make sure no one from the press or police was following her.

"You're paranoid," she muttered, catching her reflection in the rearview mirror as she stopped at a traffic light. The other vehicles seemed innocuous, no dark van or SUV with tinted windows hovering a few cars behind. She made a few extra jogs though the shady, narrow streets just to be sure, then berated herself for her apprehension. As she turned onto the main highway and cruised out of the city limits, she stepped on it, needing to get out of the city, away from the police, away from the press, away from the blackness that surrounded last night.

She pushed the speed limit, her thoughts spinning as rapidly as the wheels of her Lexus. So why hadn't Kelly called? she wondered, flipping down the visor.

Maybe she did. While you were out walking Oscar. Or while you were in the shower. You were the one who turned off the ringer on the phone. There's a chance that Kelly was one of the sixteen calls, you know.

Gnawing on her lower lip, Caitlyn realized her mistake. She should have checked the messages and tried once more to catch her sister before she faced their mother. Now, she'd have to wait several hours and she didn't dare mention Kelly's name at Oak Hill.

Caitlyn's fingers tightened over the steering wheel and her palms began to sweat as the suburbs gave way to fields and marshes. She shoved in a Springsteen CD and tried to get lost in the music of the E Street Band, but it proved impossible. She couldn't forget that Josh had been killed, that the police seemed to think she was somehow involved, and even she herself couldn't explain her whereabouts or actions at the time of his death.

And all that blood in your room . . . how did it get there? Drained from your body? Come on. If you'd lost that much, you would be in a hospital right now, probably on the receiving end of a transfusion.

She swallowed hard, nearly missed a corner, the car's wheels sliding in loose gravel strewn upon the road's shoulder. Heart racing, she eased off the gas.

So whose blood was it? Josh's? But he was blocks away in his own house.

Maybe you moved the body.

Maybe you moved it in this car.

Her stomach clenched.

Sweat dotted her forehead and she slid a glance into the back seat. No dark stains. Nor on the passenger side. Of course she hadn't killed Josh and taken him home. What was she thinking? This was crazy. Nuts.

Just like Grandma Evelyn.

She began to tremble. First her abdomen, then her calves.

Don't do this . . . don't think this way. She concentrated on the road. The ribbon of asphalt with its middle broken stripe, up and down, over small rises and into shallow gullies. Her breathing was coming in short gasps. Horrid images sped through her mind. A quick vision of Josh at his desk, of the blood. On the corner of the desk was a copy of the damned lawsuit claiming she'd been negligent in their child's death.

Negligent! As if Jamie hadn't been everything to her; the very reason for her life. "Bastard!" she spat, tears beginning to well as she thought of the hours she'd spent at her daughter's bedside, the mad rush she'd made to the hospital, the mind-numbing terror as the doctors and nurses in the ER tried and failed to get her precious baby to respond and then . . . then . . . the horrible words, wrapped in sympathetic looks, kind gestures, a gentle touch on her arm when she was told that Jamie had "passed on."

"I'm sorry, Mrs. Bandeaux," Dr. Vogette had said softly to her in the hospital's waiting room with its soothing blue and green couches, potted palms and piped-in music. His expression had been sober, his eyes behind wire-rimmed glasses, concerned. "Sometimes this happens with a virus. We did everything possible . . ."

"No," she said vehemently, nearly veering off the road. "No, you didn't, you bastard. None of you did all you could!"

An oncoming truck blasted its horn, the driver holding a hand outward with fingers extended as if to remind her that she was an idiot as all eighteen wheels sped by carrying a load of gasoline. "Yeah, yeah, I know," she muttered under her breath, trying to regain control not only of the Lexus but of her composure as well. Checking the rearview mirror, she saw the semi disappear around a corner.

You're cracking up Catie-Did. You are absolutely cracking up. She could almost hear Kelly's voice, heavy with recriminations.

"Pull yourself together." She slowed for the bridge, then caught a glimpse of the plantation just on the other side of the river.

Oak Hill.

Symbol of all the Montgomery wealth.

A reminder of days and grandeur long past.

A hint of Old Georgia and genteel Southern ways.

And a facade. A damned sham. Behind the solid oak doors, beveled glass windows and thick white siding lurked secrets and lies and tragedy. So much pain.

Don't dwell on that now. You can't. Just do what you have to do.

Determined not to fall apart, she gritted her teeth and wheeled into the long straight lane guarded by ancient oak trees. There were thirty-nine trees, one having blown over in a storm and never replaced. She and Griffin had counted them time and time again. "I'll meet you at number seventeen," he'd whispered to her often enough. Seventeen had been his favorite.

She slowed as she approached the main house. Three full stories above the ground, the first two complete with verandahs and railings, the third peeking out of dormers in the sloped roof. Once grand, it now stood in a state of disrepair. White paint had grayed and was beginning to chip and blister.

Tall black shutters, once gleaming, now baked to a dull sheen beneath the unforgiving Georgia sun, surrounded paned windows of old, watery glass. And the shrubbery was no longer manicured, but overgrown and rambling despite the work of a year-round gardener. Where once there had been parties and laughter and gaiety, there now was silence and shadow, ghosts and wraiths, tragedy and lies.

Only Berneda, Caitlyn's mother, and her sister Hannah continued to live here. There were a handful of servants, of course, and fortunately Lucille Vasquez had remained. Caitlyn understood why her mother stayed on—this was the only home she'd known in over forty years—but she couldn't fathom why her youngest sister elected to stay in this tomb of a plantation. At twenty-six, Hannah should have been out with people her age, living on her own, not holed up in this huge, decaying reminder of the Old South. But then, Hannah had always been a little off, out of step, and even out of touch.

Like you?

Caitlyn ignored the nagging voice in her mind and followed the driveway to the side of the house. Her heart sank. Troy's black Range Rover was already parked in the lengthening shadows behind her mother's Cadillac. So he'd beaten her to the punch. Great. Troy had probably hightailed it here the minute his important appointment had ended. So much for breaking the news herself.

She climbed out of her Lexus.

Hushed conversation and a hint of cigarette smoke drifted on the breeze.

". . . always trouble . . . since the accident . . . hasn't been herself . . ." Her mother's soft, dulcet tones floated over a honeysuckle-scented breeze and Caitlyn tensed. So she was the topic of conversation. Again. Today, she supposed, it made sense. Other times she wasn't so sure.

"She needs help," Troy said over the sound of clinking ice cubes. "Serious help."

"I thought she was seeing someone . . . after Jamie passed on . . . Oh, Lord, trouble just never stops, does it . . . the twins were always . . ."

Caitlyn's spine stiffened, and her mother's voice was more muted, as if she'd turned her head away.

". . . I just never knew what to do . . . so fragile, not strong like the rest of you . . . sometimes it's difficult to be a mother."

Give me that strength. Caitlyn was tired of everyone handling her with kid gloves. Yes, she'd been frail and had fallen apart after the accident and then again when her baby had died, but who wouldn't have? She ducked through a clematis-draped arbor and hurried up two brick steps to the back porch.

Conversation dwindled. Her mother turned to look over her shoulder as she sat, back to the stairs at a glass-topped table. Sipping iced tea, she fanned herself with the fingers of her free hand. She was dressed as if for a social tea—a long gauzy skirt and print top, polished pumps on her feet, a string of pearls around her throat.

Troy was standing, smoking a cigarette, one hip propped against the railing, his expression as grim as that of an undertaker as he watched a hummingbird flit through the fragrant honeysuckle blossoms. Through the partially opened window, Caitlyn caught a glimpse of Lucille, her mother's private maid. With the pretense of folding napkins, Lucille hovered close enough to eavesdrop.

It was little wonder Lucille knew everything about the family. She had raised her daughter, Marta, here. Sometimes Marta, Kelly and Caitlyn had played together long ago.

"Caitlyn!" Troy greeted her in an obvious effort to quickly change the subject and warn his mother that her difficult child had arrived.

"I thought you had an important meeting," Caitlyn told Troy.

"I did. Important but short."

"Right."

Berneda's pale cheeks colored a bit. "Oh, Caitlyn, I'm so sorry about Josh," she said, swallowing as tears suddenly glistened in her eyes. "I know you loved him."

"Once," Caitlyn admitted, determined not to break down.

"It's difficult." She patted Caitlyn's hand as Caitlyn brushed a kiss against her wan, bony cheek. Berneda was fighting heart disease and slowly losing the battle.

"I'll be all right."

"Lucille," Berneda called to the open window, her strong profile visible. She had been a striking woman in her youth, with intense green eyes, reddish brown hair and a regal carriage that hinted at snobbery and added to her allure. She'd once modeled, she'd reminded her children often enough as they'd grown up, and had she not married their father and borne seven children, which had wreaked havoc on her once wasp-thin waist, she could have posed for the covers of magazines in Europe as well as the United States. She'd always made it clear that she'd taken the higher ground, decided to have babies and yet, whenever any one of them screwed up, she threw the modeling card on the table. "Think what I sacrificed for you! A fortune of my own making and all that fame. I could have made it in movies, you know. Had an offer once . . ." But now she was playing the role of concerned mother. "Lucille, see that Caitlyn has some iced tea."

"I'm not thirsty, Mom," Caitlyn assured her.

"Nonsense. You've had a horrible shock." Berneda forced a tired smile. "Oh, Caitlyn, I'm so sorry." She held out her arms and waved her fingers inward rapidly, inviting a hug. As Caitlyn embraced her, she drank in the scent of her mother's perfume, a fragrance Berneda had worn for as long as Caitlyn could remember. They clung to each other a moment as Caitlyn heard the screen door bang shut and Lucille, balancing a tray, stepped outside.

"I think we could use something stronger." Troy eyed the glass pitcher and tumblers arranged around a small plate of ladyfingers, grapes and pecan tarts.

Lucille's expression didn't change, but Caitlyn noticed her neck stiffen a bit, and her eyes seemed a darker shade of brown as she set the glasses onto the table and began pouring, refilling Berneda's glass and offering Caitlyn a new drink with a sprig of mint in the glass. "I'm sorry about your husband," she said to Caitlyn.

"Thank you." Caitlyn's throat grew thick again even though she knew from personal experience that Joshua Bandeaux was a liar and a cheat. She hadn't believed it at the time, but now she realized that he'd married her for her name and her money, gotten her pregnant to that very end.

It hurt to think that Jamie's conception had been part of Josh's long-term plan to get at Caitlyn's money. And then, to think he would actually file a wrongful death suit against her . . . as if she would ever do anything to injure her child.

"Caitlyn?" She heard her name as if from a distance. "Caitlyn?"

She blinked.

"Are you sure you're all right?" Lucille asked, jarring Caitlyn out of her reverie.

She found herself watching the beads trail down her glass of tea, a glass she didn't remember accepting. "Right as rain," she said sarcastically. She couldn't help but catch the quick look sent from Troy to Berneda, a shared understanding that she wasn't quite all there, that she was somehow "misfiring" or "not running on all eight cylinders."

"I'm sorry," Caitlyn finally said, forcing a smile she didn't feel. "I just spaced for a second."

"It hasn't been an easy day," Berneda said.

"You don't have to make excuses for me, Mom. I just wanted to come out and tell you about Josh."

Her mother nodded and sighed. "Troy said that he thought you might stay out here for a few days."

Caitlyn shot her brother a look guaranteed to kill. "I don't think so."

"He mentioned the police might be bothering you."

"Just asking questions."

"Surely they . . . they don't think you had anything to do with Josh's death?"

Her fingers nearly slipped on the glass. So there was already speculation. Wonderful. She sent Troy another killing glance. "I don't know what they think, Mom."

"But that's ludicrous—" Berneda began as the sound of a car's engine roared up the drive. "Now what?"

Brakes squealed to a stop and for an instant Caitlyn thought the police had chased her here—that they were standing on their brakes, guns drawn, ready to arrest her just as if she were some wanted criminal in one of those action movies. Sweat broke out over her forehead. She wanted to run. Instead she took a long drink of iced tea, told herself to remain calm as fast-paced footsteps clicked loudly against the back walk.

Amanda Montgomery Drummond, Caitlyn's oldest sister, in black skirt and jacket, flew around the corner. Her short-cropped hair looked as if she'd jabbed her fingers through it a dozen times on the way over and her silk blouse was uncharacteristically wrinkled. "I've been trying to call you," she said to Caitlyn as she reached the porch. She dashed up the steps. "What the hell is going on? I saw on the news that Josh is dead. Is that right?"

Troy nodded and stubbed out his cigarette in the ashtray on the porch railing.

"And no one thought to call me?" She was furious, her eyes narrowing on her brother.

"Caitlyn called me," he explained as he plowed stiff fingers through his hair.

"That still doesn't explain why I'm sitting in my office and Rob Stanton—you know, one of the senior partners who just happened to be working today—pokes his head in and suggests I go into the conference room to catch the noon news. Jesus, couldn't someone have thought to pick up the damned phone so I might not get blindsided?" She was seething, her cheeks flushed, her lips turned in on themselves.

"It was a mistake," Troy said.

"So then I try to call you—" She turned on Caitlyn. "And all I got was your machine."

"I turned off the phone. Reporters."

"Figures. They're the worst kind of carrion eaters around. Just the hint of a scandal and they come out of the woodwork." She took in a deep breath and shook her head as if to clear it; then her expression softened. "God, Caitie, how're you doing?"

"I've been better."

"The police have been asking her questions," Berneda cut in.

"They just dropped by to tell me about Josh."

"But you said you weren't a suspect." Berneda's skin turned the color of the weathered siding.

"What she said was that she didn't know what the police were thinking," Troy explained to his older sister. "Josh may have committed suicide or . . . well, there could be foul play, right, Caitlyn? Isn't that what you made of it?" he asked, making sure he'd gotten all the facts straight.

"That's essentially what Detective Reed said."

"Damn it all," Amanda muttered.

"If it turns out to be homicide, then they'll take a closer

look at all of us.'' Troy glanced at his mother's horrified expression. ''Come on, Mom, you know the drill. The people closest to the victim are always at the top of the suspect list. We've been through this before.''

''Too many times,'' she agreed as she watched a butterfly flit near a lilac bush.

''But they're not sure it's homicide. That's good.'' Amanda was thinking aloud.

''There is nothing good about this,'' Berneda whispered.

Amanda's face was grim, the wheels in her mind obviously already turning at a rapid pace. ''Marty from Accounting knows someone on the force. Maybe he could get the guy to tell us what the police are really thinking.''

''Oh, my God, you're worried.'' Berneda struggled to sit up higher in her chair, and Lucille was at her side in an instant, plumping her pillows.

''I just can't believe Josh would kill himself,'' Caitlyn insisted.

''You don't know that.'' Amanda dropped into one of the chairs surrounding the table. ''No one knows what someone else is thinking. Look at Bill Black. From outward appearances the guy had it all—partnership in one of the best legal firms on the East Coast, a beautiful young wife, two cute, healthy kids, a house worth a fortune and another place in the Catskills. Free and clear. Then one day, for no apparent reason, he goes into the garage, puts a hose in the tailpipe of his new Mercedes and ends it all. No one knew that he was being blackmailed, no one knew that he was accused of raping and impregnating an underage client. No one, not even his best friend, thought Bill had a problem in the world. They were wrong.''

Caitlyn shook her head and stared at the hills to the west and the lowering sun. ''I know Josh.''

''Knew him,'' Troy corrected. ''And Amanda's right. Let's just wait and see what the police come up with.''

Berneda turned her attention to her eldest daughter. ''But if Caitlyn needs a lawyer, could you help her?''

''I'm not a criminal attorney,'' Amanda said, her voice

tight. "I gave that up years ago. I deal in tax law and estates. You know that."

"I know, I know, but I'm worried. You worked for the District Attorney."

"And hated it, remember? Dealing with all those low-lifes and idiots and . . . anyway, I'm glad I gave it up."

"Can you recommend someone?" Berneda asked, worrying the pearls at her neck.

"Jesus, let's not borrow too much trouble!" Troy searched in his shirt pocket for his cigarettes. "Caitlyn and I already discussed it. I don't think she should talk to the police without representation, but let's not all act as if she's a suspect." He found his lighter and clicked it several times until he was finally able to light up. "Okay?" he asked her as he exhaled.

"Of course not."

"Didn't think so."

"I just think it's good to be prepared," Berneda said as Lucille appeared again.

"Are you all stayin' for dinner?" Lucille's smile was benign, as if she had no idea how serious the conversation was.

Berneda nodded. "Of course they are."

"Not me." Amanda checked her watch. "I've got tons more work to do. *Tons.* I won't get home until midnight as it is." She caught the wounded look in her mother's eye and sighed. "I just ran out here to see that you were okay. I know this kind of thing shakes you up. When I get this project done, I'll come out for a weekend. How does that sound?"

"Like it will never happen," Berneda said, though she brightened a bit.

"Of course it will. It's a date. Promise."

She'd barely said the words when her cell phone chirped and she fished in her purse to find the phone, flip it open and put it to her ear. She walked to the far side of the porch, started talking in hushed tones and turned her back on her siblings and mother. "I know, I know . . . but there was a tragedy in the family. I'll be there. Yes. Tell him twenty minutes, thirty tops . . . hey, I get it, okay. Remind him it's Saturday. He's lucky I'm working.'' She snapped the phone shut and let out a long sigh, then squared her shoulders and faced her family again. "I really do have to run right now. But I'll be back, promise." Dropping the phone into her bag, she brushed a kiss across her mother's cheek. "I'll bring Ian, too," Amanda vowed and Berneda's smile froze at the mention of her son-in-law. Amanda's husband was a corporate pilot for a timber company. He was often away, rarely making an appearance at any family function. Good looking and fit, he was the kind of man who could charm the birds from the trees. The only trouble was that as soon as they got close enough, he'd shoot them. Dead. And love every second of it. There was a dark side to Ian Drummond, one he seldom showed, one Caitlyn had once caught a glimpse of, though she'd never admitted it to a soul. Would never.

Amanda touched Caitlyn lightly on the arm, her fingers grazing the bandage under her sweater. Caitlyn froze, hardly daring to breathe. What if Amanda felt the gauze wrapped so tightly around her wrist? She pulled her arm away. "Call me if you need to," Amanda said with the trace of a smile. "And if you're not going to answer your phone, at least turn on your damned cell. I tried that, too."

"I will," Caitlyn promised and Amanda squeezed her arm, nearly sending Caitlyn through the roof of the porch.

"Do." She slipped her sunglasses onto the bridge of her nose and hurried down the path, leaving with a roar of her car's engine, disappearing as quickly as she'd come.

"Well, that's that," Troy said, scowling as he drew hard on his cigarette. "She's done her duty."

"What's that supposed to mean?" Berneda was pushing herself upright.

"Just that Amanda does the bare minimum as far as the family is concerned."

"You don't believe she's busy?" Berneda shook her head and Caitlyn noticed a few silver hairs that had dared make an appearance in her mother's mahogany colored tresses. "You two have never gotten along."

That much was true. Caitlyn remembered the animosity between her eldest sister and her brother. It seemed to have existed from the moment Troy had been brought home from the hospital and still lingered today, over thirty years later. "Where's Hannah?" Caitlyn asked, as much to ease the tension as anything.

"Out." Berneda looked away. "She left last night."

"For where?"

"I don't know. She was angry."

"With—?" Caitlyn urged.

"The world. Me. Lucille and whoever happened to call." Berneda lifted one hand in a gesture of dismissal. "You know how she gets. Has a stubborn streak. Just like her father had. I don't know . . . I don't know if she's even heard about Josh yet, but she will." Berneda checked her watch. "There's certain to be something on the evening news. I suppose, whether we want to watch it or not, we should."

Caitlyn didn't know if she could get through an evening sitting on a couch and staring at the television while reporters dissected, rehashed, explained and made conjectures about her husband's death. But she had to. Sooner or later she had to face the truth about what happened to her husband. In the next few days, it certainly wasn't going to get any easier.

Eight

"They all belong at Warner Brothers Studios," Sylvie said as she sauntered into Reed's office bringing with her the scent of some musky perfume and a whiff of recently smoked cigarettes. She'd been home and checked on her kids, but had obviously found another sitter and was back at the station.

"Who belongs at Warner Brothers?"

"The Montgomerys, that's who. Those people are looney-effin'-tunes!" She leaned against the windowsill in his office, bracing herself with her hands.

"Effin?"

"I'm tryin' to clean it up, okay?" She rolled her eyes expressively. "My kids are seven and three, and you don't know how bad your language is until you hear it come back at you from them. What's the old saying, 'From the mouths of babes . . .?' Well it's the truth. The other night I'm doin' the dishes and the kids are in the family room, just around the corner. I hear Toby call his sister a buckin' pwick . . . probably overheard me talking about his dad." Sylvie shrugged. "Anyway, Priscilla laughed and told him how stupid he was, that girls couldn't be pricks and it wasn't

bucking but fucking . . . Oh, well, you get my drift." Her
lips twisted at the irony of it all. "I told 'em both to knock
it off, but Priscilla reminded me that my language was as
bad as a sewer rat's so we all agreed to put a quarter in the
Hello Kitty bank . . . Now wait, don't give me that look!
Surely you've heard of Hello Kitty." She stared at him as
if he'd told her he had three balls.

"I don't even get it. Hello Kitty?"

"I forgot you lived on another planet."

"What're you talking about?"

"Forget it. You don't have kids. You're out of it. The
point is, I should never have agreed to the deal. Now they
chase me around waiting for me to fuc–screw up. Damn!
Oh, geez . . ." She rolled her eyes. "I figure I'll save enough
money this year to get me and the kids to Disney World."

He leaned back in his chair until it creaked. "You had
something to say about the Montgomerys."

"Boy howdy." She shook her head. "Talk about nut
cases! It's one after another. It goes back for generations.
There's a history of major screws loose in that family. And
tragedy. Hunting accidents, boating accidents, car accidents
and enough scandals to make Jerry Springer salivate. It's
like a fuc–an effin' soap opera! Did you know that there
was a whole other side of the family? We're not talkin' a
bastard or two. No way. This is just all kinda kinky.

"Cameron Montgomery, Caitlyn's father and heir to the
cotton and shipping fortune, had himself another family.
Right around here." She swirled one long finger in the air,
apparently to indicate Savannah. "Not only did Cameron
have seven kids with his wife, but he managed to have
another one or two, maybe more, with a woman named
Copper Biscayne, a low-rent sort who lived out of town.
She's dead, by the way, along with a whole lotta other people
who were related to the Montgomerys. Josh Bandeaux is
just the latest in a long line of casualties."

"Any others that look like suicides?" Reed asked.

"Now you think he killed himself?"

He shook his head. "The jury's still out on that one. Just

thinking aloud. We know that someone was with him that night; we just don't know if whoever it was decided to kill him.''

"You think someone staged the thing, to make it look like a suicide.''

"Just one of the possibilities,'' he said, reminding himself. He rubbed the back of his neck. "But we'll find out more when we get the autopsy report and the crime scene results. My guess is there'll be some evidence pointing to the missus. She had means, motive and opportunity and she can't scare up even a flimsy alibi.''

"I'm not sure you gave her the opportunity.''

"I asked her where she was last night and she said she was out. That was about it.''

"You didn't press the issue.''

"We weren't sure we were dealing with a murder.''

"We still aren't.''

"But we do know they were separated, there was another woman, he wanted a divorce and her money and he was filing a civil wrongful death suit against her for the kid's death. A neighbor saw her car at the scene.''

"But,'' Sylvie urged. "I hear it in your voice, Reed— there's a 'but' coming.''

He picked up a pen and clicked it as he thought. "But she'd have to have been one stupid killer to leave so many clues at the scene. She didn't strike me as stupid.''

"Maybe she was freaked. Didn't mean to kill him and then took off.''

"Didn't mean to kill him? With his wrists slit? That's not the same as a gun going off accidentally in a struggle. Did you see the man's arms? Whoever slit them—and I'm not ruling out the victim—intended for him to bleed to death.'' He narrowed his eyes on his partner. "There's something about this that doesn't feel right.''

"Something? Try nothing,'' Sylvie said, as she reached into her pocket for her pager. Frowning at the numeric display, she started for the door. "Nothing about it feels right. Yet. But it will. We'll figure it out.''

"You think so?"

She glanced over her shoulder and threw him a smile. "Effin'-A."

"What a pity," Sugar Biscayne muttered sarcastically, smirking as she watched the news and slid her jeans and panties over her hips and down her legs. "Another bastard bites the dust." She kicked the faded Levi's into a corner of her bedroom and slipped into a red thong and short shorts that barely covered her butt. The reporter was going on and on about Josh Bandeaux as if he was some kind of Savannah god or something. Yeah, right. Swirling the remains of her drink, she felt a slight buzz. Probably from the vodka, but it didn't hurt that another Montgomery pig had bought the farm. And Bandeaux was the worst, weaseling into the family, trying to cozy up to the money. What a shit. She raised her glass in a mock toast. "Enjoy hell, you sick son of a bitch."

A fan moved hot air from one end of the master bedroom to the other, whirring so loudly she could barely hear the television, where the screen was filled with an image of Bandeaux at the annual policeman's ball. Handsome prick. Sexy as hell. *Yeah, and dead as a doornail.* That thought gave her a little bit of pleasure as she stared at the screen.

Dressed in what looked like a designer black tuxedo with a shirt that required no tie, Bandeaux clenched a drink in one hand and flashed his sexy grin straight at the lens of the camera. God, he loved the limelight. More than one Savannah woman had found that smile irresistible. Sugar thought that it was the embodiment of evil.

She took another drink. Felt the cold vodka slide down her esophagus to hit her stomach in a burst of flame. She shuddered, remembering how she'd felt when she'd heard the news that Caitlyn Montgomery had married the slimeball. All because Caitlyn had been naive and stupid enough to let herself get pregnant. How in the hell did *that* happen these days?

Go figure.

Any woman, herself included, would have found Bandeaux sexy enough for a roll in the hay—Sugar would admit that much—but it took a really dumb one to marry him. Pregnant or not. Tying yourself to that prick only spelled trouble of the worst order. And Caitlyn had found it. Big time. Not that Sugar cared. Sugar had always thought Caitlyn was a few eggs short of a dozen when it came to brains. Caitlyn had inherited plenty in the beauty department, but lacked something when it came to smarts.

Blessed with smooth, white-Southern-belle skin, plump lips, and wide hazel eyes, Caitlyn was tall and athletic-looking except that she had big tits. Great tits. Sugar always noticed, not because she was into women, but because she always sized up the competition. All women, even rich society types, were competition.

Especially relatives.

The picture on the screen flipped to a shot of Josh Bandeaux with his wife and daughter. The kid was probably eighteen months or so at the time the photograph was taken. They seemed the perfect family aside from the fact that Caitlyn's smile appeared strained as she stood next to her husband in an obviously posed family portrait. "Perfect, my ass," Sugar said, tossing back the remains of her vodka and biting on a piece of ice as she scrounged in the second drawer of her dresser and found a decent tank top. She tugged it over her head and smoothed out a few wrinkles so that it hugged her figure.

The reporter was saying something about the suspicious circumstances of Bandeaux's death when she heard an engine—a truck from the sound of it—pull into her drive. Who the hell would be showing up now? Inwardly groaning, she made an educated guess that her brother was paying her a visit. Dickie Ray was the last person she wanted to deal with.

She snapped off the old set with its crummy reception and walked into the living room, where she opened the door of her double-wide before her brother could start pounding the hell out of it.

Her dog, part pit bull, part lab, and one hundred percent bitch, was on her feet and let out a low growl.

"Mornin'," Dickie said, one eye on Caesarina. The dog didn't like him. Never had. But then, she had good taste.

"It's nearly seven at night and I'm late for work. *I've* got a job," Sugar reminded him, pointedly checking her watch, thinking that she didn't want to let him inside. Once flopped on the old couch, Dickie Ray had an inclination to park it and down a six-pack while staring at some kind of sports program for hours. Once he got inside, it would take a crowbar to get him out. He wasn't a bad guy, just lazy as hell.

"You call what you do a job?"

"Legitimate work," she said. He didn't so much as flinch. Thought collecting disability was as good as work. "I perform a service."

Dickie Ray snorted. "So now giving drooling, drunked-up losers a hard-on is a service."

"I dance."

"With your clothes off. Face it, Sugar, you're a stripper. Period. You can call it what you want, but what you do is show off your tits and ass so that the guys in the bar want to jerk off."

"That's their problem."

"They don't see it that way."

"Neither do I. Let's drop it." She hated it when Dickie Ray was surly, or as Mama would say, "in one of his moods." He was certainly in one now, tweaking that nerve of hers that always showed when she discussed how she earned her wages. She wasn't proud of what she did, just the way she did it. She was good at her job, in great shape, and, when she'd socked enough money away, or when she ever got her hands on the inheritance she'd been promised, she'd give it all up, go to school, learn to run a computer and become a receptionist in some big corporation. But she just couldn't swing it yet.

"Hear about Bandeaux?" Dickie Ray asked as he walked into her kitchen, opened a cupboard and found a half-eaten box of Cheez-Nips.

"I was just listening to the news."

"A shame." Dickie Ray tossed a handful of the crackers into his mouth. He could have been a handsome enough man if he ever got rid of the beer gut and stringy hair hanging down to his shoulders. He kept the sides short, but let his blond curls fall free, probably in the hopes of disguising the fact that he was thinning on the top. To offset that problem he was always wearing a baseball cap, pulled down low over his eyes, the bill nearly touching the top of the aviator sunglasses forever on his face. Probably to hide the redness in his eyes. Dickie had a tendency toward benders, alcohol and cocaine whenever he could get his hands on it. His goatee was untrimmed. "You think he was kilt?" Dickie had found himself a plastic Big Gulp cup in one of her cupboards. He opened the refrigerator and hung on the door, letting the cool air blast over his face as he surveyed the meager contents. Finally he settled on a Dr. Pepper.

"Murdered?" Sugar asked.

"Isn't that what 'suspicious circumstances' usually means?"

She turned that thought over a couple of times. "That's probably what happened. Bandeaux pissed too many people off in this town."

"Wonder who did it." He took a sip and wrinkled his nose. "You know this here soda is flat?"

"It's Cricket's," Sugar explained.

"Where is she?" Dickie looked around as if, for the first time, he realized that his younger sister wasn't on the premises.

"Working. You know, *earning* her keep. She doesn't get off until eight."

He glanced at his watch, then searched in the cupboard over the refrigerator for a bottle. "Got any scotch or rye?"

"No."

"A man could die of thirst around here."

"That's the general idea," she said and meant it. Her last boyfriend had sponged off her for a year. Her ex still came sniffing around, looking for a handout. Either money or sex. She gave him neither. No wonder she had such a bad attitude about men; she surrounded herself with losers. She had a fleeting thought about her current relationship. A relationship only Cricket knew anything about. Even then Sugar kept most of the details to herself. The affair was clandestine. Hot. Off limits.

Dickie Ray scrounged through the cupboard and found a pint of Jack Daniels with a trace of liquor in it. Frowning at the scant amount, he nonetheless drained the bottle into his cup. "Hardly worth the work," he muttered, stirring his concoction with an index finger.

"No one's got a gun to your head."

"Leastwise not today," he said with an enigmatic wink, then lifted his cup. "Let's drink one to whoever it was that had the balls to get rid of Bandeaux." With a quick nod, he took a long guzzle of his drink and wiped his mouth with the back of his sleeve.

"You talk to Donahue lately?" he asked, finally getting to the reason for his visit.

"Not since the last time you asked."

Dickie snorted. "Some hotshot attorney." Dickie's bad mood quickly got worse.

"He's doing what he has to."

"It's been months," Dickie grumbled, and Sugar picked up his empty soda can and dropped it into the overflowing trash can. Caesarina wandered over to sniff the trash, then settled on her rear on the yellowed linoleum and scratched behind an ear with a back leg. "I think he's stalling us."

"He's not stalling." Sugar, too, was irritated by all the hoops, obstacles and delays that had been thrown at them, but she refused to give up. Flynn Donahue, Attorney at Law, had promised Sugar, Dickie Ray and Cricket that he would find a way to get them their fair share of the Montgomery fortune. After all, they were all grandchildren of Benedict Montgomery, just the same as his legitimate heirs were. The fact that their grandmother, Mary Lou Chaney, had been his secretary rather than his wife was of little consequence. Blood was blood, Donahue had insisted when he'd taken their case nearly a year ago.

Yeah, and what about the rumors that good ol' Uncle Cameron could be your father? Sugar had heard nasty gossip all of her life. And now was banking on it.

"Nothin' like keepin' it all in the family," Brad Norton had teased in the eighth grade. His whiny voice had cracked and Sugar couldn't help but notice he was getting a major case of zits. Good. "I guess you all just like you all. I mean *really* like." He'd followed the comment by raising his bushy blond eyebrows before sniggering loudly, and his friends, a group of blockheads, had joined in, laughing and pointing.

"What's it like, Sugar? Is it *sweet* to think that yer uncle is yer pappy?" Billy Quentin had thrown in, hitching up his pants that were always trying to fall down beneath his big belly. He'd been a fat, stupid boy whose father had bred hunting dogs, poached deer and distilled his own whiskey. No one liked Billy so he was constantly shifting from one creepy clique to the next, hoping to score points. That hot September afternoon, Billy had been hoping that by putting Sugar in her rightful white-trash place, he'd score points with Brad and his friends and elevate his own pathetic social position.

"Better'n knowin' my dad is a jackass and my momma's a whore like yours. I'd be wonderin', if I was you, Billy, why your daddy likes his dogs so much. It might help explain why yer so stupid." She'd walked off and Brad and his friends had laughed at Billy's expense. To that she'd turned, looked over her shoulder, and said, "And I'd be careful if I was you, too, Brad. Your daddy's a preacher and you probably wouldn't want him to know that you got yerself a messa *Playboys* under yer mattress."

"I don't!" he'd yelled, outraged, but Sugar had just smiled.

"So then you lied when you were braggin' the other day

over at the gas station?'' she'd asked, and his mouth had dropped open so wide he could have caught flies. He hadn't known Sugar had been in the rest room of the gas station on the other side of the door with the broken window transom and she'd heard him boasting to his miserable pack of friends.

That had been just one of dozens of incidents when Sugar had been reminded of the incest that was rumored to be a part of her family. She'd suffered through all the painful laughs, sniggers and disparaging looks. But now, damn it, she was finally going to get her own back. If the damned rumors were true, then she figured it was her right to cash in on the Montgomery fortune.

But the wheels of justice were grinding slow enough to get on Sugar's last nerve. She was sick of living in this double-wide tin can, sick of being considered white trash by the holier-than-thou legitimate side of the family, and sick to death of dancing for a bunch of drunken middle-aged men who practically came in their work pants when she kicked up her legs. As if any of them would have a chance with her. She was a stripper. Not a whore. It took a whole lot more than a couple of twenties stuck into her G-string to get her to meet some loser in his pickup and give him a blow job.

The sooner Flynn could wrap up this lawsuit, the better. She and her siblings were contesting Cameron's will, claiming their stake of half of whatever Berneda and her brood had inherited, which just happened to be a shit-load of money. She wasn't sure how much, but it was in the millions. *Millions!* Even split seven ways between Cameron's surviving progeny, that was more money than she'd see stripping in her lifetime. What she could do with just a portion of that money! Not only her, but Cricket and Dickie Ray as well.

''You want it, too,'' Dickie Ray observed, as if he could read her mind. ''So bad you can taste it.''

''Flynn said this could take years.''

''Bullshit. I might not have years.''

"He's doing everything he can."

"That fat turd?" Dickie Ray snorted his disgust.

"Haven't you heard that patience is a virtue?"

"Don't you believe it. If you want something bad enough, you've got to make it happen. I learned that a long time ago," he said as she looked pointedly at the clock mounted over the refrigerator.

"I've got to get down to the club," she said, reaching for her purse.

"Fine." Dickie Ray squared his hat upon his head again and started across the scratched linoleum to the front door. "Tell Donahue he'd better get the damned ball rollin' and soon. Elsewise I just might have to take things into my own hands." He winked at her, and she had the uneasy sensation that he'd already begun.

"Don't do anything stupid, Dickie." She found her purse and searched for her car keys.

"Me?" he asked, raising his hands toward the low ceiling, his expression the picture of innocence.

Sugar was starting to get a bad feeling about it. Her fingers curled around the key chain.

"Anything I do, I do for us." He winked as he reached the door. "Remember that."

The screen door slammed behind him, and Sugar felt as if the devil himself had breathed against her spine. Dickie Ray was dangerous. A loose cannon. If he wasn't careful, he'd screw up everything for all of them ... she couldn't let that happen. Taking his empty cup into the kitchen and dropping it into the sink, she heard her brother's pickup start with a deafening roar. "Don't do it," she whispered as dread settled over her as tight and close as a funeral shroud. "Whatever it is, Dickie, please ... don't do it."

Josh Bandeaux.
Interloper.
Liar.
Cheat.

Dead.

So dead.

Which was as it should be. Atropos slipped the key into its lock and walked into the wine cellar where ancient, forgotten bottles climbed the walls. She crossed quickly and found the hidden lock which, when engaged, moved the rack enough to reveal the door that she slid silently through. She closed the door behind her and felt a calm come over her, here, in this secret spot.

The interior was painted stark white, the fixtures gleaming chrome, polished to a mirrored surface. No dust lingered on the tile floor, and the chair in one corner was white vinyl, the desk brushed metal. A chrome lamp, white leather recliner, stereo with a neat stack of CDs that could play softly from hidden speakers that were buffered from the rest of the old building by soundproof panels, filled the room. Every surface was spotless.

It was a private space. Closed off from the world. Away from the city and yet near enough for convenience. Hidden and isolated. Perfect. If she could only push out the noise in her mind.

She slipped surgical slippers over her feet and a cap over her head, then pulled surgical gloves from a dispenser and pushed a button on the stereo. Soft baroque music filled the room in soothing tones. If anyone found her hiding spot, she was certain she'd left no real clue to her identity, though her artwork would garner some speculation.

Carefully she withdrew a small plastic package from her purse and made her way to the desk. With her key she opened the top drawer, then stared smugly at her treasures. A clear plastic bag of photographs and a zippered case.

Humming softly, Atropos opened the plastic bag and let the snapshots fall onto the top of the desk. She sorted quickly through them, shuffling the glossy, battered photographs as deftly as a Las Vegas dealer, spying blurry images of familiar faces, stopping only when she found the photograph of Josh Bandeaux.

"Tsk, tsk. What a bad boy." She unwrapped the thin

plastic that surrounded the pair of surgical scissors. The stainless steel instrument gleamed to a mirror finish except for the dark stains that remained on the tips of the blades. Josh Bandeaux's blood . . . no longer fresh, but dried on her weapon.

Atropos remembered the look on Bandeaux's handsome face as he'd caught a glimpse of his assassin, the horror to know that it was his time, his personal Armageddon. It had been so easy. Remarkably easy. A necessary task that had offered a little thrill, not so much in the killing as in the knowledge that Bandeaux realized what was happening. His sheer terror had been evident in the twisted comprehension of his Hollywood-handsome features. Even now, remembering the fear in his eyes, she felt a sweet rush of adrenalin, a pleasant peace that helped quell the rush of noise in her head.

Unfortunately she didn't have time to bask in the thrill of the kill. She'd had to work fast. Now she studied the snapshot of Josh. Tanned, and wearing only a Speedo swim-suit, he had an arm slung around the shoulders of a beautiful woman dressed in a scanty yellow bikini. Palm trees and an incredible sunset were the backdrop for Bandeaux and the woman, who was not, of course, his wife. No, this nearly naked, bronzed blonde—wasn't her name Millicent?—was no one important. Not even to Josh. A whore. Nothing more. Nothing less. Someone unneeded.

Time to get rid of her.

Snip!

The scissors flashed under the flourescent light. With a clean cut, the photo was halved and the smiling beauty fluttered to the floor to land forgotten on the white tile. "Sayonara," Atropos whispered.

Then, in the remaining portion of the snapshot, Josh was standing alone, a drink in his hand. But not for long.

Snip!

Off with his frothy island cocktail, and oops, part of his hand as well. Oh, too bad.

But Josh was still smiling, offering up that wide, sexy, woman-killer grin to the camera.

That wouldn't do.

Snip!

No more smile. No, Josh's head floated slowly downward to join the other scraps of his body parts.

What about his dick?

Oh. The most important part. Can't leave that attached!

Snip!

Gone. Josh Bandeaux's legs and groin were neatly separated from what was left of him—just a naked, hairy chest and neck. Not very flattering. Not any longer.

And now he'd join the others. She looked at the one piece of art in the tiny space, a large family tree covered in Plexiglass.

The Montgomery family tree.

All members of the family were listed in the spreading branches, and the branches included those married, then divorced; bastard children; anyone who had married in. Like Bandeaux. Some of the branches had pictures attached, snapshots of those who had met their preordained fate.

Carefully, she removed the frame from the wall, laid it upon the desk and using a screwdriver she located in her zippered case, she unscrewed the corner pieces. After lifting off the top covering of Plexiglass, she placed what was left of the snapshot of Josh—his hairy torso—beside his name on the tree. She found his life strand . . . red and black thread carefully braided together and pre-measured by her sister, Lachesis. Gently Atropos glued his life strand to the trunk of the tree and ran it along his particular branch . . . a withered branch, one attached only because he'd married into the family. Once it was in place, she eyed her work.

Excellent.

In her estimation, Josh ''The Bandit'' Bandeaux had never looked better.

Nine

The press was camped out at her front door when Caitlyn returned home. Turning the corner into the alley that ran behind her house, she noticed a reporter and a cameraman, each smoking a cigarette, seated in a white van. The streetlights had just turned on. Twilight was settling on the city, but still they waited for her.

The day was rapidly going from bad to worse. From the sideview mirror she saw them crush their cigarettes and throw open the front doors of the vehicle. Great. Caitlyn pushed the garage door opener, turned the corner and had to wait as the door ground slowly upward. "Come on, come on," she growled at the lazy mechanism as she spied the reporter hurrying along the alley. Caitlyn punched the throttle just as there was enough clearance so as not to scrape the roof. Her Lexus shot forward. She cut the engine and pushed on the opener again. The door started downward but not before the reporter, a square-jawed, fit man with an impossibly thick head of hair, stepped agilely into the garage, placing his leg in front of the electronic eye. The door stopped abruptly.

"Mrs. Bandeaux, I'm Max O'Dell with WKAM," he said over the clicking of the jammed mechanism.

"I know who you are." She was already out of the car.

He grinned as if she'd handed him a compliment. "If I could have a word with you about your husband. I hate to intrude, but I just have a few questions."

"No comment." Caitlyn slung the strap of her purse over her shoulder just as the cameraman, toting his shoulder-held camera, jogged into the driveway.

"Please. It'll just take a couple of minutes," O'Dell insisted.

"Not right now."

"But—"

"You're in my garage and I'm asking you to leave. I have nothing to say to you." From the corner of her eye, she saw the cameraman focusing. "I don't want to call the police, but I will."

"You were separated from your husband."

"And you're trespassing." From the side door to the garage, Oscar was barking wildly. "I'm going inside. If you'll excuse me ... and even if you don't." Slapping the button, she heard the garage door start again, this time elevating. Her eyes, behind her sunglasses, narrowed on the reporter. "I'm closing the door before I let the dog out and telephone the police, so if I were you, I'd beat a hasty retreat." She didn't wait for him to respond, just jabbed the button again and walked through the side door to be greeted by Oscar, who was jumping up and down as if his legs were springs.

Caitlyn actually smiled as she reached down and picked up the fluff of wild fur. Her face was washed by a long pink tongue. "Yeah, I missed you, too," she whispered as the dog's wet nose brushed her cheek. "Big time." She half expected the pushy reporter to follow her, but she heard the sounds of voices on the other side of the courtyard wall and realized Max O'Dell and his cohort from WKAM had given up for the evening. Thank God.

Inside, she fed the dog, then hung up the telephone and

listened to the messages that had collected on voice mail. Three reporters, including Nikki Gillette, left numbers for her to call back. Caitlyn deleted each message. There were two other hang ups and a short message from Detective Reed at police headquarters asking her to return his call. Her heartbeat suddenly raced. Warning bells clanged in her mind. What could he want? What did he know? Hadn't Troy told her not to talk to the police? But she couldn't ignore them, and she wasn't about to start hunting down a lawyer today.

Squaring her shoulders, she punched the number Reed had left. An operator told her Detective Reed was off duty for the night. Caitlyn left her number then tapped her fingers nervously on the counter.

Kelly still hadn't called. Maybe she was out of town. As a buyer for one of the biggest department stores in the city, Kelly was gone often . . . but she usually checked her messages. Caitlyn walked through the house and looked through the front window. The van for WKAM was no longer at the curb. Thankfully, Max O'Dell had taken the hint and left.

But he'd be back. And there would be others.

Caitlyn had dealt with reporters before, and if they smelled a story, they kept on the trail, never giving up. They reminded her of trained hunting dogs on the scent of wounded prey.

She picked up the hand-held phone and walked into the living room where the flowers she'd bought last week were beginning to fade and drop petals on the coffee table. Falling into the soft cushions of the couch, Caitlyn glanced over at the baby grand. A framed picture of Jamie rested upon the glossy piano. *Oh, sweet, sweet baby.*

Blessed with curly brown hair, eyes as clear and blue as a June sky, and a button nose with freckles upon its bridge, Jamie had been a chubby, adorable imp. In the photograph she was staring over the photographer's head, looking skyward, her hands clasped, her smile showing off tiny teeth . . . the teeth that had made her cranky and drool as they'd appeared. Caitlyn's throat thickened. Was it possible that she was gone . . . so precious a life cut short after only three impossibly brief years?

Caitlyn remembered how quickly a runny nose had become a fever, the virus attacking so swiftly it had been frightening. Friday night. By Saturday morning, Jamie had been listless. Caitlyn called the pediatrician's office, but it had been closed. By afternoon, Jamie was worse and Caitlyn had taken her to the hospital where, despite the efforts of an emergency room team, her only child had died from a high fever and an unexplained virus. Caitlyn had never forgiven God.

". . . so leave a message." Kelly's recorded message jolted her out of her reverie. She realized that tears were drizzling silently down her face and her heart was as heavy as an anvil, sitting deep in her chest, aching so badly she could barely breathe. She clicked off the phone. Kelly was probably on a buying trip. The truth of the matter was that her twin was gone more often than she was around. No doubt because of the family's attitude toward her. *It works both ways. Kelly's attitude about the Montgomery clan is far from stellar.*

So what should she do now?

Josh was dead.

Murdered or the victim of suicide.

Josh whom she had loved so passionately.

Josh who had cheated on her.

Josh who was the father of her only child.

Josh, who in his anger, rage and grief, had lashed out at Caitlyn both privately and publicly, insisting she was an unfit mother and screaming that she should be tried for criminal negligence if nothing else.

Josh who was going to make good his threats with the wrongful death suit. Shivering, she rubbed her shoulders and the slashes upon her wrists pulled tight and itched beneath their bandages.

She stared at the cold fireplace and tried to concentrate. Last night Kelly had left a message on her cell and suggested they meet downtown. Yes, that was right. Caitlyn had been bored out of her mind, creating a website that was driving her nuts, so she'd leapt at the chance to get out of the house. She'd thrown on a pair of khakis and a T-shirt with an open blouse as a jacket, then driven to the waterfront . . . and then . . . she'd gone into the bar. One Kelly had discovered. The Swamp.

She leaned back and felt a lump between the cushions, and she dug her fingers down to find her cell phone, turned off as usual, hidden in the couch. She didn't stop to wonder how it had ended up here in the living room. Didn't care. She switched it on. The battery was fading, nearly dead, but she was able to read the Caller ID and sure enough, Amanda, as she'd said earlier at Oak Hill, had left a message.

The other one was from Kelly.

She dialed the message retrieval number and heard Amanda's exasperated voice. "Jesus, don't you ever have this turned on, Caitlyn? I'm trying to get hold of you. I heard about Josh and I'm really sorry. Let me know what I can do. Call me back."

Caitlyn erased the message and then, clear as a bell, Kelly's recording played. "Caitlyn. It's me. I got your message, but, as usual, you don't have this damned phone on. Call me back when you can. I'll be in and out, got to leave town on a buying trip for a couple of days, but I'll call you back. Pull yourself together, okay? I know you feel awful about Josh, but come on, let's face it, the bastard's death isn't that much of a loss."

"Let me get this straight," Reed said as Gerard St. Claire yanked off his latex gloves and discarded them into a trash can that was marked for medical waste. A glum assistant wearing earphones was cleaning off the stainless steel table in the autopsy room, getting ready for another corpse. It had been a slow weekend for deaths, and Bandeaux's case had been given top priority; hence the quick results. "You're saying that Bandeaux died from loss of blood, right?"

"His body was pretty much drained." The medical examiner pulled off his cap, dropped it into a basket of dirty laundry and was left in his scrubs. The rooms smelled of disinfectant and formaldehyde, death and sweat despite the cool temperature. Stainless steel sinks, tables and equipment gleamed starkly against old tile and dull paint. "And, from what the crime scene team has put together, some of it's missing."

Reed stopped short. "Missing? How?"

"Not enough blood was found at the scene to account for his blood loss. Not even with evaporation. So unless Bandeaux gave a gallon at a local blood bank or came up against a vampire or has a pooch with a blood thirst, we've got ourselves a problem. Some of the blood is missing."

"As in stolen?" That didn't make any sense. "What if the body was moved?"

"It wasn't. Diane Moses and I agree on that one, and you know that we never see eye to eye."

"So he could have lost blood somewhere else . . . and made it back home . . . then lost more."

"No blood trail. And I don't think so. Because of rigor and the way the blood settled in his body and his loss of body function—the urine that had leaked to the floor—I'd bet he died at the desk." St. Claire ran his hands over his forehead. His bristly white hair showed a little sweat. "He lost most of the blood through the cuts that were different than the others—they snipped through a small artery on each wrist. The others were pretty superficial and were made after the initial cuts."

"To make us think it was a suicide."

"That's the way I see it." He rubbed his chin thoughtfully. "And that's not the only puzzle we've got going on with Bandeaux. It looks like old Josh was allergic to something, perhaps the sulfites in a domestic wine. He had a severe reaction, went into anaphylactic shock, would probably have died from it if left alone, but we're still looking at the chemicals in his blood. He might have been able to get the antidote. However there was another drug in his system,

GHB, Gamma Hydroxy Butyrate, that would have rendered him immobile.''

"The date-rape drug?''

"One of 'em,'' St. Claire agreed.

"Which means there's a chance that even if he had an antidote kit with epinephrine, he couldn't have gotten to it.''

"Or to a hospital or to a phone to call 911.''

"Right. The final analysis of his blood will tell.''

"Why GHB?'' Reed asked.

"A street drug, relatively easy to get if you have the right connections. Easy to slip into a drink. Then Josh is putty in our killer's hands. I can't tell how out of it he was, maybe he was nearly comatose, but there's a good chance that he knew what was happening to him.''

The doors on the far side of the room opened, and a gurney with a body bag strapped to it was being maneuvered inside by a heavyset EMT. As the doors shut, Reed caught a glimpse of an ambulance parked on the cement ramp that led up to the street.

"Can I get someone to sign for this?'' the EMT asked.

St. Claire's assistant looked up and nodded as he wiped his hands. With a much-practiced toss of his head, his headset fell to his shoulders and the throb of a deep bass thrummed through the sterile room.

St. Claire said, "So, in my opinion, Bandeaux didn't die from a suicide. Something else was going on, and oh ... take a look at this. I put it in my report.'' The M.E. walked to a refrigerated drawer and opened it. There, draped in a sheet, his body bluish, was Josh Bandeaux. St. Claire pulled the sheet back carefully so that Reed got a view of the naked body with its odd color, lack of animation and incision lines where the medical examiner had made his cuts to examine Bandeaux's internal organs. St. Claire gently lifted one of Josh's hands. "Take a look at the marks on his wrists. Most of them are consistent with a right-handed person slicing his own skin. They match the blade of the knife with his prints on it; the knife you found on the carpet beneath his body. But if you look here ...'' He pointed to a spot on

Josh's arm. "You'll see that these cuts are at a different angle, as if the blade was positioned straight up—vertically. As I said, the cuts are deep, the veins snipped cleanly, made by something very sharp. Like a surgical instrument or maybe a boning knife. These are the cuts that assured Josh of dying. They would have been very difficult to make by the victim."

"So you're saying the suicide was staged."

"I'd bet my Ferrari on it."

"You don't own a Ferrari."

"Yeah, but if I did." He let the drape fall into place, then pushed Josh back into his refrigerated tomb. "The family wants me to release the body. You got any problem with that?"

"Not if you found everything we need."

"I did," St. Clair said as he braced himself on a table while leaning down to remove the green slippers that covered his shoes.

Reed's pager beeped. Glancing at the readout, he recognized Morrisette's number. "Gotta run. Thanks for pushing this through so fast."

"No problem."

Reed was already shouldering open the thick door and flipping open his cell phone as he stepped into a hallway where the floor tiles gleamed with layers of wax and the walls were painted a soft, quieting green. He took the stairs to an outside door and shoved it open. Heat, thick as tar, blasted him. The natives barely noticed, but it was hot as hell to a man who had grown up in Chicago and spent a lot of his adult life in San Francisco. Even the recent rain shower hadn't done much more than settle the dust and leave a puddle or two on the streets.

Ignoring the fact that he was already sweating, he dialed the station, asked for Morrisette's extension and was put on hold, only to be referred to her voice mail box. Damned automation. Frustrated, he left a terse message, walked the few blocks to the station and landed at her desk just as she was hanging up from a call that had brought a flush to her face and pulled the edges of her mouth downward.

"Fuck—effin' ex-husband," she muttered as Reed kicked out a side chair and dropped into it.

"Got your page. I was with the M.E."

She lifted an eyebrow. "Bandeaux?"

"Yep."

"Anything interesting?"

"A lot." He gave her a quick rundown of what St. Claire had told him. "He put a rush job on this. We'll have the complete, typed report tomorrow."

"GHB? Jesus, what's that all about? Not date rape."

"Maybe date murder. Unless Josh was experimenting."

"With Midnight Blue? Then he was nuts." She stood and stretched, arching her back as if it ached. "So you're thinking someone killed him."

"Very possibly. It's looking that way." Reed rubbed the inside of his palm with a thumb. He just wasn't sure.

"So why try to make it look like a suicide?" Morrisette asked.

"Good question. Whoever did it did a half-assed job, though. And what's with the wine? Was it a mistake? Did the killer not realize that he was allergic to certain kinds, and gave him the wine as a way of administering the GHB?"

"But wouldn't Bandeaux have been careful about the wine?"

Reed lifted a shoulder. "Maybe he didn't know it had sulfites. And there's a chance it wasn't the wine. We'll have to check with Bandeaux's M.D., see what exactly he was allergic to."

"Okay, but for now, let's assume it was the wine for lack of some other substance found in his body, right?"

"Right."

"So if it was a life-and-death matter what kind of merlot or chardonnay you guzzled," she said, lines collecting between her plucked eyebrows, "wouldn't you check to make sure you weren't drinking the wrong stuff?"

"Yeah, but probably only the bottle, not the wine itself."

"Meaning?"

"That the bottle could have been doctored—the labels switched, or someone could have poured the bad stuff in another room and carried it in to him."

"Someone he trusted," she amended.

"Yeah, so did we find a wine bottle on the premises?"

"Only about two hundred in the wine cellar, but they were full," she said, bending over the desk and reaching for a file. "I think there was a bottle in the garbage; let's see . . . I've got a list of everything collected . . ." She pulled a computer sheet from the file and ran a silver-tipped nail down the first couple of pages. "Here we go . . . a bottle of pinot noir. Imported. France."

"Did we locate a cork?"

She looked again. "Yessir, we sure did."

"Anything strange about it?"

"Not that was mentioned. What're you getting at?"

"Have the lab check and see if there's anything left in the bottle. I want to know what it is and see if the cork was tampered with, or if the wine matches what the label says . . . What about the lipstick on the wineglass?"

"Nothing yet."

Reed didn't like what he was thinking. Too many puzzle pieces didn't fit, no matter how he tried to force them. Unless the murderer was in a hurry or a complete moron, he or she did a really bad job of making the scene appear suicide. "So what do you think?" he asked Morrisette. "Suicide or murder?" She dropped back into her desk chair, nudging her computer in the process. The blank screen flickered and the image of Josh Bandeaux slumped over his desk and very dead, appeared. "Why try to kill him twice?"

"Maybe it was suicide. I know, I know, I really don't believe Josh Bandeaux would kill himself, but let's run with this theory and see where it leads us—just for the sake of argument. Maybe ol' Josh was depressed, but the wine and the GHB weren't working fast enough, so he grabbed a knife."

"And scratched himself up? The wounds that killed him

were made from another weapon, a surgical tool or hunting knife.'' Reed wasn't buying it.

"Which we haven't found,'' she said, chewing on her lower lip as she studied the report.

"And then there's the GHB. How does that fit in?''

"It doesn't.'' She shook her head and glanced at the computer screen. "But nothing does. If he was murdered, why would the killer, if he took the time to make it look like suicide, leave the wineglasses and bottle and traces of wine, knowing that we would find out that he was allergic to the sulfites?''

"If that's what happened,'' Reed said. "Either the murderer is dumb as a stone or she's flaunting it, rubbing it in our nose that she got away with it.''

"She?'' Morrisette repeated. "As in Mrs. Bandeaux?''

"She's certainly on the suspect list.''

"Along with half the denizens of Savannah. Seems like everyone Bandeaux knew had a bone to pick with our boy,'' she muttered. "The Bandit got around.''

Reed couldn't argue. Morrisette was right; there were other suspects worth examining. But as the investigation wore on, he was starting to believe that Caitlyn Bandeaux was guilty as sin. He'd read a copy of the wrongful death suit Josh Bandeaux was filing against his ex-wife. Nasty stuff. In the document Bandeaux charged Caitlyn with being neglectful to the point of being an unfit mother. And neighbors had seen her coming and going; even the maid who found Bandeaux's body swore that Caitlyn had been a regular visitor to her estranged husband's home. Despite the fact that Bandeaux had a girlfriend. "Has anyone found Naomi Crisman?''

"Not yet. One of Bandeaux's friends thinks she's out of the country. Probably doesn't even know he's dead.''

"What about phone messages? E-mail?''

"None and deleted.''

"Mail?''

"Still being sorted, along with the garbage. So far the crime scene team hasn't come up with much. Except that a button was found on the floor near the desk. It looks like it came from Bandeaux's dress shirt.''

"So it fell off?''

"Nope. Was cut. The thread was clipped neatly, not frayed, nor unraveled. Someone deliberately cut the button off that night. No way would Josh have worn a shirt without a button.''

"Why would someone do that intentionally?''

"Maybe they were trying to hit a vein and missed.''

"Or maybe not,'' Reed said aloud, not liking the turn of his thoughts. "Maybe whoever did it was making a point.''

"Which was . . . what? 'Hey, Josh, you'd look better in cuff links'?''

"No—more like, 'Hey, Josh, look what I can do to you.' '' Reed tried to imagine the scene of the crime and his thoughts turned dark as he imagined Bandeaux at his desk with a killer in the room, the victim paralyzed, the wineglasses— two of them—the music that had been playing, the open doors to the verandah. The scene had somehow been intimate. "I think it might have been that the murderer was adding a little bit of terror to the scene. Bandeaux was immobilized, couldn't move. So why not show him how sharp the weapon was? Why not take the time to scare him to death?''

Ten

The funeral was excruciating.

Caitlyn felt the weight of dozens of curious gazes, not only in the church, but also here in the graveyard as a preacher finished the service with a final prayer and sunlight streamed from between the clouds. The mourners, primarily dressed in black, had scattered among existing graves. Expressions grim, eyes downcast, they'd bent their heads to pray, all the while whispering among themselves.

It had been three days since Josh's body had been discovered, and if anything, the media interest in Josh Bandeaux's death had been intensified. Whether they were admitting it or not, the police seemed to think that Josh had been murdered; the talk of suicide had muted, though it was still a consideration, or so she thought.

Caitlyn noticed members of the press in attendance, and standing slightly apart from the rest of the crowd, Detective Pierce Reed was leaning against the bole of an ancient oak tree, dark glasses hiding his eyes, though, Caitlyn guessed, he was surveying the people who came to pay their respects to her husband. Or maybe he was watching her reaction.

The entire ceremony in the church had seemed surreal.

The organ music, the prayers, the candles and eulogy seemed as out of sync as the funeral procession that had snaked through the city streets to this remote cemetery with its ancient gravestones, tombs and moss-draped trees.

Other than his two ex-wives, Josh had no family of his own. A single, spoiled child who had come to his parents late in life, he had no siblings and his mother had died not long after her husband nearly ten years earlier. Caitlyn had never met one member of Josh's family. Other than his first wife, Maude, and stepson Gil, both of whom were in attendance. As was Naomi Crisman, dressed in elegant black. But there was not an uncle, aunt or cousin to be seen; nor had she ever heard of any. Caitlyn, as his wife, had asked that his body be released. He had no other familial ties.

Caitlyn took in those who'd shown up.

She slid a glance in Josh's first wife's direction. Maude was tall and elegant in her designer suit. She hid behind wraparound sunglasses and a broad-brimmed hat. Contrarily, her son looked as if he'd just rolled out of bed after a hard night of rock music and drugs. He wore jeans, an Ozzy Osbourne T-shirt and an attitude that suggested, "bite me." His hair was pushed out of his eyes, but he hadn't bothered to shave, and his mouth was pulled into a tight I-would-rather-be-anywhere-else-on-earth scowl. Where Maude was reed-slender, Gil was already running to fat, his stomach rolling over the top of his jeans.

A few feet from Gil, Naomi Crisman kept to herself. She was Josh's most recent love interest, another woman who'd hoped to become the next Mrs. Bandeaux, but she pointedly avoided everyone's gaze by averting her eyes and staring at the ground. Barely twenty-five, Naomi was suitably sub-dued in a simple black sheath. Her long streaked hair had been loosely piled up on her head and held with what appeared to be enamel chopsticks. She sighed often, whether from sadness or boredom was anyone's guess.

Standing a few feet away, close enough to be considered part of the mourners, but distanced so as to draw attention to the fact that they didn't quite belong, were the Biscaynes.

Sugar, Dickie Ray and Cricket. All dressed in their Sunday best, standing a little apart from the crowd, and yet blending in. For as much as the Montgomerys fought the truth, the evidence of Benedict's betrayal—the genetic stamp—was evident in the faces of his illegitimate grandchildren. Their hair might have been lighter, thanks to their grandmother's natural blond shade, but the eyes were round, their noses straight and strong, their cheekbones high, all characteristics of Benedict Montgomery.

Don't discount your own father, for God's sake.

It's possible that one or more of them are not only your cousins but half-sisters or brother.

Caitlyn's stomach turned, but she remembered playing hide-and-seek with Griffin in the carriage house and hearing the bedsprings of an old iron four-poster creak and groan in the attic above. Later, still hidden in the shadows of the tractor, she'd seen two people sneak down the back stairs. Enough moonlight had filtered through the windows for her to recognize her father, Cameron, and a tousled-haired woman. They'd paused at the foot of the steps and the woman had curled her sinuous body into him and kissed him long and hard, their mouths locking, his hand cupping her buttocks beneath the short summer dress with its button front.

"Later," he'd growled.

"Don't forget." Her voice was deep, husky, and as she'd turned to light a cigarette, the match flaring enough that Caitlyn could see her features, Caitlyn had recognized Copper Biscayne. She'd gasped and a bat had swooped out of the carriage door as Copper had searched the dark interior.

"Someone's here," she'd whispered, but Caitlyn's father had chuckled. "It's just the bats. You're jumpy. Go on. Git. Before somebody does come along." He'd patted her on her rump and she'd hurried off, her high heels crunching on the gravel path that lead to a side shed and equipment access road.

Cameron had looked over his shoulder, as if assuring himself that no one was hiding inside. Caitlyn had held her breath. Griffin stared at her with round, frightened eyes, and then her father had slipped through the open door, closed it behind him and latched it shut.

If not for the fact that she'd climbed the stairs to the attic and the room that reeked of cigarette smoke, liquor and musk to slip out the window and shimmy down the oak tree, they would have been locked inside.

As it was, she'd escaped, but had never forgotten that night and her father's betrayal. She'd been only eleven at the time, but the memory was still as fresh as if it had happened yesterday.

Caitlyn had no idea how long Copper and her father had been lovers, but certainly long enough that there could have been a child or two conceived.

A dyed-in-the-wool bastard, just like his father.

Caitlyn didn't even cringe at her emotions for Cameron. She'd come to terms long ago with the fact that she'd hated him when he was living and she could bloody well hate him now that he was dead. She didn't blame the Biscaynes for wanting their share of his estate. By blood they deserved it.

"Jesus, they're nervy," Amanda whispered as she followed Caitlyn's gaze. "Know who the man with them is? Their attorney. Hails from New Orleans, and he's as shady as one of these old oaks," she said, rolling her eyes to the branches overhead.

Caitlyn didn't respond but as Sugar glanced in her direction, she tore her eyes away and tried to concentrate on the preacher's last words. She stood at the grave site with Troy on one side, Amanda the other. Her mother and Lucille sat on chairs set up on a fake grass carpet and surrounded by floral sprays beginning to droop in the heat. Hannah, hiding behind dark glasses and a dour expression, was positioned on the far side of Troy and stared dully at the ground.

Whereas Caitlyn, Amanda and Kelly took after their mother with thin, willowy builds, deep mahogany-colored hair and hazel, near-green eyes, Hannah and Troy looked more like their father. Their features were larger, their hair darker, almost black, their eyes a sharp, intense blue. As her older brother, Charles's had been. He, as had been often stated, had been the spitting image of their father. Tall and good-looking, a natural athlete and competitor, Charles had been groomed to step into Cameron's expensive shoes.

Until he'd died.

One of the many tragedies that scarred the thick, twisted branches of the Montgomery family tree. Caitlyn had only to shift her eyes a little distance away and see the tomb for her family members. In earlier times the Montgomerys had been buried in the ancient cemetery near the old plantation house at Oak Hill. Generation after generation. But in recent times, the family had taken their final resting plots here in the city. The first to have been buried here was Benedict and later his wife. Charles rested here and Baby Parker, who had died of SIDS, at least according to Doc Fellers, before his first birthday.

"Amen," the crowd whispered as the final prayer was finished. The preacher raised his head. He motioned at Caitlyn. She stepped forward, her legs wobbly, as she dropped a single white rose onto Josh's coffin. It was still impossible to believe—really believe—that he was dead. If nothing else, Josh had always been a vibrant man, so full of life.

She'd spent the past few days making funeral arrangements, speaking briefly to the police, avoiding the press and trying to sort out what had happened. She hadn't been able to sleep in her own bedroom—the thought of the blood spilled everywhere had been too unnerving—so she'd spent the last two nights tucked under a coverlet on the sofa, unable to fall asleep without the aid of some kind of tranquilizer Doc Fellers had offered up.

"I know you hate to take pills," Berneda had said, pressing the tinted bottle into her palm, "but these will help. I had an appointment anyway and asked if he'd prescribe something for you."

"Don't you think you should have asked me?" Caitlyn had replied, but had accepted the little dark bottle anyway. The lorazepam had come in handy, helping her calm down, getting her through the days as well as the nights.

She still hadn't talked to Kelly; they just kept missing each other, but Kelly had promised to call once the funeral was over, once the press was looking elsewhere for a story, once the gossips found other fodder for their grisly mill. "You know I can't come to the funeral," she'd said. "I'm not that much of a hypocrite, and Mom would freak, absolutely freak, so I'm not gonna make any waves. Not right now. We'll get together once Josh is in the ground. Hang in there . . ."

Caitlyn was trying. But having a helluva time. Her work was neglected, piling up, clients leaving messages of condolence mixed with inquiries as to when their particular projects would be finished. Tomorrow, she thought, tomorrow she'd have to start returning calls and somehow begin living her life again.

If the police would let her.

If her conscience would permit it.

"Come on," Troy said, shepherding her toward the waiting town car parked in the shade of one of the trees. The solemn driver, a heavyset man employed by the funeral home, waited, his hips resting against a front fender. Caitlyn had focused upon him and didn't notice a stranger approach until a shadow fell in front of her feet.

"Mrs. Bandeaux? My condolences."

She braced herself. Expected a reporter to have crashed the funeral, thought a microphone would be thrust in front of her face as a camera clicked off quick shots for the local paper.

"Not now," Troy uttered.

"I know it's a difficult time, and I only stopped by because I'm a colleague of Rebecca Wade." The voice was male. Deep. The man behind it, tall and serious. Khaki pants, loose blue sweater, dark hair longer than the current rage, the shadow of a beard darkening his jaw.

Troy turned to face the intruder. "I don't care who you are. This is a very private time. If you'll excuse us—"

"No. Wait." Caitlyn paused in a patch of shade. She

squinted up at him through dark glasses. "You know Dr. Wade?"

"Went to school with her, then worked with her for years. I'm Adam Hunt." He extended his hand. "She asked me to check with some of her patients while she's away."

"You've spoken with her?"

"Not recently. But I was detained a bit." He glanced down, and for the first time she noticed that his ankle appeared to be taped. "Got into a tangle with a motorcycle. I lost." He flashed a wide smile that warmed the cool gray of his eyes. "I shouldn't have come here today, but you haven't returned any of my calls and Rebecca asked me specifically to contact you. I'm . . . I'm sorry for the delay. I know that this is a particularly difficult time for you, so if you want to talk to anyone, just call me." He pressed a business card into her hand. "I won't keep you. Again, my condolences."

Before she could respond, he hobbled off down a slight slope to a spot where an older-model Jeep was parked.

"What the devil was that all about?" Troy asked, tugging at his tie.

"I'm not sure."

"Well, for the record, I don't like him. Probably got a personal agenda."

"For the record, you don't like anyone," Caitlyn said and saw a shadow pass behind her brother's eyes. "Okay, low blow. I'm sorry," she amended. "This is just a rough day."

"Aren't they all?" he responded as the driver opened the door for her, and out of the corner of her eye Caitlyn watched Adam Hunt slide behind the wheel of the Jeep. "Who the hell is Rebecca Wade?"

"My shrink."

"Oh." Troy cast a glance at the Jeep as it drove off. "In that case, maybe you should talk to him, but check him out first. He could be a reporter with a cover story. Some of them aren't all that trustworthy, you know. Would go to any lengths to get a scoop."

"You really are paranoid."

"Not me. Just realistic." They scooted over the hot seat as the driver turned on the engine and cranked up the air conditioning. From the corner of her eye she saw her mother, Lucille, Amanda and Hannah climb into a second dark vehicle. They were on their way to Oak Hill.

"It runs in the family," she said, joking morbidly.

"Very funny. But not through me. The rest of you, okay? Remember, I'm the sane one."

She doubted it. But then she was beginning to doubt just about everything. *The sane one? Oh, Troy, get over yourself.*

As far as her family went, she'd be surprised if there was a sane one in the lot.

Atropos observed them all. The mourners of Josh Bandeaux. As if anyone really cared if he lived or died. She had watched the service, the dour expression of the preacher, the mother-in-law's weary, unhappy expression behind her half veil, as if the funeral had been some kind of fashion show . . . and then there were the others, those illegitimate, greedy Biscaynes who'd made a public show of being a part of the Montgomery family.

Sugar. Cricket. Dickie Ray . . . their names said it all. One called something sweet when she was nothing more than a whore, the other's nickname that of an insect that made a lot of noise and the third named for his claim to fame—the only one of the bastards who'd been blessed with a penis. And probably a minute one at that.

Atropos had seen their desperate expressions, their lust to be a part of the Montgomery family tree, to have a chance at a fortune they wouldn't have to earn. It pleased her to know that they'd never get any of it; nor would the rest, the legitimate side of the family.

It wasn't their fate, nor their destiny.

The strings of life had been woven and measured.

All that was left was for them to be cut at the appropriate time.

They would all have to be patient, but then they would feel the pain of Fate's razor-sharp sheers . . . but the deaths would be appropriate, the suffering acute and specific. Because Atropos knew it wasn't the deaths that were important. It was the dying.

Eleven

Sometimes those who appear the most innocent are the most evil.

How many times in his career had this proved true? Reed glanced in the rearview mirror and caught a glimpse of the black town cars that held members of the Montgomery family along with the Widow Bandeaux. He sensed that she knew more than she was saying about her husband's death, and yet he couldn't really figure her out. She was beautiful and sexy and at times appeared as shy as a frightened rabbit, while in other instances she'd proved herself aggressive and as tough as a wounded cat. One with very sharp claws.

His gut feeling was that he was missing something. Something important.

Driving away from the cemetery, he flipped down the cruiser's visor. Traffic was light but the glare off the hood was harsh enough to make him squint behind his polarized lenses. He pushed the speed limit and cut through side streets, heading toward the center of town where the smell of the Savannah River crawled upward through the Cotton Exchange and Emmet Park to hang low over the city.

Caitlyn Bandeaux must've killed her husband, he rationalized, as he passed a horse-drawn carriage filled with tourists. The beasts, palomino draft horses in thick harnesses, plodded past historic sites while a tour guide pointed out the homes and businesses of the once-leading citizens of the city. Reed barely noticed. His thoughts were filled with Caitlyn Montgomery Bandeaux and her part in her estranged husband's death. All of the evidence—no, make that *most* of the evidence—pointed straight at Mrs. Bandeaux. He couldn't ignore it.

Motive. Her old man was going to divorce her for a younger woman, plus he was planning to file a wrongful death suit against her for the death of their child. Salt on an old wound. Another round of public humiliation.

Means. As frail as Caitlyn Bandeaux appeared at times, Reed was willing to bet she was smart and strong enough to drug Bandeaux and slit his wrists. Lipstick on the wineglass indicated that someone was present, presumably a woman. The matter of getting some GHB was easy—a street drug popular at rave parties.

Opportunity. Caitlyn had no alibi, nothing set in stone, at least nothing she'd offered up. They'd talked on the phone a couple of times, and she claimed her recollection of the night was "fuzzy." Meaning she was either blotto out of her mind with alcohol or she was lying.

He'd bet on the latter.

Lying for herself? Or covering up for someone else? And if so, who?

Caitlyn's car, or one like it, had been seen at Bandeaux's house that night. Which propelled her to the top of the suspect list. More and more he wasn't buying into the suicide scenario. It seemed contrived. Clunky. Out of place.

So was Caitlyn Bandeaux a cold-blooded killer? Outwardly, she didn't seem the type.

Because there was no type.

And, face it, Reed, you're a sucker for a pretty face and a knock-out figure.

Frowning, he stopped for a traffic light. His jaw set. His fingers tapped nervously against the steering wheel.

So why not arrest her? Or get a search warrant for her house? Maybe you'll get lucky and find the murder weapon.

But he had to tread carefully. There was the issue of her mental health; she'd been in a psych ward at least once and an innocent plea by reason of insanity would be a no-brainer for any lawyer she hired. Reed wondered about Caitlyn's supposed mental illness. How handy that Rebecca Wade had conveniently pulled up stakes and moved away for an indeterminate amount of time. He made a mental note to track the missing shrink down. Pronto. Her absence was just too much of a coincidence. There was a chance that even if he arrested Caitlyn Bandeaux, a sharp attorney could fall back on an insanity defense.

The light changed and he stepped on it. He'd have to talk to Caitlyn Bandeaux again and try to pin her down about her whereabouts on the night Bandeaux died. After that he'd put a tail on her. Watch what she did. And who better than himself?

After all, whether he liked to admit it or not, he enjoyed a stakeout where a beautiful woman was involved. Which posed another problem. A major problem.

As he turned onto Habersham Street, he thought fleetingly of San Francisco and another time, a night when the fog had rolled in from the bay and he'd pulled the surveillance duty. His job had been to watch a woman suspected of dealing drugs.

She'd lived in an upper story in a loft apartment not far from Fisherman's Wharf. His jaw clenched as he remembered her undressing in an erotic dance that almost seemed as if she'd known he—or someone—was observing her. Wearing a short skirt, blouse and scarf, she'd slowly peeled off the outer layer, wiggling out of the skirt, unbuttoning her blouse, coming closer to the window, showing him more skin than was normal as she unhooked her bra and bared her breasts. Letting the scant scrap of silk fall to the floor, she'd touched her dark nipples and paraded around in the barest of panties and her scarf, then ambled up to the window, licked her lips and pulled down the shade.

Reed had seen the rest through the flimsy screen, her small shadow, then another, a much larger image, and the horrifying struggle—or had it been an embrace? Had the seductive display not been for his benefit at all, but for someone else, someone *inside* the apartment? Reed hadn't taken a chance and called for backup before flying out of his building and into the street. Up five floors to her apartment where he'd kicked the door open and found her lying on the floor in front of the window. The scarf she'd used to tempt him had become her noose.

Her assailant had escaped, had seemed to vanish into thin air.

Her killer was never located.

Reed's judgment had been questioned.

His effectiveness in doubt.

He'd taken a leave of absence and then resigned, taking the job here, in Savannah, leaving the city on the bay to start over. Here. Nearly three thousand miles away.

Or were you just running away?

Pulling into the lot behind the station, he didn't want to think about what he'd left: a smart, sexy schoolteacher who had claimed to love him, a city he'd known and liked, a job that was intriguing and a reputation that had been tarnished. And what had he gotten here, in Savannah? A couple of failed relationships, a handful of one-night stands and a job no better than the one he'd left on the West Coast. But now he was presented the opportunity to redeem himself by tracking down Josh Bandeaux's killer . . . no matter who she happened to be.

He parked in an open slot in the lot at police headquarters, jammed his keys into his pocket and walked into the cool interior of the building. Pushing all images of San Francisco out of his head, he took the stairs to Homicide and strode into his office. It seemed airless and tight. He threw open the window and let fresh air into his over-cooled, stale-smelling box of a room, then flipped through his messages and in-box, before reading his e-mail. Then he placed another call to Mrs. Bandeaux, who wasn't yet at home. Probably with the family at one of those gatherings of the bereaved after a funeral where everyone stands around lying about what a great guy the deceased was.

Rotating in his chair, he stared out the window to the red-brick building across the square, a restored Victorian home once owned by a rice broker. He had other cases to think about. There had been a knifing on the waterfront last week, the case still unsolved, and a domestic case where a wife, nearly beaten to death herself, claimed she hadn't pulled the trigger of the pistol that had shot her husband. There were a couple of others as well, but the Bandeaux case haunted him, was the one that had the D.A. frothing at the bit.

Though he sensed that Caitlyn Montgomery knew a lot more than she was telling, she wasn't alone. Not for a minute did he discount the rest of Josh Bandeaux's in-laws. The Montgomery family history read like something out of a bad soap opera.

Reed had done some checking on his own after hearing Morrisette's viewpoint. And she'd been right on the money. Mental illness and rumors of incest seemed to be the most common theme, but the police blotter was filled with reports over the years, complaints and citations, everything from traffic tickets to suicide and attempted murder . . . yet suspiciously few arrests, probably due to the fact that the rich Montgomery family had consistently contributed to the campaigns of the local D.A., the sheriff, several judges and just about every public official who ever ran for office. Even the governor.

But this time was different. If a Montgomery had killed Joshua Bandeaux, then he or she would pay for it. End of story.

He sensed Morrisette approach before he actually heard her, smelled a hint of perfume and cigarettes a second or two prior to the sound of her footsteps crossing his threshold as she pushed open the door he'd left ajar. The sounds of voices, phones, shuffling feet and whirring office machines in the open area of the department increased as she left the door open wide, crossed the small, crammed space and balanced one hip against his desk. "How'd the funeral go?"

"How do they all go? The preacher said some prayers, stretched the truth by saying what a saint Bandeaux was, then stuffed him into the ground."

"Don't sugar-coat it on my account," she drawled. "The missus there?"

"Surrounded by her family. And the bereaved."

"Both of them?" Morrisette asked, snapping her gum.

"Very funny. Actually, there were over a hundred in the church, about half that at the interment."

"Anyone laughing?"

"Nah." He felt one side of his mouth lift. "You really had it in for that son of a bitch, didn't you?"

" 'Course not."

Leaning back in his chair, he lifted a doubting eyebrow.

Morrisette rolled her eyes. "I didn't like my friend getting involved with him. Tried to talk her out of it. He was just a little too smooth. You know the type. Bad boy, playboy, rich boy, all rolled into one handsome package. Years ago he would've been selling snake oil."

"That was your friend Molly?"

"Millie, and don't try to trip me up, okay?" Her face was suddenly hard. "I don't like being tested. Not by anyone, and especially not you!"

"I was just asking about Bandeaux."

"Millie was going through a rough time, okay. Bandeaux showed some interest. The way I heard it . . . he was a good time on a Saturday night. But I don't know from personal experience, so get over it."

"All right."

"Now, if you're done with your sick innuendos, let's get down to some real police work. I talked with Bandeaux's secretary earlier this morning. According to her, nothing was out of the ordinary down at the office."

"You believe her?"

"Don't know why she'd lie. It's not like she could get fired for what she says to the cops." Morrisette picked up a pen from Reed's desk and clicked it several times. "She didn't seem that broken up about it. Said she'd already lined up another job. It was a short conversation. She had to get to the funeral."

"So you had time to go if you wanted to?"

"Not really. I got a call from Diane Moses. Seems that the lab found something interesting in the bloodstains on Bandeaux's carpet."

"What?"

"A second type." She grinned widely.

"Second type?"

"Bandeaux was B-neg. Kinda rare. That's what most of the blood was, but there were traces of someone else's. Human blood. O-positive. So I did a little checkin' around, called in a favor at the local hospital and guess what I found?"

He was already a step ahead of her. "That the poor widow has O-positive blood."

"Bingo!"

"Anyone else?"

"That's where it gets a little muddy. O-pos is common. Especially in the Montgomery family tree. Just about every Montgomery from the grandmother down to the little kid who died had O-positive, and I'm sure that a large portion of the citizens of Savannah do as well. But we can have some DNA work done and that should narrow the field a tad."

"We'll cross-match it with everyone associated with the victim. You order the DNA report?"

"Mmhmm. Now . . . all we need is something from Mrs. Bandeaux—a hair or some body fluids—and we'll be in business."

"I was going to meet with her anyway."

"So now you have another reason."

"Another one?"

"Oh, come on, Detective, don't try to bull sh—pull one over on me." Morrisette cocked her head to one side to survey him. "It's written all over that ugly mug of yours. You find the widow attractive."

"She is attractive," he said carefully.

"I mean, attractive *to you*. If she wasn't our A-number one suspect, you might just think about taking her out and trying her on for size."

"Don't think so," Reed lied, not wanting to follow that line of thinking. "She's a little wacky for my taste."

"I told you not to bullshit me. Oh, darn, another quarter." Looking disgusted with herself, Morrisette hopped off the desk. "You like 'em a little wacky. Or kinky. Maybe even a lot kinky. As long as they're at least one step out of the mainstream. Wasn't that the trouble with the schoolteacher? Helen? She was too square."

Reed didn't answer, but his jaw tightened.

"Hey!" Morrisette held her hands up to her head as if in surrender. "I'm not the one to talk about relationships. If there's a loser within a five-hundred-mile radius, I end up dating him."

He didn't comment. Didn't want to pursue this conversation. And he didn't want to think about Helen and what life might have been if he'd stuck it out in San Francisco, given into the pressure and married her. His feelings about Caitlyn Bandeaux were clear: she was a suspect. Period. The suicide theory was history as far as he was concerned, though he wouldn't admit it to the press or Bandeaux's family just yet. He snapped the chair back to its normal position. "See if you can track down her shrink. Rebecca Wade. She left town a month or so ago, and I don't like it. Do what you have to do to find her. ASAP. I want to know why she left when she did, where she is and what she can tell us about Caitlyn Bandeaux."

"There is that little problem of patient-doctor privilege."

"Work around it. It's just too convenient that she's missing."

"You think her patient killed her?"

"I don't know what to think, not until we locate her. Meanwhile, I'll double-check Caitlyn Bandeaux's alibi."

"That would be a good start," she said, slapping the top of his desk, "a damned good start."

"And that's another quarter. At this rate you'll have both kids' college tuition funded by Christmas."

"Very funny," she muttered under her breath and looked as if she wanted to cuss him out big time, but held her tongue. "I'll let you know when I find Dr. Wade. In the meantime, get over your fantasies and figure out how to prove that Caitlyn Bandeaux killed her husband."

"So I take it you don't believe in innocent until proven guilty?"

"I think that's pure, unadulterated . . . hogwash. I'll stake all of my kids' college fund that Mrs. Bandeaux is guilty as sin."

The dream replayed as it always did.

She heard her brother's voice ricocheting off of the surrounding cliffs.

"Help!" he yelled, his strong voice fading in the storm. "Someone help me!"

Caitlyn ran through the thicket of spindly pines, her boots slipping on a dusting of snow that was beginning to cover the forest floor. "Where are you? Charles!" she screamed, frantic as she scrambled over a fallen log. Was she getting closer or farther away? "Charles!"

Oh, God. Oh, God. Oh, God. Where was he? Snow fell from the sky and night was closing in, darkness seeping through the undergrowth.

Bursting through a thick copse, she caught sight of him lying in the brush, the shaft of an arrow sticking out of his chest, a red stain pooling dark upon his corduroy shirt.

Oh, no! She stumbled, then climbed to her feet, but her legs felt leaden, weighted down by the ice and snow swirling around her. Dry leaves crackled underfoot, and somewhere far off a dog howled. "I'm coming," she yelled, running forward, her breath fogging the cold winter air. As she reached him, she dropped to her knees, her icy fingers wrap-

*ping around the horrid weapon protruding from her broth-
er's torso.*

*"Don't!" a frightened voice warned. She turned to see
Griffin, pale-faced and wan, standing between two saplings.
Snow had collected on his collar and in his disheveled hair.*

"Help me!" she screamed.

*Griffin didn't move. His gaze was glued to the arrow.
"Don't pull it out!"*

*"But he's dying!" Her words echoed in the forest, swirled
in the falling snow.*

"You'll kill him sure if you yank that out."

*Oh, he was never any help. None at all. "For God's sake,
run!" she yelled, trying to propel Griffin into action. "Get
help! Go to the lodge!"*

*Charles groaned. Blood oozed from the corners of his
mouth. Though he was staring straight at her, his eyes dulled,
as if he couldn't see. Snow was beginning to cover his face.*

*"Go!" she screamed, turning to look over her shoulder
at Griffin, but he'd disappeared into the thickening curtain
of snow. As quickly as he'd come. The space between the
saplings suddenly dark and yawning.*

*There wasn't any time. She had to do something. She had
to try and save her brother. Swallowing back her fear, she
gripped the arrow shaft hard and pulled. It didn't move;
her fingers slid up its slick sides. She wrapped her fingers
around it again. Closing her eyes, she yanked with all her
might, heard a sickening sucking sound and then she was
holding the shaft aloft, the arrowhead bright with blood in
the light from the rising moon as night stole through the
forest.*

But it was too late.

Charles's breath rattled one last time.

*He let out a horrid wail that reverberated through the
trees and then was silent.*

Silent as death.

*No! He was so still. Unmoving. She scrambled away from
him, flew to her feet and began to run.*

Faster. Through the naked birches.

Faster. Across a frozen stream.

Faster. Up the hill toward the family's hunting lodge in the Appalachians.

Her lungs were on fire, her feet slipping on the icy ground. The forest was dark. Looming. Seemed to close in on her as snow and ice pelted from the heavens. It covered the familiar paths, clung to her eyelashes, stung her cheeks and changed the surrounding landscape so that she had no idea where she was, from which direction she'd come.

"Help!" she cried, the arrow frozen in her hand. "Please! Help!"

"Caitlyn?" Berneda's voice was as brittle as a winter branch.

Caitlyn couldn't see her mother through the curtain of snow. "Mama? Where are you?

"Caitlyn? Come here this instant!" her mother hissed.

Running again, trying to locate the sound, Caitlyn suddenly broke free of the woods. Gasping, her heart drumming, she finally saw the rambling old hunting lodge with warm patches of light in the windows, smoke curling from the chimney and icicles gleaming from the eaves. The door was open, music drifting into the night. Her mother stood in stark relief against the bright backdrop. A tall, dark angel glowering down upon Caitlyn as she raced up the short rise to the porch.

"Help. We have to get help. It's Charles, he's hurt!"

Berneda's face was the color of the surrounding snow, her eyes blazing with accusation as she noticed the arrow in her daughter's hand. Her splayed fingers flattened over her chest. "Oh, my God, Caitlyn," she whispered, "what have you done?"

Caitlyn's eyes flew open.

She was alone, lying upon the canopied bed that had been hers during the years that she'd occupied this room. The flowered canopy was faded now and the afghan she'd pulled to her neck smelled of must and age. She'd been tired after the funeral, had taken her mother's advice and rested, here, in her old bed.

She swallowed hard. Remnants of the dream still lingered: the sucking sound of the arrow loosening from Charles's flesh, the cold whistle of the wind, the horrid accusations in her mother's voice. This recurring nightmare had chased after her since she was a child, ever since the day when she actually had found her brother dying in the snow.

If only she'd listened to Griffin. If only she hadn't panicked and pulled that damned arrow from his chest.

But she had. So many years earlier.

It had been the day before Thanksgiving, and most of the family had gathered at their hunting lodge in the mountains of West Virginia. Her father had been alive then, and Charles had been out hunting by himself. Caitlyn, Kelly and Griffin had been playing hide-and-seek in the woods when Caitlyn had become lost and wandered farther from the house, deeper into the forest. Calling for her twin, she'd stumbled upon the half-frozen body of her brother. That was where the dream parted from reality, or at least she thought it did because from the moment she'd seen Charles lying faceup in the snow, she couldn't remember a thing, only that she'd somehow ended up back at the lodge, blood streaking her coat and insulated pants, the deadly arrow clutched in one mittened hand. She'd been catatonic for days . . . unable to talk, withdrawn inside herself. The entire episode was now a black hole, a void she could only fill in the middle of the night when her subconscious would call up a nightmare as bleak and stark as the sky on that icy November day.

"God help me," she whispered, trying to get a grip on herself. Her nerves were shot, her memory filled with holes, her life careening out of control. She couldn't let this happen. Not again. Flipping on the bedside lamp, she noticed the crisp business card that had fallen from her purse.

Adam Hunt
Ph.D.
Grief And Family Counseling

A phone number was listed on the bottom line.

She saw it as a lifeline to her sanity.

Finding her purse where it had fallen to the floor, Caitlyn leaned over the side of the bed, reached inside and dragged out her cell phone. Her battery had run down again, but there was still a little power. Without thinking twice, she punched out Adam Hunt's telephone number. She had to get help. She couldn't take this much longer or she would completely crack up. Just like her grandmother Evelyn had.

She shuddered as the phone rang.

Cold, cold Nana.

Naughty Nana.

Bad lady.

Twelve

Adam waited.

In Rebecca's office.

He'd made arrangements with the rental management company, not that it was legal. But he was able to talk his way in as Rebecca was a couple of months behind on the rent and Adam agreed to pay the money due, explaining that he was a friend. Fortunately, the building manager wasn't all that concerned about the legality of the transaction—just the cash. Adam slipped him an extra five-hundred dollars in cash, promised to vacate if Dr. Wade showed up, and the louse managed to turn a greedy blind eye.

So much for ethics in property management.

But Adam couldn't complain. He was eyeball deep in the illegal transaction, and he'd spent the past three days reading everything he could about Caitlyn Montgomery, sensing she was somehow the key to Rebecca's disappearance.

If she's really disappeared.

She could be on one of her "self-awareness trips."

Or she could have found another man; taken a lover.

It's not as if she hadn't done it before.

But he couldn't shake the feeling that something was

wrong. Really wrong this time. Rebecca had mentioned a breakthrough with one of her patients, a major breakthrough, and then she'd disappeared. True, she'd been talking about taking some time off, heading west and seeing parts of the country she'd never visited before, but to leave without saying good-bye, to never call or send a postcard? No, it didn't feel right. And yet he hadn't gone to the police again. Not after the last time. Not until he was certain. He'd already gone to her house and picked the locks. The house was deserted, but not emptied. Too many personal items had remained . . . he'd have to talk to the landlady, but he hadn't caught up with her yet. Had avoided her until he'd had a quick look for himself.

Now he heard a slight rap on the partially opened door, and then Caitlyn Montgomery Bandeaux poked her head around the corner. Mahogany-colored hair framed a heart-shaped face sculpted with high cheekbones, arched eyebrows and intelligent, troubled eyes.

He was on his feet in an instant. "Come in."

Cautiously, she slid through the door. "This is kind of weird," she admitted, surveying the surroundings.

"Because this was Rebecca's office?" God, she was beautiful. He'd remembered that from the cemetery, but it seemed that today, without the strain of the funeral, she was prettier, had more color. Not that it should matter.

"Yes." She managed a shy smile. "Because it's Rebecca's office."

"Will it make you uncomfortable?"

"I don't know." She managed a smile and smoothed the nonexistent wrinkles from a khaki skirt that buttoned up the front. Her hair was piled loosely onto her head, falling down in some places, and she looked nervous. Edgy. A little ragged around the edges. But then she'd been through quite a bit in the past few days.

"You changed things around," she said, tugging at the sleeves of her pale sweater.

"A bit." He'd replaced a couple of the lamps, thrown two new rugs over the floors, put up cheap prints he'd bought at an estate sale, and prominently displayed his degrees behind the desk. He'd repositioned the couch and chairs and thrown out the dead plants, replacing them with a couple of ferns.

"This does seem a little surreal," she admitted as she took a seat in the rocker and dropped her purse onto the floor beside her.

"I imagine."

"Kind of like a bad movie. A really bad movie."

He grinned and saw a bit of amusement in her eyes, just beneath the strain. So she had a sense of humor. That would help.

"I think I've been coming here for two-and-a-half years— well, before I stopped a few months back—and I always saw Rebecca, er, Dr. Wade, in that chair—" Caitlyn motioned toward the desk chair and shrugged, then rubbed her arms as if an eerie sensation had stolen up her skin. Crossing her legs, she flashed him a bit of calf, though she seemed unaware of the movement. Surely she knew she was a striking woman . . . then again, maybe not.

"Maybe we should just take this session to get to know each other," he suggested, reining in his thoughts. Rebecca's desk chair squeaked as he shifted in it. "How about this? I'll tell you a little about myself and then you can tell me about you."

"Kind of like that old kids' game? You show me yours and I'll show you mine?" she asked, then seemed horrified at the insinuation.

"Not that intense. At least I hope not today."

"Good. I'm not sure I'm up to intense." She shoved her hair out of her face and managed a thin smile.

So far this wasn't going as he'd planned. He wheeled the chair to a small table where a pitcher of iced tea was sweating and a small electric soup maker was warming water. "Coffee? It's instant. Hot or cold tea?" he asked, and she shook her head.

"I'm fine—well, maybe tea."

He poured hot water into a mug, then handed the cup,

spoon and tea bag to her. "Sorry, fresh out of honey or lemon or cream or sugar or even sugar substitute."

"That's fine. I'm a purist." Dunking the tea bag in her mug, she leaned back in the rocker and again he noticed that she was a striking woman. Paler than most, her fair complexion complemented a toned and supple body. A few light freckles bridged her straight nose and thick, red-brown lashes rimmed wide hazel eyes that, in the right light, looked green. Full lips turned down thoughtfully at the corners, and the space between her eyebrows puckered as if she were in deep, troubling thought. When she looked up at him, he was taken with the intensity of her stare, those hazel eyes dark with worry. "I thought you were going to tell me about yourself."

"That's right." He managed a smile. "I'm afraid it's pretty boring. Born and raised in Wisconsin, one brother, went to school in Madison, then transferred to Michigan for grad school. I taught for a few years, then went into private practice. I was working in the D.C. area and was thinking of moving when I talked to Rebecca and she suggested I come down here. Savannah sounded interesting. A real change. So I decided to go for it."

"What about all your patients in D.C.?"

His smile broadened. "I weaned them."

"They're all healed?" she asked, snapping her fingers. "Psychoses, depression, whatever. Just like that?"

"Healed? Hmm. A relative term, but yes, actually, most of them are in pretty good shape. A few I referred to colleagues."

"How long have you been here?"

"About two weeks."

"Am I your first patient?"

"In Savannah, yes."

"Do you have references?" she asked, then glanced at the diplomas and awards for service that he'd hung over the now-cold fireplace. "Oh . . ."

"You can call Michigan. Talk to Dean Billings in the

Psych Department. Last I heard he was still working, but he could've retired, I suppose."

"So why did you show up at Josh's funeral? That's kind of weird. You knew about me."

His smile stretched. "You caught me. I was looking for you. Figured you'd be there. I'd been talking to Rebecca— Dr. Wade. She'd called me specifically about you. She'd mentioned you before, then called when she read about Josh's death in the on-line version of the *Savannah Sentinel*. She thought you might like to talk about it."

"She should have called me."

"I think she tried. No answer."

"I didn't answer for a few days . . . wasn't up to it. The press was calling and I was upset." Her brows pulled into a tighter knot. "But she didn't leave a message."

"Maybe she intends to call back," Adam suggested, knowing it was a lie as he stared into the hazel eyes of this beautiful, vulnerable woman. He felt like a heel, but tamped the feeling down.

Caitlyn dunked her tea bag and didn't comment, but he knew the wheels were turning in her mind and she was second-guessing her appointment. Maybe he'd blown it. He leaned back in his chair and tented his hands. "So, now tell me about you."

She visibly started. Then placed her tea bag on a napkin. "I guess that's why I'm here, right?" She glanced out the window, appeared to struggle. "Where do you want me to start?"

"Wherever you like." When she didn't immediately respond, he said gently, "How about why you were seeing Dr. Wade and then you can go back as far as you want." He sent her a reassuring smile, knew the rimless glasses he'd donned helped soften his visage, and made him look more intellectual than intimidating. "We'll work forward or backward from the starting point. I just want you to be comfortable."

"Kinda hard to do when someone's dissecting your life."

"Not dissecting."

"Then examining."

He leaned forward, rested his elbows on his knees, his chin propped in his hands. "Look, I don't know how you did things with Dr. Wade, but let's start fresh. Don't think of me as dissecting or examining, or looking too deep into areas you want to keep hidden. We can begin with a dialogue and go from there. We can begin by talking about your family."

"My family," she said and sighed so deeply that her hair ruffled. "Well, okay. Let's start by saying we didn't put the fun in dysfunctional. The Montgomerys have been in Savannah about as long as there's been a Savannah," she said, looking away from him as she rubbed a finger over the edge of the couch. She seemed to loosen up a bit, explaining that in the first few years of her life she'd thought everything was perfect. She had a twin, Kelly, and they were close; her other siblings, five of them, were spread above and below; the twins were the middle children. One of her brothers, "Baby Parker," had died as an infant from SIDS, and the eldest, Charles, had been killed in a freak hunting accident, and she had recurring dreams about finding him in the woods. The other hunter, whoever he was, had never been found. As for the remaining siblings, her older sister Amanda, the lawyer, was "driven," her brother Troy, "controlling," and her baby sister, Hannah, a "worry."

She talked for nearly two hours and he learned that her oldest sibling, Charles, had been the heir apparent. Then he'd died. Now the duty of running the vast Montgomery wealth was split between Amanda as the oldest sibling and Troy, the next to youngest, who just happened to be the last standing male in the family.

As Caitlyn spoke, Adam observed how careful she was, how she looked him squarely in the eye, only to quickly glance away, as if suddenly shy. He'd gone through Rebecca's notes on Caitlyn, but some of them were obviously missing, the pages having disappeared. Unless Rebecca had stored them somewhere else. He hadn't found them yet, though he'd torn this office upside down and come up empty-handed. The quick search of Rebecca's house hadn't shed any light on the missing pages, either. Odd, he thought. Had she taken them with her?

Everything Caitlyn confided he already knew about her, though he played the innocent, leaning back in his chair, scribbling notes, asking the appropriate questions or nodding thoughtfully. He even made a couple of jokes and was rewarded with her lips twitching into a beguiling smile.

". . . so then I got married," she said and lifted a shoulder. "No one was happy about it."

"No one, meaning your family."

"Right."

"Why did they disapprove?"

"Josh had been married before to an older woman, Maude Havenbrooke. He'd even adopted her child from a previous marriage."

"Divorce is fairly common."

"That was only the first strike against him. Josh had a reputation for being . . . er, making reckless investments. My family thought Josh was after my money—I, um, have a trust fund." She cleared her throat. "But I didn't care what anyone thought about Josh. I was in love." She rolled her eyes and shook her head, then hesitated before adding, "And . . . and I was pregnant." She blinked and looked at her hands. "Jamie was born seven months later and she would have been five if . . ." She cleared her throat. Struggled for words. ". . . If she had survived. She died." Nodding her head as if to convince herself, she added huskily, "She was my baby and . . . and my whole life." Tears gathered in her eyes and she blinked.

He felt a pang of sympathy for this woman trying so hard to hold herself together. Without saying a word, he rolled Rebecca's chair to the bookcase, picked up a box of tissues and handed the box to her.

"I'm sorry," she whispered.

"Don't be. It's hard to lose a child."

"It's hell," she corrected, spitting out the words and

touching a tissue to the corner of her eyes. "Do you have any children, Dr. Hunt?"

"No." His ex-wife had never wanted any. It was a bone of contention and had contributed to the breakdown of his marriage.

"Then you can't begin to imagine the pain I've gone through, the guilt I've borne, the ... the desperation I've felt. I wake up every morning and think about her, wish that I could have taken her place. I would trade in an instant." Her eyes were suddenly dry, her shoulders stiffening, the tissue crumpled in her fist. "But I don't have that choice and my husband ..." She let her breath out and visibly stiffened. "My *husband* was going to file a wrongful death suit against me. Can you imagine? As if I ... I had killed my daughter, our daughter."

"I don't understand."

"Neither do I!" She shot to her feet. "He claimed I was neglectful ... that I didn't get her to the hospital in time, that I was too wrapped up in myself. It's ridiculous. I was still recovering from a sprained wrist, but I was well enough to take care of my daughter. I just thought she had the flu and ... well, by the time I got her to the hospital ..." Her words faded and she stopped talking to stare out the window, as if mesmerized by a dove roosting on the eave of the next building. Sunlight gilded the dark strands of her hair, made the red in it appear. "It was too late. Josh blamed me. And I blamed myself. I should have taken her in sooner, but I didn't know." She turned, her wide eyes red-rimmed, one small fist clenched tight. "He went to his grave believing that I'd somehow purposely endangered my child's life." Her shoulders slumped. "I went over all this with Dr. Wade—well, not about the lawsuit. I didn't know about it until after our last session." She flopped back on the couch, checked the time and said, "I think I've run over."

"I don't have that many patients yet."

"Maybe I should refer the rest of my family. We could keep you and about five other psychologists busy for the rest of your life!"

Smiling as if in disbelief, not wanting her to know that he'd read every page he could find on her already, he took off his glasses and polished them with a handkerchief.

"If Dr. Wade calls you, would you tell her 'hello?' " She tossed the wadded tissue into a trash basket at the end of the couch.

"If she calls," he promised, feeling a twinge of guilt at the deception as he slid the reading glasses onto his nose. It seemed as if all he did these days was stretch the truth, or bend it, or even break it. But he couldn't be honest with her, not until he found out what he needed to know.

She wrote a check hastily and handed it to him.

"I'll refund this when the insurance payment comes through," he promised, feeling even more guilt.

"Fine." She offered him a shy smile that touched him in a way he hadn't expected. "Thanks, Dr. Hunt."

"Adam," he insisted. "I like to keep things casual."

"Adam, then." She nodded curtly and he stood in the doorway to Rebecca's office, watching her hurry down the stairs, not once glancing over her shoulder. God, she was an intriguing woman. Beautiful, bright and troubled. So troubled.

He looked at her check, the flourish of her signature, knowing that she was building trust in him. He winced against another sharp jab of guilt.

Maybe his grandmother was right. Maybe there was never a good reason to lie. He could tear the check up right now, or he could use it to get a little more information about Caitlyn Montgomery and hence, perhaps, Rebecca Wade. He didn't hesitate a second, just folded the check with a sharp crease and slipped it into his wallet.

Seated at the table in her private space, Atropos closed her eyes. She needed peace. She needed rest. She needed to calm the rage that burned and clawed. She thought of ice and snow, of a serene time when her hectic work would be done. Slowly, starting with her toes, she relaxed each muscle in her body, up her legs and torso, letting her arms and shoulders go limp, easing the tension from the muscles of her face, clearing her mind.

She had to be clearheaded. Calm. Deadly. She couldn't afford to make a mistake. Not now . . . not after so many years of planning. When her mind was free again, she stood and stared at the skeletal family tree she'd erected. There, on the appropriate, unforgiving limb, was Cameron.

The son.

And the father.

Now the not-so-holy ghost.

He'd died at the wheel of his Porsche when it missed a corner and slid into the swamp, where he drowned. He'd been on his way to visit Copper Biscayne, his lover, and as fate would have it, Cameron in the freak accident had not only lost his life, but one of his balls as well. It appeared to have been sliced off when he'd been thrown through the windshield; shards of glass had still been imbedded in his scrotum. That piece of information had never made it to the press; there was no mention of the lost testicle in any of the articles that Atropos had so meticulously clipped from every paper that reported Cameron's death. Cameron's picture had been sliced, then pasted onto the family tree. The colors had faded somewhat, but the snapshot had been taken of Cameron with his three bastard children . . . Sugar, Dickie Ray and Cricket. Atropos wasn't certain they were all his, but it was possible, if not likely.

Yes, Cameron had deserved his end.

Another limb belonged to Charles. The eldest son. The golden boy who could do no wrong. Gifted athlete, college graduate, and honed into the image of his proud father. Charles had been set on a course from a young age to run the family businesses. Unfortunately, he'd been shot by an errant bow hunter one Thanksgiving holiday. Atropos smiled as she stared at his reconstructed picture. He'd been standing over the top of a trophy kill, a very dead bear, the first beast Charles had killed with his bow. The picture had been sliced up, of course, then carefully pasted back together so that it seemed as if the bear had killed Charles.

How fitting. It just seemed more like the natural order of things.

There were other limbs that were filled in as well, but Atropos didn't have time to bask in each murder. Not when there was so much work to be done. She wondered if anyone, the police or Montgomery family members, realized that the killings were not random, that the causes of death were planned to perfection, that there was a bit of irony in each. How easy it would have been to buy a stolen gun and shoot her victims while they were alone. But that wasn't the point. It wasn't just the erasure of a life, but the artistry of the killing that was important, so that every victim realized they were about to die, at her hand. In those last, gasping, terrifying moments of life, the doomed needed to know that their fate had been sealed. They'd had no chance of escape.

That was the thrill.

That was the artistry.

That was the magic.

That was the brilliance.

She felt better as she stared at the death tree. Her blood sang through her veins. She felt her heart beating, tingled with anticipation of the next kill.

She glanced again at the snipped torso of Joshua Bandeaux. A truer bastard had never walked the earth. He deserved much worse than he had gotten. And the stupid police hadn't even figured out for certain that he'd been killed. Which was frustrating. A little press would help sate her need for recognition . . . the need that had always propelled her. The few clippings already gathered were meager, not worthy of her acts.

She glanced at the tree once more. Soon its gnarled and deadly branches would be filled. The clock was ticking. There was much to do. On quiet, padded footsteps, she walked to the desk and retrieved the snapshots from her drawer. Gently, as if they were a frail deck of Tarot cards, she shuffled them and fanned them out facedown on the desk. *Eeny, meeny, miney moe . . . Pick a victim soon to go . . . if he hollers . . . make him pay . . . with his life that very day . . .*

Carefully one photograph was selected and turned over.

A picture of Amanda.

Second born. Smart, beautiful, successful.

Amanda Montgomery Drummond. With her own little demons . . . or demonettes. Yes, it was the eldest daughter's turn.

In the snapshot Amanda, in a tennis skirt and top, was leaning against the polished fender of her pride and joy, a little red sports car, a cherry-red 1976 Triumph—make that TR-6—a gift from her father long before his untimely accident. Her eyes were shaded behind sunglasses, her smile wide, her mahogany-colored hair snapped back into a ponytail. Tall, athletic, gifted . . . with double majors in college, she had graduated summa cum laude and had given herself the choice of medical or law school.

Not a compassionate woman by nature, one who had an eye on making money, she'd chosen the law. Which was probably just as well. She would have made a horrid doctor.

"It's your time," Atropos whispered to the smiling Amanda in the picture. "Won't the family be surprised? Or maybe, just maybe they'll be relieved. You really are a bitch, you know." She found the thread of life for Amanda Montgomery, already clipped and ready.

What Atropos had planned for Amanda was guaranteed to get the family's attention. She started to pick up the pictures, but in her haste knocked two of them onto the floor. They fluttered and turned upright as they hit the tiles.

Two pictures. The first was of Caitlyn as a child. She was laughing, her head thrown back as she swung on the old rope that had hung from the sturdy limb of a live oak with branches that spread over the river. The second was of Berneda, the mother, her hands clasped over her heart in front of a birthday cake with seventy-five candles burning bright. Lucille stood just behind her, one step out of the spotlight, where she'd always been. Always tending, never tended.

Well, it was about time Lucille was released.

The mother would have to meet her own personal destiny. She found Berneda's life braid . . . it was cut just perfectly.

As for Caitlyn?

Atropos found the red and black thread of her life and sighed.

For the moment, Caitlyn would be spared. But only for the moment.

And not for long. Atropos glanced at the picture again and at the frayed rope that the unsuspecting Caitlyn clung to as if for dear life. How fitting. Atropos fingered Caitlyn's thread of life . . . it was only slightly longer than that of her mother.

The child in the snapshot seemed to smile at her.

Foolish, foolish little girl.

Thirteen

"Where were you on the night of your husband's death?"

The question wasn't unexpected and yet Caitlyn, absently ruffling Oscar's fur, had been dreading it. Seated at her own kitchen table, with Officers Reed and Morrisette across from her, she said, "I thought I told you I was out," she clarified, second-guessing herself. When Reed had called and asked to come by, she'd agreed. Now she wondered if she should have insisted she have an attorney present. "My sister and I were supposed to meet at a bar called The Swamp, down on the riverfront, but she got tied up and I was alone."

"So you never went to your husband's house that night?"

"It was my house once," she said automatically and sensed both officers' suspicion. And why not? Wasn't it usually someone in the family who turned out to be the killer? "Look," she said, standing. "I think I'd better call a lawyer."

The woman with the spiky hair lifted a shoulder. "If you think you need one. We're just asking a few questions."

Caitlyn's skin prickled with dread. "The truth of the matter, which I think I told you before, is that I'm kind of fuzzy about that night."

"Why is that?"

She thought about explaining about the blackouts, about the loss of time she sometimes experienced, about the lapses in her memory, but it sounded like a lie. These cynical and jaded officers wouldn't believe her. "Sometimes I drink too much," she said.

"So you were so drunk that night that you can't remember what you did?"

"I think I should call my attorney." She pushed Oscar off her lap and stood. It was time to end this.

Reed scooted back his chair. "If you think you need one."

"You tell me, Detective. You're the ones asking the questions."

"We're just trying to find out what happened." Reed offered what was supposed to pass as a smile, but there was no amusement in his eyes. None whatsoever.

"Fine. You can do it when I have a lawyer present," she said and walked to the door. Oscar, toenails clicking, followed after.

"Mrs. Bandeaux, did you see your husband on the night of his death?" Detective Morrisette asked.

Did she? Could she tell them she wasn't sure?

"A neighbor saw your car, or one like yours, in the driveway around midnight."

Every muscle in her body tensed. Her heart began to pound with a new, unnamed fear. *So you did go there . . .*

"And there was more than just Bandeaux's blood at the scene."

"Someone else's?" she asked, her knees nearly giving way as she felt the scars on her wrist grow tight.

"O-positive. We'll be doing DNA analysis of it, so we'd like a blood sample from you."

"You think I killed Josh."

"We're just trying to narrow the field." But Reed's eyes were cold, and even Detective Morrisette was grimmer than usual. No good cop–bad cop routine. Just the facts, ma'am.

"I'll have my attorney contact you," she said as they stepped over the threshold and she shut the door behind them. She was shaking inside, a headache pounding behind one eye, the same kind of pain slicing through her brain that preceded the blackouts that ate away huge chunks of her time.

The first time she realized that she had holes in her memory had been when she was a child, recovering from a sinus infection that had landed her in the hospital. She'd been six or seven at the time and had found herself on the school playground long after dark. Her mother had been frantic and she'd not been able to explain herself, couldn't remember her whereabouts. No one had known how she'd missed the bus and lost track of time, not even Griffin, who had been the last person she'd seen, the one who had suggested they walk the three miles home.

Funny she should think of that now as she climbed the stairs and passed through her bedroom to the bathroom and noticed the slight discoloration on the carpet. What the hell had happened the night that Josh had died? Why had there been blood all over this room . . . and why had her type of blood been in Josh's home?

Not that it proved she was there, she thought. Millions of people had O-positive blood. Including most of her family. And yet a new fear, deep-seated and dark, gripped her. Could she have . . . was she capable of . . . in one of her blackouts, could she have killed her husband?

Don't even think that way! She held on to the sides of the sink for support and waited until she'd forced the panic back. *Don't let this get to you. Do something! Be proactive, for God's sake!* She found a bottle of Excedrin Migraine in the mirrored cabinet and popped two tablets, then walked into her office, sat at the desk and picked up the phone. She needed a lawyer, a defense attorney, and fast.

What about an alibi? Isn't that what you really need?

"Oh, shut up," she muttered as she sat at her desk chair and quickly scanned her e-mail. Nothing from Kelly or anyone else. Wondering how to get hold of her twin, Caitlyn dialed Amanda's office, but it was after hours and a recorded message asked her to leave her name and number. "Great," she muttered under her breath. She slammed the receiver down. Where the hell were her sisters when she needed them? Kelly was never around, and Amanda was oftentimes buried in her work. Well, she'd just have to unbury herself. Caitlyn couldn't afford to wait. No telling what the police had up their sleeves.

Amanda had worked for the D.A.'s office for a couple of years before deciding the low pay, long hours and "working with every low-life slime who decided to crawl out from his personal, perverted rock" wasn't for her. Years ago Amanda had seen the corporate light and transferred into domestic law, switching gears easily. Now she worked with low-life slimes when they wanted a divorce. But she would know the name of a good criminal defense attorney.

Caitlyn punched out Amanda's home number and leaned back in her desk chair, waiting for yet another machine to pick up. "Come on, be home," she said under her breath and heard a noise behind her. She froze. Fear crawled up her spine as she hazarded a glance over her shoulder only to see Oscar ambling into the office. Relief washed over her but she noticed her own reflection. The door was slightly ajar, the mirror hanging upon it catching her image as she sat in her desk chair. And she looked horrible. Frazzled. Undone. Her hair was mussed from countless times pushing it off her forehead, her complexion pale, dark smudges visible beneath her eyes. She shifted her gaze to Oscar. "Hurry up," she whispered, patting her lap impatiently as a machine answered and Amanda's recorded voice asked the callers to leave their names and numbers. The recorder beeped.

Oscar catapulted into her lap.

"Amanda? It's Caitlyn," she said, hating to leave this particular message. She scratched the dog behind his ears. "Look, I need your help. Unlike Mom, I *do* know that you're not a criminal defense attorney, but I was hoping you could give the name and number of someone you would recommend—"

Click.

"Caitlyn?" Amanda asked, her voice worried. "Are you

still there? I just walked in and heard you leaving a message. What's going on?''

"The police were just here,'' Caitlyn said, relieved to actually be speaking to her sister.

"Uh-oh.''

"Yeah. Big time uh-oh. They want a DNA sample from me,'' she said, hoping to hide the panic that was creeping up her spine. Her fingers clamped over the phone. "They seem to think I was at Josh's that night. They're not saying much, but I think they don't believe that he committed suicide and that someone killed him, and even though they didn't come out and tell me, I'm sure I'm the primary suspect and . . . and . . . I need a lawyer and oh, God, I can't remember and—''

"Caitlyn! Get a grip!'' Amanda snapped, then added more softly, "I'm sorry, but you're scaring me to death and I can't really follow what's going on. Take a couple of deep breaths and start over, okay? Now, from the beginning, tell me what's happening. Start with when the police arrived. Tell me everything.''

As best as she could, Caitlyn recounted the entire conversation. The horrid sense of panic that had been with her since the morning she'd woken up to a blood-smeared bedroom burrowed deeper as she recounted Detective Reed's pointed questions and her own feeble answers. She began to shake inside. She was going to be accused of Josh's murder, she was certain of it, and she couldn't remember what she'd done that night.

"He didn't charge me with anything, didn't out and out accuse me, but . . . I'm sure he believes I did it.''

"What about the suicide angle? I thought he left a note . . . isn't that right?''

"I don't think the police believe it . . . maybe they think the killer left it . . . Oh, God, I don't know.''

"Maybe this isn't as bad as it seems,'' Amanda said thoughtfully.

"Well, that's a relief because it seems pretty damned bad to me.''

"I know, and I'd be lying if I said you weren't a suspect. Geez, you could be the number-one suspect, but you're not the only one. I don't believe they're narrowing the field as Reed told you. I think they're concentrating on you."

"I thought you said it wasn't bad."

"We just have to remind them that there are other suspects. Now, get your story straight and your alibi down pat."

"Alibi?" She couldn't believe the words. "You want me to lie?"

"No, of course not. Let's not add perjury to the potential charges. I know several good criminal defense attorneys, people I didn't want to come up against when I was working with the D.A.'s office. They're expensive, but worth it."

"Criminal defense attorneys," Caitlyn repeated, disbelieving that she would ever need their services. She glanced again to the door and saw herself as she was—tired, beaten, scared out of her wits, not even certain if she'd killed her husband or not. "Okay, give me their names."

"John Ingersol. He's fabulous." Caitlyn scratched a note on the back of an envelope. "And Marvin Wilder. Or, if you feel more comfortable with a woman, then Sondra Prentiss in Atlanta is great. It all depends on their schedules. Tell you what, sit tight, have a stiff shot of something if that helps, and I'll make some calls in the morning. In the meantime, don't talk to the police, okay?"

"What if they come back?"

"Refuse to talk to them. Insist on having a lawyer with you."

"Okay." She felt slightly better.

"Do you want me to come over tonight?" Amanda asked. "Ian's out of town, and I was just going to go over a deposition, but I can do it later."

"Thanks, but I think I'll be okay."

"Are you sure? Maybe you should go out to Oak Hill. Troy thinks you should stay out there until this all blows over and really, it's not such a bad idea. Besides, if not for you, then for Mom. She could use the company."

"She's got Hannah."

Amanda snorted. "A lot of comfort that is. Mom doesn't have Hannah," she said with disgust. "No one does."

"Maybe no one has anyone."

"Pessimistic, Caitlyn. Very pessimistic. Oh—I've got another call, someone's trying to beep in and I'm waiting to hear from Ian. I'll phone you in the morning after I connect with one of the defense attorneys. Until then, avoid the police."

"I'll try."

"Don't just try. Do it! You don't have to speak to them. If you want to talk, call me or that shrink of yours, but not to anyone with a badge. Got it?"

"Got it."

"Good. Now try to calm down."

Oh, yeah. Right. Caitlyn figured there wouldn't be any calming down, for a long, long time.

"She's lying." Reed squinted through the windshield, certain that Caitlyn Bandeaux was hiding something, something about her husband's death.

"Yep." Morrisette was at the wheel, her foot as leaden as always as she shot down the narrow, shaded streets on their way back to the station.

"You ever locate her shrink?"

"Still working on it, but get this, her office is being sublet by another psychologist. A guy by the name of Adam Hunt."

"So the first shrink, Rebecca Wade, isn't coming back?"

"Who knows? Not for a while. I talked to the manager of the building, a guy who had to be a descendent from one of the last Neanderthals or Attila the Hun, and he didn't want to give me any information, of course, but I strong-armed him a bit, suggested I'd check his record, find out if he was checkin' in with his parole officer if he had one, the whole nine yards, but he stuck to his story, claimed she didn't leave a forwarding address, so I checked with the utility companies. Ms. Wade stiffed the phone company for the past two months and up until that time was a perfect customer, paid all her bills on time. So I checked with the real estate management company who handles the house she leased. Same deal. She owes two months' back rent. Before that she never missed a payment. In fact, she usually paid early.'' Morrisette tapped her fingers on the steering wheel. ''The woman I talked to at the real estate company said that Rebecca Wade had intended to move out as of June first, but left early. Half her stuff was packed, half not.''

''So what the hell happened to her?''

''That's what we have to find out. I checked out the house, and a neighbor, Mrs. Binks, stopped by. Said she was worried.''

''Has anyone filed a missing persons report?''

''No one even knows if she's missing.''

''What about relatives?''

''The neighbor said she was single, but divorced, she thought, and that she might have an aunt in Kansas or Wisconsin or somewhere in the Midwest.'' Morrisette shot through a yellow light. ''I'm looking into it. Apparently the lady shrink is a very private person. I have a theory about 'em, you know.''

''About who?''

''Shrinks. I think they're all in the business because they need mental help themselves.''

Reed grinned. ''You think?''

''Absolutely.'' She reached for her pack of cigarettes. ''And the management company checked their records, said Ms. Wade had left town once before, just took off for a few months, but that time she paid her rent in advance.''

''You think this has something to do with Josh Bandeaux's death?'' Reed asked, the wheels turning in his mind. It was an odd link. With Caitlyn Bandeaux as the cornerstone. But stranger things had occurred.

''Probably not.'' She punched in the lighter. ''You asked what happened to her and I told you. I did manage to get Rebecca Wade's Social Security number from the management company, so that should speed things up. Already put it into the database.''

''Good. Let's go down to The Swamp. See if anyone remembers her.''

''Your wish is my command,'' Morrisette mocked as she sped toward the waterfront.

''Just as it should be.''

Caitlyn felt a sharp chill. Suddenly cold to the bone, though summer heat was blistering the sidewalks of Savannah. Maybe it was because the police had stopped by earlier or maybe it was because she'd gotten another call from Nikki Gillette at the *Sentinel*, but whatever the reason, she was suddenly ice-cold. Amanda had suggested that she rest, and though it wasn't yet dark, was closer to dinnertime, she avoided her bedroom and stretched out on the couch. She pulled her afghan over her shoulders and imagined she could still smell the hint of Nana's perfume in the complicated stitches. Nana Evelyn, who had painstakingly knitted and purled, keeping her stitches even, concentrating on the pattern, sitting in front of a television that blared everything from Lawrence Welk to the evening news, making sure her mind wouldn't wander to forbidden territory.

Knit a row, purl two rows, or was it the other way around? Nana had tried to teach Kelly and Caitlyn the art of knitting and they'd both failed miserably. The last time had been at Christmas in the lodge. . . . Caitlyn shivered, drew the knitted blanket up closer to her neck. She'd been little. Five . . . Or was it six . . . and snow had covered the ground. She'd played outside all day, her snowsuit and mittens discarded and drying near the fire. But it was nighttime and she was supposed to sleep in the room with Nana. Cold Nana. Knitting Nana. Weird Nana.

''I don't want to sleep there,'' she'd told her mother.

''That's nonsense. You and Kelly always sleep with Nana when we come up here.''

''Not tonight,'' she'd whispered, for Nana had been quiet

all day long, knitting, her needles clicking, her eyes following Caitlyn as she'd played outside and then later when she'd warmed her hands by the fire.

"Don't be silly." Berneda had dismissed her, and both she and Kelly were tucked into the bunk beds in the large room. Nana had her own bed, a bigger bed with curtains around it and she'd peek through the folds of dark cloth while she was awake, or snore loudly as she slept.

But that night, she left the drapes open and lay propped up on the pillows. Oh, she'd pretended to be asleep, but Caitlyn knew she wasn't, caught a glimpse of a slit of eyeball beneath her lowered lids. She didn't snore, didn't say a word, and as the fire died and the night grew dark, Caitlyn stayed awake as long as she could, but eventually sleep overtook her and she'd drifted off.

That was all she remembered until she felt a hand upon her shoulder, an arm around her waist. Drowsy, she opened an eye as Nana picked her up. She'd started to say something, but Nana pressed a bony finger to her lips. "Don't wake Kelly," she'd whispered, but Caitlyn looked over at Kelly's mussed bed. A bit of moonlight filtered through the windows, and Caitlyn saw that Kelly's bed was empty.

"Where is—?"

"Shh! Didn't I say to be quiet? That's a good girl, Caitlyn," Nana whispered, carrying her to her bed. "Nana's cold." She bustled Caitlyn into the bed with her and drew the curtains tight so that it was dark.

Caitlyn whimpered.

"Oh, don't make a sound, honey. Don't you know you're Nana's favorite?" An icy hand smoothed Caitlyn's hair off her face. Colder lips brushed a kiss on her forehead. "That's it, snuggle closer. You'll warm old Nana up . . ."

Now, nearly thirty years later, she shuddered and threw Nana's blanket off.

Hateful old woman with her cold eyes and cold hands and cold, dark secrets.

* * *

"Yeah, that's the woman who was here," the bartender said to Reed and Morrisette as he studied the black-and-white photograph of Caitlyn Bandeaux. A burly man in a polo shirt and slacks, the bartender wore a single earring and a graying ponytail that didn't make up for the fact that male-pattern baldness was definitely setting in.

The afternoon was young. Happy Hour was still fifteen minutes away, and The Swamp was nearly empty aside from the stuffed alligators, egrets, fake frogs and catfish that were suspended from the ceiling. An overturned canoe and paddles were mounted over the bar. Fishing reels and life preservers gathered dust on the walls. In one corner music stands, amps, cords, mikes and stools were stashed behind a drum set.

Two regulars were nursing beers at stools near a couple of pinball machines, and a kid who didn't look twenty-one was busy sweeping near the hallway that led to the rest rooms and a back exit.

"I remember her because she ordered two drinks at a time. Not two of the same like most folks. She took 'em over to that table there." He pointed to a booth of tufted black leather surrounded by mirrors, then grabbed a towel and swabbed the top of the bar. "Had herself a Cosmo and a . . . martini, I think. Yeah. Sat there and waited for someone . . . well, I assume it was someone . . . sat there and drank and smoked and spent her time looking at the door or the mirror . . . I mean, I didn't pay a lot of attention when it got busy. She left after a while."

Reed glanced at the booth. "You remember what time she arrived?"

The bartender grimaced. Rubbed harder at a ring on the bar. "Let's see. I think it was after the band came on at nine . . . maybe even after the first set . . . I'm not sure. Like I said, things were starting to hop around here, but I think she hung around for a while. Can't be sure how long . . .

No, wait, the band was taking a break so it should of been ten-thirty, maybe a quarter to eleven. That's their usual routine.''

"Did she talk to anyone?"

"I don't know. She's a good-lookin' woman. I imagine someone might have tried to hit on her, but . . . hey, I don't keep track of that kind of thing. I just remember looking up and catching her reflection in the mirror. She was sitting and smoking a cigarette. Then I lost track. It got crazy in here that night. Always does on Friday nights.''

"If you think of anything else, call me,'' Reed said and left his card as he and Morrisette walked outside, where sunlight cut through the narrow streets.

"So she was here.'' Morrisette unlocked the cruiser.

"For a while.''

"But she had time to do the deed and return.''

"Seems as if.'' She slid behind the wheel as Reed strapped himself in on the passenger side.

"Bandeaux's place isn't too far from here. Let's time it,'' Reed suggested, "and go easy on the speed, okay? Caitlyn Bandeaux had downed a couple of drinks but, unless she'd been drinking before, should have been clearheaded enough not to want to be pulled over or attract any attention, so she would have obeyed the speed limits, driven to his house, shared a glass or two of wine with him to numb him.''

"Or throw him into anaphylactic shock. Then slip him a mickey, slit his wrists and hightail it back to the bar. To make sure she had an alibi.''

"Yeah . . .'' Reed wasn't certain. Morrisette pulled away from the curb and he checked his watch. She somehow managed to keep her speed right at the limit and didn't run any yellow lights. "But if she was going to use the alibi, why admit to us that she was bombed out of her mind and couldn't remember?''

"Because the time frame isn't gonna work. She's covering up.'' Morrisette maneuvered the cruiser through traffic as if she was on a Sunday drive. It took less than twenty minutes to reach Bandeaux's home in the historic district. "Traffic would have been lighter at night. She could have made it door to door in about fifteen minutes." She parked in Bandeaux's driveway, and Reed stared at the yellow crime scene tape still stretched around the wrought-iron fence. It was loosening, had ripped in one place, would soon be taken down. Unlike the noose surrounding Mrs. Bandeaux's long neck. With each of her lies, the rope just kept tightening.

"So what do you think?" Morrisette asked.

"Since she wasn't exactly candid, I think it's time to get a court order for a sample of Mrs. Bandeaux's blood."

"Sounds good to me. And while we're at it, we'll ask for a search warrant for her place. We could get lucky and might just find the murder weapon."

Adam leaned on the time-worn railing of the verandah and swirled his drink. From this vantage point of the house he'd rented, he had a bird's-eye view of Washington Square. It was near dusk, sunlight fading with each passing second. Traffic was light, a few cars rolling past, and the promise of darkness was near. And he was feeling like crap. Lying to Caitlyn had been harder than he'd imagined. He should come clean. Now. He took a long swallow from his glass and knew the reason he was wavering. Because he was attracted to her. Which was asinine. Could cost him his license if he let things get out of hand. He'd have to be careful.

It's just because you haven't been with a woman in a long time.

Nope. That was only half of it. He hadn't been attracted to a woman in a long time. Probably because of his ex-wife. Had he ever really gotten over her?

Maybe finally.

At least he'd found someone else to fantasize about.

Except that she's your patient.

"Oh, hell," he growled, staring at the square.

A couple was strolling hand in hand under the trees, and an old, emaciated man was seated on a bench, hands folded on the top of his cane, fedora angled jauntily upon his head. Overhead two squirrels pirouetted and dived, scrambling nimbly through the branches and whispering through the leaves.

What had Rebecca said the last time she'd called?

"I've got a breakthrough on this case that you won't believe. This is it, Adam. Remember I wanted to write a book about a case? I finally found it. I'll be taking a couple of months off, going to try and organize my notes, and then, with the client's permission, I'll write it. You're going to be so jealous!"

She'd been laughing, almost flirty, and he'd felt that there might be hope for their relationship after all. It had been so long since he'd heard any hint of gaiety in her voice, any trace of lightheartedness, and he wondered with more than a measure of guilt how much of that had been his fault.

He missed her lighthearted banter. Or he had.

After the last phone conversation, he'd never heard from her again. He'd called, leaving messages, hoping to recapture that hint of breathlessness and resurrected youth he'd heard in her voice.

It hadn't happened. She'd never returned his calls, and when he'd come down here he'd found her landlady distressed, her clients disbursed, his own silly dreams of rekindling a fire long dead, dashed.

Then he'd met Caitlyn Bandeaux.

Beautiful, sexy, recently widowed Caitlyn Bandeaux.

And she presented a whole new problem.

The ice in his glass clinked softly. He didn't know what he was going to do with her. She'd called tonight, had sounded shaken up and had asked to meet with him tomorrow. He'd agreed.

In fact he was looking forward to the session. Couldn't wait to see her again.

So you're gonna play the shrink again?

His jaw slid to one side and guilt scratched at his conscience. He should stop this charade right now; go to the police and be done with it. But he couldn't. Not yet. He had a job to do, a promise he'd made to himself. Even if Caitlyn Bandeaux held a fascination for him.

It was the kind of fascination that was certain to cause a man grief, but it was there just the same. He just had to figure out what do to about it. What to do about her.

The trouble was that no matter what he decided, he knew he'd regret it. He took a long swallow of aged Kentucky whiskey.

Like it or not, he'd just stepped into a lose/lose situation. And it was only going to get worse.

Fourteen

Sugar stood in the shower and let the cool water wash away the dirt, smoke, sweat and sin that seemed to cling to her body. Closing her eyes, she leaned into the spray. Her head echoed with the loud music she'd heard for three hours, and a few of her muscles ached from the high heels she'd worn as she'd gyrated to the music, making love to the damned pole while the perverts watched from their darkened tables. God, she was glad when a night was over.

If it wasn't for the money, she would stop. Dickie Ray actually had the gall to insinuate that she worked at Pussies In Booties because she enjoyed dancing nude, that she was enough of an exhibitionist to get off on the leers, jeers, hoots and hollers from the crowd, but he was wrong. It was just for the money. Nowhere else in this town could she bring in the kind of cash that she was making at the club. But then, her younger redneck of a brother didn't understand that. In fact, he didn't understand much. Oh, he was motivated by money, all right, but he expected it to come knocking on his door. His only ambition was to buy a lottery ticket every week. It was a wonder she put up with him. Because he was kin. The whole "blood is thicker than water" thing. Which she was beginning to think was a pile of crap.

She shampooed her hair and used the runoff suds to wash her face, shoulders and back. Then she splashed on some violet-scented body wash and took special care around her breasts and abdomen.

Though she didn't get off on displaying her body for the nameless Joes in the audience at the club, she did enjoy showing off her curves and "spectacular breasts," as she'd been complimented endless times, but only to one special man . . . the one who had promised to come by. As exhausted as she was, there was a certain frisson of excitement just at the thought of being with her new lover. She tingled at the thought. Not that the relationship would ever go anywhere. *You don't know that. Why not dream a little?*

She felt sexy and naughty and a little wicked and she loved the feeling. She also experienced a twinge of superiority when she was with him, as if she was pulling a fast one on the bluebloods of Savannah. Supposedly the city had a reputation for being the stepsister to Atlanta, a Southern lady with a dirty hem on her antebellum gown, but if that was true, Sugar Biscayne never wanted to set foot in the state capital. There was plenty of snobbery here in Savannah to suit her style. Now finally, she was getting a little of her own back.

She twisted off the shower, toweled off and rumpled her hair with perfumed mousse. Body gel and lotion followed before she slipped on a black thong, piled her hair on her head loosely and let one wayward, damp curl slip free. A little rouge on her nipples, a brush of mascara and a quick sheen of lip gloss—he liked her to look young and innocent and hot. His ultimate fantasy was for her to play the role of seductive virgin, an untouched woman/girl who wanted him to give it to her . . . well, maybe that was every man's fantasy, but for this one, she'd do anything.

You're his love slave and he's playing you for a fool, her conscience nagged, but she didn't listen, already heard the sound of a finely tuned engine roaring ever closer and the crunch of expensive tires in the gravel drive. She gave her nipples one final pinch to make certain they were red and hard, then slipped her arms through the sleeves of a short white robe, the one he'd bought for her, the one that just barely covered her ass.

Beams of headlights splashed light on the wall as she hurried through the bedroom and down the short hallway, only pausing for a second at Cricket's door. It was ajar and as Sugar pushed it open, she eyed the mess—rumpled bed with the sheets sagging to the floor, glasses and plates littering every surface—stereo, dresser, window ledge, night stand. Towels and clothes were dropped haphazardly on the floor, slung over the vanity chair or tossed casually over the open closet door. A bag of chips spilled and crushed into the carpet, shoes kicked off and left.

A pigsty.

Cricket had better clean up her room *and* clean up her act if she didn't want to be kicked out on her butt. Sugar paid the bills, so she set the rules. Her baby sister could damn well abide by them no matter what form of current depression, obsession or dependence Cricket was into. Sugar would be damned if she was going to pick up after Cricket. The kid was old enough—nearly twenty-four, for crying out loud—to clean up after herself. She wondered if her sister would show up at all. It was already pushing three in the morning.

Sugar shut the door to Cricket's room. The rest of the house could pass a military inspection. Aside from the couch showing signs of wear, cat-claw marks compliments of Cricket's cat, Diablo, and a couple of stains no amount of cleanser and elbow grease could erase, the double-wide was clean enough, just a little shabby, showing signs of age.

The purr of the engine stopped.

Caesarina growled low in her throat.

"Stop that!" Sugar ordered, but Caesarina was on her feet, big and glaring at the front door as Sugar swept by. "Be good," she warned the dog as she flung open the door.

He was already up the steps, his warm hands anxiously parting the robe to slide familiarly around her waist.

"You smell good," he growled, lips at her nape, fingers cupping her buttocks to pull her tight against him. His erection pressed against the zipper of his slacks and she felt a little thrill, the beginning of desire firing her blood. Oh, this was good. So good. She wrapped her arms around his neck and kissed him, feeling the warmth of his lips and the slick promise of his tongue.

He let out a soft moan, then walked her backward and managed to kick the door closed. Slowly his fingers scaled her ribs, inching up her skin until he cupped her breasts. "Do me," he growled, nibbling her earlobe.

"Don't you want a drink first?"

"Later."

"Then come into the bedroom—"

"Just do me." It was an order, one that held a desperate edge. He pushed her head down and she slid to the floor, kneeling in front of him, the hem of her robe fanning around her. "That's it, baby, that's what Daddy wants."

This and a whole lot more, she thought, slightly disappointed as he angled his hips toward her. But she wouldn't be unhappy for long. This was part of their usual routine. First she serviced him as if she were some kind of whore and then he might take the time to spank her just until her cheeks were hot, as if she was supposed to be a young innocent, but in the end he always, without fail, became an eager, indulgent lover, someone who would satisfy her every need.

As long as his were taken care of first.

She told herself she really didn't have any room to complain.

He treated her better than any other man she'd ever been with.

She glanced up at his handsome face and ignored the dog watching her. Making eye contact with her lover, Sugar offered him a naughty smile, licked her lips and then, slowly, oh, so slowly, her long fingernails tracing the metal teeth, she slid the tab of his zipper down.

Atropos lurked in the shadows. It was dark, still night, but dawn was threatening to the east. Soon gray light would steal across these weed-choked, dry acres and the thicket of scrub oak that provided her with cover. Her car was hidden half a mile down the road. No one knew she was here.

Watching.

Waiting.

Listening to the feral, animal grunts and moans that emanated from the trailer. Her mouth twisted with disgust. Even she needed a smoke after all the screwing that went on inside the old tin can. She checked her watch. Nearly five a.m. and Sugar Biscayne's lover was still inside, still going at it. He was as bad as she, sneaking around at night, visiting his white-trash whore in this dump of a double-wide.

The sounds of rutting soon ceased and within minutes, the door to the mobile home opened. The lovers' silhouettes were backlit by garish flourescent bulbs that flickered an eerie blue. His suit was wrinkled, his shirttail hanging out of his pants, and Sugar was standing barefoot, the short little robe not hiding much of what she so proudly displayed down at the Pussies In Booties, her hair mussed . . . pathetic cunt. Sugar Biscayne was a low-life whore who showed off her glistening, sweat-soaked body for a few lousy bucks. She was the worst kind of woman.

And her lover was perfect for her.

Because he was the worst kind of man. One who was caught in the trap of sex and lust she so brazenly displayed. And he bought into it. The married scumbag dropped one last kiss on her, grabbed her ass, then dashed to his expensive car and his other life. What would he tell his wife? What excuse would he make? How would he hide the smell of sex, booze and another woman? But then, the wife probably knew. And no doubt the husband wouldn't return home until he'd stopped off at a motel somewhere, shaved and showered, ready with excuses. Either his wife didn't want to face the truth or was afraid to admit that her man had strayed.

He was in his car now, already preparing his alibi. Headlights splashed twin beams across the thicket and Atropos froze, her heart drumming. But he didn't see her, no, he was already making his frantic escape. The expensive car's engine turned over, raced, and he twisted on the steering wheel, backing up quickly, gravel crunching beneath spinning tires.

Sugar stood in the doorway, her lipstick long faded, her robe gaping. She lifted a hand to wave, expecting her lover to flash his headlights or honk or roll down the window and blow a kiss. Desperate, needy cunt. Didn't she know he was already gone, his alibi set, ready to wash away any hint of lingering scent or feel of her?

The entire situation was sickening.

But soon over.

Sugar's days and nights of lovemaking were numbered. Atropos reached into her pocket and felt the braid within— Sugar's life had been measured and soon would be cut. It was only a matter of days. Atropos was feeling smug, ready to slink back to her car, when she heard Sugar's voice.

"You want to go out?"

What? Atropos felt a whisper of fear crawl up her spine.

"Well, come on . . ." Sugar opened the door wider, and the dog shot out of the trailer.

Oh, shit! Atropos didn't move a muscle. The dog lifted its nose into the air, then looked her way. Atropos didn't dare breathe. The animal was large, with a massive neck and shoulders. It let out a growl. Started her way.

This wasn't in the plan. Definitely not in the plan. Reaching slowly into her pocket, Atropos's fingers curled over the handle of her surgical scissors. They were long, the blade thin and deadly.

"Caesarina! Stop it! Get to your business." Sugar was impatient in the doorway, holding the lapels of her robe together with one hand.

The dog glanced at Sugar, then, lowering its head, growled again and started toward the thicket.

"Quit foolin' around!" Sugar ordered.

Atropos's heart nearly jumped from her chest. This was no good. No good . . . Sweating, she reached into her pocket again. Found her cell phone and, glancing at the illuminated dial, pressed a preset number.

The dog was advancing, its beady eyes centered on the thicket, her white teeth bared.

"Oh, for Christ's sake, get in here!" Sugar said, but her eyes were trained on the thicket and dawn was offering a little more light. Soon Atropos would be visible. "You see somethin' in there?" Sugar asked, her gaze centered on the tiny copse.

Come on, come on. Ring, damn it.

"Caesarina?"

From inside the trailer, Sugar's phone jangled loudly.

"Who the hell—?" Sugar wondered, but then turned, expecting, no doubt, to hear her lover's voice on the phone. She hurried out of the doorway and Atropos started backing away, inching out of the thicket and toward the low slope and fence she'd have to vault to get to her car parked on a seldom-used lane. Never once did she take her eyes off of the advancing dog. But she dropped her phone into her pocket and searched again with her fingers . . . it was in here . . . surely she hadn't forgotten . . .

"Hello?" Sugar's voice could be heard on the phone. Atropos was backing up faster and the dog, head low, was starting to break into a lope. Closing the distance.

"Hello? Who is this?" Stupidly Sugar called her lover's name. *Fool!* Atropos had the scissors pointed at the mutt and the fingers of her other hand found the canister.

The dog leaped, its huge maw wide. Teeth like razors. Atropos pushed hard on the spray button.

"Hey! Who is this? Hello? Hello?" Sugar was yelling, angry now, her voice muffled in Atropos's pocket.

Mace hit the dog square in her eyes. It squealed.

"Die, bitch!" Atropos struck. Her scissors were a dagger.

She plunged the deadly weapon into the side of the beast's huge neck. Once. Twice.

Caesarina gave off a pained yip and fell back.

"What?" Sugar screamed, her voice muted.

The dog, whimpering, trailing blood, ran back to the double-wide, and Atropos took off running toward the car.

"Caesarina? Oh, God . . . what happened?" Sugar's voice was suddenly concerned. Panicked. "Did you get into a tussle with a possum? Jesus, you're bleeding! Oh, God . . . we've got to get you to the vet!"

As if that would help.

As the first light of dawn spread over the fields, Atropos raced over a final rise and saw her car. She'd made it. The dog was probably dead, but that was good. It would give the Biscayne bitch something to think about.

Rapping lightly on the door to Adam's office, Caitlyn steeled herself. *This is necessary,* she told herself, *you need to talk things out.* She was here to get help, not because she thought Adam Hunt was the slightest bit attractive, or sexy, or even a tad interesting. This was a professional meeting, counselor and client.

"Come in," he called as the door, already ajar, inched open.

She walked inside and found the desk pushed out at an angle, Adam on his knees behind it. He looked over the corner of the desk and smiled as if he were a kid with his hand in the cookie jar. "Excuse me." He stood and dusted off his slacks. "Something fouled up with the computer. I thought the surge protector might have switched off. No such luck." He edged the desk back against the wall with his hips and she couldn't help but notice his buttocks. Nice. Tight. Damn it, what was she thinking? "Now, before we get started, can I get you something?" He motioned distractedly toward the small table with its pitcher and carafe.

"Coffee, if you've got it. And, yes, instant's fine."

"Good."

Within seconds she was cradling a warm mug and sitting on a corner of the couch. Adam slipped his glasses onto his nose and leaned back in his desk chair, a pen in one hand, a legal pad balanced on one knee.

"I called you because I'm having bad dreams." She blew across her mug and didn't let her gaze linger on the lines of his face, didn't want to wonder where he'd gotten his high forehead or straight hair, dark as the coffee crystals he'd poured into her cup.

He waited. Clicked his pen.

"Sometimes they recur. Other times they're new, but they're always horrible, always nightmares."

"The same, or different?"

"Different, but always awful." She shuddered. "I mean, graphic and emotionally wrenching."

"How often do you have them? Every night?" He began writing.

"Just about. Sometimes I wake up in the middle of the dream and I'm covered in sweat and gasping for breath, confused even though I'm in my own bed. Other times, the dream plays out and I wake up with only a hint that it was there. Then later in the day, it'll hit me." She managed what she knew was a feeble smile. "They always involve some member of my family and a life-and-death struggle and . . . and while I'm in the dream I know something bad is happening. I try to help, but I can never stop what's happening. Sometimes I'm the age I am now, other times I'm a little girl. The last one I remember was the dream with Charles."

"Your older brother?"

"Yes."

"Who's deceased, right?" His eyebrows had drawn together, and all sense of humor had evaporated from his face.

"Yes. I dream about the day he died. I was the one who found him." She took a sip from the coffee and tried to keep her voice calm, without emotion. "You see, there was this horrible bow-hunting accident," she said, shivering as she remembered the day that she'd been playing in the woods and had stumbled upon her dying older brother. She told Adam everything she could remember about the accident, about the snow, about being lost while playing with Griffin and Kelly, about finding Charles near death and about pulling the ghastly arrow from his chest.

"I guess I shouldn't have done that. I was just a kid and I didn't know any better, but Griffin, my friend who was with me, he told me not to. I ignored him. Thought I was saving Charles's life." Her voice caught and she took in a deep breath. It was over. Long over. She had to deal with it. "Anyway," she said, staring at the floor, "the upshot was that Charles died. The doctor assured me and my mother later that Charles would have died anyway, but I think . . . I mean, I wonder . . ." She sighed and shook her head. "I think Doc Fellers might have been protecting me."

"Why would he do that?"

"Because I was only nine at the time and I—I've always felt somewhat responsible, but maybe it's all just part of the Montgomery curse."

Adam was writing notes. He looked over the top of his glasses. "The curse?"

She blushed. Hadn't meant to bring it up. "It's probably just . . . talk. Superstition. But I've heard about it for as long as I can remember. Lucille—she's my mother's maid and was as much a nanny to us kids as anything—she swears it's true. But then . . ." She took a sip of her coffee. "Lucille believes in ghosts, too."

"And you don't?"

Caitlyn shrugged. "I don't think I do and I swear to anyone who asks that I don't, but . . . sometimes . . . well, I just don't know. It's kind of the same position I have about God." Leaning back into the soft leather, she closed her eyes. "That's not really right. I mean, I *want* to believe in God, but I'm not sure I actually do. I don't necessarily want to believe that there are spirits walking around, invisible beings who haven't yet decided to pass on, but sometimes I think . . . I mean I sense that I'm not alone."

''When you really are?''

''Yeah,'' she whispered, nodding. ''At least it seems that way.'' She let out a little laugh. ''You know, this even sounds nuts to me. A lot of my family thinks I'm losing it, like my grandmother . . .'' Her voice faded as the last image she remembered of Nana—her waxen face and sightless eyes—sliced through Caitlyn's brain. Her skin curdled and she sucked in her breath.

Adam's eyes narrowed on her. ''You okay?''

''Yes . . . no . . . I mean, I don't think I'd be here if I was really 'okay.' '' She looked him steadily in the eye and pointed out, ''You *are* my shrink.''

''So let's get back to the Montgomery curse.''

''Oh. That.'' Setting her coffee on the table, she stood and walked to the window. Outside, clouds covered the sky, threatening rain. As ominous and dark as the damned curse. On the verandah of the house across the alley, a woman in a big hat was refilling her bird feeders with seeds.

''Yes, the curse.'' Caitlyn hesitated, felt the same sense that the family's privacy was about to be breached, the same sensation she'd experienced when she'd confessed everything to Dr. Wade. Absently she rubbed the inside of her wrists, felt the slits that were beginning to heal—cuts she didn't remember making. There were people who self-mutilated, who inflicted pain on themselves. Surely—Oh, God, please—she wasn't one of those. ''My family is plagued with mental instability . . . well, okay, so I'm here, telling this to a shrink, I guess you know that much.''

He smiled a little. ''Why don't you tell me about it?''

''I don't know how many generations this goes back, but my grandmother Evelyn, she suffered from some kind of . . . dementia for lack of a more precise medical term. Her condition was never diagnosed, not officially, or if it was, it was one of the family's skeletons that was locked away in the closet with the rest of them.'' She glanced over her shoulder and arched an eyebrow. ''That poor closet is getting pretty full, I think. The Montgomerys might have to rent out another one, or one of those storage units, or a whole damned attic. Anyway, my grandmother and grandfather, Benedict, had two children, my father, Cameron, and his sister, Alice Ann. She was, well, as the family so kindly puts it, 'never quite right,' meaning that she suffered from severe depression and was what I think they might call bipolar today. I don't remember her, as she was institutionalized. Meanwhile, Evelyn—''

''Your grandmother, correct?''

''Yes. Nana,'' Caitlyn said, feeling that same skin-crawling sensation she always did when talking about her grandmother. ''She turned out to be kind of crazy herself. Even before the dementia set in, but then it could have been because she was dealing with my grandfather, who was . . . oh, there's no nice way to put it. He was a womanizer. Big time.'' She stared out the window as the first drops of rain began to hit the panes. How many times had she, as a child, listened to whispered conversations between her older siblings, or Lucille and Berneda. ''His name was Benedict Montgomery, the man responsible for the creation and success of Montgomery Bank and Trust. He had a long-term affair with his secretary, Mary Lou Chaney, and she got pregnant and did the then-shocking thing of having the baby out of wedlock. I wasn't alive then, of course, but I'm sure my grandmother Evelyn was mortified. Mary Lou wasn't one to go quietly away to some home for unwed mothers, oh, no. She had the baby and named her Copper Montgomery Chaney. The way the family tells it, that scandal was the start of all Nana's mental problems.''

''Do you believe that?''

''You know, I don't know. I never knew my grandmother as anything but . . . weird. Bitter, I guess.'' She stared outside to a ledge where pigeons were sheltering from the storm. The rain had gathered speed, spitting against the window and chasing the lady on the terrace across the way inside.

''The scandal didn't stop with Copper's birth. According to all my family, she grew up wild and tough and married a guy named Earl Dean Biscayne. They had three children, who should be my half-cousins or something, but no one's real sure about that because Copper died a few years back in a fire in her home.''

"Why isn't anyone sure that her kids are your half-cousins?"

God, this was hard. She watched a drop of rain drizzle down the glass. "Maybe I should amend that statement. We're all sure they're at least our half-cousins. Maybe more." She turned to face him and expected some kind of censure in his eyes, a hint of revulsion, or, at the very least judgment, but his expression was the same as it had been, serious enough to etch lines across his forehead, but not enough to pinch the corners of his mouth. "You see, my father, Cameron, opted to pick up where his father left off. He met Copper through Benedict, who doted on Mary Lou until the day she died. Meanwhile, my father, who's already married to my mother, decides to have a fling with Copper. His half-sister.'' The thought turned her stomach. "There's even a rumor slinking through this city that at least one of Copper's children was sired by my father, maybe all three.'' Caitlyn leaned her hips against the windowsill and didn't let herself think about the times she'd stood at her open window and had seen shadows on the lawn, silhouettes of illicit lovers meeting, heard the soft moans of passion along with the wind stirring the field grass. "I guess there's a reason my grandmother went batty,'' she said. "First her husband cheating on her, then her only son involved in incest. I think she used to talk a lot about 'bad blood' running through the family.''

"What happened to her?"

In Caitlyn's mind's eye, she saw her grandmother's coffin as it was lowered into the ground, felt an overwhelming sense of relief as she'd stood huddled with Kelly, her eyes dry. "She lived in Oak Hill, that's the name of the family home. It's a big house, one of the few plantations close to Savannah. We all grew up there, and Nana lived with us. She died when I was around five. On Christmas Eve. At the hunting lodge the family owns in West Virginia.'' She considered leaving it at that, but couldn't. After all, she was here for a reason. She couldn't doubt him. If she wanted to get better, she had to tell him the crux of her problems. "I have trouble with my memory sometimes, Dr. Hunt—"

"Adam. Remember? We're going to keep things informal. I'll call you Caitlyn and you call me Adam, if that works for you."

"That would be fine. Adam." She tested out his name, managing the weakest of smiles, and then plunged on before she lost her nerve. "As I said, I have trouble remembering things, periods that are unclear and not even blurry—just missing. Holes in my life. It's frustrating and scary and I never know when it'll happen. It's . . . it's beyond a worry. Way beyond. It's the primary reason I was seeing Rebecca . . . Dr. Wade."

"I know," he said with a kind smile that she found surprisingly sexy. "I did see that in one of her files."

"Did you?" she asked, surprised. "I thought you said you didn't have any files." *Don't be suspicious, don't be suspicious, don't be so damned suspicious! This man is trying to help you.*

"You must've misunderstood." He was calm, staring straight at her through his rimless lenses. "What I said was that there wasn't anything on the computer. The computer files, if there were any, are completely erased."

"That's impossible. I saw her typing her notes . . . maybe she put them on disks."

"So far I haven't found them."

"Wouldn't she want you to have them if you're going to help her patients?"

"I would think so. As you said, maybe they're on disks somewhere." He mentioned it casually, but she noticed a new hardness in his features, a hint of determination bracketing his mouth. "I did find some of Rebecca's handwritten notes. But they're incomplete."

"That's so odd. She seemed meticulous to me . . . was always clarifying things."

"When I talk to her again, I'll figure it out."

"She's going to call you?"

"I would hope," he said but there was a trace of a shadow in his eyes, a lie, she sensed, buried in the truth.

She was suddenly uncomfortable. Wary. What did she know of him? "So if you've got the files, why am I going over things you probably already know about?"

"Because the information in the files is spotty at best and I would like to get my own impression of those things you're telling me." He slid his pad and pen into the desk, then leaned forward, hands locked and dangling between his knees, his gaze as friendly as it was seductive.

That was the problem with her, she was attracted to the kind of men born to hurt her. Like Josh Bandeaux.

"Listen, Caitlyn, if what we're doing here doesn't feel right, then I think I should refer you to someone else. There's a chance you'd be more comfortable with a woman."

"Why's that?"

"Because it's what you're used to with Rebecca."

She couldn't start over. Not again. This was tough enough. Besides, whether she wanted to admit it or not, she liked being with him. Felt safe and sheltered, which, of course, was silly. What did she know of him? To reassure herself, she glanced at the degrees hung on the office walls.

He must've read the indecision in her eyes. "I really want to know what you feel is important to talk about. A lot has happened since you saw Dr. Wade."

That much was true. Truer than he realized.

"But if you want to see someone else . . ." he offered.

"No," she said quickly. Decisively. The next unknown shrink could be worse, far worse, and then where would she be? On to the next counselor and then the next. It had taken her nearly a year to find Rebecca, and not because she was the highest priced, but because she was a warm and caring person. She and Caitlyn had clicked immediately. Now Caitlyn felt a connection to Adam. She'd stick it out. For now. "Let's go on," she said. "I need to get some things off my chest."

"If you're sure."

"I am," she said, but it was a bald-faced lie. She wasn't sure of anything anymore. Not one damned thing.

"Okay, so tell me about your grandmother, Evelyn." Adam offered Caitlyn a reassuring smile, showing just the hint of his teeth, then glanced down at his notes again as he picked up the legal pad. "You mentioned her and your lapses of memory just about in the same breath."

"That's right," Caitlyn said, and her voice seemed to reverberate in her head. That cold, dark morning had stretched into an eternity. "What I was about to say was that even though I sometimes don't remember things, I'll never forget the night Nana died because I was locked in the room with her, sleeping in her bed. I woke up and she was there—icy cold, just staring at me. I freaked, I mean really freaked. I screamed and cried and pounded on the door, but her room was located over the carriage house, away from the other bedrooms, and the windows were covered with storm windows. No one missed us. No one heard me." Her throat tightened, and her voice cracked as she remembered curling into a ball near the closet and sucking on her thumb. "No one came for a long, long time."

Fifteen

"This damned case—and I'm not including damned in the swear-word piggy bank," Morrisette announced as she slung her purse over her shoulder and hurried down the back steps of the station. Reed was half a step ahead of her. "This damned case just gets screwier and screwier."

"Amen." He'd been thinking the same thing. Too many people had a connection to Josh Bandeaux. Too many people hated him. Too many women had been involved with him. Too many pieces of evidence didn't fit. He'd talked to Diane Moses and was supposed to meet with her later to sort through her theories on the evidence the crime scene team had collected.

On the first floor, he shouldered open the door to the parking lot. It was late afternoon, and the station's shadow crawled across the rain-washed asphalt, but despite the recent shower, the temperature was still hovering somewhere near ninety. He didn't want to take a stab at how high the humidity was. He was sweating by the time he reached the car. "Tell me what you've got. I'll drive."

"I'll drive."

Reed flashed her a smile as he unlocked the door to the cruiser. "Next time, Andretti."

Scowling at his smart-assed reference to a race-car driver, she slid inside. "I'll hold you to it."

"I know you will." He twisted on the ignition and wipers, letting the blades slap away the remaining raindrops. Morrisette leaned against the passenger door as he backed the cruiser out of its slot. "Okay, we know that the wife had reason to hate Bandeaux's guts, but he had a few more enemies. Not only business types, but ex-girlfriends by the dozen." He slid a glance her way.

"Oh, don't even go there, okay? I'm not an ex-girlfriend. And Millie's *not* a suspect. Jesus, Reed, I wish I'd never said anything!"

"I would have found out anyway."

"Of course you would have," she said sarcastically. "A crackerjack detective like you."

He winced as he pulled out of the lot and headed past Colonial Cemetery. Sylvie Morrisette was one of the few people in Homicide who knew about his botched stakeout in San Francisco. "Does Jesus count as a swear word?"

"I was praying, all right."

"Sure."

"Damn it all to hell. There's another thing I wish I wouldn't have said anything about. You're worse than my kids."

"Is that possible?"

"Very funny. I have *great* kids."

"They're not teenagers yet."

"And what would you know?" She snorted and rolled her eyes. "You know, I get damned sick of every dam— er, stupid single cop on the force offering me up advice on my kids. I've got it waxed."

"If you say so."

"They're *great* kids," she repeated.

"No argument here," he said, hoping her motherly feathers would soon be unruffled. They were going to be spending a lot of time cooped up in the car together today, so it would

be best not to start out irritating each other. Reed wanted
to double-check a few alibis and witness reports for the
night of Josh Bandeaux's death. First on the agenda was
Stanley Hubert, Bandeaux's neighbor who reported spying
a white car in the driveway. Next he hoped to catch Naomi
Crisman, Josh's elusive girlfriend, and finally he planned
on visiting Oak Hill to talk to a few members of the Montgomery clan, see what they had to say about the man Caitlyn
had married.

It all could prove interesting.

"You've totally tossed out the idea that Bandeaux offed
himself?" Morrisette asked, scavenging in her bag until she
found a mutilated pack of gum.

"Pretty much."

"So whoever killed him just did a half-assed job of covering their tracks?"

"That's the way it looks," Reed said, easing onto the
narrow street where Bandeaux's house stood. He pulled into
a spot near the curb and cut the engine. "But then, looks
can be deceiving." As Morrisette plopped the gum into her
mouth, he climbed out of the car and made his way up
Stanley Hubert's walk. She was only half a step behind.

He'd barely punched the doorbell when there was a gruff
bark from inside and the door swung wide.

"I saw you pull up," a stiff-backed man admitted as they
flashed their badges. A graying bulldog stood bristling at
his side.

"We're looking for Stanley Hubert."

"You found him. Come in, come in." Hubert was probably in his late seventies or early eighties, wore thick glasses,
a panama hat and seersucker suit. He stepped out of the
way, and the grumpy dog with a grizzled muzzle let out a
raspy growl. "Hush, General," Hubert commanded, then
poked at the dog with the tip of his cane. "Ignore him,"
he said to the officers. "He's just upset that you ruined his
nap. Come on out to the back porch. We can talk there."

Hubert whistled to the dog. Then, using his cane, he
headed toward the back of the house. Through a door

scratched to the point of losing its stain, they walked outside
to a verandah completely encircled by a six-foot brick wall.
Birdhouses were suspended from the limbs of a giant oak
tree planted in one corner of the enclosed yard while ivy
climbed tenaciously up the uneven brick and mortar of the
fence. "Sit," Hubert suggested and they all took seats
around a glass-topped table. A few drops of rain still lingered
on the smooth top. "What can I do for you?"

Reed said, "We just want to double-check some facts
about last Friday night."

Hubert was only too glad to comply. His story hadn't
changed an iota. Around eleven-thirty, just after watching
the local news, he'd walked outside with the dog. He'd seen
a white car, one that seemed identical to the Lexus Caitlyn
Bandeaux drove. He'd recognized the make because Caitlyn
had been driving the same car before she'd moved out of
the house next door a few years back. He hadn't actually
seen the driver as he'd smoked his cigar and waited for his
dog to "do his business" that night, but Hubert was ready
to testify that the car was identical, if not the very car owned
by Josh Bandeaux's estranged wife.

"I'd hate to take the stand against her," he admitted,
fishing inside his jacket for a cigar. "I like that woman.
She's . . . troubled, I'd guess you'd say, but a decent enough
person. Always managed to wave and smile at me when she
lived next door and oh, did she love that little girl. A shame
about Jamie." Hubert let out a sigh and some of the starch
seemed to fade from his muscles. "That child was the glue
that held that marriage together and even she wasn't enough
in the end." He adjusted the brim of his hat against the sun.
"I don't understand it, you know. I was married for forty
years before the Good Lord took my Aggie. I would've
given my right arm and probably my left for a few more
years with her and today . . . most marriages are thrown
away before they've even begun. A shame, that's what it
is, a damned shame." He snipped off the end of his cigar
and scowled. From the corner of his eye Reed caught Morrisette, four times divorced, tensing.

"Did you ever talk to Mr. Bandeaux?" she asked, masking her irritation. "Did he seem depressed?"

Hubert scoffed. "You mean, do I think he'd commit suicide? I doubt it. Seriously doubt it. Stranger things have happened, I suppose, but he didn't seem the type to end it all. Not Josh Bandeaux. He was just too interested in self-preservation."

"But you think his wife would kill him?" Morrisette kept pushing.

"I didn't say that."

"Well, do you?"

He frowned, studied the end of his unlit cigar as he fumbled in his suit pocket for a slim gold lighter. "I wouldn't think so, no. But . . . sometimes when a person's pushed too far, he or she will go to extreme lengths, take matters into their own hands, do things they or anyone else never thought they were capable of. I've seen it time and time again. I was career military before I went corporate. I've seen some men I'd thought were weak overcome incredible odds and watched other stronger, bigger men crumble into a heap when they were called upon to do something they couldn't. It's just damned hard to say."

They'd learned nothing new, but Reed felt confident in the witness as they finished the interview. Hubert promised to call the police if he thought of anything else that might be relevant; then, with General huffing ahead, he'd escorted both detectives through the front door. Hubert was older, his glasses thick, but he was as sharp as a tack. Reed doubted that Stanley Hubert, retired major and nuclear engineer in private business, made too many mistakes.

"So Caitlyn was here," Morrisette observed, chewing her gum thoughtfully as they walked next door. "She just doesn't remember it."

"Seems like."

"That's way too flimsy and way too handy of an excuse if you ask me."

Reed wanted to argue, but couldn't. It wasn't that he didn't want to get on Morrisette's bad side again. That happened on a daily basis and was just part of dealing with her. But he couldn't argue with her logic. Not when it mirrored his own.

They walked through the iron gate leading to Bandeaux's front door. The yellow crime scene tape had been stripped away and a silver Jaguar was parked in front of the garage.

"Somebody's home," Morrisette observed halfway up the walk when the front door banged open.

Naomi Crisman flew down the steps, her hair billowing away from her sculpted, worried face and the skirt of her wraparound dress opening with each long stride. She nearly barreled into Morrisette. "Oh!" She stopped short. "I'm sorry, I didn't see you . . ." Her expression changed instantly when she recognized them as cops. Annoyance drew lines in her forehead and pulled her finely arched brows together. "Detective Reed." She inclined her head and adjusted the strap of her purse, seeming to pull herself together in the same motion. "Is there something I can do for you?"

"Just answer a few more questions."

"I thought we went through this."

"Just double-checking some facts." Reed flashed her a disarming smile as slow-moving traffic eased down the narrow street in front of the house. "Can we talk inside?"

Naomi made a big show out of checking her watch, then sullenly walked into the house without nearly the enthusiasm she'd felt while bolting out the door a couple of minutes earlier. "This place gives me the creeps," she admitted, leading the detectives to the right of the staircase and into a cozy parlor that was directly across the foyer from Bandeaux's den.

Statuesque but small boned, Naomi Crisman had a knock-out figure with big breasts, tiny waist and well-rounded hips. Her hair was streaked several colors ranging from dark brown to white-blond and cut in fashionable layers that accented her high cheekbones and large eyes. *A body that women would kill for,* Reed thought and noted that she showed off the whole package in the shocking pink dress and five-inch heeled sandals. Not the usual mourning attire for a grieving girlfriend. It seemed Naomi was already moving on.

Once inside the parlor, she motioned to a couple of Queen Anne chairs for the detectives, chairs that were upholstered in the same sage green print as the drapes. She stood in the archway to the foyer, her arms folded under her breasts, her lips pursed in irritation. "I've answered tons of questions already," she said as Reed took out his notepad and Morrisette switched on her recorder and placed it on the table.

"I know, just a couple more. To clarify things," Reed said. "Let's start with your boyfriend's wife."

"Which one?"

"The one he was still married to, Caitlyn Montgomery."

"Oh, *her*." Naomi made an impatient sound. "The nutcase."

"What makes you say that?"

"Because she's crazy. It's a matter of record. Come on, you *do* know that." When neither one of them responded, she rolled her eyes. "Check the local hospitals. According to Josh, she was in and out of mental hospitals or psych wards or something. She's tried to commit suicide at least once, maybe more, and every time she seemed to get better, you know, like mentally—if you really can, I don't know about that—she ended up regressing again. She's a lost cause. Once a fruitcake, always a fruitcake."

"How about her relationship with the deceased?"

" 'The *deceased?*' Oh, for crying out loud, is this some kind of cheesy courtroom drama? 'The deceased.' Josh would love that." For a second her attitude faded and sadness stole over her features, as if she actually had cared for Bandeaux. "Their relationship wasn't great, okay? He was divorcing her and suing her for their kid's wrongful death, so how good do you think it was?" She rolled her eyes as if she were speaking with morons.

Reed tried not to get angry, but he felt Sylvie's temper rising with each of Naomi's sarcastic comments. He was content to let Ms. Crisman rant. Sometimes suspects said more in their commentary than they did when actually answering a question.

"Was he going to marry you?" Reed asked.

"Of course! Why do you think *she* was so upset?"

"She was still in love with him?"

"Oh, who knows with her? Probably. Ask her." For the first time Naomi cracked the barest hint of a smile. "Lots of women were in love with him." Her gaze slid to Morrisette, and Reed felt his partner begin to seethe.

"Where were you on the night he died?" Morrisette asked calmly as she popped her gum.

"I've already answered this. I was visiting friends on the island."

"St. Simons Island?"

"Yes. They have a place on the water down there. I had a little too much to drink and didn't want to risk the drive home, so I spent the night in their guest room."

"And you can verify that you were there all night?"

"God, yes! I thought I already explained what I was doing. I was staying with Chris and Frannie Heffinger. I have their phone number if you need it." Her eyes narrowed. "Do I, like, need a lawyer or something? Am I a suspect?"

"We're just working things out."

"Then arrest Caitlyn, okay? We all know she did it. She's still got keys to the place, for God's sake and Josh was divorcing her. I already told you that she is totally mental. Really, this isn't rocket science."

Morrisette just about came out of her chair. "What would you know about rocket science?"

"Are we finished? I really do have an appointment. And just so you know, I'm moving. This place makes me edgy. Just thinking about Josh being . . . slaughtered over there—" She hitched her head toward the den and nervously scratched at her neck. "It's too much for me."

"So you don't think he committed suicide?" Reed asked again though he'd already made that call himself. Bandeaux had been murdered.

"Josh? Are you kidding? He had too much to live for.

Too much money to make, too much booze to drink and too many women to sleep with.'' She must've seen Morrisette stiffen because Naomi looked straight at her as she said, '' 'For the record,' I know Josh . . . has had a few indiscretions in the past year or so. It's not as if he really cheated on me. We were broken up at the time.'' She lifted a slim shoulder. ''That was going to end, once we were married.''

''Was it?'' Morrisette asked. ''How do you know?''

''Because he promised me. He was nuts about me.''

''Or just plain nuts,'' Morrisette said under her breath. Reed shot her a warning glare.

''Look, I really have to go. Is there anything else?''

''How about the names of the women he slept with, if you know them.''

''I don't. They were all just cheap one-night stands.''

Morrisette wasn't convinced. ''Well, think real hard, would you? Sometimes a woman scorned is the best suspect.''

''Then you've got your killer, don't you? No one could be any more scorned than Caitlyn. It's pathetic really. Kind of sad.''

''You really think she was capable of killing Josh?'' Reed asked.

''I don't know what she's capable of. But I think she's just off enough that she might, okay? And don't ask me about proof, cuz I don't have any, but she's . . . freaky.''

Naomi adjusted her purse strap as Reed stood and pocketed his notes. ''If you think of anything else''—he handed Naomi his business card—''call me.''

With a don't-hold-your-breath smile, she dropped the card into her purse.

Morrisette snapped off her recorder and they all walked outside. The afternoon was even hotter than before. Steamy. The air so thick it clung to your skin. Reed was already sweating as he climbed behind the wheel. Naomi took the time to lock the house, then slid behind the wheel of her

Jag. She flipped a pair of sunglasses over her eyes, started the sleek car, and took off in a roar, barely braking as she entered the street. Her tires actually chirped at the corner and she had to be ten miles over the speed limit within a block.

"Arrogant bitch." Morrisette stared after the rapidly fleeing car. "And don't even say it, okay? I get one free swear word a day and this is it. What's she doing? Forty? Fifty in a twenty-five? It's almost as if she's begging for us to pull her over, a real in-your-lousy-cop-face attitude."

"That's something coming from you, Andretti."

Reed put the cruiser into gear and pulled away from the shady curb.

"I'm not just talkin' about her driving. It was her entire holier-than-thou, or at least smarter-than-thou attitude. It sucked."

"That it did," Reed admitted as he headed out of town.

"I'd love to bring her down a notch or two."

"Wouldn't we all, but before that you'd better level with me about Bandeaux. If you were involved with him, I need to know it and toss you off this case. We can't taint it. Can't give a defense attorney any reason to throw this case out."

She reached into her bag and pulled out a pack of Marlboro Lights. "Don't worry about it," she said, popping her gum as she found her lighter. "I told you I wasn't involved with him, not personally."

"And if I find out differently?"

"You won't."

"I hope you're not lying to me," he said as he cut across town. "I assume you're too good a cop for that."

"You assume right."

"I'd hate to have to tell the D.A. that we fucked up because one of the detectives on the case was involved with the deceased."

"Just drive," she muttered, lighting up and pushing her sunglasses over her eyes in one motion. "And quit hassling me. We'll both live a lot longer."

* * *

Caitlyn slid her car into the garage and told herself she could not, could *not* fall for her shrink. That was crazy. Nuts! Exactly the reasons she'd gone to him to begin with. She walked into the house and greeted Oscar, stooping down to pet him for a second before checking her messages and deleting them one by one. Not a peep from Kelly.

"The suddenly silent twin," she muttered to herself as she started for the stairs and stopped in the foyer. Something felt wrong . . . a little off. A scent. Someone's perfume?

Or was she imagining it?

On edge and telling herself that she was losing her grip, she walked up the stairs and into the den. Everything was as it should be . . . or was it? She always pushed her computer mouse to the side of her monitor and today it was in front, a few inches out of place.

Or had she, distracted these past few days, left it where it was?

"Odd," she whispered and clicked on her e-mail.

At last a message from Kelly.

Caitlyn sat in the desk chair and opened the letter. It was short.

Sorry I haven't reached you. Been out of town. Work, work, work! Wish I could say I was sorry about Josh, but really, Caitie-Did, we both know he was a prick. Good riddance. Hope this doesn't offend. xoxo, Kelly.

That was it. The entire message. Offend? Since when did Kelly worry about offending anyone? Caitlyn clicked off the computer, set the mouse back in its place and told herself that she was just tired; she'd forgotten where she'd put the damned mouse after the last time she used the computer.

No one had been in her house.

She was almost certain of it.

Almost.

Sixteen

"Caitlyn! Caitlyn Bandeaux!"

Kelly inwardly cringed as she handed the girl behind the counter two bucks and accepted her cup off iced coffee. "Keep the change." Maybe the woman who had confused her with Caitlyn, whoever she was, would realize her mistake and leave her be.

No such luck.

"Remember me?"

Kelly glanced over her shoulder. The answer was a definite no. "I'm sorry."

"Nikki Gillette." The woman, around thirty with wild strawberry-blond hair, sharp features, and confidence oozing from her, extended her hand. "With the *Savannah Sentinel.* I called you once, remember? Asked for an exclusive. I'd really love to talk to you."

"You've got the wrong person," Kelly said. She was wearing sunglasses and her hair was pulled away from her face. She didn't bother to smile but, carrying her coffee, headed for the front door.

"But if I could have just a few moments of your time." The woman was trailing after her.

"I told you I'm not Caitlyn Bandeaux." Using her hip, she pushed open the glass door and, from the corner of her eye, caught the look of disbelief on Nikki Gillette's face.

"You're not? Wait a minute. But . . ."

"I said, 'I'm not.' "

"You've got to be related." She paused, her eyebrows drawing together as if she was puzzled. "You know, you look enough like her to be her twin."

Kelly offered a smile that was meant to convey *no shit, Sherlock.* "You must be an *investigative reporter.* Look, I *am* Caitlyn's sister and she's going through a really rough time right now, so do everyone a favor and just back off, okay? Maybe when she's . . . out of mourning or whatever she's going through, she might talk to you. I wouldn't, but she might."

"Listen, I'd love to talk to you or someone in the family."

Kelly sent her a look that said more clearly than words, *drop dead,* and kept walking. The pushy reporter started after her, and Kelly ducked around a corner, through a back alley and into the next street. Quickly she slipped into a shop displaying "collectibles," where she caught a hard, unhappy glare from a salesclerk with blue cotton-candy hair and lips that were painted far beyond their natural line. The woman cleared her throat and glanced at the cup in Kelly's hands just as she realized drinks weren't allowed in the store. The persnickety clerk couldn't do much about Kelly's breaking one of the store's golden rules as she was involved with another customer and a discussion of the value of some knock-off of the Bird Girl statue that Kelly figured was worth less than half of what it was marked. Nonetheless, Blue Hair was giving Kelly the eagle eye. As if she might try to shoplift some of this touristy stuff. *Great. Just . . . great.* With one eye on the front display window where she could view the sidewalk and street, Kelly pretended to show some interest in a faux antique telephone and an Elvis clock complete with swiveling hips. Blue Hair negotiated the deal and was ringing up her sale.

Kelly made her move while the clerk was dealing with

the credit card transaction. "Excuse me, do you have a rest room?"

The clerk's first inclination was to snap a quick, "No." It was evident in her eyes, but she didn't want to risk an argument in front of her customer, or to be confused in the middle of the sale. "Just a minute."

"Don't bother yourself. I'll find it," Kelly said.

"Wait a second. It's not for public use—"

Kelly had already dashed through a door near the back of the store that led through the storage room. Just to the side of the rest-room door, tucked between shelves loaded with boxes of merchandise, she discovered the back door. In a second she was outside, past a small loading zone and across the square.

This was ridiculous. Running from reporters. Because she looked so damned much like her twin.

As a kid she'd found it fun to play pranks on people who didn't know them well, pretending to be Caitlyn. As a teenager she'd hated being confused with her identical sister. As an adult it was a just a pain in the butt. A big pain in the butt. Especially since Caitlyn was such a wimp. And a fool. Kelly didn't know which was worse.

She lit a cigarette and sipped from her drink as she headed back to the car. What the hell was she going to do about Caitlyn? Just wait for her sister to be arrested? Or until Caitie-Did opened her mouth to the police? Because she would. Kelly knew it, could sense that Caitlyn was cracking up again. Oh, sure, she was going through the motions, seeing a shrink, probably even on her way to taking antidepressants, or tranquilizers or some other mind-numbing drug. How about Valium? Or Prozac? Or a frontal lobotomy?

Jesus.

She took a drag on her cigarette and tried to think. She didn't have time for Caitlyn to fall apart. She had her own life to live. Things to do. Some with her twin, some alone. But first things first. She had to make sure that she wouldn't run into the damned reporter, or a policeman or an acquaintance of Caitlyn's who couldn't tell them apart. She just didn't want to deal with all of that crap right now.

Carefully, she backtracked a bit.

It seemed that Nikki Gillette hadn't managed to follow her, so she took a circuitous route back to the car, stubbed out her cigarette on the street and climbed inside. The leather interior was hot against the back of her legs, the steering wheel nearly burning her fingers. Quickly she twisted on the ignition and turned the air-conditioning up full blast while opening the sun roof, hoping to push the hot air outside. A woman pushing a stroller passed by on the street, and Kelly felt a tug on her heart. It seemed she'd never have a child of her own. It just wasn't in the cards.

Before you could have a child, you needed a man, and Kelly wasn't in the market for one of those. She'd been through her share of heartaches, and most of the men she knew were losers. Take Josh Bandeaux. *May he rest in peace*. What a joke. There was no rest for the likes of her dead brother-in-law. A bastard if one had ever walked the earth. He'd even had the gall to come on to her. To *her*. His wife's twin sister, for God's sake. She'd put him in his place, of course, but she had the creepy feeling that he'd wanted not only to get her into bed, but to have Caitlyn there waiting for them. As if either she or Caitlyn would be interested in a threesome. What kind of sick male fantasy was that? Well, forget it!

She managed to put the car in gear and ease into the afternoon traffic. Damn that Caitlyn anyway. Had she always been weird? Well, maybe a little bit. But things had gone from bad to worse after the boating accident. Kelly's jaw tightened at the memory. An explosion in the motor, Caitlyn's terrified screams, the boat collapsing in on itself and then all that water. Long, dark stretches of water.

Her throat suddenly tight, she slowed for a red light.

The boating accident.

That's when everything had really gone to hell.

* * *

Adam was missing something. Something vital. And he was running out of time. He sat in the desk chair long after Caitlyn had left the office and stared at the corner of the couch where she'd sat. Sometimes frail, other times remarkably strong, she bared her soul to him and he had to fight the oppressive feeling that he was using her unjustly, that she was leaning on him, depending on him, trusting him, not suspecting that his motives were far from pure.

"Hell," he muttered.

He needed to speed things up.

His sessions with Caitlyn had gone well enough, but he hadn't uncovered anything that he was hoping for. In fact he was beginning to think he was treading in waters that were rapidly deepening and darkening. Emotionally turbulent waters. Waters that could easily drown a man. He glanced at his wall of credentials and winced.

Does the end justify the means?

In this case, yes. And yet . . . he remembered her huddled on the couch, her arms drawn around her knees as she looked at the floor, studying the patterns of the carpet as she explained about her family. There was more to learn about her, so much more. She was complex and compelling and contradictory.

And fascinating as hell. But she may not be the one. She may not be able to help.

He turned in the chair and stared at Rebecca's computer. There were no backup disks with Caitlyn's name on them. Nonetheless, Adam had searched through them all. And nothing on the hard drive. At least nothing he could find. But there was a way to retrieve deleted files; he'd heard that from one of his computer-nerd friends. Always a way to get old information, sometimes even if the hard drive crashed. So all he needed now was some help. He wondered vaguely if there was a book entitled *Computer Hacking For Dummies.* If so, he needed a copy.

He glanced back at her untouched coffee cup and remembered her holding it as if for warmth. In a room where the temperature was pushing eighty. He suspected she wanted to talk about her husband. All the preliminary stuff about her family was important, to him, as a psychologist, and surely if he wanted to treat her, but she really wanted to talk about Josh Bandeaux, her marriage to him and his death . . . but first, Adam thought, to seem legitimate and to balm his conscience a bit, they had to lay the groundwork.

So she was coming back tomorrow. He tented his hands and rested his chin on his knuckles. He'd encouraged the appointment. He needed to move things along faster.

But there was another reason as well, one that he hated to admit to himself, one that he didn't want to face. Caitlyn was a troubled and troubling woman. The simple truth was that he wanted to see her again and not necessarily as a psychologist to a patient, but more in the line of a man to a woman.

Which was totally out of line.

Dangerous to them both.

If he were to get involved with her—with a patient—it could cost him his license.

And if she were to get involved with him—with someone she trusted—it could cost her everything.

The phone jangled.

Sugar, dusting the television, stuffed her rag into a back pocket and snagged the receiver before the third ring. "Hello?"

Nothing.

"Hello? Hello? Who is this?"

Again no answer. She thought about those incessant telemarketers trying to sell her everything from new telephone service to dildos. "Listen, I'm hanging up now!" She had another thought. Maybe it was some pervert who was in the club last night and had watched her dance. She'd had it. "Drop dead!" she ordered.

"You drop dead," someone whispered on the other end.

Her blood turned to ice. She slammed the receiver down. "Shit." She glared at the phone. Who had found her? She paid good money to have her number unlisted, but that didn't keep the telephone sales people from finding her. Or the sickos. "Shit." Then there was the weird call she'd gotten when no one had answered, but she'd thought she'd heard "Die, bitch," just before Caesarina had come into the house injured. Her skin crawled. Were they related?

The front door opened, then slapped closed.

Sugar nearly jumped out of her skin.

Cricket, looking as if she'd gone to hell and back twice in the last twenty-four hours, wandered in, dropping her backpack near the dining-room table.

"Where the hell have you been?" Sugar demanded, still unnerved.

Caesarina, thumping her tail from her hiding spot under the kitchen table, climbed to her feet. She stretched and yawned, then ambled over for Cricket to scratch her ears.

"Jesus! What happened to her?" she asked, looking at the dog's shaved neck and the stitched cuts. Yellow antiseptic and dried blood stained Caesarina's skin. "Did she lose a fight with a grizzly?"

"Don't know. It was weird. I let her out in the morning and she came back all cut up and sniffing and snorting and scared as hell, which you know, isn't like Caesarina. I ran her to the emergency vet, who claimed she was lucky . . . I thought maybe she'd been in a fight with a possum or a raccoon, but the vet thought the cuts looked like they'd come from some kind of blade, glared at me like I enjoyed spending my early mornings slicing and dicing my dog. She thought she'd gotten into something toxic, that she was acting like she'd gotten a snort of something she was allergic to or something. Oh, hell, the vet didn't know."

"They're all quacks down there," Cricket said, patting the dog's head.

"Anyway, she's alive and, even though she looks like hell, in pretty good shape." Still, it was weird. The phone call, the attack on her dog . . . Sugar was unnerved. "So," she said, turning back to the subject Cricket was avoiding. "Where were you?"

"What's it to you?" Cricket's hair was in dire need of a brush, her makeup was all but worn off and her peasant blouse had a couple of stains on it. The edge of a tattoo peeked from above the waistband of hip-hugging jeans that needed to come face-to-face with a scoop or two of Tide. When she stretched, a belly-button ring glittered against her flat abdomen.

"Don't start with me, okay? As long as you live here, you answer to me and I've been out of my mind with worry."

"I'm not nine anymore."

"Oh, yeah, all grown up."

"Jesus. What's got into you?"

Sugar decided to wait a few minutes, until she'd calmed down, to tell Cricket about the phone call. It was probably just some loser from the club, someone getting his jollies by scaring her. No reason to spread the panic around. Not yet. Not until she'd calmed down. "I'm just jumpy today."

"So that's *my* problem? I don't *think* so. Just chill out."

"You could have called."

"And you could quit nagging," Cricket shot back. "Leave me alone, okay?"

Sugar took a deep breath. Shook off the terror that had, for a second, spread over her. "I didn't mean to jump all over you."

"Good. Then just stop, would ya? Enough with the surrogate mom routine." Cricket yawned. "We got any coffee?" She ran a hand through her short hair. Dyed red with magenta streaks, it was weird, but didn't look bad. When it was styled. Which it wasn't this morning.

"It's cold."

"Doesn't matter as long as it's got caffeine." She half sleepwalked into the kitchen, found a cup and poured in some of the sludge that had been coagulating in the glass pot. Yawning again, she put her mug into the microwave and hit the start button.

"You could make fresh."

"This'll do."

"Where were you?"

"Out." Her gaze hardened, but she didn't elaborate.

"That much I know. Who were you with?"

Cricket just stared at her. She looked so small and tired, almost world-weary, and Sugar felt a needle prick of guilt. She hadn't done her job right; had failed. When their mother was killed, Sugar had sworn to take care of her younger siblings, but she'd made a mess of it. Dickie Ray was basically a small-time crook and con man, while Cricket, a hairdresser who had trouble keeping her appointments, had never blossomed to her full potential. But . . . if they could get their hands on their fair share of the Montgomery fortune, all that would change.

Or would it? There was a chance that it was already too late. Damned Flynn Donahue. It was time to give that lazy lawyer a kick in the butt. She'd call him later today, but at the thought of picking up the phone she remembered the harsh, ugly voice so recently on the line.

You drop dead.

Who the devil had called?

"Guess who came into the shop yesterday?" Cricket asked, completely oblivious to Sugar's panic attack. She kicked off her sandals as the microwave dinged.

"Who?"

"Hannah-friggin'-Montgomery, that's who." Sugar's stomach knotted. As it always did when she thought of the Montgomerys.

Cricket chuckled as she grabbed her cup and padded barefoot to the back door. "I guess Hannah didn't know that I'd switched over to Maurice's."

Sugar grabbed a bottle of Diet Dr. Pepper, whistled to the dog and followed Cricket to the porch. Dickie Ray had rigged up a ceiling fan a couple of years back. Sugar switched it on while the dog walked down the wooden steps to nose around the fence line and scared up a couple of startled birds.

Sampling her coffee, Cricket took a seat in the flimsy chaise, a relic from a particularly bountiful garage sale spree. "Hannah nearly fell off Donna's chair when she saw me."

"What did you do?"

"Made monkey faces at her in the mirror the entire time she was getting her foil weave." Cricket slid a glance at her older sister to see if she was buying her story. Sugar wasn't. "Okay, so I said 'hi' and ignored her for the rest of the two hours. What did you expect me to do?"

"Make monkey faces," Sugar joked.

"I should have, but I don't want to lose this job. As it is, I probably cost Donna a major client. Got a cigarette?"

"I thought you quit."

"I did. Mostly. But I'm tired and I could use a buzz."

"Have more coffee."

Cricket scowled into her cup. "It's not the same."

"You'll survive," Sugar predicted and glanced at the weed-choked yard. The wheelbarrow was where she'd left it two days ago, half full of weeds, the bark dust thin around the shrubbery flanking the house.

Curling one leg under her, Cricket asked, "You see him last night?"

"Who?"

"You know who. And don't look so surprised. I figured it out on my own." Cricket took a long drink, but her gaze was fixed steadily on her sister's face. When Sugar didn't answer, she added, "He's using you, you know. If you think he's gonna come in here and sweep you away and marry you, you've got another think comin'."

That much Sugar knew. "At least I was home last night."

"Too bad." She ran a hand through her hair and grimaced. "I'm gonna shower and get down to the shop. Did I get any calls?"

"No one who left his name."

"What's that supposed to mean?"

"We're getting more and more hangups."

"Wrong numbers?"

"Maybe . . . some of them, but . . . ." Sugar lifted a shoulder and decided not to worry her baby sister about the recent call that had made her skin crawl. "It's probably nothing."

"I'll bet it's a weirdo from the club. You don't exactly get the highest class of 'clients'—isn't that what you call 'em?—down at Pussies In Booties."

Sugar bristled. Felt that same old knife of shame, but pushed it down deep. "It pays the rent and puts money in the bank."

"Yeah, yeah, I know, I've heard it all before." Cricket drained her cup and forced herself to her feet. "Someday I'm going to have clients who tip me a hundred dollars, and I won't have to take off my clothes to do it."

"I won't hold my breath," Sugar said, then immediately regretted the words as Cricket muttered something obscene and headed inside. A few minutes later Sugar heard the old pipes creaking as the water was turned on. She leaned back in her chair and closed her eyes. She'd had it with Cricket's bad attitude. Where did she get off looking down at her older sister? If it hadn't been for Sugar, Cricket would have been kicked around from one foster home to the other after their mother died. Worse yet, she could have landed in juvenile court half a dozen times for drinking under age, marijuana possession and other miscellaneous infractions. Cricket and the police had a long history.

But so did Sugar. Fortunately she had a friend on the force—her own personal leak. She'd even called him Deep Throat behind his back. He, thinking he might someday get into her pants—or more likely her thong—kept her informed. Even about the Joshua Bandeaux case. He seemed to think the detectives in charge of the investigation were leaning toward murder rather than suicide, which Sugar found interesting. She wanted more details, but her leak had been a little reticent, and she figured he was just angling for another shot at getting her into bed. Fat chance. The likelihood of her sleeping with him was about the same as the old snowball's chance in hell.

She stared across the surrounding fields. Dry. Weed-choked. This five-acre patch wasn't exactly prime Georgia real estate. But it was hers. She'd bought out Dickie Ray and Cricket when they'd inherited it. Both of her siblings could make cracks about her job at the club all they wanted, but she made more money in three months than the two of them did combined for an entire year. Maybe that wasn't such an accomplishment considering that Cricket could barely hang on to a job and Dickie Ray spent most of his time as a welfare and disability cheat. When he wasn't being a small-time crook who spent most of the pathetic money he made on loose women, booze, cock fights, video poker, and when he could afford it, cocaine. Why she put up with him she didn't know.

Because blood is thicker than water.

Yeah, go tell that to the Montgomerys.

Sugar scowled as she thought about it. Took a long pull on her diet soda. It was funny, and kind of sick, how the Montgomerys and Biscaynes were all tied in together. Sugar looked enough like the Montgomery sisters—Amanda, the twins and Hannah—to pass as their full-blooded sister. Dickie Ray and Cricket, too, but the whole damned thing was so incestuous. There was a reason Dickie Ray wasn't all that smart. She'd heard someone say, "the lights were on but no one was home." In Dickie Ray's case, the lights had burned out long ago.

For years Sugar had heard the whispers, the rumor that her mother, Copper, had been involved in an on-again, off-again affair with Cameron Montgomery, who was, in fact, Copper's half-brother. How sick was that? And if the old scandal was true, that Sugar might be the spawn of that union, it made her nauseous. That would mean she'd have more Montgomery blood running through her veins than the legitimate side of the family.

The legitimate side of the family. What a joke. There was not and never had been anything remotely legitimate about the Montgomerys, who, in her opinion, all playacted at working and lived off their damned trust funds, all the while pretending as if the Biscaynes were white trash or worse—like damned lepers. That Grandpa Benedict had kept Mary

Lou Chaney as his mistress wasn't scandal enough. That he'd sired a daughter out of wedlock along with his children, Cameron and Alice Ann, was only the tip of the iceberg. From that point on it got chilly, with Copper, hellion that she was, determined to embarrass the old man to all lengths, including engaging in an affair with Cameron.

Could he be her father? Sugar didn't know, but her options weren't all that great because the man Copper had married, Earl Dean Biscayne, was a loser of the lowest order, a liar, a cheat, a man who thought a "whuppin' " was the only answer to disobedience. His cruel streak ran deep, and Sugar wasn't unhappy that he was out of their lives. He'd disappeared at the same time that his wife had been killed, here on this very plot, when her single-wide trailer had burst into flames. Careless smoking had been the official cause, according to the fire department, but Sugar knew her mother well enough not to believe that she'd dropped a cigarette in her bed. Copper had never smoked much in the house— and only in the kitchen. Then Earl Dean had disappeared. Hadn't even shown up for the funeral. But Earl Dean had never put much stock in appearances or protocol. And some people figured he had found out about her cheating, killed her and taken off. Even Sugar wasn't sure if that was true.

But if Earl Dean wasn't her daddy, then most likely Cameron Montgomery was, and so she had a double dose of the Montgomery blood. She didn't want to think too much about that or the mental illness that seemed to run rampant in the family because she might have double the genes. There were those times when she just couldn't seem to think straight, when she got all screwed up with what she remembered, when reality seemed out of kilter, as if there were some electrical wires crossing in her mind. Then she was scared to death that something was wrong—really wrong—with her brain. But right now, for the moment, it was working fine, clicking along.

She'd have to call that lazy-ass lawyer and tell him to start pushing harder for a settlement. He needed to start earning his two-hundred-dollar-an-hour fee. She figured that if Flynn Donahue couldn't handle the job, she had one last resort to try and get money from the Montgomerys. If the legal road was suddenly blocked, then they would take a different path. Dickie Ray was more than willing to work behind the scenes with the Montgomerys on what he called "a more personal level." He'd smiled his toothy wicked smile and suggested, "Let me handle those rich snobs my own way."

Which worried her.

Heretofore Sugar had reined him in.

But it might be time to let the reins slip a notch or two.

With one last look around the yard, Sugar took a final pull from her near-empty bottle and heard the pipes moan as the water was shut off. She pushed herself to her feet and considered the phone call again. Someone repeating her own words. Maybe it was nothing, a natural response.

But she sensed it was more. Something deadly and evil.

As if it was lurking nearby, just out of sight, hidden in the lengthening shadows that stole across the marshy acres, slipping through the reeds and cattails.

Caesarina felt it, too. The battered old hound stared across the unmoving landscape, and the skin beneath her coat quivered. Her stitches were an ugly reminder of something not quite right. Something evil. Caesarina let out a worried whimper, and Sugar's heart turned as cold as death. The warning whispered through her mind and skittered up her spine again:

You drop dead.

Atropos drove like a maniac. The wind whipped her hair. Adrenalin fired her blood. She'd heard the fear in Sugar Biscayne's voice, *felt* her terror. God, what a rush! The little bastardess was getting some of her own back. Big time.

A semi with a load of chickens was blocking the road, so Atropos shifted down and nosed into the oncoming lane. It looked clear and so she floored it, shooting past the stacked cages where doomed foul were huddled and losing feathers onto the roadway. As she reached the cab of the truck, the driver, who damned near looked the part of a redneck chicken farmer, with gray hair poking out of a baseball cap, stared down from his cab, grinned and blasted his horn in an attempt to flirt.

As if!

Atropos looked up, gave him a dirty little smile, then flipped the bastard off as she saw the oncoming pickup and swerved in front of the semi, earning herself another blare from the trucker's horn.

Oh, bite me, she thought, the speed exhilarating, replaying in her mind Sugar Biscayne's terror at the last phone call. She was becoming unhinged and wasn't that fitting. All of her life Sugar wanted to be a Montgomery so badly she could taste it, and now she was getting the feel of what it was like to be one. Atropos wasn't biased. She'd mete out her punishment to everyone connected to the Montgomery money in equal parts . . . and wasn't that what Sugar had always desired, to be treated like a true, legitimate Montgomery?

Well, now, it was happening. She was going to get exactly the same treatment as the rest of the family.

Atropos switched on the radio . . . and a song was playing that gave her a little inspiration. Who was the artist? Def Leppard . . . that was it. And the song? "Pour Some Sugar On Me."

Now, there was an idea.

A damned good idea.

Seventeen

"Tell me about the boating accident," Adam suggested as Caitlyn settled onto the couch for her next session. Some of the weirdness of being back in Rebecca's office had vanished, but Caitlyn still felt odd. She didn't want to think it was because of Adam, because he was handsome, because there was an air of mystery about him, because she found him too damned sexy for *her* own good.

"What happened?"

She thought back, remembered the calm sea, the bank of clouds that had seemed so far away. So peaceful. So benign. "I'd gone sailing with my sister, Kelly. Just the two of us. Kind of a birthday celebration. We'd just turned twenty-five, and that's when our trust funds kicked in. Anyway the boat was Kelly's birthday present to herself," Caitlyn said, the words coming out as she remembered the hot, muggy day that had started out with so much promise.

"Where are we going?" Caitlyn had asked when Kelly had shown up on her doorstep and insisted they celebrate their newfound financial freedom.

"It's a surprise."

"I'm not sure I like surprises."

"Quit being a spoilsport, okay? For once, unwind. Come on." She'd convinced Caitlyn to get into the car, and she'd driven to the marina. After parking, she'd stuffed a beach bag into Caitlyn's arms and pulled a small padded cooler from her trunk.

"You rented a boat?" Caitlyn asked as they walked along the sun-baked planks of the pier.

"Not rented."

"What do you mean?"

"I bought myself a birthday present." She paused in front of a slip where a gleaming cabin cruiser was moored.

"This?" Caitlyn's had asked, shocked. "It's huge."

"Hardly a yacht."

"But—do you even know how to drive it?"

"Steer it. Of course. I've been given lessons. Now, hurry up or we'll be late for the party."

"Party?" Caitlyn had felt as if she'd just stepped onto another planet. "What party?"

"The one I'm throwing for us."

"You didn't tell me about any party," Caitlyn had said, eyeing the sleek craft as it rocked against its moorings.

"Sure I did. Ages ago! Now, come on, let's take her out for her maiden voyage, just the two of us. I've got some champagne to celebrate." She'd climbed into the boat and opened the cooler to show the long necks of two green bottles capped in foil. "Dom Perignon," she said, as if that would add to the allure. Then she stepped lithely out of her shorts to reveal the bottom of a yellow bikini. "We'll go over to Hilton Head and dock in at the resort. I've rented a banquet room for our party."

"You're serious about this?"

"Abso-frickin'-lutely. We can't turn twenty-five without a party. It's kind of our last hurrah before we become real adults."

"I thought we were real adults."

"Speak for yourself. Come on." Kelly had flashed her naughty smile, and her hair glinted red in the shafts of sunlight piercing the clouds. "We deserve this. Finally we've got our share of Grandpa Benny's money. God, how long have we heard about it?'' She stood on the deck, one hip thrown out as she'd taken a long, appreciative look at her purchase. ''You know what I think?''

''I'd hate to guess.''

''I think, no, I believe that old bastard would have liked nothing better than for his favorite granddaughters to do a little celebrating.''

''What makes you think we were his favorites?''

Kelly had laughed and winked as she'd squinted at Caitlyn. ''Who else? Amanda? Hannah? Or those damned Biscaynes? Come on, I'm sure we were his favorites. Not that it matters. Now, come on, Caitie-Did! Let's go.''

Of course, she'd been unable to resist. Kelly's enthusiasm was and always had been infectious.

Now, sitting in the psychologist's office, Caitlyn remembered the day vividly, and whereas she'd rarely spoken of what had happened on her twenty-fifth birthday to anyone, not even the members of her family, she told Adam. About sailing through the darkening water, about the clouds rolling in, about the friends and family that had gathered. There had been a band and a birthday cake and champagne and they'd partied long and hard into the night. By the time they returned to the boat, the wind had come up. Kelly had been drinking, but had insisted she could maneuver the craft back to the mainland, and Caitlyn had consumed too much champagne to argue. Looking back, it was a situation set up for tragedy.

On the way back to the marina it had begun to rain, but Kelly had been undaunted at the helm of her new craft. She'd turned on her running lights, and Caitlyn had felt more than the light buzz from her champagne. But beneath the euphoria ran a darker sensation, a headache threatening to throb, a tightness in her skull. However, if Kelly had felt any hint of her own upcoming hangover, she didn't show it. She had still been laughing at the weather, standing at the helm, the wind tearing at her hair when the boat just stopped, the engine sputtering and dying.

"What the hell?" Kelly had muttered but was still laughing as she tried the ignition. The engine ground and then nothing. "Jesus . . . this isn't supposed to happen. I had the thing checked over by a mechanic. When I see him again I swear I'm going to wring his fat neck!" Suddenly it seemed darker than it had been, which, of course was impossible. But the lights of shore appeared miles away, the wind picking up eerily. "Shit."

"Did you run out of gas?"

"I don't think so. Christ, it's dark out here." She'd fumbled in a compartment for a flashlight and managed to switch it on. The boat had rocked on a swell and the night seemed eerie and stark . . . as if they were alone in the world.

Caitlyn's nerves were strung tight. "Maybe we should call for help," she'd said.

"Who?"

"I don't know. Maybe the Coast Guard." The wind had quickly died, and the water was quiet. Deathly quiet. Too quiet . . . just the lap of the water against the hull accompanied by the gentle rocking of the craft. Caitlyn stared out at the water, imagined she saw dark shapes shifting below the surface.

"There's nothing wrong with the engine." Kelly was still cranking on the ignition, muttering under her breath, when the damned thing started again. She gave it some gas. The engine roared. "See! It was nothing!" She turned to look smugly back at Caitlyn, but there was something in the air, the feel of electricity that Caitlyn sensed. Just a trace of smoke—the scent of electrical wires burning.

"And you wanted to call for help!" Kelly laughed.

"I think we should still—"

BAM!

The explosion tore through the boat. Smoke and fire erupted. Crackling loudly over the splintering of wood. Caitlyn was thrown off her feet. Her head banged against the deck. Pain blasted through her brain. Her head reeled.

From somewhere faraway Kelly screamed in terror.

The boat pitched and shuddered.

Caitlyn struggled to stay conscious. Frantically she wrapped her fingers through the railing.

"Kelly!" she tried to scream, but no words came. "Kelly!" She was swirling, the blackness trying to pull her under.

With a slow, ominous groan, the hull cracked, wood splintering, fire burning on the spilled oil and gasoline. The cruiser trembled, then crumpled in upon itself.

"Kelly!" Caitlyn forced out, but it was barely a whisper. Oh, God, where was she? "Kelly!" Panic strangled her, and blackness threatened to swallow her. She clung to a piece of the railing, her eyes narrowing through the smoke and darkness as Kelly's dream boat sank deeper into the surrounding void. Cold water tumbled over her, pulling Caitlyn downward as she flailed and tried to stay afloat. *God, please don't let me lose consciousness, don't let me drown here. Kelly! Kelly, where are you?* A seat cushion floated past and she grabbed wildly for it, wrapping her arms around the bobbing piece of plastic and foam. "Kelly," she cried, desperate, coughing and sputtering. "Kelly!" She couldn't breathe, couldn't keep her eyes open. And then the blackness consumed her. She felt the cold water pulling at her and from somewhere far away she thought she heard a bone-chilling, agonized groan, but she couldn't locate the sound.

Water filled her lungs. She could no longer fight.

She closed her eyes and sent up a prayer to a God she didn't trust and then she let go. . . .

The accident had been a horrid experience, one she still couldn't think about too long. Now, ten years later, as she sat in Adam Hunt's office, she felt a chill as cold as the sea had been that night. Shivering, she looked up at him leaning back in his chair, his hand propping his chin, his note pad balanced upon a leg, his eyes centered on her. "Are you okay?" he asked when she stopped talking. Only then did she feel the tears in her eyes. She blinked. Looked away and heard the chair protest as he stood and picked the tissue box off the table.

Sitting next to her, he handed her a Kleenex.

"I'll be fine," she said, grabbing the damned tissue and swiping away the stupid tears. Why was she such an emotional wreck? Why couldn't she pull herself together? She knew he saw people in this condition all the time. It was his job, for God's sake. This was what he dealt with. Worse, if that was possible. Yet she felt like an idiot as he sat there all concerned.

"Do you want to talk about it?" Adam asked, his voice soft with concern as she threw Kelly's nagging worries out of her mind.

"There's nothing more to say." She managed to stem the flow of those damned tears. "I was comatose when a passing boat found me, and I woke up three days later."

"And Kelly?"

"Kelly always manages," Caitlyn said. "She was picked up, too, and out of the hospital before me. I think she was more ticked off about the boat than anything else. She hadn't bothered to insure it, and she's been kicking herself ever since." Managing a smile, she added, "And I haven't heard her talking about buying another one."

"Can you tell me anything else about her?"

Caitlyn rolled her eyes. "Tons. She's the interesting one. The adventurous one. The bright one. She was always getting me and Griffin, my friend growing up, into big trouble. Now she's a buyer for Maxxell's. Isn't around as much as I'd like and she . . . she and the family don't get along."

"Why is that?"

"Because of the boating accident. She not only blew through a big chunk of her trust fund but she nearly killed me and herself." Caitlyn tore at the corners of her tissue.

He waited and she bit her lip. There were some things that were private.

"Caitlyn?" His voice was so close, a whisper that changed the cadence of her heartbeat. Which was absolutely foolish. She smelled soap and some kind of aftershave, a musky scent that disturbed her on a very basic and female level. "There's something else, isn't there?" he asked, and for a moment she wanted to curl up against him and cling to him.

"I don't know if I should tell you," she admitted, shredding the Kleenex.

He waited. "Whatever you think. It's your decision."

She expected him to touch her, to pat her on the shoulder or give her a hug. And she wanted him to. Just the feel of a man's concerned touch. She saw the hesitation in his eyes, the spark of something dangerous, then it quickly disappeared. Adam pushed up from the couch as if realizing that being in such close proximity to her was a mistake, that there was something perilous about being so close to her, and he returned to his desk chair.

She'd come so far, she couldn't back off now, Caitlyn decided. She was here because she needed help. No matter what else, she had to get better, and Adam was going to help her. Come hell or high water. She drew in a deep breath. "Kelly made some charges a few years back. Right after the boating accident. About my older brother, Charles. That he . . . well, he used to come into her room and . . ." She let out the breath that she didn't realize she was holding. Shuddering, her stomach roiling at the thought, she said, ". . . that before he died, he'd molested her."

Adam didn't move. "Do you believe her?"

Slowly she nodded. Remembered Charles as he had been. Ten years older. Trusted. Her father's favorite. Her stomach twisted so hard it cramped.

"Because?"

She felt the hot rush of tears burning behind her eyes but wouldn't release them, refused to shed one single drop.

"Because he molested you, too."

She nodded again and she couldn't stem the flow as the memories of hearing footsteps outside her bedroom door, listening in horror as the doorknob turned, dying a thousand deaths as he crossed the room, nearly silently. But she'd heard every muffled step, smelled him, the scent of sourness—whiskey, she now knew—mingled with the dirty musk of male sweat. Sometimes, when the moon was just right and the curtains were open, she saw his shadow stretching forward, dark, angular, and foreboding as it crawled across the carpet and up the wall. She had squeezed her eyes shut tight, her body rigid, as she tried to feign sleep. Her hands had fisted in the sheets and she'd prayed. *No, God, no . . . please don't let him do this!*

Then he had touched her, his hands trembling, his breathing a raspy pant. She had cringed and cowered, begged and cried, but he'd never stopped.

"Caitlyn?"

Startled, she opened her eyes and saw Adam kneeling in front of the couch. She was in his office—Rebecca's office. What had happened was long ago, in a past she kept locked away. Her face was wet and she was trembling.

Adam's head was at the same level as hers. She hadn't heard him approach. "I'm sorry," she whispered, sniffing and wiping at her nose.

"You don't have to be. What happened to you is criminal."

Again tears collected in the corners of her eyes. "It—it happened a long time ago. I was seven . . . maybe eight. He was ten years older."

"But it never really goes away," he said kindly and sat on the couch next to her again. This time he wrapped one strong arm over her shoulders. "I think this is enough for today."

She swallowed hard and leaned into him, smelled the slight scent of his aftershave. It was probably a mistake to touch him, to become too close, but she rationalized it by telling herself she believed she could trust him, believed the official degrees lining the walls, believed that Rebecca Wade would not have recommended her to someone who would take advantage of her.

How do you know Rebecca actually recommended him? All you have is his word.

That much was true. But for now, it was enough.

"Before I go knocking on Caitlyn Bandeaux's door again, let's go over what we've got," Reed said as Morrisette slid into the opposite side of a booth at a local bar. Smoke was heavy in the air, voices hushed, laughter sprinkling conversations. A couple of guys were shooting pool near the back, and the television over the bar was tuned into a Braves' game. Atlanta was up 3 to 1 over Cincinnati, but it was only the bottom of the third inning

A waitress ambled over and took their orders. Morrisette ordered a patty melt with a Diet Coke, and Reed opted for a cheeseburger with fries. He was officially off duty, so he decided on a Budweiser. "Okay, what do you know? Top to bottom, what the hell's going on with that family?"

"I know a lot. I've been doing a lot of checking. I mean a *lot*. And most of it ain't pretty. My gut instinct tells me they're all frickin' nuts. Every last one of 'em. And more than just minor league loco. We're talkin' the majors here. And they're cursed, too. Or at least it seems like it. Just one catastrophe after another. The father, Cameron, died in a car wreck about fifteen years ago. He lost control of the wheel on his way to St. Simons Island and ended up in the swamp. Hurtled through the windshield. He was drunk out of his mind at the time, his seat belt failed and bam-o, right through the glass. He was pretty messed up, broken ribs, femur, jaw and pelvis and punctured lung—and get this— his right testicle was completely severed."

"What?"

"Yep. Never found."

"How could that happen?"

"A freak accident. They think glass."

"From the safety glass of the windshield?" He didn't buy it.

The waitress deposited their drinks and promised to bring the sandwiches soon. As she left, Morrisette tossed the straw in her drink onto the table and took a sip. "Old man Montgomery was a car enthusiast. Loved older ones and he was driving one of his toys. An old model Jaguar. Before safety glass."

"Bad luck," Reed observed, taking a sip of his beer. He was getting a bad feeling about this.

"And that's just the tip of the iceberg." Morrisette took a long swallow from her Diet Coke just as the Braves scored, drawing a shout of approval from a fan perched on a stool at the bar. Morrisette glanced at the television, then continued. "A few years later the eldest son gets it. Another 'freak accident.' Now how many of those can one family have without it being freak anymore? Anyway, the family was up in West Virginia at their hunting lodge. For Thanksgiving. Charles is out hunting. Ends up with an arrow in his chest. Guess who found him?" She took another swig of the Diet Coke. "Caitlyn."

"Mrs. Bandeaux?"

"Yep. She'd been out playing and gotten lost. Claims to have stumbled upon him, and he was nearly dead. She pulled out the arrow, and good old Chucky boy didn't make it."

"How old was she?"

"About nine or ten, I think."

"Jesus."

"The doctor, a quack by the name of Fellers, was there. Nothing he could do, he claims, with the arrow being yanked and all. Too much trauma. Too much blood loss." With a lack of enthusiasm, the waitress put down their platters. Reed got her patty melt, and his burger was slid beneath her nose.

Morrisette switched the plates. "How the hell can they screw up every time?" she asked loudly enough for the bored-looking waitress to hear. "It's not like we're a big group. There's only two of us, for Christ's sake, and it's not as if the place is busy."

"Maybe she does it just to bug you."

"Well, it's working." She found a plastic bottle of catsup on the table and squirted a long stream of the red condiment over his fries. Somehow it reminded Reed of Bandeaux's wrists. Cut at odd angles, leaving streams of blood. Morrisette plucked one fry from the pile and took a bite. "I love these things. Never order 'em. Too fattening."

"Help yourself," he said.

"Didn't think you'd mind. This way neither one of us overeats."

"And I pay for it."

"Even better." She snagged another fry, dredged it through the pool of catsup and said, "There's something else no one mentions much and maybe it's nothing, but one of the kids died of SIDS. He was the kid born between Troy and Hannah . . . is that right? Yeah. Parker. He'd be in his mid-twenties if he'd survived."

"You think he was murdered?"

"I don't know. It's pretty bizarre, but then what isn't in this case? Doc Fellers was the attending physician and he's a bonafide quack, would have done anything to cover up something indiscreet in the family. And don't forget there's the mental illness angle of the whole Montgomery clan. The great-aunt was pretty much retarded—and yeah, I know that's not politically correct, but she was so slow she had to be placed in one of those fancy-schmancy homes. Anyway, somehow she ends up falling down the stairs and breaks her neck. No one saw the accident, that's what it was ruled, but a few of her friends—now, remember, these so-called friends are patients in the looney bin, too—claim she might have committed suicide. She was depressed—well, duh, who wouldn't be?—and had talked about death quite a bit."

Morrisette plowed into half of her patty melt. Reed had yet to take a bite.

"What about Caitlyn?"

"You think she might have pushed her aunt down the stairs?"

"No, but there's a thought. I was wondering if we can get a court order to have her shrink's files opened. You ever locate her—Dr. Wade?"

"Nope." Morrisette scowled as she chewed. "It's almost as if she was planning a trip, then didn't go. I've requested her phone, cell phone and credit card statements. Got one from a local bank. Dr. Wade made a reservation at a pretty expensive resort in New Mexico, never arrived, never called and lost her deposit." Reed listened and tore into his burger.

"The last couple of purchases she made were at an outdoor store in town for hiking boots and some other athletic gear. Over the Internet she ordered some books and maps. They were delivered, but by the time they arrived, she'd disappeared. The landlady has them."

"Maps of where?"

"Arizona, New Mexico and Southern California, just where she was planning to go."

"Where's her car?"

"Gone."

"What about her office?"

"Haven't got that far yet, but I'm working on it." She stole another French fry. "You think this is connected with Bandeaux's death?"

He didn't know, but he didn't like it. "Seems like a helluva coincidence that Caitlyn Bandeaux's shrink goes missing a few weeks before her estranged husband's death."

"You really want to nail her, don't you?"

"I just want to clear it up." He took another bite of his burger. Washed it down with beer. He'd nearly convinced himself that Caitlyn was the killer, but something held him back. Something didn't quite feel right about it. "The D.A.'s on my ass."

"She's on everybody's ass. Up for reelection this fall. But we have to tread carefully with the Montgomerys. They have a habit of buying off judges and senators and the like. It keeps their records clean. You know the rumor that the grandfather was banging his secretary, Mary Lou Chaney. She had a kid by him, Copper Chaney. A real wildass. She, Copper, ended up marrying a local tough, Earl Dean Biscayne, and they had three kids." Morrisette swiped at the corners of her mouth with a paper napkin, then finished her drink. "Copper was killed when her single-wide caught fire because she was smoking in bed and her husband, Earl Dean, disappeared around the same time. Some people think he caused the fire, others think that he was already missing when Copper died, but what is really interesting is that

Copper had herself an affair with Benedict's legitimate son, Cameron.''

"Caitlyn's father?"

"Yep." Morrisette signaled to the waitress with her empty glass. "So she was really screwing her half-brother.''

"If it's true.''

"Welcome to the South, baby.''

"Give me a break.''

"You're right. We don't have the corner on incest around here.''

Reed was bothered just the same. Morrisette was a smart-ass, but she was a good cop, did her job. "Did Montgomery have an alibi for the trailer fire?''

"Ironclad. At home with the wife, Berneda, or so he claims.''

"What does she say?''

"That he was there, according to her statement, but she's had all kinds of health problems for years. The woman's a walking pharmacy. Who knows if she even slept with the guy. My guess? She said what she had to. Kept the press at bay and her husband off the hot seat. I doubt if we'll ever know what really happened.''

"Would you all like another Diet Coke?" the waitress said as she wended her way through the empty tables.

"Yeah." Morrisette nodded.

"How 'bout you?" she asked Reed. "Another Bud?''

"That would be good.''

"It'll just be a minute." She managed a smile for Reed and ignored Morrisette.

"She's got the hots for you," Morrisette observed, watching the leggy waitress saunter back to the bar where two men in baseball caps, work shirts, blue jeans and cowboy boots had taken stools.

"How do you know it's not the hots for you?''

"Oh, I don't know, maybe it was the way her eyes said, 'fuck me' when she looked at you.''

"Maybe she was just playing hard to get.''

Sylvie actually smiled as the two new guys checked the

score on the television before carrying their drinks to a pool table and racking up. "She's not my type. I like big blondes with even bigger tits." She winked at Reed. "Give me an Amazon any day of the week."

"You're sick."

"So they say, but not as sick as the Montgomerys. Get this. I think Hannah, that's the youngest sister, might have been seeing Bandeaux, too. May have even given him some money. Her trust fund doesn't really kick in until she's twenty-five, but she's got a shit-load of dough anyway. I've been trying to talk to her, but so far, I've run up against the ol' brick wall. Only been able to leave messages. And she's not the only member of the extended family that had a financial stake with our deceased. Remember the name Dickie Ray Biscayne, one of Copper's kids? He did some work for Bandeaux, too, but nothing ever recorded on the books. Just provided security for the prick, kind of a low-class bodyguard."

"Didn't do a very good job," Reed observed, but was thinking hard. The damned Montgomerys and Biscaynes were too interlaced. "This is worse than a nighttime soap."

"Are you kidding? It's worse than a *day*time soap." Morrisette finished her sandwich just as the Reds scored and the man at the bar muttered an obscenity and ordered another beer in disgust.

The door to the bar opened and Reed noticed Diane Moses bustle inside. Not a hair out of place, her expression forever harsh, she glanced in their direction. "Look at this, we just got lucky. Maybe the crime scene can shed some light on this."

Morrisette waved her over.

Nodding, Diane held up one finger, then paused at the bar long enough to order a glass of wine before carrying it to their booth. "I suppose you want me to give you the definitive clue to crack the Bandeaux case," she said, scooting in next to Morrisette.

"That would help." Reed finished his beer.

"Have you talked to His Highness?"

"St. Clair?"

"That would be him." Diane took a sip of her wine and scowled. "Just a minute. They poured me vinegar here, and I'm not in the mood." She walked to the bar, had a heated conversation with the bartender, and returned with another glass of merlot. "Much better," she said after taking an experimental sip and sliding into the booth next to Morrisette.

"You guys find anything new in the evidence collected at the Bandeaux scene?" Reed asked.

"Just got all the results of the chemicals in his body. I faxed it over to you. There was alcohol, GHB, traces of Ecstacy and get this . . . traces of epinephrin, as if he managed to get to his allergy kit and inject himself."

"Before he or someone slit his wrists."

"Yep."

"So it appears that Josh got high with Ecstasy and maybe had some wine with a friend, but the wine was the wrong kind, the kind that put him into shock. Someone definitely switched the labels. But he used the allergy kit, gave himself a shot of epinephrin, and, just when he thinks he's home free and not gonna die, he types up a suicide note on the computer, then slits his wrists."

"Or the friend does just to throw us off."

"After having watched Bandeaux save himself." Reed's eyes narrowed. "You know, it's almost as if someone tried to kill him twice. Once with the wine, but he somehow figured it out and gave himself the antidote, but then the killer struck again and this time finished the job."

Reed pushed his plate away as the waitress brought the second round of drinks. "Anything else? What about the lipstick on one of the glasses?"

"It's called *In The Pink* by New Faces. Ironic, don't you think, considering Bandeaux's condition?" Diane asked, her eyes gleaming a bit. "It's sold at all your major upscale department stores. The good news is that it's a relatively new shade, only been available for the past two years."

Reed glanced at Morrisette.

"I'm already all over it," she said, then took a big swallow from her glass. "We'll check all the local markets and the Internet."

Diane Moses said, "You already know about the other blood there, and we found some other hairs in the vacuum bag. Hair that we're comparing to Bandeaux and Naomi Crisman along with some kind of animal hair. Looks like dog. We're still checking."

"Bandeaux and his girlfriend didn't have any pets," Reed said, sipping his beer.

"The ex-wife does." Morrisette finished her second drink. "Maybe she'd been playing with the pooch and he'd shed on her and before she could grab one of those sticky rollers they have to clean your clothes and upholstery from pet hair, she visited Josh and dropped the hairs on his carpet."

"Or it could be that they had the dog together when they were married and she took the mutt over to visit. The neighbor seems to think she was over there a lot." Reed swiped a napkin over his lips. "Or maybe it's another dog. Either way I think it's time to get a search warrant, see if the missus has any weapons around." He didn't think they'd have trouble getting the warrant. Caitlyn's blood type had been found at the scene, a car like hers had been spotted at Bandeaux's place that night, she was going through a messy divorce with the deceased and things had gone from bad to worse with Bandeaux's threat of an unlawful death lawsuit over the kid's demise. Caitlyn Bandeaux also had a history of mental problems, as both Morrisette and Naomi Crisman had mentioned. Reed wasn't certain the dog hair meant anything, but he couldn't ignore the fact that Caitlyn Bandeaux was smack-dab in the middle of it. He just had to figure out how.

It had been a long week.

But it was nearly over.

Thank God.

Amanda stepped on the throttle of her little convertible

and the TR-6 sprang forward, buzzing along the highway, past the marshes where snowy white egrets were visible in the long grass and gators hid in the murky water. The wind tore at her hair, and she felt some of the tension from the office and the mess with Josh Bandeaux ease from her shoulders.

Shifting, she passed a guy in a BMW, left the guy standing still and it gave her a rush. She glanced in the rearview mirror and grinned at herself. Ian would be home tonight and she might just cook. Something with lobster, his favorite. And crusty French bread. And wine.

It would be good to see him, she thought as she spied the sign for her exit. Her marriage was far from perfect. Ian could be as big a jerk as any man, but then she wasn't exactly a piece of cake to live with either. For today, she'd forgive him his faults.

She roared off the exit and braked for the turn.

Nothing happened.

She sucked in her breath. Adrenalin pumped through her blood. She hit the brakes again, the corner rushing at her ever faster. "Shit!" She shifted down, stood on the useless brakes and swerved, her tires hitting gravel. Hard. The car tried to spin out. She fought the wheel and blew through the stop to squeal around the corner, swinging wide into the oncoming lane. Her heart was pounding like crazy, but fortunately no one was speeding toward her, no head-on collision imminent. "God help me." With all her strength she pulled hard on the emergency brake, then shifted into a lower gear. The little car flew off the shoulder, bounced down a slight slope and headed straight for the small sapling she passed each day on her way to work. Amanda braced herself. Here it comes, she thought wildly, holding fast to the steering wheel, bracing herself for the collision. It was the only tree near the highway. And it was small. Surely she'd survive. If only she didn't hit it squarely.

Wham!

The little car bucked.

Amanda flew forward, her head bouncing on the steering wheel.

Her seat belt snapped tight.

Glass shattered. Metal crunched.

Pain erupted behind Amanda's eyes. She groaned, looking into the cracked rearview mirror, where she thought she saw a vision . . . one of another woman advancing upon her, a woman she should recognize.

Then there was nothing, no woman, no pain, nothing at all as her consciousness slid into darkness.

Eighteen

"It looks like someone tampered with her brakes," Deputy Fletcher said from his end of the telephone connection. "I've had a mechanic take a cursory look at the undercarriage of Amanda Drummond's sports car. We've impounded it, and it's here at the police lot if you want to take a look."

"Tampered with them?" Reed repeated, slipping into the sleeves of his jacket and juggling the phone. He was still in his office, working a few extra hours, when the call had come in. "So you're saying the brake line was cut? That sounds like something straight out of an old movie. A bad old movie."

"Come on over here and take a look for yourself."

"I'll be there in half an hour."

He walked out of the station, climbed into his cruiser and rolled out of the city. He made it to the lot in twenty-five minutes, where Deputy Fletcher met him and walked him to the garage. Amanda Montgomery's mangled Triumph was inside, elevated by a hoist. The front end was bashed in, the cherry-red hood crumpled, the wheels twisted on the axle. "It looks as if she's lucky to be alive," Reed observed, though most of the damage was sustained on the passenger side.

"Yeah. If she would have hit the tree dead-on, it would've been a whole lot worse." As it was, the driver's side looked relatively unscathed. "Now, take a look at this," the deputy said, pointing to a long tube running from under the engine. The undercarriage was filthy with grease and dirt. "See right here, this is the brake line." He pointed with the tip of a pen he pulled from his pocket. "It's runnin' right out of the reservoir and it's been snipped."

"Cut."

"Yep."

"Couldn't it have happened in the accident?"

"Maybe, but we don't think so. We figure someone cut the brake fluid line and when the fluid drained out, she lost her brakes. Cutting the line is relatively easy." His expression was sober. "Someone wanted to mess up the car and whoever was driving it real bad. She's damned lucky she wasn't worse off."

"Where is she?"

"Ambulanced to Our Lady of Hope Hospital. She'd passed out, had a few scratches and probably a bruise from her seat belt, but she woke up as the EMTs were putting her into the ambulance and had a fit. Said she was fine. I was at the scene, and we convinced her to go in and have herself checked out for a possible concussion."

"Who called in the accident?"

"A witness. She was following Mrs. Drummond as she turned off the highway and saw her start to have trouble. When the Triumph tore off through the field, she called 911. She was waiting at the scene, and that's when things got a little dicey. Mrs. Drummond woke up, took one look at the witness and started screaming at her."

"Who was she?"

"A woman by the name of Christina Biscayne. Goes by Cricket."

Reed's radar went up. "She was following Amanda Drummond?"

"Yeah, on her way to a friend's house when she saw the accident." Reed made a mental note to speak with Cricket Biscayne, talked a few more minutes with Fletcher and didn't learn anything new. From the police impoundment lot, he drove to Our Lady Of Hope, a small private hospital, but the closest one to the accident scene. As luck would have it, Amanda was about to be released. She was seated in a wheelchair, a few cuts on her face, her hair a little mussed as she waited near the door. "What's the hangup?" she asked, glaring at the nurse.

"Just getting the doctor's signature on the release," the RN told her.

"I thought you had that all done."

"So did I."

"And what's so hard about getting his signature? He said I could be released, didn't he?" Amanda demanded, her fine features pulled into a don't-give-me-any-crap expression.

"Yes, he did. I'm sure it'll be just a few minutes. We're busy tonight. There are other patients," the nurse replied with a long-suffering and extremely forced smile, then looked at the pager strapped to her belt. "Just wait here." She walked across the blue carpet to a house phone and picked it up while her patient seethed in her wheelchair.

"Mrs. Drummond?" Reed asked, flipping open his wallet to show his badge. "Pierce Reed, Savannah Police Department."

"I know who you are," she said impatiently. "What're you doing here?"

"Heard you had a mishap."

"A mishap? Is that what you guys call it? Jesus, my damned brake line was cut, or so the officer at the scene said when he phoned my husband. If it's true my brake line was cut, then someone deliberately tried to kill me." She shoved her hair out of her eyes. "Again." Angling her head up to get a better view of him, she asked, "You do know about that, right? That I was nearly forced off the road about six months ago? No one seemed to care then, but now, after I almost die, you show up." She folded her arms over her chest. "So it wasn't a mishap, Detective. It wasn't even an accident." She started to rise to her feet. "Someone tried to kill me!"

"Please, Mrs. Drummond, stay in the wheelchair. It's hospital policy," the nurse said.

"I don't need a wheelchair, I just need to get out of here," Amanda snapped. She was on her feet now, her gaze never once leaving Reed's face. "And I need police protection. Someone's taking potshots at my family and it seems like I'm next on the list."

"Do you have any idea who?"

"Isn't that *your* job? You're the detective."

"I'd like to take a statement about what happened," he said and wondered why her jabs got under his skin. Pampered, rich bitch.

"Good. It's time you guys took what's happening seriously. Before the rest of the family ends up like Josh Bandeaux!" She watched as a car slid into the patient loading area near the double doors. "If you'll excuse me, my husband's here." She cast a disparaging look at the nurse. "I'm leaving, with or without the release."

"No problem. Dr. Randolph just signed it." The nurse handed her an envelope just as a tall, thin man in a pilot's uniform approached.

"What the hell happened?" he demanded, then, more quietly, asked, "Are you okay?"

"What happened is that someone tried to kill me and I ended up totaling the TR. And . . . no . . . I'm not okay." Amanda seemed to soften a bit, even blinked and cleared her throat as if she were near tears. Somehow she managed to pull herself together and find that razor-sharp tongue of hers again. "This is Detective Reed, Ian." She motioned to Reed. "He's going to nail the bastard who did this before he gets another crack at me. Isn't that right, Detective?"

"We'll do our best."

"Mrs. Drummond. Please sit down." The nurse was firm, and reluctantly Amanda dropped into the wheelchair. The nurse began to push Amanda through the automatic doors.

"I hope you do your best," Amanda said to Reed as she left the hospital. "Because the next time I might not be so lucky, and you'll find yourself in the middle of another unsolved homicide."

Caitlyn couldn't shake the feeling that she was being watched. She was in her office, working on a project she'd pushed aside for nearly a week. Her desk lamp and monitor provided soft light, and smooth jazz was playing from the speakers. Standing, she squinted to look through the lacy curtains, searching for hidden eyes. It was night; the street lamp in front of her house illuminating the fenced gardens in an eerie blue light. A fine mist was falling, fogging up the windows a bit, softening shadows, glistening on the street. From the corner of her eye, she noticed movement, a darker shadow in the shrubbery.

Her heart slammed against her ribs.

Leaves moved. She could almost hear the rustle of footsteps.

That's because you're paranoid. There's no one out there. No one.

She swallowed hard and saw the gleam of two beady eyes, low to the ground.

She tensed. The shrubbery shivered. A possum waddled into the lamplight, and Caitlyn, feeling foolish, breathed a little easier. Now she was jumping at shadows.

Still, she felt the weight of some unwanted gaze, and she snapped the shade down and leaned back in her desk chair. Maybe the police were following her; she wouldn't be surprised. Whether Detective Reed said it or not, he'd zeroed in on her as Josh's killer, and the trouble was, she wasn't able to defend herself. Or maybe someone else was silently stalking her, the same person who had been in her bedroom on the night of Josh's death, the one who was in some way responsible for all that blood.

You, Caitie. You're responsible.

"No," she whispered, trying to concentrate on her work,

refusing to believe the horrid thought. Maybe she should call Adam. She was so restless, and it felt right talking to him.

As a patient, or as a woman? Face it, Caitlyn, you just want to see him again.

"Damn." She was tired of listening to her nag of a conscience that sounded so much like her twin's voice.

She glanced at the computer monitor. On the screen an image she'd been working on, a vampire bat in flight, mocked her. The deadline for the artwork to be submitted for approval to the local zoo's board was only a week away and she was behind.

She adjusted the bat's movements, trying to concentrate, hoping that the image of the creature flying over a silvery disk of moon and through iron gates would help draw in the website's visitors. She wanted this opening page to be intriguing, hinting at all the old myths and superstitions while being scientifically accurate. She was tired, the muscles of her back beginning to ache from sitting so long in the chair, her nerves jangled as they were every night. She stood up and stretched, still staring down at the screen, and Oscar, who'd been sitting at her feet, barked.

"Yeah, and what do you want?" she asked, managing a smile.

Another bark. Oscar jumped up at her, then settled back on his haunches and looked up at her with eager, dark eyes.

"You okay?" He twirled in one spot. "You want to go outside?"

Another bark and his tail brushed the floor.

"Okay, okay," she said. "I get it. Finally. Come on, then."

The dog was already hurrying down the stairs. "Why do I think I'm being conned, that you saw the possum and want a piece of him?" she muttered, trailing after her dog.

Oscar was leaping at the back door by the time she reached the kitchen. She unbolted the lock and he shot through, barking like mad and running to the fountain in the corner. The verandah was shadowed but warm, and Caitlyn stood at its edge, waiting for the dog to settle down, listening to the insects humming and noticing the faint hint of cigarette smoke in the air. It was warm. Humid.

"Caitie?" a voice called from behind her.

"Jesus!" She nearly jumped out of her skin. Turning quickly, she looked into the shadows as she recognized the voice. "Kelly?"

But there was no one there . . . the verandah was empty. Other than Oscar nosing in the flower beds and the gurgle of the fountain, not a sound. She glanced at her dog and noticed that he hadn't looked up, didn't come wiggling over to have Kelly pat his head.

Caitlyn was jumpy. That was it. Imagining sounds.

She let out a long breath, tried to slow her heart rate. Maybe she really was cracking up. Losing it. God, no. "Come on," she said to the dog as he sniffed the base of a magnolia tree. "Oscar. Now." He hesitated, glanced over to the dark corner from where she'd thought she heard Kelly call her name, and he let out a whimper. Caitlyn looked again. No one. Nothing . . . just her overactive imagination.

"Get a grip," she told herself, but threw the dead bolt once she'd closed the door. From the kitchen she stared into the dark backyard and felt a another sliver of doubt. Had someone been outside with her . . . or not? Was someone watching the house, lurking in the shadows . . . stalking her, for crying out loud?

She backed away from the window and tried to shake off the feeling that something wasn't quite right. Halfway up the stairs, she heard the phone blast.

Taking the remaining steps two at a time, she flew into the den. The rudimentary drawing of the vampire bat was still floating on her monitor. She clicked off her computer and slid out the compact disc, silently counting to ten before taking a chance that the caller wasn't a reporter. "Hello?"

"Caitlyn?" Troy's voice crackled over the line. She nearly melted with relief to hear him. "Can you go out to Oak Hill?" His voice was serious. Grim.

"Now?" She glanced at the digital clock glowing in the semi-dark room. It was nearly ten.

"Yes."

"Why?" Caitlyn asked, her heart pounding with dread. "What's wrong?"

Troy hesitated a second, then said, "Amanda was in an accident. Single car. A few hours ago."

"Oh, my God!" Caitlyn braced herself for the worst. "Is she all right?"

"I guess so. Ian's picking her up now. A good samaritan phoned 911 when she saw her go off the road, and I don't have all the details, but I think she blacked out. Anyway, the EMTs arrived and hauled her by ambulance to the ER. She's already seen a doc, had a couple of tests and she's insisting that she be released. She was lucky. But Mom's not taking it well. You'd better get out to the house."

"I'm on my way," Caitlyn said, hanging up and scooping up her purse. She had her keys in her hand and nearly tripped over Oscar as she raced down the stairs.

The ghosts were talking again. Whispering between themselves as they dashed through the old house and outside. Lucille trembled as she stared out the window, looking past the trees lining the drive to Oak Hill. She rubbed her arms, tried to shake off the chill, but she couldn't.

Evil was coming.

Riding fast on a black horse with hooves aflame.

Coming straight for her.

If only she hadn't promised the old man she'd stay. If only she could leave. But she'd sworn to take care of Berneda Montgomery as long as that woman drew a breath. So she had to stay. Muttering a prayer, she made the sign of the cross over her ample bosoms, and as she did she heard the ghosts laughing at her.

There was no escape.

Nineteen

"Okay, now wait a minute. Catch me up," Caitlyn demanded once she'd reached Oak Hill. The family had gathered. Including Amanda. Aside from being paler than usual, Amanda seemed fine. She was pacing the length of the parlor, her husband Ian sitting on a tall stool near the cold grate of the fireplace.

Berneda, looking wan, lay on the chaise. Lucille was seated next to her, Doc Fellers in attendance. Positioned near the window and staring out the watery glass panes to the darkness beyond, Troy was as tense as a bow string, his eyes narrowed on the lane, as if he expected a gang of bad guys from an old Western to appear in a cloud of dust. Even Hannah had shown up and was slumped in one of the plush side chairs. Her skin was tanned, her expression bored, her eye makeup dark, her hair streaked blond. A neglected can of diet soda was sweating on the coffee table. "What happened?"

"Someone cut the brake line of my TR," Amanda said as she plowed stiff fingers through her hair. She was worked up, walking from one end of the room to the other. "You know, the police didn't take me seriously when I said someone tried to run me off the road a few months ago, but they'd better do it now.''

"You were run off the road?'' Berneda struggled to sit up a little higher.

Lucille's hand strayed to her shoulder. "Shh. You rest.''

"Yes!'' Amanda said emphatically. "Run off the damned road. I could have been killed! And no one seemed to care. I brought it up again today when Detective Reed showed up.''

"He was there?'' Caitlyn asked, starting to panic again. He was hovering so close to her family. Of course she wanted him to find Josh's killer, yet the thought that he was ever present bothered her.

"He came to the hospital just as I was being released and I basically told him to get off his ass and find whoever it is that's doing this.''

"Amanda thinks her accident and Josh's death might be connected,'' Ian said.

"I'd bet my life on it,'' Amanda said.

"Connected? Why?''

"It's just a little too coincidental that someone fiddles with my brakes a week after Josh was killed.''

"If he didn't kill himself,'' Ian said.

"Oh, come *on!* Only a moron would think that! We all knew Josh. Let's not even go there, okay? Suicide my eye! I'm just lucky I wasn't killed today!''

"You weren't hurt,'' her husband reminded Amanda. The tight corners of his mouth suggested that her histrionics were too much for him. Though over forty, Ian Drummond's hair was jet black, his eyes nearly as dark. He had the physique of a twenty-five-year-old countered by the sullen, angry expression of a man who had lived unhappily too long.

"It doesn't matter, Ian. Someone tried to kill me last winter—right before Christmas, remember? And they tried again today! Next time they might just get away with it!''

Berneda gave a little squeak of protest.

"Perhaps you should talk elsewhere,'' Lucille said, her

eyes flashing a warning that Amanda was in no mood to accept.

"I just thought it was best if everyone in the family found out from me. It'll probably be in the news, on the television tonight or in the paper tomorrow morning. I thought you'd all want to hear it from me yourselves."

"What did Detective Reed have to say?" Caitlyn asked.

"Not much more than the rest of those idiots. I've spoken to someone there three times since that damned black Explorer nearly pushed me into the swamp, once the day it happened, another time a week later and now again today, but you know what? I don't think anyone there really gives a damn."

"Except Detective Reed did show up today. You didn't call him," Ian reminded her.

"But I will. If he thinks that little interview today was enough, he obviously doesn't know me."

"Maybe the police have bigger fish to fry. You came out of it unhurt," Troy offered, stuffing his hands into his pants pocket.

"Bigger fish as in the Josh Bandeaux murder?"

"I thought they were still trying to figure out if he committed suicide," Berneda said.

"I told you I don't think it was suicide." Amanda couldn't hide the exasperation in her voice.

"What do you think?" Hannah asked Caitlyn.

"I don't know, but I agree with Amanda. I can't imagine that he would kill himself. The police seem to think it was murder."

"I agree." Hannah's blue eyes darkened a shade, and Caitlyn held her tongue. There had been rumors about Josh and Hannah, but there had been rumors about Josh with just about any female within ninety miles. So Caitlyn had become inured, she supposed. His affairs had become more embarrassing than painful. But to think that her own sister had . . . "Josh loved himself too much to end it."

"Must we speculate?" Berneda asked, running a shaky

hand over her lips. She looked pale and shrunken on the chaise.

"Of course not, Mom. Why don't you go upstairs and rest?" Caitlyn suggested.

"So you all can talk about me?"

"We won't."

"Of course we will," Hannah said. She slid out of the chair, her legs appearing longer than they were because of her short denim skirt and boots with five-inch heels. "That's what this family does best. Gossips. About each other." Hannah had never been afraid to speak her mind. The baby of the clan, she'd been coddled and spoiled and thought it was her God-given right to blurt out whatever she thought. "I need a drink." She walked through the foyer to the dining room where an antique sideboard had been converted into a wet bar. "Anyone else?" she called, her voice echoing against the coved ceiling.

"Spoiled brat," Ian said under his breath, but loud enough that everyone in the room caught it.

"This is all so much to take in." Berneda wrung her hands nervously.

"You've upset her," Troy accused Amanda.

"Oh, I know, I shouldn't have come here, but I thought it would be best if I came over in person and she saw that I was all right. Isn't that better than catching a sound bite on the eleven o'clock news?" Amanda glanced at Berneda. "Mom, I'm okay, really," she said, though she didn't sound as if she'd convinced herself. "Everything turned out all right. Except for the TR Daddy gave me. It's totaled."

Hannah strolled back to the family room and was sipping from a short glass.

"All this in one week," Berneda said, her voice shaking as she reached for Amanda's hand. "It's a little much. First Josh and now you. I swear sometimes I do believe this family is cursed."

"Cursed? Oh, God, Mom. Now you're starting to sound like her," Hannah said as she threw a pointed look at Lucille. "Seen any ghosts lately?"

"Hannah!" Berneda responded.

"I don't see 'em, I only hear 'em," Lucille said in a voice so cold it sent a shiver down Caitlyn's spine.

"What about you?" Hannah twirled on the heel of her boot to stare at Caitlyn. "I thought you heard ghosts, too."

"That's enough!" Berneda was shaking, and Doc Fellers stepped between Hannah and her mother. "Let's all try to calm down. I've given your mother a tranquilizer."

"How thoughtful," Hannah said with a sneer. "I think I'll have one myself." She lifted her empty glass and wiggled it in the air.

"Stop it," Troy warned.

Lucille's lips tightened at the corners. Her dark eyes reflected pinpoints of light from the lamps glowing from the end tables, and she seemed distant and cold.

"Come on, Mom, let's get you upstairs where you can lie down. Ian, can you help me?" Amanda asked and seemed none the worse for her accident.

Lucille was on her feet in an instant. "I'll take her to her room."

But Amanda was already helping Berneda off the couch. "Come on, Mom . . . Ian?"

"I'll get her," he said and picked Berneda up to carry her up the stairs. Amanda was right behind him, and Lucille, never one to be far from her charge, followed at a slower pace as she gripped the handrail and eased up the steps.

"I think she'll be all right," Doc Fellers said as he zipped up his medical bag. "This week has been hard on her. I've left a prescription for a tranquilizer with Lucille, and I want it filled if Berneda becomes agitated again."

"Mom was agitated?" Caitlyn asked, worried all over again.

"Upset," Troy explained.

"You can call me day or night," the doctor said. That was the way it had always been. For as long as Caitlyn could remember. If there was a medical problem or emergency, Henry Fellers was telephoned. Sometimes they'd meet him at the hospital, or he was called in to the emergency room, but more often than not, he came here, to this old plantation home. Like an old horse-and-buggy doctor of a hundred and fifty years ago. Which was odd. In this day and age of HMOs, specialized medicine, high-tech treatments with MRIs and CT scans, along with laser surgeries, computer images, and conference calls to specialists all over the country, Doc Fellers was a throwback to the nineteenth century.

Odder still, Caitlyn was nearly certain that the Montgomery clan were his only remaining patients. He'd been semi-retired for fifteen years or so and yet, no matter what time of day or night, if needed, he raced to Oak Hill. Berneda's migraines and heart condition, Caitlyn's sinus infections, Charles's broken collarbone, Amanda's concussion, Hannah's abortion . . .

He'd been the medical doctor who had admitted Caitlyn to the mental hospital after Jamie died, and a few weeks later he'd lobbied with the psychiatrists to secure her release.

"I'll check on Berneda tomorrow," he said now as he started for the door only to pause to touch Caitlyn on the shoulder. "And how are you doing? I was real sorry to hear about Josh. I didn't like him much, you know that, never thought he treated you worth a damn, but I know it's a loss just the same."

"I'm okay," she said.

"You're sure?" Sincere eyes regarded her from beneath shaggy white eyebrows. "Sometimes we all need a little help. I can write a prescription for you as easily as I can your mother. You've been through a lot, Caitlyn."

"I'll be all right."

"You sure?" The doctor was far from convinced.

"As sure as I can be," she said as he walked outside and squared his hat upon his head. She closed the door and found Hannah stirring her drink with her finger and staring at her.

"You know, we're a pathetic lot," Hannah said.

Caitlyn wasn't in the mood for her baby sister's dark sense of humor. She needed to go upstairs and say good-bye to her mother before she drove home. "Speak for yourself."

"Merely an observation. My opinion."

"So keep it to yourself."

"Uh-oh, look who just got tough," Hannah taunted, holding her drink aloft in mock salute, then offering a not-so-nice-girl grin and taking a long sip. "I'm soooo scared."

"Good." Caitlyn grabbed her purse and shot her youngest sister a look guaranteed to kill. "Scared is an improvement, Hannah. A *big* improvement."

Reed didn't like the turn of his thoughts. No matter how he tried to mold it, he kept coming up with Caitlyn Bandeaux as the logical suspect. He was waiting for the judge to issue a search warrant and the D.A., Katherine Okano, was getting anxious. She was pushing. Hard. That was the trouble with women in high places. They got impatient and became bitches. Throw menopause into the mix and all hell was sure to break loose. Men, on the other hand, were just plain tough.

That's the misogynist in you, his conscience reminded him as the phone rang and he picked up. "Reed."

"Yeah. This is Detective Reuben Montoya, New Orleans Police Department, Homicide. I've got a missing person with a connection to one of the cases you're investigating."

Reed was surprised. "What do you need?"

"Her name is Marta Vasquez. She's been missing since last December. She's thirty-three, five-seven, a hundred and thirty pounds, Anglo-Hispanic. Last seen in a bar on Bourbon Street where she was out with friends. I'll fax you a picture and detailed description."

"What case is this connected with?"

"That's the kicker. Marta is the daughter of Lucille Vasquez, who lives at Oak Hill outside of Savannah. I know that technically Oak Hill is out of your jurisdiction, but I've already talked to the sheriff out there and he gave me your name." Reed's interest sharpened. "I've been reading the *Savannah Sentinel,* so I knew you were working on the

Joshua Bandeaux case. Lucille Vasquez knew him. She's the housemaid to your victim's mother-in-law.''

"How do you think the cases might be connected?'' Reed was sitting up, clicking his pen as the wheels turned in his mind.

"I don't know. I don't see how, but I'm running out of options down here and a couple of friends thought Marta might be going to visit her mother. I'm not sure how this all works out as Marta and Lucille were estranged, but I'm checking everything out on this end. I've called Marta's mother myself, but Lucille Vasquez is the proverbial brick wall. Won't give me any information.''

Reed had heard as much from the detectives who had interviewed the staff at Oak Hill. He leaned back in his chair again and glanced to his computer monitor where a list of all of Josh Bandeaux's known acquaintances flickered. "You said you were with Homicide. You think Marta is dead?''

There was a weighty pause on the other end of the line, and Reed thought he heard the click of a cigarette lighter before the expulsion of a long breath. "Is she dead? Hell, that's the real question. I hope not. For now I'm just looking for answers.'' Before Reed could ask another question, Montoya added, "I've got a personal stake in this one. Any help you could give me would be appreciated.''

He sounded straight. "You got it. But I don't know what we can find out.''

"Just keep me posted. I'll fax you a picture, her stats and the pertinent information.''

"Fair enough. The fax number is—''

"Already got it. Thanks. I owe ya, man,'' Montoya said.

Reed hung up the phone and wondered about any possible connection between Marta Vasquez's disappearance and the murder of Josh Bandeaux. Coincidence? Or a clue?

He jotted a note and heard the familiar sound of boots heading for his door. From the cadence he knew it was Morrisette and she was on a tear. He looked over his shoulder just as she burst through the door.

"Guess what?" she said, hoisting her little butt onto his desk.

"I couldn't."

"You're no fun."

"So I've been told. Many times."

"Our favorite family is in the news again." Morrisette's eyes actually twinkled. She really got off on all this stuff. Reed, on the other hand, felt as if a brick had been dropped on his gut.

"The Montgomerys?"

"Whoever said you weren't an ace detective?"

"You for starters."

She grinned far enough to show some teeth.

"If this is about Amanda Drummond's accident yesterday, I already heard about it and talked to her in the hospital. She thinks someone's trying to kill her. I was about to call you and see if you wanted to go with me to get her statement."

"Shit—oh, damn ... oh ... I should have known you would already have gotten wind of this. And yeah, I wouldn't miss this interview for the world," she said, a little deflated that Reed was one step ahead of her.

The telephone jangled and he punched the button for the speakerphone. "Reed."

"You've got a couple of faxes," a secretary told him.

"I'll be down to pick 'em up in a few." He was in the process of hanging up when he saw Amanda Drummond storming through the cubicles, heading straight for his office.

"Looks like we'll be doing that interview here," he said under his breath as Amanda pushed through the already half-open door.

"You said you wanted a statement," she said without so much as a greeting, "so I thought I'd make it official. I know this is Homicide, okay, and I probably technically should be talking to that yahoo of a deputy with the Sheriff's Department, but since you stopped by the hospital yesterday and seem to agree that what happened to me might be related to Josh's death, I thought I'd talk to you."

"That'll work," he said. "This is my partner. Detective Morrisette. She'll sit in. If you don't mind, I'm going to tape this." He reached into his drawer for a pocket recorder and noticed that Morrisette had pulled a small notepad and pen from her pocket.

"Fine." Amanda gave Morrisette the once-over, hesitated a second when she checked out her hair, then turned back to Reed as she settled into the chair near his desk. Morrisette rested a hip on the windowsill. "For the record, I think someone is picking off Montgomery family members one by one. Someone tried to run me off the road, and if you check the records you'll see I made a statement with the police to that effect. Then he waited, killed Josh in the meantime and took a crack at me again yesterday!" Her jaw was set, her eyes bright as she leaned across the desk. But she didn't look scared. Just angry. Such was her personality. "Look, Detective, I want whoever the bastard is caught before my luck runs out." She pointed a manicured nail straight between his eyes. "So I expect you to nail the S.O.B. before he gets another chance."

"I can assure you that we're doing everything possible to close this case, Mrs. Drummond."

"Oh, sure. The company answer. That'll make me sleep better tonight." She let out her breath in a huff, and as she did some of her rage seemed to dissipate. "Let's get one thing straight. I don't like unleashing the bitch in me. It . . . it shouldn't be necessary. But sometimes I feel it is." As she leaned closer to the desk, making the conversation appear more intimate, Reed was reminded that she was an attorney, used to putting on a show in a courtroom, to playing to an audience. "Look," she said, "I know Kathy Okano. We were both assistant D.A.s together years ago before I couldn't stand it any longer. But I'm sure she would agree with me."

"Where do you usually keep your car?" he asked.

"In my garage at my house. I live out at Quail Run. It's a gated community, complete with security guard."

"When's the last time you drove the car?"

She didn't miss a beat. "Three weeks ago. It's a sports car, and I only use it once in a while. I usually drive my Mercedes. The TR is just for fun, a convertible."

"Who else drives the sports car?"

"Just me."

"What about your husband?" Morrisette asked.

Amanda shook her head. "Never. Just me."

"But he has access." Sylvie Morrisette wasn't about to back down.

"Yeah, he even has a key so that he can move it if he has to or wash it. But trust me, *Ian* didn't sabotage my car!"

"Then who did?" Reed asked.

"I don't know. That's what worries me."

"You have anyone over to your house lately?"

"No . . . well, not really."

"What do you mean not really?" Morrisette countered. "Either someone was there or not."

"What I mean is no one I don't trust. My brother, Troy, and my sisters Caitlyn and Hannah have each been over . . . and my friend, Elisa."

"How about since the time you last drove the car. When was that?"

"Two . . . no, more like two-and-a-half weeks ago. I had to go pick up some paperwork I'd left at the office, so I drove into town, then came directly home."

"So who's been to your house since?"

Amanda scowled. "I don't know. Some friends, neighbors, workmen. I had some maintenance done on my air conditioner and a chimney sweep come to clean out the flues."

"Did they go into the garage where your Triumph was parked?"

"I suppose so. I don't really know."

Reed said, "It would be helpful if you made a list of everywhere the car has been and the names of everyone who had access to your garage over the last two-and-a-half weeks. I'd also like copies of the last couple of invoices from the shop who did the work on your car, including if you went to one of those quickie lube places.''

''I'll get those for you.''

''Good.'' Reed and Morrisette asked more questions, and she gave a rundown of the events leading up to the accident, how the brakes had failed.

Amanda gave them a list of names of the people who regularly worked for her—the lawn service, the maid, the neighbor next door who had a key to the house—and promised to get the other information they'd requested, but she wasn't satisfied. ''You know, I'd check out Cricket Biscayne if I were you.''

''She called 911 for you.''

''So I heard, but I'm sure you already know that there's a lot of bad blood between my family and hers.''

''The way I hear it, you're all part of one big extended family.''

Amanda bristled. ''That's not how I see it, and it seems pretty damned coincidental that she's the person who sees me lose control of the car. You know the Biscaynes are white trash, and I don't care if that's not PC or that my grandfather was involved with their grandmother. They're just a bunch of lowlifes with their hands out. It wasn't just a lucky set of circumstances that Cricket was following me.''

When the interview was over, Amanda left a business card with her home and office numbers printed on it. ''You can reach me at either number,'' she said as Reed clicked off his recorder and she, wincing, slung the strap of her purse over one shoulder. ''I'll fax you the invoices you wanted along with a list of the people who work for me, or who have been to the house and seen the car, with their addresses and phone numbers.''

''I'll look for it,'' Reed assured her. The lady was nothing if not efficient.

''Good.'' She started for the door but hesitated. ''Thanks,'' she added, as if it was an afterthought, then left, sweeping out the door and through the cubicles.

''She gives new meaning to the word bitch,'' Morrisette

observed, not seeming to care if Amanda Drummond was out of earshot. "Jesus, did she climb all over us or what?" Morrisette glared through the open door. "You know what? She just about made me want to turn coat."

Reed raised an eyebrow.

"After that, I'm thinking of joining the other team. Anyone who's trying to get rid of her is my kind of guy."

"Or gal," he thought aloud. "She said her sisters had been over."

"Oh, wait a minute. I see where this is going. You think Caitlyn Bandeaux slid under the Triumph and snipped the brake lines? Are you nuts? Have you ever seen one of those cars? They're just a few inches off the ground, and I don't think Mrs. Bandeaux is the mechanical type. Whoever did this would have to know what he—or she—was doing. Nah, Reed, you're way off base with this one."

Reed wasn't convinced. "I want what's left of the car dusted for prints, and we need to see the area where it was parked. Check and see if any brake fluid had dripped onto the garage floor or anywhere else she may have parked it, and as I told her, I want to see the mechanic's records."

"Anything else?"

"Yeah, I think Amanda's right. We need to talk to Cricket Biscayne to begin with and then have another chat with our favorite widow."

"I'll call on Cricket—Jesus, what's with these people? If you were named Copper, would you name your kids Cricket and Sugar? I mean, I *know* they're nicknames, that Cricket is really Christina and Sugar is Sheryl, but you'd think, by the time they were adults, they would have started calling themselves something a little more sophisticated . . . classy. Sugar's a stripper and Cricket's a flake of a hairdresser who can't stay in one shop for more than a month or two at a time." She slapped the heel of a hand to her forehead. "Forget I said that."

Her pager went off. "Shit, if this is my babysitter—" She pointed a finger at Reed. "Don't even say it—I know. I've got the quarter already." She was looking at the readout on her pager. "Oh, fu–fudge. It's Bart. Probably another reason he can't make the child support. I wonder what it is this time? His truck broke down? He lost another job? He's a little short. Crap! Every damned month!" She took off down the hall swearing a blue streak and Reed, still thinking about Amanda Montgomery and her claim about the attempt on her life, decided to pick up his faxes.

There were several, none yet from Amanda Montgomery, but the one that caught his attention was from the detective in New Orleans, Montoya. It was a photograph and description of Marta Vasquez. The picture was grainy black and white, but showed a pretty woman with short, dark hair, nose that turned up just a bit and wide, sensual lips. Reed couldn't help but wonder what had happened to her and how, if in any way, it could be connected to the Bandeaux case. According to the information, Marta had a scar on her abdomen from an appendix surgery and a tattoo of a hummingbird on her ankle. She'd been a student off and on and had recently worked at an insurance company before quitting suddenly with no explanation.

A lot like Rebecca Wade, Caitlyn Bandeaux's shrink.
Coincidence?
Unlikely.
Marta Vasquez was the daughter of Lucille Vasquez, maid, housekeeper, and general nanny for the Montgomery brood. So Marta would have known the Montgomery children. He frowned. She'd disappeared . . . that was all anyone knew. No one had seen her for six months. He stared at the picture as he walked back to his office where his phone was ringing loudly.

"Detective Reed," he said, tossing all the faxes into his already overflowing in-box. First things first.

Cricket was the last one in the shop. Her final client, a rich woman who "would have died" if she hadn't been able to make an evening appointment, had left, driving away in a new Cadillac and finally satisfied with a foil weave of no less than seven colors and a difficult cut that had taken nearly three hours. Cricket looked at the dirty towels piled high on the washer, but figured Misty, the girl who started at some ungodly hour—eight? Nine? It didn't matter. Misty, with her irritating bubbly personality, fake boobs, and unending case of the giggles, could damned well wash and dry the towels.

Crap, this job was getting the better of her. On her feet all day listening to women bitch about their husbands or their kids.

But they weren't really complaining, Cricket knew, hearing it in the tone of their voices; they were proud of their spouses or their brats, the "oh, woe is me, long-suffering wife and mother" act, was just for show. Cricket put up with it because it was part of the job and there was usually a tip involved, though some of the women were so tight they squeaked.

Cricket's muscles ached and she cracked her neck as she swept up around her station at the salon, swabbed out the sink, then hung her apron on a hook near the back door. Her Coke was where she'd left it by the color-mixing sink. She picked it up and took a sip from the straw. Caffeine, that was what she needed. Well, and maybe a shot or two of tequila . . . or maybe a joint. Maybe all three. Her tips for the week would buy a couple of drinks and maybe an ounce or two of weed.

She walked outside to the stoop where she and the other girls smoked. Against Maribelle, the owner of the shop's orders, they'd leave the back door open and stand outside for a quick hit of nicotine.

Now, as she locked up, Cricket fished in her purse for a pack of cigarettes and her lighter. Only one filter tip left in the crumpled pack. And the cigarette was kind of broken. Shit. She managed to light the damned thing as she walked down the lane that cut between two main streets. Basically, it was an alley cluttered with dumpsters, crates and strictly enforced no-parking zones. Maribelle insisted the girls park a block over, allowing every tiny parking space for the clients.

Not that Cricket gave a rat's ass where she parked.

Maribelle also hinted that she should get a percentage of the beauticians' tips. Yeah, right. What a stingy old bat. Cricket had half a mind to quit. She finished her Coke and tossed the empty cup into a Dumpster. The night was thick and dark and hot, no sign of stars or a moon, just street lamps offering an eerie glow and attracting insects. A mosquito or no-see-um was bothering her.

Cutting behind a gas station, she slapped at the mosquito, and the aches that had been with her most of the day seemed to melt away. In fact her legs were rubbery, not working quite right. And her vision was fuzzy. She was working too hard. That was it, way too hard.

With more difficulty than usual, Cricket found her little hatchback where she'd left it, under a street lamp, only the light tonight wasn't working right, flickering on and off, and the street was deserted. Not that it mattered, she thought thickly. God, what was wrong with her? She'd unlocked the car when she heard a footstep, sensed someone behind her. Without much concern, she looked over her shoulder and saw something, a figure—man or woman—crouching behind an old station wagon.

She slid into the car and caught the heel of her shoe on the door frame. "Crap," she muttered, but found she didn't really care. Her vision was really blurry now and . . . and she couldn't sit up straight, was half in and half out of the car, unable to punch the key into the ignition. Jesus, what was going on? It was if she was drugged as if someone had what . . . doctored her Coke?

She heard footsteps and rolled one eye back to see the figure dashing across the lane . . . it was a woman and she seemed familiar . . . someone who would help her. Cricket tried to speak, attempted to hold on to a clear thought as the woman in black drew nearer. *Help me, please,* she tried to say, but couldn't form the words. They died in her throat as she recognized the stranger.

What was she doing down here? Why? Had she been waiting? Expecting her? Oh, God. Sudden, blinding truth hit Cricket like a ton of bricks. She noticed the woman's tight-fitting gloves and white slash of a smile.

Like the Cheshire Cat in *Alice in Wonderland*.

Or worse. This smile was cold, the eyes gleaming in anticipation. She reached into her purse and withdrew a small glass jar, which she flashed in front of Cricket's eyes. In the glow of the interior light she saw them. Insects, all sorts and kinds were packed inside, desperately crawling up the sides of the jar, thin legs and wings and antennae moving, pulsing against the glass, segmented bodies crushed against each other. They scrambled over each other, fighting to the top of the heap, as they tried to escape.

"Friends of yours?" the woman inquired, her gaze menacing as she rolled the vial between her gloved fingers. "I think so."

In that instant, Cricket knew she was going to die.

Twenty

You shouldn't be here.

Her own voice taunted Caitlyn as she switched off the ignition and listened to the engine of her car die, then tick as it cooled. The wind was brisk, rattling the branches of the live oaks and stirring the fronds of the thick shrubbery.

"I know, but it's Jamie's birthday," she said aloud as she stared up at the house. Three stories of red brick, trimmed in white, accented with narrow, paned windows and black shutters, the house stood quietly, its lights glowing warmly in the darkness.

Jamie's house. Caitlyn's throat was thick as she conjured up her daughter's cherubic three-year-old face. But she didn't cry. Had wept her buckets of tears years before. Quickly, before the morbid thoughts got the better of her, she pocketed her keys and slid from behind the steering wheel of her Lexus.

The night was warmer than she'd expected, the air a gentle kiss on her cheeks as she made her way up the walk to the wrought-iron gate. She thought it would be locked, but the latch gave way and the old hinges creaked. Mist rose from the ground like smoke, swirling at her feet and wafting eerily through the lacy branches overhead. In front of the home that used to be hers, her doubts mushroomed and she second-guessed herself. She was alone. But then she always had been, hadn't she? One of seven children, but alone. A twin, but alone. Married, but alone. A mother and now alone.

The wind was gusty, tugging at her hair, hot as midday, though it was night. She was vaguely aware of the sound of a car's engine as it drove past and the yapping of a neighbor's dog over the sound of the steady, painful drumming of her heart.

It was now or never.

Either she was going to face Josh or let the marriage die.

Forcing starch into her spine, she walked along the brick path just as she had hundreds of times during the short span of her marriage. Up the three steps to the wide front porch, where baskets of petunias hung and the scent of honeysuckle was strong. She raised her fist to rap on the door, but it was open, hanging ajar.

An invitation.

Don't do it! Don't go in there! She heard Kelly's voice as surely as if her sister were standing next to her in the shadows.

Seduced by a sliver of light spilling onto the dark porch from the cracked door, she stepped inside, her footsteps echoing on the smooth marble foyer with its twenty-foot ceilings. The grandfather clock began to chime over soft music playing from hidden speakers . . . something haunting and classical, coming from the den.

She stepped over the threshold and saw him, slumped over the desk, one arm flung over the edge of the desk, blood dripping from his wrist, pooling onto the plush pile of the carpet.

"Josh!" she cried as the phone began to ring.

One ring. She stared at the phone on the desk near Josh's head.

Two rings. Oh, God, should she answer it?

Three rings.

* * *

Caitlyn's eyes flew open. Her heart was pounding wildly, her skin soaked in sweat. She was home. In her own bed. But the horrid image of her husband lying dead across his desk still burned through her mind.

Josh dead in his den with the wrongful death papers, the wine and open verandah door. She knew without asking to see photos of the crime scene that she'd duplicated it in her subconscious. But how? Unless she'd been there? Unless she'd actually witnessed his death? But that was impossible. It had to be!

The phone blasted. She scrabbled for the receiver. "Hello?" she whispered.

Nothing.

Her skin crawled.

"Hello? Is anyone there?"

Not a sound. Not even a dial tone.

Terrified, she slammed the receiver down. Dear God, what was happening? She wiped a trembling hand over her forehead.

What she'd experienced was just a bad dream. A *really* bad dream.

So who had called at three-fifteen in the morning?

Who had refused to answer?

A wrong number?

Forcing herself to calm down, she took several deep breaths. Oscar was lying at the foot of her bed, yawning and stretching. "Come here," she said, patting the pillow next to her, and he slowly inched upward to curl against her. There was something calming in stroking his bristly fur, in listening to the whirring of the ceiling fan moving overhead.

The bedside phone rang again.

What now? Every muscle in her body tensed.

Reaching blindly, she snapped on the light and picked up the receiver. "Hello?"

No answer.

"Hello?"

Her heart was hammering as she waited, though she heard shallow breathing.

"Who is this?"

Nothing. No response.

Her skin crawled . . . was there the faint hint of music in the background? Why wasn't the person answering? She hung up the receiver and checked Caller ID. *Unknown caller.* That much she'd already figured out. She rubbed a hand over her forehead. The phone jangled again.

Damn! She started. Looked at the Caller ID before answering. Troy's number. She picked up. "Hello?"

"Caitlyn. It's Troy. I know it's late and I hate to call you, but I think you should know that Mom's on her way to the hospital. It's her heart."

"No! Oh, God, is she okay?"

"Don't know. I just got a call from the EMT. He asked me to meet them at Eastside General. I'm on my way."

"Me, too," she said without thinking. "I'll meet you there. Oh, and Troy, did you try to call me a couple of minutes ago?"

"No. Why?"

"The phone rang and I answered, but no one was there."

"It wasn't me," he said.

Her fingers clenched around the receiver. "Probably a wrong number," she said, not believing it for a second as she hung up. She stripped out of her nightgown, pulled on a pair of jeans and a sweatshirt, then slid into a pair of sandals, the bottoms of her feet encountering something crusty. "What the devil?" she groused, then saw the dark splotches on the insoles, two purplish drips that she knew instinctively were blood. Her stomach turned over as she realized these were the shoes she'd worn on the night Josh died. She'd obviously kicked them toward the back of the closet and hadn't noticed the stains when she'd cleaned up her room the next day. Now she scrambled out of the sandals as if her feet actually burned. She felt a wave of panic and found a pair of running shoes that she wormed her feet into, then hurried down the stairs. As she reached the back door, the phone began to ring again. She checked Caller ID.

Unknown caller.

Her heart froze.

She should answer; it could be news of her mother.

She picked up. "Hello?"

No response.

"Hello?"

Nothing, just the static of an open line. The hairs on her nape rose. She had to quell the fear that threatened her.

"Who is this? No, wait, I don't want to know. Whoever you are, just go to hell!"

"You go first." The voice was a harsh whisper and had the same effect on Caitlyn as if she'd heard her own death sentence. She slammed the phone down, her heart racing, cold sweat breaking out on her back and face. Who was it? Why were they calling?

Calm down!

Caitlyn backed up and stumbled against the counter. She had to get to the hospital. She didn't have time to think about whoever it was who was harassing her. But as she stepped outside to the sultry Savannah night, the three chilling words followed her.

You go first.

The hospital loomed in the night, eight very modern stories in sharp contrast to most of the historic buildings in the area. Caitlyn parked and paused long enough to leave a message on Kelly's cell phone. "Kelly, it's Caitlyn. I just got a call from Troy. About Mom. It's around four in the morning, and she's been rushed to Eastside General Hospital. I don't know the details, but when I do, I'll call again." She hesitated, staring out the windshield to the deserted parking lot. "I, um, I just thought you'd want to know. It wouldn't kill you to visit her. Maybe it's time to mend a few fences." She clicked off, figured she'd probably pissed off her sister, but didn't really care. A crisis was a crisis.

Sliding out of her Lexus, she stepped into the thick, warm night. There was a slight breeze off the Savannah River and the rumble of a few engines as solitary cars, headlights cutting down the city streets, rolled past. Her footsteps echoed across the pavement as she spied Troy's black Range Rover and, beside it, Hannah's Honda.

Glass doors opened as she stepped under the covered portico. Inside the lights were turned low, the corridors hushed except for the ER, where lights blazed. The night staff was on duty, and several members of her family were waiting.

Grim faced, Troy stood near the admissions desk while Hannah sat on a long couch and absently flipped through a magazine. Lucille sat on a small chair near a potted palm and looked straight ahead, either dead tired or stricken, Caitlyn couldn't tell which. Amanda, none the worse from her recent accident, perched on the edge of a plastic chair and Ian, dressed in his uniform, his shirt crisp, his cap lying on a table, seemed distracted and edgy. He constantly glanced at his watch or bit at a thumbnail.

"How is Mom?" Caitlyn asked, approaching her brother.

"Better." Troy tried to angle a look past the drapes of the private rooms as some sleepy elevator music played from speakers set into the walls.

"Thank God," Amanda said with a sigh. "I don't know if I could take another tragedy."

"You could take anything," Hannah said without looking up from a six-month-old edition of *People* magazine. "You're tough as nails."

"How would you know?"

"I know." She flipped another page slowly, and Caitlyn caught a glimpse of Julia Roberts on an inside page.

"Fine, so you're psychic."

"Nooooo, I just know people. I leave all that psychic crap to Lucille."

Amanda looked about to shoot back a retort but decided to hold her tongue. Lucille didn't so much as glance in Hannah's direction.

Troy ignored his sisters' bickering. "Once the ambulance got her here, the doctors were able to stabilize her."

"She had another one of her 'spells,' " Amanda offered.

"Her heart?"

"Umhmm. Angina attack."

"Angina pectoris," Hannah clarified, looking up briefly. "You know, as opposed to just angina, which can be anything. You're talking about her heart."

"What about her nitroglycerine pills? They're supposed to help."

"They didn't work this time."

Lucille sighed heavily as she wrung her hands. "This time nothing helped, so I called 911." Guilt kept her eyes from meeting Caitlyn's. She stared at the coffee table. "Nothing worked. I was walking her upstairs to bed, and she began to have trouble, breathing hard, complaining of pain. I managed to get her into the bed and give her the pill, but she just kept getting worse." The older woman's lips pursed, and she shook her head. "I called Doc Fellers, and he didn't answer. Your mother, she was fit to be tied and in so much pain, but she didn't want me to call anyone else. Finally, I couldn't take it anymore. I called 911, and they sent an ambulance."

"You did what you could," Troy said.

Hannah rolled her eyes.

Amanda shot Hannah a warning glare, but their youngest sibling didn't seem to notice as she tossed the glossy magazine onto the table.

"I should have called sooner," Lucille said.

"Where were you, Hannah?" Troy asked.

"Out," Hannah said sullenly, then grabbed her bag. "I'm going out for a smoke."

"I'll join you." Troy was already reaching into his jacket pocket and jogged to catch up with her. The glass doors parted and they stepped outside, huddled together near the ash can.

Caitlyn looked over at Amanda. "How're you feeling?"

"All in all? Just peachy," Amanda said flippantly. "All in all, it's been a helluva week."

Caitlyn couldn't disagree, but as the first light of dawn seeped through the mist, she had the gnawing feeling that it was only going to get worse.

He had to work fast.

Adam slipped into his office and made sure the door was closed tight behind him. He'd missed something; he was sure of it. Although he'd searched this room top to bottom, he was going to do it one last time, scouring every nook and cranny, tearing up the damned floorboards if he needed to. Time was running out.

And you're scared. Not just for Rebecca but because of Caitlyn. Face it, Hunt, you're interested in her and not just professionally.

Ignoring that thought, he went to work. He looked through everything. Drawers, files, bookcases, tables, even the pillows on the couch and chairs. He searched the closet and the dry planters, behind the pictures he'd taken from the walls and through all the pockets of the coats he found in the closet.

He rolled up the carpet, looked through the bathroom next door and finally, as the sun rose steadily in the east, was about to give up. If the information he sought wasn't on the computer's hard drive, then he was sunk. But something bothered him; something about the office didn't seem right. He sat down on the couch and viewed it again, remembering where the furniture had been placed when he'd first walked in, thinking of the few objects he'd removed . . . what was incongruous about the place?

Think, Hunt, think!

His gaze skimmed the desk and furniture, the decor. All recent. Made to look older, yes, but acquired in the past few years. Aside from a few books, a pair of boots, a jacket and the backpack, the items were fairly new.

But so what?

Frustrated, he sat on the corner of the couch where Caitlyn always took her seat. He thought he smelled the hint of her perfume, and his heart raced a little. Innocence and sexuality all rolled into one seductive package.

Stupid, stupid, stupid. That's what his attraction to Caitlyn was. Professional dynamite. Personal disaster. And yet when she appeared in this room, he couldn't deny the physical allure of the woman. Slim, but not bony, she carried herself with a slightly aloof air, a facade that shattered in their sessions when she, fighting to maintain control of her ragged emotions, would refuse to break down, or try and laugh off her own case of nerves. Her smile was sexy. Her movements sensual. Her worries deep. Shadows darkened her eyes, and confusion occasionally tugged at the corners of her mouth, but beneath the layers of anxiety and tragedy, he sensed there was an intelligent, sharp, deep woman that she rarely allowed out.

He was an idiot. Plain and simple. He didn't have time for a woman and certainly not a complicated one like Caitlyn Bandeaux. Already the police were nosing around, asking questions about Rebecca. It was only a matter of time, days or possibly hours, before they figured out that he was subleasing her offices and using her equipment. Then he'd have some explaining to do. Her disappearance would be a matter of record, and they would seal up the office and house. Not that their investigation would necessarily be a bad thing, just a hindrance, and he would be looked upon with suspicion. His movements would be restricted, and he really believed that he was more likely to find her than any other person on the planet.

He'd lived with her.

He knew her.

He understood her.

He knew he could find her.

But he was beginning to worry that it wouldn't be fast

enough. Too much time had slipped by. With each passing day he felt with growing certainty that she was dead.

Worse yet, he had the chilling premonition that Rebecca's disappearance was somehow tied to Caitlyn Montgomery Bandeaux.

Twenty-One

"I don't know where she is," Sugar said, blocking the cop's entrance to her home. Caesarina was standing next to her, growling a warning at the detective on her doorstep.

"But Christina Biscayne does live here."

Sugar nodded. She usually hated cops. Didn't trust them. But this one seemed a little different, with his rugged good looks and intense gaze. More interesting than the green yahoo who had interviewed her after Josh Bandeaux's death. That cop had been a kid, but this one, he was definitely a man. He had a woman with him—tight-packed body, tons of attitude and really bad hair. What was with that? The department must have loosened its dress code. "Cricket's an adult. Sometimes she doesn't come home."

"Will she be back later?"

"Who knows? I hope so."

"Doesn't she have to work?" the woman cop asked.

"Yes. But I don't know her schedule."

They seemed to want to ask more, but settled for asking Sugar to have Cricket call the police station once she turned up. Sugar lingered at the door, watching Detective Reed climb into the passenger side of the vehicle. He had a nice walk. Easy strides that were long enough to stretch his slacks over a tight butt. As he settled inside, he flipped on a pair of dark aviator glasses. He wasn't exactly handsome, not in Hollywood terms, but there was something innately sexy and male about him. Maybe a hint of danger, which, of course, she was always drawn to. The driver lit a cigarette, backed the car up, and as the dust was still settling, stepped on it and roared down the rutted lane, leaving a plume of dust and Sugar to wonder where the hell her sister was.

Where the hell was she? It was dank, dark . . . and she was lying on what felt like a dirt floor. Cricket couldn't move, couldn't lift her head, didn't know how long she'd been here. Her hands were bound behind her, her feet wrapped, her mouth covered with tape. Not that she could do anything. Ever since she'd been brought here, driven in her own car and hauled in a child's cart to this dirty, stinking hole in the ground, she'd been drugged, unable to move. She'd seen flashes of light from beneath a door and her captor, who called herself Atropos, had come and gone. Hours—maybe days—had passed. Cricket couldn't tell, but she had a bad case of the creeps here in this godforsaken cellar.

''You awake again?''

Cricket started. She hadn't heard her captor approach.

''Well, it won't be for long, now will it?''

Up yours, you bitch! Cricket thought, her mind disjointed. It seemed as if she'd slept, or been knocked out, but she didn't know; she resided in a kind of netherworld that was foul smelling and dark. It had been a long while and she was thirsty and thought she might have wet her pants . . . her bladder had been full and now wasn't.

If she had the chance she'd kill the bitch, but so far she hadn't had the opportunity or the strength. Any time her mind had cleared and she'd thought about trying to lash out at her attacker, she'd suddenly been overcome with drowsiness. She was being drugged, no doubt about it. But if she ever got a clear head . . . the bitch was dead. Dead!

"Here we go. I thought you might be lonely." Atropos squatted near Cricket's head and flipped on a flashlight, the narrow beam showing off old rotten wood and bits of broken glass. There were bottles as well and what looked to be rat poison on a shelf. Oh, no . . .

Atropos placed an old glass milk jug on the floor. It seemed to be moving, breathing inside, growing.

Cricket began to sweat. Couldn't take her eyes off the milk bottle. Her heart was pounding, adrenalin laced by fear, kicking through her bloodstream.

"Watch this." Atropos trained the flashlight's beam directly on the jar. Inside were nests of spiders, cottony-looking drifts and lacy webs, crawling with hatchlings, tiny spiders moving everywhere, elder arachnids as well, their many eyes ever watchful, some with front legs upraised, ready to eat each other's young. "I've been incubating them for weeks," she explained.

Cricket began to shake.

Atropos retrieved a smaller vial from a pocket in her jacket and placed it in the light. Within, atop a cotton ball, were insects . . . no, not just insects. Crickets. Three or four of the dark bugs.

Oh, for the love of God! Cricket's guts turned to water.

Carefully, Atropos unscrewed the lid and then, using a pair of tweezers, pulled one of the tiny pests from the jar. It struggled against the tight forceps, but it was no use. Adeptly Atropos retightened the lid, opened the milk jar, held the cricket over it for a heart-stopping second, then opened the tweezers and let the cricket fall.

Horrified, her gaze glued to the milk jar, Cricket watched the cricket land in the cobwebby pit, where it was stuck on a web.

It struggled but a second.

The spiders pounced.

With new terror, Cricket watched the spiders fight over

the struggling insect, a large brown arachnid becoming the victor and piercing the cricket's tiny body with deadly fangs.

Cricket recoiled in terror. Her heart was pounding. She wanted to throw up, but she was gagged in this macabre place with its broken bottles, dark corners and sick, sick inhabitant.

"Mmmm. Not a pretty sight," Atropos said as she tied a braided cord—red and black strands—around the neck of the milk jar, then rescrewed the lid. "Oh, well, show's over. Now remember, 'sleep tight and don't let the bed bugs bite.' "

Atropos flipped off the flashlight and walked up stairs that creaked and moaned.

Cricket was plunged into darkness once again.

With the jar of spiders only inches from her nose. She didn't have to be a brain surgeon to guess what fate Atropos had decided for her. Tears filled her eyes; terror stole through her heart.

And, in the darkness nearby, the spiders waited.

Did you do it?

Did you try to murder Amanda?

The horrid voice in her head, sounding so much like Kelly's, was at it again, pushing Caitlyn as she drove through the city streets. Distracting her so that she nearly ran a stoplight. She bit her lip, turned up the radio and switched on the headlights. It didn't help. The damning voice couldn't be sidetracked.

What about Josh? Did you kill him . . . it's just so damned convenient that you can't remember.

You dream about seeing Josh dead and slumped over his desk. So what about Amanda? Don't you remember being in her garage? Running your fingers over the smooth finish of her little red sports car? Fingering the tiniest tear in the rag top?

Then there's Berneda's attack. The doctors are saying that she didn't get her medication, that there was no trace

*of nitroglycerine in her body, though Lucille swears Berneda
took her pill after the angina attack. You were there the
other day. You helped say good night to her. You saw the
bottle of nitroglycerine pills on the bedside table. You even
touched the bottle when you reached for a tissue ... did
you do something else? Something you've tucked into one
of those holes in your Swiss cheese of a brain? What kind
of person would try to kill her own mother?*

Heart in her throat, recriminations echoing through her
mind, Caitlyn pulled into the small lot off the back alley.
She looked up at the elegant old Victorian house that was
now cut into private offices. From the car she found the
windows of Adam Hunt's office, the very rooms that Rebecca Wade had used. The third floor, near the roof line, with
only the dormers of the attic above. It was near evening.
She'd been at the hospital most of the day, but Adam had
agreed to meet her after the scene at Oak Hill, and the
shadows of the buildings and surrounding trees were lengthening, promising dusk and twilight.

Could Adam not be trusted? Could he have some kind of
ulterior motive in seeking her out?

The scene at the plantation home with her mother, Lucille,
Ian and her siblings, then Berneda being rushed to the hospital, had been more than she'd been able to handle. All the
melodrama. All the secrets. All the damned innuendoes.
No wonder the family was cursed with mental problems;
everyone seemed to feed on them.

And it was time to put a stop to it. At least for her.

She had to get better. To end the demons in her mind.
Adam Hunt was a psychologist; what transpired between
them was private, and she had to trust somebody. Not the
police. Not her own family. Not her own mind. Not even
Kelly.

So you're going to spill your guts to a total stranger?

Caitlyn could almost hear Kelly mocking her.

You are *nuts. Bona fide and certifiable. Just like Nana!*

"Stop it!" Caitlyn screamed, pounding a fist on the steering wheel. The horn blared and she jumped. Shocked herself

out of the rage that consumed her. She couldn't put up with this another second. Couldn't stand listening to the doubts in her mind. Wouldn't be a victim any longer. For years she'd been a prisoner of her own mind, but no more.

Either Adam Hunt was salvation or he was destruction, but he was damned well *some*thing, her only hope.

She had to push forward, to find a way out of the trap that was her mind. Whether it turned out to be the biggest mistake of her life or her deliverance, she was going to go through with it. She swung out of the car. Before she could second-guess herself, she strode up a short path and up the back flight of stairs to Adam's office.

The door was ajar.

She tapped lightly on the old painted panels; the door creaked open to a darkened, empty room. Caitlyn felt a chill. As if it were a warning reminding her that she shouldn't be here, shouldn't step across the threshold. Which was silly. She was just a few minutes early. And she had to change the course of her life. Today. Before she lost what fragile hold she had on her own sanity.

You'd better take a seat outside, in one of the chairs clustered around the corner at the landing, where all the patients who visit this floor wait until they're invited in. It was a cozy spot. Magazines littered the small table, and water was available from a cooler. She knew Adam would expect to find her there.

But tonight, after hurrying up the back staircase, Caitlyn saw no reason for that kind of protocol. Tonight she was a new person. Bold rather than timid. Forthright rather than shy. She stepped into the darkened office and noted the empty coffee cups on a small table and the crumpled tissues in the wastebasket tucked discreetly behind one arm of the couch. Were they hers from her last visit, or did Adam have more clients, other people he was trying to help?

She heard a creak and turned to the open door, but no one arrived.

Ghosts, she thought, remembering how Lucille had told her that if she listened very hard and concentrated, wasn't distracted by outside noise or even the sound of her own heartbeat, she could hear them.

No one arrived. She ran a finger along the edge of Adam's desk and wondered what he thought of her, what notes he'd jotted about her and her family. Did he think she was truly going out of her mind? His legal pads were stacked in a corner of the desk. All she had to do was lift one up and start reading. What was the harm in that? As long as she only looked at her file, what kind of trouble could she get into? After all, it was *her* life and she was paying him to help her.

Biting her lip, she picked up the first tablet, but dropped it as if it burned her fingers when she heard footsteps on the stairs. Quickly, making as little noise as possible, she flew to the couch and had just sat down when Adam walked in and flipped on a light switch. He visibly started, his body flinching as he saw her in the corner of his couch.

"Caitlyn?" Glancing at his watch, he said, "I didn't realize I was late."

"You aren't. I got here early and the door was open, so I decided to park it." She smiled and hoped she didn't look as guilty as she felt. All her doubts seeped away as she saw the ghost of a smile touch his lips. He seemed so genuine. So caring. "I hope that was all right."

"Of course it is." But his voice didn't sound as warm as it usually did. "I just ran out to get some more coffee." He held up a small brown bag, then opened it and pulled out a jar of coffee crystals and non-dairy creamer. He carried the soup heater into the bathroom and filled it with water, then plugged it in. As the water heated, he took his chair and reached for his notepad. The one on the top of the stack.

"You want to tell me about what happened to your sister and your mother? You sounded pretty shook up when you called."

"I was. Am," she admitted, refusing to back down, to listen to the warnings in her mind. Tonight. She was going to start reliving her life. Right now. This very moment. Her fists clenched so hard she felt her nails bite into her palms.

Slowly uncurling her fingers, she started with her sister's accident and its aftermath. She explained the family dynamics, about Ian's anger, Berneda's frailty and Hannah's bad attitude. She mentioned that Lucille had been bristly and that the whole family treated Caitlyn with a hands-off attitude.

"It's as if they not only think I'm addled or feeble-minded," she said, standing to walk to the window and watch night descend over the city, "but they treat me as if I'm some kind of scary creature and they're afraid that if someone says or does the wrong thing, I might completely flip out and end up in the mental hospital again."

"Are you afraid of that?"

"Yes!" She turned to stare straight at him. "Yes! Yes! Yes! I've been in one and let me tell you, it's no picnic. The people in there . . ." She lifted her hands toward the ceiling, as if in supplication from heaven. "My God, for as long as I can remember I've heard people whispering about me, about how I'm some kind of freak. Some people think I killed Charles, even members of my family, because I pulled the damned arrow from his chest and they think . . . Oh, I don't know what they think. Just that I'm crazy, I guess." She flopped back onto the couch. "Looney Tunes is the favorite phrase. I guess that's not quite as harsh as insane, and please, don't ask me if I'm insane, okay? Because I don't really know." Tossing her hair out of her eyes, she fought the urge to crumble completely. "You should have seen them at the house. All of them. Mom included. It was just plain weird."

"Well, let's try to keep you out of the hospital, okay?" He offered her a smile that somehow cut through all of the shadows in her mind.

"I'm all for it."

His gaze held hers, maybe a second longer than necessary, and she experienced that little jolt of excitement, the sizzle in her nerve endings, whenever she met a man she found interesting.

"You said something about your mother being in the

hospital,'' he prodded. His voice seemed a bit rougher than it had been.

"Because of all the anxiety over Amanda's claims that someone was trying to kill her, I think, she had an angina attack as she climbed the stairs for bed. It was touch and go for a while, but she's stabilized.''

"I'm glad to hear it.''

"Me, too,'' she admitted, then pulled herself together. It was now or never.

"Adam,'' she said and her voice sounded unnatural, even to her own ears.

His eyes found hers again, his pupils darker with the shadows in the room.

"There's something you should know. I don't think I'm crazy—I mean, I pray that I'm not, but . . .'' How could she explain what she herself didn't understand? Her palms were suddenly damp, her heart racing. Slowly, she forced an unnatural calm to settle over her.

"What is it?'' Any hint of a smile had left his lips. His expression was wary, his muscles tense. As if he knew what she was about to say.

Still, she plunged on. "Strange things have been happening. Not just to the family, but to me specifically.'' Her chest was so tight she had to force the horrid words out. "Aside from the bad dreams, I have flashes of memory or a sense of *déjà vu* about certain events, things tied to some of the 'accidents' that have occurred. I remember flashes, little glimmers that don't make a whole lot of sense. Like touching my sister's car, the one she nearly died in, or seeing my mother's medication in her room.'' She swallowed hard and felt the quivering inside, the feeling that she was about to step into a dark void, like opening the locked doorway to the forbidden cellar stairs and taking the chance that the door would slam behind her and she'd hear the turning of a key, that she'd be trapped forever in the terrifying void.

Closing her eyes, she plunged on. "The morning after Josh was killed, I woke up and . . . and there was blood all over my bedroom. I mean, all over.'' She began to shake as she pushed up the sleeves of her sweater. "In the bed, on the curtains, pooled on the floor, in the bathroom . . . oh, God, it was all over. On the walls and carpet, smeared on the sink and tiles. The glass shower door was cracked . . . but I don't remember pushing my arm through it. And there was blood on the curtains, oh, dear God . . ." Her voice had risen an octave, and she had trouble forcing the words out.

Opening her eyes, she saw that Adam's face was a mask, but beneath his controlled expression, in the tightness at the corners of his mouth, she sensed his shock. No reason to stop now. Plunging on, Caitlyn said, "I had a nosebleed that night and I discovered . . . these." She held out her arms, palms rotated to the ceiling, displaying the ugly scabs on her wrists. "I don't remember making them. I don't recall a nosebleed, and even if I had done this . . . mutilated myself, I don't think I bled enough to make all that mess, and I'm afraid . . . oh, Jesus, I'm afraid that somehow I'm responsible for my husband's death."

Twenty-Two

"You think you killed him?" Adam asked, the skin on his face drawing tight.

"That's just it. I don't know. I don't remember. But the police are saying that my blood type was at the murder scene and then there was the blood all over my room. I kidded myself into thinking that it was all mine, but that would have been impossible." She took in a long breath, not certain if she'd made the right decision to confide in him.

"What do you remember?" His voice was gentle, not filled with accusations, no hint of judgment in his tone.

She explained everything that she could, from waiting for Kelly at the bar to drinking too much and not remembering if she'd left and gone to Josh's house, only to somehow wake up twisted in blood-stained sheets.

". . . It's been awful. Hideous. I was scared and I couldn't stand looking at the mess, so I cleaned it up as best I could, washed the linens, walls, bedclothes, sinks, carpets, anywhere I saw the blood. I just had to get rid of it." She plowed the fingers of both hands through her hair, fought a headache beginning to throb at the base of her skull. "I think I'm cracking up. I think I should go to the police, but

I'm afraid to. Detective Reed already has me pegged as his number-one suspect.''

"Do you think you're capable of murder?''

"No! Of course not." She shook her head as she pulled the sleeves of the cotton sweater lower on her arms, covering the wounds. "But I don't know what to think. I have glimmers, little fragments of thoughts, about the crime scene. In my mind's eye I see Josh dead at his desk—and there's more." She related her feelings of *déjà vu* and her bits of dreams, little pieces of memory that connected her to the accidents and tragedies within her family. "And that's not all. I feel that I'm being watched and I don't know if the police have set up a surveillance of my house or if someone sinister is stalking me or if it's just my own wild imagination." She let out a weary breath. "I feel like I'm running, but I don't know where I've been and I have no idea where I'm going. It's disconcerting. Crazy-making.''

"You're not crazy.''

"Stick around. You don't know me that well.''

"Well enough to know you're not crazy, so let's not even go there.'' He was serious as he laid down his pen. "Let's take a break. This is pretty heavy stuff. Why don't we go out for real coffee or dinner? My treat and the professional time clock will be turned off.''

She was wary. "I don't know.''

"Come on," he said, "I'm hungry. I promise we won't talk shop.'' Setting his notes on the desk, he stood. "There's a great restaurant just around the corner. Guaranteed authentic local cuisine. We'll walk.''

"But—''

"My treat. Come on." He was already walking to the door, jangling his keys.

What could it hurt? So he was her counselor. That didn't mean they couldn't get to know each other, did it? *Oh, Caitlyn, this is trouble. Big trouble.*

But then, it wasn't as if that was anything new.

Outside, he took her hand and led her through an alley and across a square to a house built two hundred years earlier.

Up the front steps to a reception area, where a waitress led them upstairs to what had once been a bedroom and covered verandah outside the glass French doors. Potted plants decorated with tiny white lights separated the tables. From their vantage point, they could observe the square and look down the tree-lined streets. A warm breeze carried with it the smell of the river, the warm scent of baked bread and a trace of cigarette smoke.

"Can I get you something from the bar?" the waitress asked after she rattled off the specials.

"Caitlyn?" he asked and she thought about the last time she'd had a drink. The night that Josh had died. The night her memory was riddled with huge holes. "Iced tea with sugar," she said.

One side of his mouth lifted, a hint of a smile touching his eyes. "I'll have scotch. Neat."

As the waitress disappeared, he glanced at the park where a few people strolled through the pools of light cast by the street lamps and the oaks grew tall and dark. Caitlyn wondered who lurked in the shadows, if anyone was watching. She opened her menu, realized she had no appetite and scanned the list of entrees without much interest.

"Do you think I should go to the police?" she asked, pretending to study the appetizer choices.

"I thought we were leaving all that talk back at the office."

She lifted a shoulder. "I'd like your opinion."

"I don't have a law degree." He snapped his menu shut and dropped it onto the table. "I think you might need a lawyer."

"I'm getting one. My sister's an attorney, remember, not criminal law, at least not anymore, but she gave me some names and I've got an appointment with one of them the day after tomorrow."

"Good."

"This is such a mess." She felt that pressure again, the one that felt like a two-ton weight on her chest, the one that didn't allow her to breathe.

Adam reached across the table. Placed one hand over the

back of hers. His eyes were dark with the night, his pupils dilated. The hand over hers was warm. Calloused. Strong. It gave her more comfort than she expected. More than she wanted. "It's time to relax," he said softly. "We'll figure it out."

"Will we?"

"Yeah." Again the hint of a smile in a jaw that was darkening with beard shadow. He was handsome, not in a bold, rugged way, but more quietly good-looking. Not the first man you would notice in a room of strangers, but one you might gravitate toward, one you would trust, one, if you looked beneath his aloof veneer, was a strong, passionate man with a few secrets he kept locked away.

"Do you have any other patients?" she asked, withdrawing her hand as the waitress, a slip of a girl with streaked blond hair and a mouth too big for her face, returned with their drinks.

"Have you decided?" she asked.

Adam motioned to Caitlyn. "What would you like?"

"Red rice with shrimp and fried okra." Caitlyn managed a smile. "My father's favorite. Real Southern cooking."

Adam chuckled. "And I'll have pork chops with corn bread and country gravy."

"Anything else?" the waitress asked.

"Wine?" Adam lifted an eyebrow in offering, but Caitlyn shook her head, couldn't take the chance. "Maybe a slab of praline pecan pie for dessert," Adam stage-whispered to the waitress as he handed the girl their menus.

"I'll see to it." She sauntered to the next table.

For the first time since Josh had been killed, Caitlyn felt safe. Could unwind a bit. Adam made a couple of corny jokes, caused her to laugh, and she managed to quit worrying, at least for a while. By the time the waitress returned with steaming platters, Caitlyn's appetite had returned and she dug into the plate of spicy rice and succulent okra.

"I think I owe you an apology," Caitlyn said when she caught him observing her.

"For?"

"Being a wet blanket. This"—she gestured to the verandah and restaurant—"was a great idea."

"I thought so."

"I think I could make it even better," she said as she sipped her iced tea.

"How so?"

"We could play doctor." She lifted her eyebrow in a naughty invitation, and when she saw him turn serious, added, "I'll be the doctor and you be the patient." He set down his fork.

"Caitlyn?"

"I'm talking about the kind of doctor you are. You know, a Ph.D. My turn to psychoanalyze you for a change."

"Oh." He grinned. "You did that on purpose."

"Gotcha!" She laughed. "I do have a sense of humor, you know, though the past week or so it's been pretty much dead."

Setting his utensils down, he cocked his head and studied her. "You're a fascinating woman, Caitlyn."

"You think?" she teased, but was flattered.

"Complex."

"Uh-uh. I'm the doctor, remember? My turn." She pointed her fork at his chest. "Turn it off for a while. You know, the trouble with psychologists is that they're always working. Every time they meet someone, it's like a new case study ready to be pounced upon."

"That's a pretty general statement."

"But true."

He lifted a shoulder and she saw the amusement in his eyes, the slight upturn of the corners of his mouth, the intelligence etched in the features of his face. "Okay, *Doctor,* what do you want to know?"

"First of all. Have you ever been married?"

The smile tightened. "Once."

"Hmm."

"It was brief. A long time ago. As I said before, no kids."

"You ever see her?"

"Rarely."

"Any steady girlfriend?"

"At the moment?" He shook his head. "No. Remember, I just got into town."

"But I thought there might be a woman waiting for you at home."

"In the Midwest? No. No woman waiting."

"I thought you might have been running from something; some deep, dark, shady past, and that's why you're here."

"Maybe I was running *to* something."

"What?"

"That remains to be seen now, doesn't it?" he teased, his smile stretching more widely now that they were out of dangerous conversational territory. "Maybe it was kismet, or fate, or the alignment of the planets."

"You think?" she asked, amused.

"Who knows, but I am here and right now I think it might have been one of the best ideas I've ever had. I mean, how great is it to be sitting outside in Savannah, eating fabulous food and spending time with a fascinating, beautiful woman?"

"One who told you she can't remember if she was involved in her husband's death," she reminded him, and some of the magic of the evening seemed to dissipate.

"Hey—for the rest of the meal, let's put that aside."

"It's not as easy as that."

"Try." He motioned to the waitress and ordered the pie with ice cream and two forks. "Just a few more minutes."

"Okay." And she did her best. Laughing, joking, letting him feed her a bit of the sweet confection, looking into the dark square across the street and trying not to imagine hidden eyes staring at her from inky hiding spots. She was safe with Adam. She trusted him, and when he paid the bill and refused to let her help, she didn't fight him. Together they walked to his office, and when he took her hand as they cut through a back alley she didn't fight him. They reached her car, and she felt a little disappointed that the evening was over.

"Maybe you should come by tomorrow," he suggested.

"We can discuss anything you want. And you have my home number, right?"

"On your card in my purse."

"Good. You can call me any time." They were standing beneath a security lamp for the small parking area. He squeezed her fingers. "Any time."

"You might regret those words."

"I don't think so." His teeth flashed white against his dark skin. His eyes found hers, and her breath stopped short in her lungs. He was going to kiss her. She was certain of it. A tingle of excitement swept up her spine, and he leaned down and brushed his lips against her forehead. "Take care." He opened the car door for her.

"You, too." Ignoring the open door, she stood on her tiptoes and put her face next to his. "Thanks for a lovely evening." She pressed a quick kiss to his lips and then slid into her Lexus. While he was still standing there, looking stunned, she slammed the door shut, jabbed her key into the ignition and put the car in gear. She backed up, waved, then nosed into the alley. She was grinning at her reflection in the rearview mirror when she glanced back and saw him standing just where she'd left him under the street lamp. Kissing him had been a bold move. Unlike her. But, then, she was doing a lot of things that weren't like her these days.

And she loved it.

Berneda opened a bleary eye. For a moment she was confused by the quiet surroundings. The only light was from a few backlit fixtures in the outer hallway. Then, slowly, she remembered that she was in a hospital, sleeping on an uncomfortable bed, tubes running in and out of her body. Her mind was sluggish, her thoughts not running in any particular order, except that she wanted to go home. To the big plantation home that spoke of more genteel times, to her own room, her own bed.

She wanted Lucille to wait on her. Lucille was patient

and kind, unlike some of the snippy young things that poked and prodded her all in the name of health care.

What was she doing here in this private room? Another spell? Yes . . . that was it. Or was it? Her brain was moving at far less than light speed. She reached for a tissue on the stand but couldn't make her hand obey her mind. She realized that her vision was distorted, that the shiny fixtures in the room were out of proportion, stretched to impossible shapes. She licked her lips, and her tongue was thick. Whatever they'd given her was powerful.

She needed more sleep. That was it. She started to close her eyes when she noticed a movement near the door. Without a sound, a figure appeared as if on cat's silent paws. A woman. Maybe another nurse. More torture. Berneda half expected some pert young thing to try and take her temperature or blood pressure, but as the silhouette of the woman loomed closer, her face in shadows, Berneda sensed something was wrong. Squinting against her blurred, distorted vision, she started to say something, but as swiftly as a cottonmouth striking, the woman pulled something from behind her back. A pillow. Berneda opened her mouth just as it was covered. She tried to scream, but only managed to flail like a marionette. The woman was strong, surprisingly so, and Berneda was weak and drugged.

Help me, she silently screamed as her lungs burned, feeling as if they would burst. Pain screamed through her body and the angina kicked in, the heavy oppressive weight on her heart reminding her of her condition. She tried to gasp for air and felt the cotton cover of the pillow pushed down her throat. No! This couldn't be happening! Who was trying to kill her?

The edge of the pillow partially covered her eyes and her eyesight was already warped, but as her attacker pressed harder on her chest, shoving the horrid pillow over her nose, as her lungs turned to fire, Berneda caught a death's-eye vision of her murderess. A familiar if distorted face.

"I am Atropos," the killer whispered harshly against Berneda's ear. "And you have met your fate."

Twenty-Three

He woke up covered in sweat. His cock was rock-hard, his skin drenched, his breathing erratic. Adam threw off the covers and walked into the bathroom, where he found a washcloth and wiped it over his face. He'd been dreaming, and in the dream he'd been with Caitlyn, kissing her, touching her, nearly making love to her. He'd wanted her as badly as he'd ever wanted a woman.

But it was only a dream.

The vision of her lying on a chaise longue on the deck of a sleek cabin cruiser had been nothing more than a figment of his imagination. She'd been naked aside from a pair of sunglasses. Her skin had been gleaming in the hot tropical sun, and she'd looked up at him with a sly, seductive smile. He'd been walking on the oiled teak planks. He, too, was naked, ready and knowing that she wanted to make love to him.

He'd reached her and knelt, kissing her belly button as she'd moaned and arched upward. Her skin had tasted salty; her flesh had been warm. He'd slid upward and run his tongue over a hard, expectant nipple.

"Ooohh," she'd moaned and he'd looked up to her face,

watched as she'd languorously removed her sunglasses and stared at him in amusement. Except that when she'd uncovered her eyes, she was no longer Caitlyn Montgomery Bandeaux, but Rebecca, and the smile that had curved her lips had turned to stone, her eyes growing glassy, her features waxen, her body as cold as marble.

Now, as he stared into the mirror, he faced what he'd feared for weeks. That Rebecca wasn't off on one of her flighty sojourns, that she hadn't even left him to find a new lover, that, in fact, there was a very real possibility that she was dead.

And the answer was tied to Caitlyn.

From all the notes Rebecca had written, he'd pieced together that Caitlyn Bandeaux was Rebecca's most fascinating client, that she was planning to do more research on her and her twin sister Kelly, but the information was spotty. Tantalizing, but incomplete. Pages and pages were missing.

Wrapping a towel over his neck, he walked into the den. It was four in the morning, but he wasn't tired. He pulled out his desk chair and turned on his computer. Caitlyn's image came to his mind as the machine whirred to life. He imagined her dark hair spread upon a pillow, her face turned up to his, her skin as soft as silk . . . oh, hell, it had been too long since he'd been with a woman. Way too long. Turning his thoughts away from the provocative image, he checked his e-mail. He was hoping for word that the hard drive he'd taken to a private company could be reconstructed, that any information that had once been stored on it might be retrieved. So far his friend at the company had not responded.

So he'd have to wait.

But he was running out of time.

Soon he'd have to come clean with Caitlyn. With the police. With himself. Because he was getting in far too deep. His involvement with Caitlyn had already gone past the bounds of professionalism; he was skating on thinner and thinner ice. Soon it would break and he'd be plunged into the black oblivion, a whirlpool of emotions dragging him under.

He found her intriguing. Extremely so.

And it wasn't just because of her circumstances.

It was because she was a damnably sexy woman; one he couldn't pigeonhole. She was shy one minute, bold the next. Her worries seemed real—or were they a part of a deeper psychosis?

I'm afraid . . . oh, Jesus . . . I'm afraid that somehow I'm responsible for my husband's death.

A murderess?

Nah.

So how did she get the slashes on her wrists?

What about all the blood she said had been in her bedroom? Real? Or hallucination?

And which was worse?

He dabbed at his forehead with the end of his towel, then walked to the kitchen and pulled a beer from his refrigerator. He could not get involved with Caitlyn Bandeaux. Could *not*. He popped the tab on his Millers and took a long pull. Who the hell did he think he was kidding? He was involved. Big time.

It was already too late.

Atropos rowed silently through the water; the boat skimmed across the current and even though she was tired, she smiled. Her car was tucked away, and with the light of the moon to guide her, she'd hurried down the path to the river. Her canoe was where she'd left it and she pushed off into the dark current. She'd always felt at home on the water and thrilled to the night; like a vampire, she thought, rowing steadily against the pull of the river. Looking up at the moon, she was reminded of her task. It had been unclear once, but now she knew her path. Sensing a storm brewing, she guided her sleek craft to the dock. Quickly she cut up the path. She was tired and exhilarated at the same time. The killings were always exhausting as well as replenishing, but she needed a little time to rest. To consider what she'd done. To reflect.

Quietly she slunk through the shadows to her private

space, then hurried down the stairs. She didn't have much time. Soon it would be dawn. She found the flashlight where she'd left it and shined it on her captive. Cricket blinked hard, and her gaze moved from the flashlight's beam to the jar of spiders. She blanched and squirmed, trying to shout through her gag. She'd have to be subdued again.

"I took care of another one," Atropos said, reaching into her pocket and withdrawing a life cord.

Cricket froze.

"Berneda. You know, the mother." Atropos sighed and shook her hair over her shoulder. She could use a cigarette . . . but not yet. Cricket was squirming away on the dirt, trying to put distance between herself and the milk jug. Pathetic. Such a brazen girl turned to jelly—all by a few little spiders. How easy it was to know their fears.

Haunted eyes looked up at Atropos. "That's right. She's dead."

The eyes rounded and there was a gasp, a muffled intake of breath. "How? Oh, she had a bad heart and then . . . well, a little trouble breathing."

Why waste her breath? The pitiful illegitimate spawn of the father would never understand. "But don't worry. You won't have to wait long." She touched the cord surrounding the neck of the milk jug. "See."

She didn't, of course. Cricket just stared up at her as if she were insane. Her! A little niggle of doubt, the fear that was always just under the surface, wormed its way up and for a heartbeat she questioned her own sanity, but then she pushed that scary idea far back in her brain, past the pain beginning to pound. She glanced down at the frightened piece of filth bound, gagged and shivering with fear. "It's almost your turn," Atropos said, just to keep Cricket in her place.

She trained her light on the bookcase and found the hidden lever. She flipped off the flashlight and heard Cricket's mewling again. It was enough to make her break the rules and kill her before her time.

Not yet. Not yet. Not yet.

Patience is a virtue.

Yeah, whoever came up with that stupid saying?

Atropos had learned early on that a person had to make her own way; she couldn't wait for it to be handed to her.

She stepped into her surgical slippers and slid into the clean white room, her sanctuary, away from nasty spiders, nastier white-trash prisoners, and into the coolness where she could regroup and find inner peace.

For a while she could bask in her accomplishments.

Until the next time.

Which, she knew, would be very, very soon.

"... oh, God, Caitlyn, she's dead. Mother is dead!" Hannah's voice quivered, and deep, heart-wrenching sobs tore from her throat as she wailed into the phone.

Caitlyn froze at her desk. She'd been working, trying not to freak out about her meeting with the lawyer scheduled for this afternoon and pushing aside all her jumbled thoughts and conflicted emotions about Adam Hunt. "Wait a minute," she said. She couldn't believe what she was hearing. Steadied herself against her desk. "Just calm down." There had to be some mistake. Had to. Maybe Hannah was tripping out again. She'd already overdosed on LSD once before; there was a chance that she was hallucinating, having a really bad trip. "Mom's in the hospital. Remember? She's getting the best care available and—"

"And she's dead! Don't you get it? Dead!"

Caitlyn couldn't believe it. Yes, her mother had been frail, but Berneda was in the hospital where she was monitored as she recovered. "This can't be true."

"It is, for God's sake! Someone probably killed her."

"Whoa. That's a pretty big leap." Caitlyn was still trying to sort fact from fiction.

"Is it, Caitlyn? You really think so? Haven't you been paying attention to what's been happening?" Hannah was frantic, her voice rising. "Look, I know she was okay, stable, that's what the doctors and nurses at the hospital said and then . . . and then . . . Troy got a call from Eastside this morning, the doctor in charge, I can't remember his name, and he claims that Mom died in her sleep. Why? How could that happen?''

Stunned, Caitlyn leaned back in her chair. "I don't know. You're sure?''

"Call the damned hospital yourself, if you don't believe me.'' Hannah was crying again, and for the first time Caitlyn started to believe her, to think that her mother had died. The pressure on her chest doubled. Berneda—dead? Was it really possible? "She . . . she was sick. Maybe she just passed away.''

"Oh, yeah, right!'' Hannah sniffed loudly. "I think some-one helped her along. Why didn't the fucking nitro pills work at home, huh? And Amanda—someone just happened to run her off the road the week after Josh was killed. No, this is being done on purpose. Someone's picking all of us off, one by one.''

A chill settled into Caitlyn's blood. Wasn't Hannah just verbalizing what she herself hadn't wanted to face? Hadn't she, alone at night, suspected that someone was systemati-cally killing off the members of her family? But who? Who would want to kill them all?

What about you, Caitlyn? You're the one who has trouble remembering. You're the one who found blood all over your room the morning after your husband was killed.

"What does the hospital say?'' Caitlyn demanded, shut-ting off the accusations running through her mind.

"I don't know. Troy's calling the doctor in charge as well as Doc Fellers, but I think they're probably scurrying around at Eastside General trying to cover their asses.''

"Are you alone?''

"Yeah—unless you count Lucille.''

"She counts. How's she handling this?''

"She's already packing her things,'' Hannah said, her voice shivering with disapproval.

"What?''

"You heard me. The first thing she did was buy herself

a one-way ticket to Florida. Said she had no reason to stick around here. No family left. Her daughter never calls or shows up even when she's supposed to, and now that Mom's gone, Lucille's going to move in with her sister.''

"Already?"

"I think she's been planning for it for a long time. She knows that Mom left her a nice little inheritance, so she's outta here. Her plane takes off tomorrow. How about that? She didn't even wait and get a cheaper fare by planning a couple of weeks in advance."

"But the funeral . . ." Caitlyn murmured, beginning to accept everything Hannah had told her. "I'd think she'd want to attend."

"Who knows? She's an odd duck. Weird, always talking about the ghosts hanging out here. I say it's high time she goes. Good riddance."

"But that leaves you alone in the house."

"Just me and the ghosts," Hannah replied, some of her old sarcasm returning. "Christ, I can't believe this." She paused and Caitlyn heard the sound of a lighter clicking.

"I can be at the house in half an hour."

"No. I'll meet you at the hospital. Troy's already on his way, and he said he'd call Amanda. I'll see you there!"

She hung up before Caitlyn had a chance to say that she'd call Kelly. Not that Hannah would care. None of them did. Ever since their mother had proclaimed Kelly dead to the family, everyone but Caitlyn had quit seeing her or even mentioning her name. It was odd, Caitlyn thought, but then estrangements always were. She dialed Kelly's cell phone, waited while it rang and left a message.

Not that Kelly would want to know.

She always acted as if she didn't have any feelings for anyone in the family.

Face it, Caitlyn, they're all a bunch of goddamned hypo-crites. Mom was mad that I blew my trust fund on the boat and hadn't bothered to insure it. She blamed me for the accident, and all of my wonderful siblings fell into line, taking sides with her, thinking that the fact that Mother acts as if I'm dead will make them richer in the end; that they'll inherit my share as well as their own. It's sick. But then, what else is new?

What, indeed, Caitlyn thought as she grabbed a sweater, made sure her wrists, which were healing day by day, were covered. Oscar caught sight of her reaching for her keys. "Not now," she apologized. "It's too hot. But when I get home, we'll take a run, how 'bout that?" The dog whined and bounced against the door. She let him out and he immediately raced to the magnolia tree, where a lizard was sunning himself on the trunk. The frightened critter scurried into the safety of the branches, and Caitlyn took the side door into the garage and climbed into her car.

She had to face her family again.

Kelly would think she was a hypocrite like the rest of them.

But Kelly could take heart, Caitlyn thought as she backed out of the garage; the family was definitely getting smaller. Hannah and Amanda were right—one by one the Montgomerys were dropping like flies.

She had to wonder who was holding the swatter.

God?

Or someone close to the family? Someone who wanted them dead.

Reed hung up the phone and hankered for a cigarette. He'd given up the habit years ago, but there were still times like these when he needed a hit of nicotine. He'd been working around the clock, busting his chops on the Bandeaux case. Hell, when the department hadn't authorized a man to watch Caitlyn Montgomery, he'd done it on the side, keeping track of her comings and goings as best he could, around his other cases.

You're obsessed; you need to get out more. Get a fuckin' life!

But he didn't. His stabs at relationships had all been mistakes, and so for a while, when he'd returned to Savannah, he'd done the bar scene, even had a couple of one-night stands, none of which was so bad aside from the fact that he hadn't much liked himself for it. The sex had been fine at the time, but like cheap whiskey, had made him feel tired, worn out and just plain old the morning after. So he'd sworn off. Didn't need the bloodshot eyes and recriminations.

How many times could he say, "I'll give you a call?" when he knew, even after too many drinks, that he was lying through his teeth, that one roll in the sack was all he wanted?

Maybe he should take up bowling.

Or golf.

Or even rock climbing. Just something.

He rubbed two days' growth of beard, downed the rest of a cold cup of coffee and decided to mosey on over to Kathy Okano's office. Hit her face-to-face with questions. She'd been the one pushing the Bandeaux investigation and now she was backing off. Like a virgin in the backseat, all ready to go until the moment of truth.

He cut through the offices and down a short hallway and was about to step into her office when he was roadblocked by her secretary, Tonya. Who looked like a card-carrying member of the World Wrestling Federation. Tons of makeup, black wild hair, sharp tongue and a sculpted, slightly bulging and, in Reed's estimation, not very feminine physique. "She took off."

"Where?"

"Had a lunch date," the secretary said.

"But I was just on the phone with her."

"That explains the mad dash out of here," Tonya said. "I'll tell her you stopped by."

"Thanks," he groused, stuffing his hands in his pockets and jangling his keys. He made his way back to his office and picked up the pace as he heard his phone. He snagged the receiver and heard Morrisette's voice, breaking up a little on her cell phone, as she swore at, he assumed, another driver. "Goddamned asshole! I should write you up!"

"For what?" Reed asked.

"Hey! You heard the news?" she asked over the roar of background noise. The police band was crackling and the sound of traffic rushing by competed for airspace. "Berneda Montgomery kicked the bucket last night."

"The mother?"

"Yeah, she's admitted to Eastside General for heart problems and within twenty-four hours, she croaks. How's that for bad luck? Hey! Watch it! That old lady cut me off! Son of a bitch!"

"You'll live. Tell me about Berneda Montgomery."

"Don't know much, but the hospital is in an uproar. It looks like Berneda didn't just die in her sleep. She struggled. There's speculation that someone slipped into her room and killed her. Either suffocation or drugs."

"Shit." He remembered Amanda Montgomery's warning that someone was trying to knock off the members of her family. It was beginning to look like she was right. "Meet me at the hospital."

"I'm already on my way."

He reached for his jacket as he saw a movement from the corner of his eye. Turning, he spied Sugar Biscayne, some of her bravado from the day before missing.

"Detective Reed? Can I talk to you a minute?"

He checked his watch, more to make a point than to note the time. "Sure. Come in." He waved her inside.

She was a pretty woman and wasn't afraid to flaunt her assets. A tight T-shirt sprinkled liberally with sequins stretched over impressive breasts and was cropped short enough to show off a nipped-in waist. Her long legs were accentuated by platform sandals and shorts that barely covered her ass.

"It's about my sister, Cricket. You wanted to talk to her and I blew you off. Well, the truth of the matter is that I haven't seen or heard from her for a couple of days. That, unfortunately, sometimes happens, but . . . with all that's been happening lately, I'm worried."

"Have you called her friends? Boyfriends?"

Sugar nodded and he noticed that her hair barely moved.

Platinum blond, it feathered around her face and down her shoulders.

"Have you filed a missing persons report?"

"No. I thought I'd talk to you first."

"I'm listening."

She sat in a side chair and crossed her long legs. "I'm not going to bore you with family history. You know that we're related to the Montgomerys and that they've been having a passel of trouble. That's why you were at the house the other day. You also know that we're suing the family for part of our grandfather's inheritance."

"He died a long while ago. Why sue now?"

"Because it's all caught up in trusts with provisions and all. Some of it was distributed, but some wasn't. It's held until all of his children and their spouses are dead."

Reed perked up his ears.

"So it's just a matter of time. Both of his legitimate children, Cameron and Alice Ann, are dead already, as is Berneda and my mother, who was . . ."

"His illegitimate daughter."

"Ugly word, illegitimate," she muttered, and her foot started to swing, bobbing up and down, the heel of her sandal slapping her foot. "Anyway, we hired an attorney, Flynn Donahue, to help us claim what we think is our rightful share of the estate."

"What does this have to do with Cricket?"

"I'm not sure, but I've been getting some threatening calls at home. At first I wrote them off. I work at a club downtown, and there's a certain amount of risk involved. Weirdos who follow you home or get your number or address. I'm pretty careful, don't give any information out, and neither does the owner of the club, but there are ways around that. If a creep really wants the information and has any brains at all, it's just a matter of bribing one of the employees or taking down my license plate information or whatever. The point is that these recent calls, they're not the usual 'I'm gonna give you what you really want, baby' type of calls. They're . . . darker somehow."

She wasn't looking at him any longer, but staring at the floor and rubbing her arms. "Evil . . . that's the right word. They feel evil. Not just some horny old bastard getting his rocks off by talking to a dancer, no . . . this is different." She lifted her face to stare at him and he saw that she was scared. Really scared. She swallowed hard. "I'm afraid . . . I'm afraid that the creep who called might have gotten to Cricket."

Twenty-Four

"Detective Reed, is it true that Berneda Montgomery was murdered while she was a patient at this hospital?"

Reed was just climbing out of his cruiser when he saw that pain-in-the-ass reporter, Nikki Gillette, barreling his way. She was wearing faded jeans, a T-shirt and running shoes, and he figured she must've camped out here at the back side of the hospital while most of her contemporaries were setting up shop near the main entrance.

"No comment."

"This is the second homicide and third attempted, if you count what happened to Amanda Montgomery's vehicle, to occur in two weeks. What does that mean to you?"

"It means two people are dead. One's not." She didn't seem to get his drift and kept up with him as he walked briskly to the back door. She had to half jog to keep up with him, but keep up she did. Well, hell, she was in good shape—make that great shape with her trim, athletic body. She was short, with the figure of a runner and a tight little ass. Add to that wild strawberry-blond hair and a dusting of freckles she didn't try to hide with makeup and you got trouble. Big-time trouble. She was looking at him through dark lenses, and her pert little mouth was knotted in frustration. But she didn't give up. Not Judge Ronald "Big Daddy" Gillette's little girl. It wasn't in her genetic makeup.

"But do we have a serial killer on the loose in Savannah?" she asked.

"No comment."

"Look, Detective—"

"No, Ms. Gillette, *you* look. I've got a job to do and I don't have time for any of this bull. Got it? When and if we have a statement, you can talk to the Public Information Officer. He'll be more than glad to fill you in. Until then, I've really gotta go." The glass doors parted and he walked inside, surprised she didn't follow. He jogged up two flights of stairs to the third floor, where another female lay in wait. It just wasn't his day.

"About time you showed up," Morrisette muttered under her breath.

One of the regular beat cops, Joe Bentley, rolled his eyes behind Morrisette's back, and Reed imagined she had just about given everyone involved a few lashes with her razor-sharp tongue. Another cop with a reddish flattop and a crooked nose sent Morrisette a dirty look. To Reed, he whispered loudly enough for everyone nearby to hear, "The wife's been lookin' for you and man, is she pissed."

"Bite me, Stevens," Morrisette shot back.

"Oh, I forgot. *You* wear the pants in the family and you're—"

"Stuff it," Reed snapped. "We don't have time for this."

"Thank you, honey," Morrisette cooed, just to add fuel to the fire, then turned serious on him. "Looks like someone couldn't wait for the Grim Reaper to come along." They walked into Berneda Montgomery's hospital room. She was lying on the bed, staring sightlessly at the ceiling, cards and flowers filled with wishes for a speedy recovery decorating the windowsill and tables. But Mrs. Montgomery wouldn't need them in her current state.

Diane Moses and her team were already present in full force, and the rooms around the one Berneda Montgomery occupied had been sealed off with crime scene tape. "We're working fast, but it's slow going. The hospital administration's already putting the pressure on for us to wrap this up. They don't like the groupies camped out with their cameras in the hall and think how much money Eastside General's losing when they're not able to charge rent for these beds. Do you know how much it costs to spend a night here? A lot. Thousands. Just to stay here. Before any medical procedure. So even though they're not saying it, Eastside's in a big rush to free up this here bed. They want this gal moved down to the morgue. Pronto."

"Won't be long now," Diane said as her team swept the room and Reed took a closer look at the victim. "Check this out." Diane showed him Berneda's wrists. "Looks like she struggled. One of her arms was strapped down, something to do with keeping the IV in, and it was ripped off. She's got marks on her wrist where she tried to pull her hand off the railing."

Reed stared at the bruises on Berneda's wrists, hated to imagine what she'd gone through at the time of her death. "Any other marks?"

"Nah, but we're scraping under her nails. Hoping she got a swing at her killer with her free hand and we end up with some skin for a DNA test."

"How'd this happen? Wasn't she on a heart monitor?"

"Yeah, but the nurse who was supposed to be watching it got called to another patient whose monitor had gone off. So my guess is our killer slipped into Room 312, unhooked the guy there, then when his machine goes off bleeping like an effin' nickel slot with a hundred-dollar payout, everyone rushes down there." She pointed to a room not thirty feet away from Berneda. "The killer slips into Berneda's room, unplugs the monitor, and offs Berneda. It wouldn't take much. She was near dead as it was."

"Her monitor didn't go off?"

"So it appears. Turned off. Someone knew what they were doin'. None of the nurses or hospital staff did it or know who did."

"Great," he grumbled. "The other guy—312—okay?"

"Barely. Doesn't remember anything. But we're already checking that room, too, and we're asking everyone on the night shift what they remember. So far no one saw anything remotely suspicious."

"Except that heart monitors were going off like car alarms in a bad part of town."

"Just one. Berneda's didn't make a sound."

"Time of death?"

"Three-fifteen to three-twenty; at least that's when the other guy's monitor started going off like crazy. By the time the staff got to the desk, it was over."

"What about before she was killed? The victim was here a while before the killer got to her. Did she ever come out of it enough to talk?"

Morrisette shook her head. "Not really. She kind of opened an eye last evening, and her speech was slurred. The nurse thought she was asking for something, but it didn't make any sense. She seemed to be saying 'Sugar' over and over again. But of course she couldn't have sugar as she was slightly diabetic."

"Slightly?"

"Not on insulin. The maid, Lucille, took care of her and then took off. According to Hannah the daughter who lived with her, the maid's on her way to live with a sister in Florida. Her job here is done now that the old lady croaked."

"She's not close to the family, I take it."

"Seems not, though she helped raise all of 'em. From what I understand, she'll get a cut of the estate. Maybe that's the cause of the current friction."

Reed didn't like it. Especially when he considered that according to Detective Montoya of the New Orleans Police Department, Lucille's daughter was missing. "Is she coming back for the funeral?"

"Who knows? I chalk it up as weird, but then everything about this case is."

He wouldn't argue that particular point. "So is the family still here?"

"Gathered in the waiting room. I thought you'd like to talk to them."

"That I do." He followed her down the hallway to the room in question. As she'd said, the Montgomery family was waiting. And none too happy about it as they slumped on uncomfortable couches, their features tortured with grief. All eyes looked his way as he opened the glass door.

"I told you," the oldest, Amanda, said as he stepped into the private area, "I told you this would happen!" She'd been standing near a potted palm and practically flew at him when he showed up. The bruise over her eye had turned a shade no amount of makeup could hide, but other than the obvious discoloration, she seemed to show no ill effects from her accident—well, aside from her current state of agitation. Reed was willing to bet the wreck didn't have much to do with that. Amanda Montgomery Drummond was just hardwired in a natural state of turmoil. "Look what happened!" she insisted. "Mother's dead. My God, are you guys ever going to catch this creep?"

"We're doing our best."

"Well, it's not good enough. Can't you see? You're running out of time. Whoever is doing this is stepping up his pace. I think we'd be better off hiring a private investigator."

"Amanda, calm down," the brother, Troy, ordered. He sat on a corner of the couch, hands clasped between his knees, his face a mask of grief. His shoulders drooped and he looked as if he hadn't slept for days.

"Don't tell me what to do. Someone killed our mother. And I think a PI would be a good idea. Obviously there's a maniac loose and he's picking us off one by one. For some reason he's got this thing for the Montgomerys. None of us are safe."

The youngest one, Hannah, was sniffing loudly and wiping at red-rimmed eyes with a tissue. Huddled in a corner near Caitlyn, she eyed Reed as if he were the enemy. Caitlyn visibly tensed at the sight of Reed. Dry-eyed, she stiffened as he approached. "I'll need to take statements from all of you."

"Oh, great. Because you think one of *us* did this?" Amanda checked her watch. "I do have a job, you know, and there are people who need to be contacted and a funeral to be arranged . . ." Her throat caught at that and some of her tough-as-nails exterior crumbled a little. "I wish Ian was home."

"Just bear with us. I know it isn't easy, but we are trying to figure out what's going on," he said, trying to keep the frustration from his tone. These people weren't the only ones feeling the pressure. He wanted to put an end to this immediately. "Let's start with you," he said to Caitlyn. He reached for his pocket recorder, and Morrisette opened up her notepad. They'd take the statements, one at a time, add them to those already extracted from the hospital workers and try to narrow the field.

"Where were you last night around three?"

I feel badly about Mother, in a way, but I'm not coming to the funeral, so please, don't try to talk me into it. I would have called but knew I'd get a guilt trip about why I should show up.

Kelly's curt e-mail message was waiting for Caitlyn when she got back from the hospital. It had been grueling, talking to the police when they were treating her like a suspect, then battling late-afternoon traffic that had been stalled for an accident. She'd had the sunroof open and the air-conditioning on and still baked, only to arrive home to this. Great. So much for mending fences. Didn't Kelly get it? Mother was dead. As in forever. Everything else seemed small in comparison. Gone. Forever. Caitlyn's heart twisted, and she blinked back tears. She'd made it through the damned interview with Reed, hadn't broken down, had maintained her cool, but now driving home, she was beginning to fall apart again. She had never been her mother's favorite child, but there had been times, happy childhood times, that couldn't be forgotten.

She needed to get out. To do something. To find a way

to keep the grief at bay. Though she'd never been as close to her mother as some daughters were, she still felt a loss, a tremendous hole in her life. She'd go for a run. If she could manage to dodge the media. Shuddering, she remembered how they'd gathered at the hospital. Bloodsuckers. First the police and then the reporters. It had been an onslaught. Sometimes she thought she should come clean with Detective Reed about the night Josh was killed, tell him about waking up in her room and finding all the blood. Just let the damned chips fall where they may.

Are you crazy? She could almost hear her twin's reaction to that idea.

And the truth was, she didn't know. Every day she seemed to slip a little deeper into the dark abyss. "Get over it, Caitlyn. Pull yourself together." Until tomorrow. Then she'd meet with Marvin Wilder, the attorney Amanda had set her up with. He'd advise her on what her best course of action should be. She sat in her desk chair and clicked off the computer. "I didn't do it—I didn't kill Josh," she said aloud, but her confidence was crumbling fast and she couldn't help but wonder, was it possible? Could she have killed her husband, attempted to kill her sister and then when that didn't work, murdered her own mother? Her hands were shaking, her breathing shallow and rapid. She gripped the side of the desk. *Help me,* she silently prayed, *please help me.*

God helps those who help themselves.

Where the hell did that come from? Some old sermon she'd heard as a kid? Or had it been her father's advice coming to the surface after all these years, after his wife's murder? She closed her eyes for a second. She wouldn't fall apart. Not now. Not ever again.

What you could use is a positively wicked martini.

This time it was Kelly's advice she heard.

"Not just a plain martini?" she said aloud and, of course, there was no response. If Kelly had been there, she would have grinned impishly, her eyes lighting as she replied:

No, Caitie-Did . . . it definitely has to be wicked.

"Of course it does," she said to the empty room. "Is there any other kind?" The suggestion sounded so full of possibilities that she clicked on the computer and answered Kelly's e-mail by asking her over for a drink. Maybe she could talk her into going to the funeral. Stranger things had happened.

Yeah, all the time, and always to you!

She almost crumbled into a million pieces again as she thought of Jamie, Josh and her mother . . . no, she couldn't let herself be destroyed. She had to pull herself together. Quickly, she composed the e-mail and sent it off to cyberspace before changing into running clothes. There were still a couple of hours before dark and she needed to work out a lot of things. Get her mind straight. Not be confused. Things had changed forever. She was in a new phase. Life without her mother. Her heart ached painfully at the thought, for although she and Berneda had never seen eye to eye, she'd loved the older woman, cared for her even though years before, Berneda had refused to believe her when Caitlyn, haltingly and embarrassed, had told her about the things that had happened to her . . . how Charles had come to her room late at night, how Nana had touched her. . . .

"Oh, God," she whispered, as a flash of memory tore through her brain. Her throat tightened and she bit her lip. Shadows, dark and murky, flitted through her mind, but they were impossible to catch hold of, sifting through her mind as quickly as cold sand through her fingers. Charles. He'd come to her room, she remembered that, but not much of what happened once he'd slipped through the doorway and crept silently to her bed. "No. Don't . . ." Caitlyn's throat tightened. Her voice sounded weird, distant, as if it hadn't come from inside her. Her lungs barely moved and she couldn't so much as draw a breath. She leaned hard against the door to her room.

Call Adam. Let him help you.

She wanted to. Oh, God, she wanted to, but she couldn't lean on him at every turn, not until she sorted some things out for herself. Later . . . then she'd call.

And why would you do that, Caitie-Did? You kissed him last time and you liked it, didn't you? You're hoping for more. You want to kiss him, hard. See if he'll respond. Feel his touch.

No. This would be a professional appointment, she told herself as she forced herself down the stairs.

Oh, sure. Then why is your heart pumping in anticipation? Hmmm?

She could almost hear her twin's accusations as she snapped on Oscar's leash and took off jogging south, tried to run from the accusations burning through her mind. She stayed on the sidewalk, avoiding pedestrians, strollers, dogs and bicyclists. It was late afternoon, the sunlight losing ground to thick purple clouds that were rolling inland, chasing after her, just as her painful thoughts ran through her mind.

"Hey! Watch out!"

Caitlyn nearly stepped in front of a rickshaw pulled by a bicycle, but pulled back onto the curb just in time, jogging in place until there was a break in the traffic. A kaleidoscope of images spun ahead of her, graphic mental pictures of Josh at his desk, her mother lying dead in the hospital bed, Jamie gasping in her arms, the arrow in Charles's chest, bedsprings bouncing in tempo to Copper Biscayne's moans . . . Faster and faster she ran, trying to outrun the painful pictures, Oscar panting as he raced to keep pace with her. She didn't know where she was going, didn't care. Faster. Her blood thundered through her veins. Her lungs burned. Her calves ached. Still she ran, her feet slapping the pavement. But no matter how fast she ran, she couldn't outrun the images; they caught up with her. She remembered kissing Adam, vamping with him and desperately wanting to rely on him; she recalled in vivid, nightmarish hues her bedroom on the morning after Josh had been killed and she'd woken up to all the blood.

A horn blasted and she realized she'd lost track of traffic.

"Hey, watch where you're going!" the driver yelled from his pickup. "Next time you might not be so lucky!"

She jerked out of the way, pulling on Oscar's leash, nearly stumbling against the curb. Her lungs were on fire and she doubled over, gasping, her hands on her knees as she dragged in long drafts of air. "I'm sorry," she apologized to the dog and, finding a couple of crumpled bills in her pocket, tied him to a parking meter and went into a corner quick mart, where she bought a bottle of water.

What're you running from, Caitie-Did? Is it what happened to you or is it that you can't face who you really are, what you've done?

"No," she whispered. Outside again, she opened the bottle, took a long swallow and knelt near her pet. "Here ya go," she said, helping him drink by holding some of the water in her cupped hand. "It's not every mutt who gets—let's see"—she checked the label—"oh, the finest natural spring water from the mountains of France." She laughed and Oscar wagged his tail. "Come on, let's hike on back. No running," she said as a breath of wind tickled the back of her neck, chilling the beads of sweat.

She looked over her shoulder, expecting to see someone. There were other pedestrians bustling along the sidewalk, two old men in hats eyeing the sky warily as they talked, a group of people with shopping bags waiting for a bus and a woman jogging while pushing a stroller, but no sinister pair of eyes looking at her. Taking note of her surroundings, she realized she'd run much farther than she'd intended, angling through the streets without much thought. She knew where she was, but it was a long way back. "I think we'd better get going," she said to the dog and headed toward the house. By the time she got there, maybe Kelly would have called or e-mailed back.

"Come on," she said to Oscar and noticed how dark the sky had become. The temperature hadn't dropped, but the air had become more dense. Traffic had picked up as commuters drove out of the city and more pedestrians filled the streets. She sensed she was being followed, but told herself that she was just being paranoid. Again. It seemed to be her new way of life . . . well, not new, but certainly more permanent.

Ever since Josh's death she'd had the skin-prickling sensation that she was being watched. Maybe even stalked.

A surreptitious glance over her shoulder and she saw no one other than bustling pedestrians heading home. No one following her. The first drops of rain fell, splashing on the pavement and sliding down her neck. The wind picked up, shimmering through the branches overhead, and pedestrians ducked inside or sprung umbrellas.

Which she didn't have.

What she did have was nearly a mile to go. Before she got drenched. Oscar was trotting along beside her and despite her promise to him, she picked up the pace. Started jogging. The little dog was right on her heels. Faster she ran, though her legs burned. Through puddles, around curbs, the rubber soles of her running shoes slapping the pavement. She concentrated on her breathing as she ducked through alleys and under trees. As she ran by a storefront window, she thought she saw Kelly inside, but she broke stride and blinked and Kelly was gone . . . had evaporated . . . it was just her imagination. She ran on, ignoring her thundering heart and lungs that felt as if they were aflame. Sweat mingled with rainwater and ran down her face.

Through the back alleys she raced until she spied her house. Finally. She felt as if she might collapse as she rounded the corner, pushed open the gate and flew up the stairs. Picking up her wet dog, she walked inside. She found a towel in the continental bath downstairs and dried Oscar with it before giving him fresh water; then she looked in her liquor cabinet and found the makings for martinis and left them on the counter.

Dashing up the stairs, she began peeling off her clothes and headed for the shower with its still-shattered glass. She'd managed to place tape over the hole in the glass and along the cracks, but it wouldn't last forever even though she was careful not to let the force of the spray hit it. Gratefully she stepped under the hot spray, letting the water run down her face and back. Closing her eyes, she let the hot water pulse into her muscles and refused to think how eerie it was to shower here, to sleep in her bedroom, to live in this house that had been so violated. Without the aid of sleeping pills, she doubted she would be able to rest knowing that something very, very wrong had happened here, something that she was a part of.

Somehow, some way, she had to figure out what happened. She couldn't rely on others. Not the police. Not Kelly. Not Adam. No . . . she had to figure it out for herself. She had to unlock her memory . . . maybe hypnosis . . . Rebecca had once used hypnosis on her, and though Caitlyn hadn't remembered what had transpired when she was under, Dr. Wade had assured her that it had been very good progress.

"I think you'll be pleased," Rebecca had said with a smile as Caitlyn had climbed step by step out from her hypnotic state.

"Will I?"

"Yes."

"What happened?"

Rebecca had looked at her watch. "Let's just say it's a breakthrough. I'm not sure what it all means yet. Let me do some research, but rest assured, I think you're going to feel much better."

There had been several more sessions of hypnosis, more evasive answers, and had Caitlyn not felt so refreshed, so much better about herself, she might have been angrier about the doctor's reticence.

"Sounds like hogwash to me," Kelly had told her when Caitlyn confided in her sister. "What reputable shrink hypnotizes someone and then doesn't divulge what happens while she's out? For all you know she could have you hopping around like a chicken with your head cut off."

"It's not like that."

"How do you know?"

"I know, okay? If I was doing something really weird, I'd feel it. As it is, I just feel refreshed."

"For the record, I think it's mumbo jumbo. Freaky stuff, Caitie-Did. Freaky stuff."

Had it been? Now, as Caitlyn picked up a bottle of shampoo, she wondered. And why had Dr. Wade left so suddenly without a word? Yes, she'd said she was leaving for a while to organize her notes on the book she was writing, and she'd promised Caitlyn she'd return and when she did they would resume their sessions, but she needed to do some research.

But Dr. Wade had left early. Suddenly.

Or so Caitlyn had assumed.

Now she was getting a bad feeling about it. Real bad.

What if something had happened to the psychologist? But that was foolish. Adam had said he was in touch with her. All she had to do was demand Rebecca Wade's phone number. That was it and then . . . and then . . . whether she wanted to face it or not, she had to go to the police.

The police? Are you nuts? For crying out loud, Caitie-Did, they'll lock you away! Don't do anything crazy! Wait. Just wait one more day. For God's sake, just chill.

But no matter how she tried to slow her racing heart, she couldn't. She went through the motions of shampooing her hair and lathering her body, but her mind was racing as quickly as her heartbeat, spinning round and round. She felt the urge to pass out. She had to support herself against the wall as she stepped out of the shower and reached for a towel. Her knees felt like rubber.

The phone shrilled.

She shouldn't answer it; it was probably the reporters again.

But it could be Kelly.

Or Adam.

She squeezed the excess water from her hair.

The phone jangled again.

Dripping, wrapping the towel around her middle, she forced her legs to support her as she ran across the bedroom and scooped up the phone. "Hello?" she said breathlessly, her heart still hammering as she tried to keep her towel from falling onto the carpet.

"Mommy?" a child's voice called. It was soft. Muted . . . as if coming from a long distance.

Caitlyn nearly collapsed. "Jamie?" she whispered. Her

heart jackhammered in her chest as she slowly lowered herself onto the mattress and tried to think.

"Mommy? Where are you?" So faint. So blurry.

"Jamie!" No, that wasn't possible. Jamie was dead. *Dead!* Snatched away when she was barely three. Her jaw started to chatter. "Who is this?" she forced out. "Why are you doing this to me, you bastard?"

"Mommy?" the little voice called again. Softer this time. Confused.

Caitlyn's heart wrenched. Her free hand clenched into a fist, fingers curling into her quilt. "Jamie!" It couldn't be. It couldn't. And yet. If only . . . "Honey?" she whispered, her mind spinning wildly as she lost track of time and space. "Jamie, are . . . are you there?"

Silence . . . just a hum . . . the sound of a television?

Oh, God. Caitlyn felt split in two. She swallowed against a suddenly arid throat and forced words past her chattering teeth. "Honey? Mommy's here. Mommy's right here—"

Click!

The line went dead.

"No!" she cried desperately. "Don't hang up! Jamie! Baby!" She was panicked, but she knew better. The voice on the other end couldn't have been her precious child. Her daughter was dead. Along with all the others. Tears sprang to her eyes. Her bedroom swam in her vision and she thought she might pass out. The call had been a ghastly, cruel trick made by someone who wanted to push her over the edge.

Blindly, Caitlyn struggled to hang up the phone, slapping at the bedside table. The receiver rocked in its cradle.

> *Rock-a-bye baby*
> *In the tree top*
> *When the wind blows*
> *The cradle will—*

"No!" She sat bolt upright, the towel falling away, her damp skin exposed to the air. This was all just a bad, macabre joke. Shaking, she tried to get to her feet. Couldn't. The room seemed darker, and she remembered the bloodstains that had smeared the walls that Saturday morning . . . the handprints on the door casings. The smears on the curtains. The sticky pool on the floor.

Her head pounded. Her heart raced.

When the bough breaks
The cradle will fall
Down will come baby
Cradle and all.

Tears rained from her eyes. She couldn't move as the blackness came and above it all, in the faintest of childish whispers, she heard her daughter's voice.

"Mommy? Mommy? Where are you?"

Twenty-Five

In his office, a cold, congealed cup of coffee sitting on a stack of unread policies and procedures just handed down from the brass, Reed studied his list of suspects in the Joshua Bandeaux murder. Not suicide. Murder.

The list was long enough. More than long enough. He scanned the now-familiar names. All the Montgomerys were included along with the Biscaynes, Naomi Crisman, Maude Havenbrooke Bandeaux Springer, Gil Havenbrooke, Lucille Vasquez, Flynn Donahue, Bandeaux's clients, his ex-partner, Al Fitzgerald, Morrisette's friend Millie Torme . . .

Pretty damned much half the citizens of Savannah.

But most of them did have alibis that were confirmed. He'd had people working around the clock checking and double-checking, and he'd narrowed the field considerably to close friends and, of course, the Montgomery family. Even Millie Torme had checked out, and though she'd expressed no regret at Bandeaux's untimely passing, she'd sworn she'd been spending the weekend with her feeble mother in Tallahassee. Which had checked out, unless all the senior citizens in Laurelhurst Adult Community happened to be consummate liars.

Millie had also indicated that Morrisette had never approved of her fling with Josh Bandeaux, had insisted that Morrisette hadn't had her own quickie affair with the cad. But Reed, suspicious by nature, wasn't convinced. Not with Morrisette's track record. As far as he was concerned, the jury was still out on that one.

However, he had a new little wrinkle in the Bandeaux case. Some of the suspects who had wanted The Bandit dead would have had no reason to kill Berneda Montgomery or to make an attempt on Amanda Montgomery Drummond's life, at least none that he knew of.

But the others?

Who the hell knew?

More than half had O-positive blood, and the department wasn't even certain that the secondary blood at the scene had been spilled that night. Even the maid, Estelle Pontiac, couldn't convincingly say that the few drops hadn't been in the den earlier.

The person most tightly connected to the deceased was, of course, Caitlyn Bandeaux. She had talked to or been seen with each of the victims and potential victims within forty-eight hours of their untimely demises. She had called Bandeaux on the night he was murdered. Her car, or one like it, had been spotted at the scene by the neighbor. It seemed as if she was the person who had last seen him alive. The police had gone over Bandeaux's last forty-eight hours and nothing had been out of the ordinary. He'd seemed normal, according to his secretary, whatever the hell that meant. Then there was the evidence. Caitlyn Bandeaux wore the kind of lipstick smudged on the wineglass in his dishwasher, she had a dog with hairs that probably matched those found in the den. Her damned blood type had been found mixed with that of Bandeaux. Her fingerprints had been found on the premises, though she had, once upon a time, lived there and visited often enough. Probably with that damned mutt of a dog. The yappy little thing had belonged to Josh Bandeaux once as well.

There wasn't a lot of hard evidence, no murder weapon,

no witness to a fight, no accusations, no DNA yet, but there was the divorce and wrongful death suit, and she did have a history of mental problems. He figured he had enough circumstantial evidence to arrest her and take the case to the grand jury, but he would like something more. A substantial link that would make the case airtight.

As for Berneda Montgomery's death, no one suspicious had been at the hospital. But Caitlyn Bandeaux, along with her brother and sister, had been at Oak Hill, the Montgomery mansion by the river, and any one of them could have doctored the nitroglycerine tablets.

But someone else could have done it, as well. The doctor, or an intruder, a repairman or servant.

Rubbing the back of his neck, he considered bumming a cigarette from Morrisette, but fought the urge. He'd quit once before and then, after the debacle in San Francisco, had started up again. It had only taken one drag and he was hooked, doomed to the weeks of nicotine withdrawal once more when he'd quit again, just before rejoining the force here in Savannah.

He walked into Morrisette's office and found her talking on the phone.

"... okay, okay, I'll be there. Give me twenty minutes." She hung up and rolled her eyes expressively.

"I've got to go home. Looks like Priscilla might have a case of the chicken pox. It's a big panic. The sitter's freaking out." Morrisette was picking up her purse. "I'll be back once I calm her down. Maybe I can find someone else . . . someone who's not afraid of a damned virus to watch the kids. Oh, shit . . . Oh! This is *such* a pain." She reached into her purse and scrounged in the bottom until she came up with two quarters and a ruined piece of gum. "At this rate I'll be in the poorhouse by the end of the month and the kids'll be rich, collecting fucking dividends on their stocks." Wincing at her own language, she pulled another quarter from her fringed bag and dropped all three in the pencil shelf of her desk drawer. The coins joined enough change to buy beer for the department for a week—well, maybe for one round. "Don't say anything, okay?" she asked as the quarters clinked together when she slammed the drawer shut. She tossed the stick of gum into the trash. "At least I'm trying self-improvement."

"And for once it's not another piercing."

"You know, Reed," she started, shooting him a look that had made stronger men cower, "there are other body parts that could be used for adding metal. And it's not just a female thing. For Christmas I think I'll get you an engraved dick stud and it'll either say 'This dick's a stud' or 'This stud's a dick.' Depends on my mood. That is if you don't piss me off. And what's the chance of that? Zero? And piss is *not* a swear word."

"If you say so."

"I do," she muttered irritably. "Now, did you want something or did you drop by just to yank my chain?" she asked as they headed through the reception area filled with desks and cops. Telephones jangled, pagers beeped and conversation buzzed over the hum of computers and the shuffle of feet. They walked toward an outside entrance, passing a couple of beat cops escorting a surly-looking suspect with stringy hair, dirty jeans and a don't-fuck-with-me expression tattooed over his face. His hands had been cuffed behind his back and he reeked of booze as he struggled to walk without stumbling.

In an outer hallway, Reed said, "I was on my way to visit Caitlyn Bandeaux again. I went through her phone records. On the night Bandeaux died, she called him. Eleven-eighteen. They talked for seven minutes. Wonder what that was about?"

"Could be interesting," Sylvie said.

"Thought you'd like to tag along."

"Let's get something straight. I don't 'tag along' anywhere. I'm not just around for the company."

"Prickly today, aren't we?"

"We sure as hell are. Single parenthood will do that to you."

"So I've heard."

"But it's worse when the ex sticks his nose in where it doesn't belong. Bart's coming over later," she said with a smile that looked as if she'd been sucking on lemons. "I can't fuckin' wait." Rolling her eyes, she shouldered open the outside door and started walking across the wet, steamy parking lot. "I'm gettin' out of here before I say something that costs me my next month's pay." She was already at her little truck with its V-8 engine, standing in the dripping rain when she stopped and snapped her fingers. "Oh. Rita from Missing Persons called a few minutes ago. She was contacted by the Sheriff's Department out in St. Simon's Island. They pulled a body out of the water down there. A woman. In pretty bad shape. No ID that I know of. They're checking with all the local areas where there have been reports of missing persons, and we've got a couple."

"Including Cricket Biscayne and Rebecca Wade."

Morrisette slipped her sunglasses onto the top of her head. "We should have a report by tomorrow."

"Maybe we'll finally catch a break on this one," Reed said, but he didn't believe it. Not for a second.

"Yeah, right." Sylvie yanked open the door of her little truck. She was already behind the wheel, had lit a cigarette and roared out of the lot before Reed had dashed the short distance to his car—an old El Dorado that, if he ever put some money into it, might be considered classic. As it was, with its seat covers, dents and nearly two hundred thousand miles on its second engine, it was little more than a tired old piece of crap. But it was paid for. And it still ran. His only two requirements.

He got behind the wheel and felt the old springs in the seat give. No doubt he needed another square of foam padding to shove under the seat cover, but he didn't have the time or the inclination for restoring the thing, at least not now. For the moment he intended to show up on Caitlyn Bandeaux's door unannounced and catch her off guard. He'd watched her place off and on, seen nothing out of the ordinary, followed her a bit, but he hadn't had much time and felt as if he'd done a half-assed job of it.

That would change. He'd hit up Katherine Okano in the morning, find out what the holdup on the search warrant was. He had a feeling it was more about privilege than protocol. The Montgomerys were big supporters of the police department and had lined the pockets of more than their share of judges. From old Benedict to Troy, the Montgomery men had made the right kind of political contributions, some above board, others under the table. The great irony of it all was that the more the Montgomery clan greased the wheels of justice, the slower they turned.

But all of that was about to change.

He'd make sure of it.

He turned on the ignition, and his beast of a car had the balls to cough a couple of times before finally catching. "That's better," he muttered, realizing that the scent of Morrisette's last cigarette clung to the interior. Figured. He couldn't seem to get away from that woman. He flipped on the wipers and cracked the driver's window in one motion.

It wasn't yet twilight, but the dark clouds overhead turned the usually bright city to gloom. Trees dripped, rain pelted, people dashed and cars threw up sprays of dirty water. And it was still blasted hot enough to steam the windows. With a flip of a switch, the air conditioner roared to life, defogging the glass as he backed out of his spot and nosed out of the lot.

It only took him a few minutes to drive the short distance to the Widow Bandeaux's place. A nice little nest, he thought, gazing up at the gracious old home all nicely redecorated to the period in which it had been constructed, sometime after the Civil War . . . or, as the locals insisted, The War of Northern Aggression. That would never fly in San Francisco, but here, where the city's pride rested in its rich Southern history, it was a local way of thinking—or, perhaps, to some a joke.

Caitlyn's home had been updated with all the modern conveniences, he knew. He'd been inside before. And this house in the heart of the historic district with a view of the square had cost her a pretty penny. Which wasn't a problem.

She had a lot more tucked away. He'd already checked bank statements. She made a little money at her job designing web pages, but the bulk of her income, and it looked like a lot of Josh Bandeaux's, was the result of the investments in her trust fund. But there was something odd as well . . . big monthly disbursements that didn't look like regular bills. Perhaps another kind of investment? Or something else?

Like what?

Blackmail?

Or hush money?

He pulled around the corner and parked on a side street a block away from Caitlyn's house. No reason to let his less-than-inconspicious car be noticed. Jaywalking, he cut through an alley to the back of Caitlyn's house and her garage, where he peeked through a narrow window. Though the garage was dark, he was able to make out the lines of her white Lexus.

So the lady was home.

Good.

That made his job easier. He felt a little satisfaction as he rounded the house and walked through the front gate. A squirrel, hidden in the leafy branches of a sassafras tree, had the nerve to scold him as he walked up a brick path through a small garden. "Get over it," Reed mumbled as the squirrel launched himself from one quivering branch to the next. Things only got worse when he climbed the front steps and pressed on the front bell. Caitlyn's ratty-looking dog went ape shit, barking like mad, as if Reed were some kind of burglar stupid enough to ring the bell.

He waited.

No one came.

But the smell of cigarette smoke wafted in the air—thin and high.

Again he rang the bell. He was sure she was home. The dog was running loose, lights were turned on and then there was the Lexus parked smack-dab in the middle of her garage. He wiped the rain from his face, silently cursed his luck and hankered for a cigarette. There were times when he still yearned for the calming effects of nicotine.

Still nothing.

"Son of a bitch."

He nailed the doorbell again. Leaned hard and insistent.

He was about to give up when he heard the footsteps. Quick, light footsteps, tripping down stairs. A face and body appeared in the long window next to the door. A beautiful face and great body.

Intriguing hazel eyes met his and instead of the usual fear that flitted through her gaze, he found steely, angry determination. Her chin was thrust defiantly, her mouth curved into a hard-as-nails frown. Quickly she unlocked the door but barred his way in with her body. It was hard to believe, but she actually looked intimidating, or tried to. As if she'd had some positive reinforcement training along with a couple of marital arts lessons.

"Detective," she bit out, managing a smile that didn't reach her cold eyes.

"Mrs. Bandeaux."

"What can I do for you?"

"I have a few more questions."

She didn't move. Her hair was wet and piled on her head, little makeup remaining on top of the attitude that didn't quite fit. "For me?"

"Yes."

She didn't move. "I think they'll have to wait. I don't want to answer any unless I have a lawyer present. And he's not here right now."

Smart-assed bitch. "It's just about your phone records."

She dropped the smile. "Didn't you understand me? I've been advised not to speak to you without my attorney. So I don't think we have anything to discuss tonight." With that she slammed the door in his face. Through the window he watched her disappear into the back of the house.

What the hell was that all about?

He pressed the bell and waited. The dog went crazy again. No one came.

Damn it all to hell. He felt like a fool standing on the damn porch like an unwanted suitor. "Come on, come on," he said under his breath. "I *know* you're in there." He glanced at his watch. *What the hell kind of game was she playing?*

He jabbed hard on the bell again.

And waited. Checked his watch again. Three minutes passed, then five.

"For the love of St. Mary." If only he had the damned search warrant, he'd break the door down. The dog was putting up enough of a ruckus to wake the dead in the next block. Christ, what a disaster. Another jab on the bell.

She suddenly reappeared, though as she opened the door, he noticed she'd changed her demeanor along with her clothes. She'd let her wet hair fall to her shoulders, and she looked at him as if she'd forgotten he was standing on her porch. She'd taken the time to change from jeans, sweatshirt and bad-ass attitude into a fluffy white robe cinched tight at her small waist. He caught a glimpse of cleavage, then kept his eyes on her face. "Oh, Detective," she said, seeming confused, tucking the wet strands of her hair behind her ears. She didn't bother trying to smile and looked as if she could sleep for a million years. "I'm sorry . . . I didn't hear the bell. I—I was in the shower . . . I'd been caught in the rain earlier and . . ."

"Your dog was barking his head off."

"He does that a lot. And the water was running. I was upstairs and . . ." She stopped short as if she realized she was rambling. "Was there something I could do for you?"

"I wanted to ask you questions. Remember?"

Her eyebrows drew together. "About Mother, I assume, but I already answered them at the hospital. Were there more?" With a shaking hand, she brushed a stray strand of hair from her eyes, and she looked suddenly vulnerable. Undone. As he would had expected a woman to appear if she'd just lost her mother.

"Not yet. I'm here about your husband's death."

"Oh." One hand fluttered to her throat and she clutched the lapels of her robe, closing the gap.

"Your phone records," he said, hoping to jog her memory, but she stared at him blankly and he wondered if she was stupid, confused, or acting. What better way to avoid a murder rap than to plead temporary insanity? With her history, the insanity defense was a given.

"What about my phone records?"

"They prove that you called your husband that night, talked for about seven minutes, then went to visit him."

"No. Wait a minute. They prove someone used my phone—right, my phone? Not my cell?—and then *someone* visited him after that time. Not necessarily me."

"I have an eyewitness who saw your car there."

She stared at him hard. "Did you come here to arrest me?" she asked suddenly, and he noticed that she looked pale and drawn. Sick.

"No. I just wanted to talk to you."

"I don't think that's a good idea. Until I speak with my lawyer. Or have him present. I could call him if you'd like to wait."

"That would work."

She opened the door and he followed her inside to the kitchen. "Could I get you some coffee . . . or . . ." She glanced at the counter, where a half-full bottle of gin, a smaller flask of vermouth and a jar of olives were gathered around two stemmed glasses. A drink had been poured, and, from the looks of the empty toothpick resting against the side of the glass, half consumed. "I'm expecting company," she explained and frowned at the open back door. She pulled the door shut. "If you'd like a martini . . ."

"I'll pass."

"I figured." She managed what was the ghost of a smile, then reached for the telephone with one hand and picked up a business card she'd laid on the windowsill over the sink. Growling and snorting his disgust, the dog settled in beneath the table, head resting on his paws, distrusting gaze ever vigilant, never once leaving Reed.

Caitlyn punched a series of numbers, then stood on the other side of a bank of cupboards, fingers tapping nervously on the counter as she waited. She glanced at Reed and shook her head, then said into the phone, "This is Caitlyn Bandeaux. I'm a client of Mr. Wilder's. Would you please page him and have him return my call? I'm at home." She added her phone number and hung up. Looking at Reed, she confided, "His office is closed for the day. I don't know when he'll phone. So let me answer your one question. If you're asking me about calling Josh on the night of his death, I don't remember it. I already told you everything I do recall about that night."

"Did you visit your mother at the hospital last night?"

"No, I—" She stopped. Her eyebrows knitted in confusion and color washed up her wan face. "Wait a minute. Are you asking me if I visited my mother in the hospital and then killed her? My God, that's what you're getting at, aren't you?" She threw up her hands and sighed, looked as if she was fighting tears. Of anger? Regret? "Listen, Detective, I really think you'd better go. If you're going to arrest me, just do it and charge me and get it over with, okay? Otherwise, please leave until I can get hold of my lawyer." She was firm, her skin stretched tight across her face, her small fists clenched, but beneath her show of bravado, he sensed something else, something akin to desperation. This woman was definitely at the end of her rapidly unraveling rope.

From beneath the table her little dog growled.

"Oscar, hush!"

He knew when he'd pushed it as far as it could be pushed. For the moment it was game over. "I'll be in touch," he said as he walked to the front door and swung it open.

"I don't doubt it, Detective."

Reed stepped onto the porch, but turned to face her. Across the threshold she was standing ramrod stiff, her shoulders square, her gaze level. Hard again. He had the feeling he was in the company of a great actress; one who could not only make him question his own convictions, but one who would be able to play a jury any way she liked.

"I only wish I could say I was looking forward to it." She slammed the door in his face.

Again.

But it was the last time.

It wouldn't happen again.

He'd make certain of it.

Twenty-Six

Adam's grandmother had always told him there was more than one way to skin a cat. He'd thought it an odd analogy for a woman who at any given time kept five or six strays on the back porch and even allowed them to stay in the kitchen around the stove in the cold Midwest winters. Nonetheless, with her cat-skinning example, she'd taught him to look at different ways to solve a problem.

Which he was now doing in his rented rooms, sitting at his computer, searching through the Internet for any mention of the Montgomery family of Savannah. But he'd been at it for hours, he'd finished a pot of coffee and the information on the screen was starting to blur. He was getting nowhere. Fast.

Sooner or later the police would figure out that Rebecca was missing.

And then they'd come knocking on his door instead of the other way around.

So he had to work quickly, to gather as much information as he could. Some of that important data only he could retrieve because he was Caitlyn Bandeaux's psychologist of record. He was privy to information the cops weren't.

Guilt wormed its way into his brain. He was using her. For his own purposes. No matter how altruistic they might be. On top of it all, he was falling for her. Or thought he was. This was one helluva time to play the role of the romantic. He couldn't get involved with her, not even a quick dalliance. It wasn't his style, nor, did he think, hers. She was his patient, for God's sake, and he was having trouble keeping his hands off her. Which was just plain stupid. It served no purpose and yet he couldn't seem to stop wanting.

And yet it was her face he'd seen as he'd woken up sweat-drenched, his groin aching, his cock rock-hard. Her body he'd been fantasizing about as he'd lain on his bed staring up at the ceiling. He'd wondered what it would be like to kiss her. Really kiss her and touch her intimately. In his mind's eye he'd imagined parting her lips while running his palms down her spine, his fingers curling in her firm buttocks.

It had been torture.

He hadn't dreamed of another woman in years. The last had been Rebecca, but her image was finally fading, had all but been erased by Caitlyn. What was it about her? Not just her beauty and certainly not the weak part of her. He'd never considered himself for the role of great protector; he certainly didn't see himself as some kind of white knight, ready to ride his charger to her defense so that he could take care of her. Nope. It was more than sex and had little to do with a need to defend and protect.

He closed his eyes for a second. Damn it, he just liked being with her. Too much. It would have to stop. Along with his damnable fantasies. He felt as if he was walking a tightrope high over a dark abyss that seemed to have no bottom. One misstep and he'd fall, and if he wasn't careful, he'd take Caitlyn down with him.

With difficulty, he turned his thoughts to the problem at hand, dismissing his lingering visions of Caitlyn, refusing to walk down that dangerous path. Even the slightest bit of sexual or romantic contact with her would spell disaster; potentially taint and ruin everything.

Jaw tight, he glared at the computer screen. Since he hadn't yet been able to find any of Rebecca's missing notes, he'd started surfing the Internet looking for articles on the Montgomery family. He'd read through all of Rebecca's other patient files and found nothing in them worthy of her excitement and claim that this case was sure to make her a millionaire as well as gain her national recognition.

Which he didn't care about. But he had to find out what it was about Caitlyn Bandeaux that had Rebecca dreaming fantastic dreams. Therein lay the key to her disappearance. He was certain of it.

He grabbed his keys and hurried down three flights of creaky stairs. Outside it was still overcast and gloomy, but he barely noticed. He drove to the offices of the *Savannah Sentinel,* where a bored-looking receptionist with nails polished in different colors, sleek glasses and a short-cropped, windblown head of hair asked to help him, then looked pointedly at the clock. It was after four.

When he asked to see the archives, she made a quick call, then led him to an area where all of their old editions were kept on compact disk. "The real old stuff is on microfiche," she added, pointing to a viewer and giving him a long once-over before leaving him to his devices. "But we're closing soon."

"I'll be quick," he promised and settled into the musty room with its single broken-backed office chair. He started with the most recent articles and went back in time, using important dates as a reference. He read about Caitlyn's daughter's death, about her marriage, about a merger with a smaller institution and Montgomery Bank and Trust. There was information on Hannah Montgomery's drug arrest and later acquittal, and Troy Montgomery's short-lived marriage. There were also articles about Amanda's marriage to Ian Drummond and, long ago, the death of Charles Montgomery. He printed all the articles, but the ones that held his interest, the information that caused him to sit up and take notice,

were the line inches dedicated to the boating accident involv-
ing both of the Montgomery twins. It was a series of articles,
starting with the date of the accident, complete with pictures
of both girls, identical as far as he could see, and some of
the boat wreckage.

Caitlyn's recollection of the string of events was intact.

The two girls were going out to a party to celebrate their
twenty-fifth birthday. They'd drunk and danced until after
midnight, then headed back to the mainland. On their way
home, there had been an explosion, the cause of which was
under investigation. The boat sank.

That was where the story veered sharply from Caitlyn's
account.

One hundred and eighty damned degrees.

As Adam read the article, every muscle in his body tensed.
His jaw was rock-hard, his stomach churning.

According to the front page of the *Sentinel,* some ten
years earlier, Caitlyn Montgomery, injured and knocked
unconscious, was found by a couple on a sailing boat who
witnessed the expensive cruiser being blown to smithereens.
But just Caitlyn. No Kelly. In fact, Kelly was never found.
Not that night, not the next day, not in the next week.

Adam's heart beat faster. Caitlyn had altered the truth.
Bald-faced lied to him.

As you've done to her. From the get-go.

"Mr. Hunt?" The receptionist was poking her head
through the doorway as he pressed the print key. "We're
locking up."

"I'll just be a second," he promised and she, rolling her
eyes, jangled her keys impatiently, but left him alone.

There was article after article about the search for Kelly
Montgomery. Adam printed them all as he skimmed each
page. He read where the Montgomery family had gone into
seclusion, that the police feared the worst and hoped for the
best.

After a week the search was called off, and the articles
became fewer and far between.

Until the last newspaper mention of Kelly Griffin Montgomery.

Her obituary.

Her headache was immense. Clanging. Making it impossible for Atropos to concentrate. Even her quiet place with its cool white walls and sparkling clean floor didn't help. She'd tripped over that awful white-trash girl in the other room and almost forgot to put on her surgical slippers. Almost. But before she made that mistake, she slid them on, then quickly walked to her desk and tried to think. She was Atropos, that was it . . . Atropos the inevitable.

She had Cricket held hostage for a reason. A reason. *Think!*

Remember your mission. You are one of the Three Fates, the most important.

Yes, that was it. Atropos. She cut the string of life that her sister, Klotho, the spinner, had spun for each person's life and her other sister, Lachesis, the apportioner, had measured so carefully. The sisters . . . three strong, all of one mind . . . But that mind hurt right now, it hurt like hell.

She opened the drawer. The strings of life were waiting, red and black, symbolizing blood and death, braided and wound intricately together. Fate. Destiny. Kismet.

Think! You are here for a purpose.

She found the two pictures of her latest victim, the mother . . . In the still frame, Berneda was young, a slim woman in a knee-length black dress. Her head was turned coquettishly to one side to show off her stunning profile, her red-brown hair piled on her head and pinned with a diamond tiara. Silk gloves hugged her slim arms, and a cigarette in a long-stemmed holder smoldered, sending a curl of smoke aloft. It was a posed picture, the backdrop solid white, and it was entirely unmotherly.

She who had borne seven children; she who had time and time again complained at her loss of figure, of the sacrifices she'd made for her brood. She, the once beautiful and often betrayed by a philandering husband, had lamented her loss of beauty, vitality and youth. She whose weak heart had been her downfall. She who had hated the bastards her husband and father-in-law had sired.

Poor long-suffering Berneda.

Finally she suffered no longer, Atropos thought as she pulled at the strands of the mother's life, seeing where it had been measured. Unfolding her unique instruments from their soft sack, she found her cherished surgical scissors. With a clean snip of stainless steel, she clipped off the strands of Berneda Pomeroy Montgomery's martyred life.

So how to mold the photograph to properly reflect the deed? Hmmm. It was her hourglass figure that Berneda had prized and later mourned in life, and so it would be robbed of her in death. Yes, that would do. Satisfied, Atropos went to work. With two clean snips Atropos clipped Berneda's head from her body, then sliced off her legs. Yes, yes, perfect. The pieces drifted to the desktop.

Picking up the head and legs, Atropos held them together, then carefully pinned them where they belonged on the gnarly Montgomery family tree. And there was Berneda, just a small profile of a beautiful face and glittering tiara resting upon knees and calves supported by four-inch heels. The cigarette and arms were still intact, giving Berneda a skewed though elegant, eye-catching look. The kind she'd always wanted. Atropos smiled. The newly cut-and-pasted Berneda stood on the branch next to the husband, the Betrayer. He was dressed in hunting clothes for he had always been a hunter, though women were his usual prey. His body was intact, aside from a hole at the juncture of his legs, to one side, a small jagged perforation where his testicle had once been. She scanned the others who lived on the tree as well . . . Little Parker robbed of his stupid little pacifier and crying his lungs out, Alice Ann with her head cut off and placed at an impossible angle, just as it had been when she'd hit the bottom of the stairs at the upscale institution where she'd been hidden away.

If only she had more time to look at her artwork, to sit

back and enjoy her work. But not yet. Atropos was running out of time.

Finding the picture of Amanda, the eldest, she snipped the car away from Amanda's slim body. The eldest was still alive—an act of God—and would have to be dealt with later. That thought made her smile. Yes, yes ... it all fit perfectly. For the moment, she placed the picture of the little crumpled sports car on Amanda's branch. For now it would have to do, but Amanda's life string could not yet be cut.

The sister of fate had decided.

Now it was time to choose again. She sat in the chair and began to shuffle the pictures. Quickly she flipped the old photos, and as she did she realized that some of the pictures were no longer flawless. Some had faded, others had yellowed, still others were bent and cracked from all the handling.

Too much time had passed. Too many years. She felt a new anxiety. Where once she'd been patient, she was now nervous. Edgy.

From the other room she heard her victim moving ... God, was it not her time yet?

Time. Atropos was running out of it. She needed to finish this, and yet there was so much work to do. She didn't even have the luxury of taking time to pick her victims at her leisure. Where once she could wait months or years, now she felt an impending sense of panic to get the job done. Faster ... and faster.

She flipped a photograph over and saw Caitlyn's face. Again. It seemed as if destiny was pointing in the weaker twin's direction. But was it the right, precise moment in time? Atropos had planned for Caitlyn to be the last, to accept the blame for all of her doings, but perhaps that was a miscalculation.

Now where the hell was the wimp's life cord?

Sorting through the strings in her drawer, the braided cords marked appropriately, by inches and in years, Atropos noted that Caitlyn's time was just about due. There were others as well, and as she flipped up the next pictures, she felt a cooling sense of satisfaction. Her anxiety eased.

Two more victims . . . one looking sullen, the other trying to shy away from the camera, her image in the background. *Too late. You can't hide.*

Atropos smiled peacefully even though she heard Cricket thumping and pounding, trying to free herself. The girl was terrified. Sensed what was coming. Good. Maybe it was time for a little reminder. Yes, that was it. Atropos had never before taken a hostage; her victims knew they were dying at her hand, and she'd dragged it out beautifully with Josh Bandeaux, but now the slow mental torture of the captive was a new high, a rush, one she couldn't indulge in too often for fear of being caught. But . . . while she had Cricket as her guest, she might as well enjoy it.

And she knew just how. She heard the girl kicking and attempting to scream, so maybe it was time to give her something to think about. She unwrapped her packet of surgical instruments and found the forceps. They should do. She donned a pair of gloves, then quickly left her slippers at the door and found her flashlight. Her gloved fingers curled around the flashlight's handle, and she felt the thrill of anticipation run through her body. This basement was so foul, so perfect. Cautiously, in case Cricket was able to throw her body or kick out, she walked toward her, clicking on the flashlight and training it on the girl. She looked bad. Dirty. Wan. Probably from lack of nutrition and water . . . it had been several days. Cricket showed some spunk. It was time to drug her again, but first . . . yes, first it was important for her hostage to understand.

Atropos squatted down by the jar teeming with spiders. The girl was angry and scared, shouting behind her gag, and Atropos could only imagine the words. Ugly words. Not that it mattered. Slowly Atropos unscrewed the lid of the milk bottle and checked the life cord . . . time was fast running out. Then, using her gloved hands, she slid the forceps into the bottle, gently angling them around a particularly thick webbing where tons of the tiny spider babies were crawling.

"You know, you're lucky your nickname is Cricket," Atropos said and glanced back at the girl. Her eyes were round with fear. She couldn't take her eyes off the surgical tongs as they extracted a slowly elongating silken sac that was pulsing with life. "If you'd been called Bunny, or Rosebud, or Chrissy, I would have had a lot more trouble determining your fate, but as it is . . ." She turned, waving the bit of spider web into the flashlight's beam and dangling it over Cricket's head.

The girl was sweating now, scooting back farther into the corner. "I wouldn't go there," Atropos warned. "I've seen rats and snakes in here and . . ."

Cricket was going nuts. Kicking and screaming behind her gag. Atropos would have none of it. She held the bit of fluff over the girl, then let it drop. Cricket screamed. "Now . . . let's see. We wouldn't want to separate a mother from her babies. Which one do you think it is . . . oh, here she is." She found a particularly nasty-looking creature staring at her through the glass, all of its eight eyes reflecting the light, spinnerets visible. "Oh, here we go." With the precision of a surgeon, Atropos slid her forceps inside the milk bottle again, and while Cricket wriggled and shrieked behind her gag, she gently grabbed the silken tuft on which the dark creature resided. A bit of red, in the shape of an hour-glass, showed on the glistening black abdomen. Atropos was pleased . . . She'd had to gather some of the creatures herself, others she'd found on the Internet and had shipped to a post office box, paid by an anonymous check, and this one, the black widow, with its pear-shaped egg sac, had been her favorite. "Come to Mama," she said, nudging the shy creature into her tongs. *Black Widow.* How appropriate, for surely Caitlyn Bandeaux would be blamed for not only her husband's death but all the rest.

All according to plan.

Cricket was screeching now. Scooting and shaking as if she could feel each and every little spider and mite on her.

Tears raining from her face. Slowly Atropos turned, holding the tongs over Cricket's head, watching her tremble as she closed the gap until the forceps with their wriggling prey was just inches above the panicked girl's nose, the red hourglass visible. "They're not as poisonous as most people think," Atropos said. "But, with enough bites—"

The girl squeaked pathetically.

It was time to end this.

Atropos opened the forceps.

Twenty-Seven

Rolling over, Caitlyn opened one eye and squinted at the bedside clock. Eight-thirty? Was that possible? She glanced at the French doors to the verandah, where shadows were lengthening over the flagstones, promising night. She must've dropped off after the drinks with Kelly and . . . oh, the heart-wrenching phone call from a child. Dear God, she'd thought it was Jamie. Who would play such a sadistic trick on her? Who would derive pleasure from making her think even for a fleeting moment that her daughter was still alive?

Someone who hates you.

Someone who wants you to crack up.

Someone who knows you intimately.

Unless you dreamed the whole damned thing. Maybe you imagined it.

Groaning, she reached for the handset and checked Caller ID, but there were no numbers in the memory bank. As if she'd erased them. Had she?

Think, Caitlyn, think!

She remembered coming back from the run and she remembered showering . . . and . . . and . . . and what? *What?*

"Damn it all to hell." Try as she might, she couldn't recall the last few hours. Not clearly.

She did recall that Detective Reed had shown up on her doorstep, though. Right? Yes . . . she was certain and she remembered slamming the door shut, telling him she needed to see her lawyer, but she didn't doubt he'd return. It was only a matter of time before he'd come with handcuffs. Oh, Lord, how had she gotten herself into such a mess? Everyone in her family was dying . . . one by one they left this world. Sadness stole over her when she thought of her daughter and her mother and even, a little, about Josh. He had been a bastard, but he didn't deserve to die so horribly . . . at his desk. She blinked. Remembered the tiniest bit of conversation.

"Wine, Josh?" she'd teased. "But you're allergic . . ."

"Not to this kind. Now get the hell out." He'd smiled, so sure of himself as he'd drained his glass.

What a fool.

Now her skin crawled.

What had she done that night? She'd been there, at Josh's home, in his den . . . but he'd been alive . . . So the blood . . . how had the blood gotten here?

Maybe you brought it back here, you crazy loon. You're just about nuts enough to do something like that. Didn't the bloody handprint fit your own?

Oh, God, oh, God, oh, God. Her heart thundered, and she imagined the room as it had been: the sticky sheets, dark smudges on the tile and carpet, cracked shower door.

Fingers scrabbling on the bedside table, she knocked the remote control for her television to the carpet, then snapped on the bedside light. The hairs on the back of her neck lifted as she took a quick look around just to make sure there were no half-open doors, no smeared bloodstains, nothing out of the ordinary. But all seemed quiet. Maybe too quiet.

Don't start this, Caitlyn. Don't start jumping at shadows.

The dog lying beside her stretched and yawned, displaying his black lips, pink tongue and sharp teeth. "Lazybones," she said, scratching him behind his ears as she tried to quell the rising panic clawing at her. "Both of us. We're just two lazybones." But her pulse was leaping erratically, her nerves jangled, her peace of mind stretched beyond its limit. Forcing herself from the bed, she managed to make her way to the bathroom, where she caught sight of her terrified expression. "Get hold of yourself," she growled, her fingers curling over the rim of the pedestal sink. "Don't fall apart. Don't!" Shaking, she ran cold water, leaned forward and took a drink, then splashed her face, hoping to shock herself out of the panic attack. Then she slammed her eyelids shut and dragged in several deep breaths. *Slow down, don't listen to the voices in your head . . . don't.*

Slowly opening her eyes, she glowered at her reflection. So weak. So scared. So frail. *Pull yourself together!* Determined not to succumb to the fear, she brushed her teeth and finger-combed her hair. She began to calm down, saw her reflection in a different light. A little lipstick would help. She opened the medicine cabinet and sifted through the tubes. Only three. Not the usual four. And the pink shade she liked best, the one that was sold exclusively at Maxxell's, was missing. Was she right? A little disconcerted, she sorted through the cupboard, decided it wasn't worth the stress and settled for a soft berry shade. The lipstick had to be in her purse, that was it.

Lately she was always losing things, misplacing her cell phone, her makeup, her favorite pair of shoes . . . "Comes with the territory, nutcase," she grumbled as she threw on a pair of shorts and T-shirt. The marks on her wrists had faded enough that she didn't need to be so careful, she decided, as she walked past the door to Jamie's room. It was closed . . . how odd. Caitlyn didn't remember shutting it; in fact, she rarely did, but kept it ajar so that she could look in and remember.

But then Kelly had been over, right? Or had she? She opened the door and was instantly assailed by memories of her daughter. "Mommy, Mommy, read me a story. The bunny one!" she had insisted, all smiles and ringlets and bright eyes. Caitlyn's heart wrenched and she started out the door when she glanced at the bed . . . it seemed wrong somehow . . . something was missing . . . the bunny. Jamie's favorite stuffed animal wasn't on the bed, or on the bookcase or . . . Caitlyn felt a breath of fear slide down her back.

Mommy? Where are you?

Again she heard Jamie's frightened voice resonating through her mind. Had her daughter . . . No, had someone *posing* as her daughter really called, or was it all in her mind? What had Lucille said once? "You hear 'em, too, Caitlyn, I know you do. The ghosts, they talk to you." Well, Lucille was a bit off, everyone thought so, that's the only reason she stuck it out with Mother. Or had stuck it out. But Jamie's voice had been real. She'd called . . . Caitlyn ran back to the bedroom, checked Caller ID, but all the old numbers had been erased. She froze. Someone had been in here. Someone had done it. She hadn't. She would have remembered.

I told ya, Caitie-Did, you're crazy as a fuckin' loon! How many times had she heard Kelly's recriminations thundering through her brain. Hundreds? Thousands? Way too many to count.

Shaken, she walked across the landing to her computer. She flipped on her e-mail in-box and saw several messages from Kelly.

Hey, sleepyhead. What's the deal? I have to make my own martinis now? I stopped by but you were doing your Rip Van Winkle routine. Call me later. xoxoxo, Kelly.

Kelly had been here? Had she taken her lipstick and Jamie's bunny? Or . . . *or what?* She must have. She clicked on the second message.

Forgot to mention I took care of Detective Dick. While you were sleeping.

What? Oh, God. Caitlyn's gut clenched.

He showed up while you were sleeping and, in so many words, I told him to get lost. I pretended to be you and said I wasn't going to talk to him or anyone else without my attorney.

No, that couldn't be right. Caitlyn remembered Detective

Reed showing up. *She'd* asked him to leave. Or had she? She'd been asleep and then . . . and then, oh, no. Panic bells began bonging in her mind.

And before you start lecturing me about pretending to be you, don't worry. The cop bought it and so did that irritating reporter, Nikki Gillette, the other day.

Caitlyn felt sick inside. Kelly had always loved the overly dramatic, the cloak and dagger, mistaken identity stuff. It was all a game to her.

See ya soon.

xoxoxo,

Kelly.

Caitlyn clicked off the computer and let her head fall into her hands. Kelly was becoming difficult.

Hasn't she always been?

Okay, more difficult.

If only Kelly would give up the charade. The pretense. Make amends with the family. Life would be so much easier. But it would never happen. Never. She tried to call her twin and ended up getting the damned machine. This time, Caitlyn didn't bother leaving a message.

Why would Kelly steal things? Things as personal as her lipstick and Jamie's favorite stuffed animal. It didn't make sense unless . . . unless Kelly was somehow trying to confuse her . . . but why?

Because she killed Josh and wants to frame you, to make it look like you're cracking up and—

"No!" Caitlyn wouldn't believe it. She hurried down the stairs. In the kitchen she hit the lights. Two empty martini glasses and an open bottle of olives sat on the counter. She froze in the doorway. Her skin crawled. She didn't remember having drinks with Kelly.

You didn't. You slept through it.

But she'd talked to the detective. Before or after Kelly? Oh, God. She dropped into a chair in the nook and Oscar, lying on the rug beneath, looked up at her and thumped his tail. "She has to quit this," Caitlyn said to the dog as she absently reached down and scratched him behind his ears. "She has to."

But she'll never do it on her own. She's having too much fun. She'll just keep on the way she has been since the accident. Until someone stops her. That someone will have to be you.

"I can't," Caitlyn said. "I just can't !" She had too much to do already, and her life was unraveling strand by strand, faster and faster. It was true. The Montgomery curse, the mental illness, was deep in her genes, in her blood. There was no escape. Panic spurted through her, her heart pounded, her pulse was out of control.

For God's sake, don't lose it. Not now!"

The phone rang and she jumped. *Damn the reporters!*

On her feet in an instant, she snagged the receiver before the second blast. "Hello?" she barked.

"Caitlyn?" Adam's voice was as near as if he was in the room with her.

Tears sprang to her eyes. Relief washed over her. He was just the balm she needed. So why did she want to break down and cry at the sound of his voice? "Hi," she managed, fighting tears, but the sound was strangled.

"Are you all right?" he asked.

No! I'm not all right. I never will be. You, of all people should know that! Cradling the phone to her ear, she slid down the cabinets, sinking to the floor. "I heard about your mother," he was saying. "I'm sorry."

"So am I," she admitted and struggled against hot tears. She wasn't used to kindness from a man; it was hard to accept, harder still to understand.

"I thought you might want to talk."

"I do. Yes." She nodded, as if he could see her. She had to see him, touch him, feel something solid in her life. Someone she could trust.

Trust him? Are you nuts? A guy who flashes his business cards at a funeral, for God's sake, a shrink culling clients out of the obits? Come on, Caitie-Did, this is crazy. You want to see him cuz you've got the hots for him. That's it.

Kelly's voice echoed through her head. These days it seemed as if her twin was her conscience as well as her tormentor.

"I can be at your place in half an hour," he said, and the timbre of his voice touched her heart. He cared. She knew it. "Or would you rather come here?"

She looked around her home, the empty glasses, half-filled bottles, mud the dog had tracked through the kitchen. Beyond all that there was the restlessness she'd felt here lately, the feeling that she was being observed.

"Maybe somewhere in between—neutral ground," he prodded. "Either the office or a coffee shop?"

"Tell you what, why don't you come by and pick me up?" She dashed the remainder of her tears away with her fingertips. "We'll decide then."

"I'll be there," he promised.

She hung up and, forcing herself to her feet, she gritted her teeth. She couldn't fall apart. What good could a nervous breakdown do? No, she had to find some inner strength and sort all this out herself. Forcing herself, she pushed all the demons in her mind back into their dark cobwebby corners as she raced around the kitchen, putting glasses in the dishwasher, stuffing the bottles back into the cupboard and swiping at the countertops and floor with a wet dishrag.

"Mission accomplished," she told the dog as she did a cursory survey of the room. "Make that Mission Impossible accomplished." Tossing the dirty rag into the hamper in the laundry room, she headed upstairs, then threw on a long cotton dress and found a matching sweater that covered the nicks on her arms. Then she frowned at her reflection. A couple of passes with a mascara wand over her lashes and a quick brush of blush was all she had time for. Her hair—well, forget it. She hurried downstairs and dialed the plantation. Hannah was alone, really alone, for the first time in her life, and Caitlyn wanted to check up on her baby sister. Oftentimes Hannah was a pain, but then, who wasn't? Kelly, Amanda and Troy weren't all that great at times either. One ring. She waited, checked her fingernails. Two. "Come on." No such luck. Three. "Great." On the fourth ring the answering machine clicked on, and Caitlyn froze as she heard the soft, dulcet tones of her mother's drawl instructing her to leave a message.

"You all have reached the Montgomerys out here at Oak Hill. If you'd be kind enough to leave your name and number, we'll get back to you . . ."

Caitlyn's knees threatened to buckle. *Oh, Mama. How could this happen?* She remembered sitting on her mother's lap, smelling the scent of her perfume mingled with smoke, the look of sadness that seemed to linger in her green eyes. Then there had been the nights Caitlyn had awoken to hear the creak of footsteps in the hallway. Sometimes they were a dangerous, scary tread that would pause at her door, open it and steal inside; other times they belonged to her mother as Berneda, an insomniac without her sleeping pills, would pace the upper hallways and stairs . . .

A sharp beep brought her back to the present as the recorder's tape clicked.

"Hannah? Are you there? It's Caitlyn. I just wanted to see how you were doing. Pick up if you're home, okay?" She waited. No answer. "Hannah? Give me a call, okay? Uh, if I'm not here, try my cell. Please. Call me."

She hung up with the uneasy feeling that something was wrong, but then, what else was new? Everything these days was wrong with a capital W. She heard a car pull up outside about the same time Oscar started barking like a maniac.

"You stay here," she said as footsteps sounded on the porch and the doorbell chimed. Peering through the narrow window near the door, she caught a glimpse of Adam, his dark hair shining in the glow from the porch lamp, his eyes sober. In jeans, a dark sweater and tennis shoes he stood, hands in his pockets.

Her stupid heart skipped a beat when his gaze collided with hers. She couldn't help but smile and feel a little thrill of excitement thrumming through her veins. There was something sexy and slightly mysterious about him, a secretive side he'd tucked beneath his college-athlete good looks.

It intrigued her. Seduced her. Made her want to find out more about him.

Face it, Caitlyn, you're attracted to him on a very basic animal level. Female to male. For a split second she imagined what it would be like to make love with him, then caught herself. That was nuts. She couldn't allow her wayward mind to go there. Hastily she unlatched the door. Before Oscar, hovering at her heels, could make good his escape, she stepped outside and pulled the door shut behind her.

"Hi. You look—" He let his gaze move up and down her body, then shook his head. "You look damned incredible, but maybe we shouldn't go there."

"What? Forget compliments? No way." She winked at him and blushed. "You look pretty incredible, too."

He threw back his head and laughed, then took her arm in his. "Enough already. We still have a patient-doctor relationship to protect."

"What a bummer," she muttered and he laughed again.

The night was quiet. Few pedestrians on the streets. No breath of wind ruffling the leaves of the trees overhead. "Where to?" she asked.

"Wherever you want to go. This time it's your choice."

She considered for a second. "What about Nickelby's? It's three blocks over, past the square. Great coffee. Even greater drinks."

His smile was a slash of white. "Lead the way."

"Your wish is my command," she joked, taking his hand and tugging on it.

Together they walked across the street, making small talk as they angled through the night-darkened streets to the little bistro. Several couples and a few singles were hanging out at small round tables positioned beneath low-wattage bulbs covered with blue shades. A single musician softly strumming an acoustic guitar stood behind a solitary mike. He didn't sing, just hummed occasionally to a song, presumably of his own creation and obviously without end.

They took a table positioned near the windows, then ordered iced tea and lemonade laced with vodka. When the waitress had disappeared, Adam asked, "So how are you and your family holding up?"

"How do you think? Someone seems to want all of us dead. Or at least part of us. It tends to make a person nervous." She plopped a peanut into her mouth and rubbed the salt from her fingers. "And that's not all of it. Then there's the grief to deal with. A double whammy."

A goateed waiter with a napkin wrapped around him like an apron brought their drinks. He wore a beret he'd angled over the back of his head in either a fashion statement or to hide the beginnings of a bald spot.

"I'm waiting for a call from Hannah. She's all alone at the house now. Lucille took off for Florida—no, don't ask." She held up a hand to ward off the obvious question. "I don't know why. And now Mom's gone ..." Her voice trailed off and she sighed as she reached for her drink. "I'm sorry. I've been advised not to play the victim and so I won't. But it would be a lie to say that I don't feel vulnerable and in some kind of shock."

"A lot has happened lately."

"That it has," she said, and it was almost a whisper.

"And even before. Your family seems particularly prone to tragedy."

"Just like out of a Greek play," she agreed as she took a swallow from her drink. "What about yours?"

"My family? Not much of one. My father took off when I was little. I don't remember much about him, don't know where he ended up. My mother, brother and I lived with my grandmother until Mom died. It was sudden. A brain tumor. I was eleven at the time. My brother was sixteen. Grandma took over from there."

"So where's your brother?"

"Brussels the last I heard. In the Navy. Intelligence. We aren't that close."

"No sisters, huh?"

"None that I know of. My father could have spawned a whole sorority for all I know."

She felt foolish. At least she'd had parents. Siblings. A

real family. Such as it was. "You make me feel like a crybaby."

"I don't think that."

"If you don't, you're the only one," she admitted. "I'm *always* accused of playing the victim, of not bucking up, of crying in my beer." She flashed him a smile. "It tends to give one a complex, you know. Maybe that's why they all think I'm not playing with a full deck. Don't get on my case about putting myself down, I'm not. My siblings seriously think I'm losing it, or have lost it, or will soon lose it." She smiled sadly. "It's just a matter of time."

"Who says so?"

"All of 'em. Hannah. Amanda. Troy. Even Kelly."

"Doesn't your twin stand up for you?" he asked, his gaze thoughtful.

"She doesn't talk to the rest of the family. I thought you knew that."

"Why is that?"

"Didn't I tell you? Mom cut her off after the boating accident. Blamed her for blowing her inheritance and almost killing me."

Adam frowned, rubbed at a bead of sweat on his glass. "Tell me again about the accident."

"Why?"

He was careful. "Because I'm trying to help you."

"What's to tell? You know what happened."

"Okay, what about afterward? When is the first time you saw Kelly?"

"After I was released from the hospital." Where was this going? Why was he now so serious?

"And when she was released, right?"

The musician had finally stopped, and the bistro seemed suddenly quiet. No glasses rattled, no buzz of conversation; only the very quiet whisper of the overhead fans made any noise whatsoever. She hated to talk so intimately about Kelly. Even to Adam. But he was waiting. Staring at her with those intense eyes. She put down her glass and took in a deep breath. It was obviously "come to Jesus" time, as her mother had always called those moments when it was imperative that all secrets come to light. Shakily, she drew in a deep breath. "Yes."

"How often do you see her?"

"Not as much as I'd like. She works out of town a lot."

"What does she do?" he asked.

"She's a buyer for a big department store."

"Which one?"

"Does it matter?" she demanded. What were all these questions about her twin? "Kelly doesn't like me talking about her personal life. She's a private person."

"But she does live in the area."

"Yes. When she's here. She has a place out on the river."

"You visit her?"

"Sometimes, though most of the time we leave messages for each other on the phone or e-mail."

"What about the rest of your siblings, do they have much contact with her?"

"No, I told you they took Mother's side." She felt it start deep inside, a tiny quiver that she knew would turn into a rumble, her heart beginning to race unnaturally. "They all . . . they all act as if she's dead."

The world seemed to stop.

The words hung in the air between them.

Adam didn't say anything, just stared at her, and she felt compelled to explain. "It works both ways. Kelly wants nothing to do with the rest of the family either. The feeling's mutual."

"Caitlyn." His voice was low. Ominous.

She swallowed against a throat suddenly as dry as sand.

"I read Kelly's obituary today."

She closed her eyes.

"She's dead."

"No." Caitlyn had known it would come to this. She took a swallow of her drink. Shook her head, vehemently denying his every word. "Her body . . . her body was never found. Not officially. But she survived the accident. It was a miracle . . . or maybe not." She forced the quivering of her insides to subside, the roar in her head to quiet. "I only know what she told me."

"Which is?" If he was skeptical, he managed to hide it.

"That she was in and out of consciousness, that she floated downstream, that she was fished out of the river by a drug runner who saved her life, but wanted to remain anonymous as there was a warrant out for his arrest. So she built a new life for herself. But the family . . . when I tried to tell them she was alive, they wouldn't hear of it. As you know, they think I'm suffering some kind of mental disorder . . . no, wait, a 'condition,' I think that's the term my mother used."

"I see." He leaned back in his chair and the music started again, a slightly different version of what sounded like the same song.

"You don't believe me."

"I didn't say that."

"You didn't have to. No one believes me. Or they don't want to. My family's pretty greedy and with Kelly dead, there are fewer people to divide the spoils, or split the estate, or pick my grandfather's bones, whatever you want to call it."

"Caitlyn—"

"I know this sounds far-fetched, but anytime she's recognized, she pretends she's me. She has her own identity now, a new one. She goes by K.C. Griffin. K for Kelly, C for Caitlyn and Griffin, as it was her middle name."

"As well as your friend's name, the boy who lived on the neighboring estate," he prodded.

She understood where this was going. "Yes." Studying the burn marks on the table, she whispered, "I know what you're going to say, that there was no Griffin, no childhood friend. But you're wrong. He existed." She blinked hard, remembered those long, lonely years growing up. "He existed for me."

Adam reached across the table. Took both her hands in his. Rubbed the back of her knuckles gently with his thumbs. "If he was real to you, he did exist. Then. But now?"

She shook her head, fought the tears. "Now I know he was imaginary."

"But necessary then."

"Oh, yeah." She sniffed and bit her lip as she thought of the nights she'd slipped out of her window, climbed onto the roof and sat staring up at the stars, Griffin beside her, ready to catch her if she fell, ready to tell her everything was going to be all right, never letting her down, not like the other people in her life, not like her older brother who had crept the halls, slipping into her room, into Kelly's room, brushing foul kisses across her cheeks, smelling of beer as he'd slid a hand beneath the covers to touch her. Not like her mother who doubted her and suggested that she was making up tales. Not like her father who was rarely around, never took the time to know her or any of his children. "Griffin was real necessary," she admitted.

"Just like Kelly is now?" he asked gently, but she shook her head, wouldn't go there. He didn't understand, but then, no one did. Not when it came to her twin.

"Kelly's real, Adam," she insisted. "As real as I am."

Twenty-Eight

Reed leaned back in his La-Z-Boy and tried to pay attention to the Braves' game playing on his new 36-inch flat-screen TV. The thing had cost him an arm and two legs, but he loved it. He figured he'd finish his "Man-Sized" microwave meal that tasted like shit, then hit the streets again, taking a swing by Caitlyn Bandeaux's home. He'd asked Morrisette to watch the place, which she had agreed to even though her daughter was in the throes of a "major case of chicken pox." Reed needed a break. He'd been working the Bandeaux case round the clock and it was time to step back and gain some perspective.

Before Caitlyn Bandeaux slams the door on your face again.

Hell.

The Braves were down seven to one in the bottom of the eighth with two outs. It didn't look good. The Mets were on a roll.

Reed washed the remains of his meal down with the rest of his beer, did his dishes by tossing the plastic plate into the garbage, flicked off the set and was out the door just as his cell phone chirped. He answered as he climbed into the El Dorado. "Reed."

"Hey, it's me," Sylvie Morrisette said from her cell phone.

"I'm on my way."

"About time. The sitter's called twice."

"Where are you?"

"On the side street catty-corner from a little bistro called Nickleby's," she said and gave him the street number. "Get this. Our widow seems to be on a date. Her and that shrink of hers. Having drinks together. Real cozy."

Interesting. "I'll be there in twenty," he said as he pulled out of his drive and headed into town. He turned on the police band and was slowing for a red light when his phone jangled again. No doubt Morrisette's sitter was pressuring her. He hit the talk button. "Reed."

"This is Deputy Bell, down at St. Simons. You said you wanted to know when we got a positive ID on the Jane Doe we pulled from the water on the north side of the island."

Reed tensed, hung a left. "That's right."

"Rebecca Wade. The M.E. got her dental records and matched 'em up."

Reed was beginning to get a bad feeling about this.

"Any idea on the time of death?"

"She's been in the drink a while. Weeks. Maybe months. Hasn't been determined yet."

"Cause of death?"

"Still workin' on it. I'll have a copy of the autopsy report faxed to you the minute I get one. But there is something odd about the case," he added and the tone of his voice had grown heavier, a precursor of more bad news. "Something you probably ought to know."

Reed took a corner a little too fast. His tires screeched. "Shoot."

"Well, her body was pretty decomposed as I said . . . but one thing the M.E. noticed, and it'll be in the report. It looks like her tongue was cut off. Clean out of her mouth."

Reed's jaw clenched. His hands tightened over the wheel.

"You're sure that it wasn't some kind of animal, a predator that got to her?"

"Don't think so. According to the M.E., the tongue was sliced off clean as a whistle and found wrapped in plastic in a makeup bag in her purse. The only thing in the little case. Just her tongue wrapped up like a goddamned ham sandwich."

She let him kiss her on the doorstep.

That was Caitlyn's first mistake.

The second was inviting him in for another drink.

And the third was the fact that she wanted to make love to him. Right here in her house, while the rest of the world crumbled around them, Caitlyn wanted to feel Adam's strong arms around her, needed to know that he cared, was desperate to find some meaning in life, to feel alive when so many people were dying.

"I don't know if this is such a good idea," he said as they sipped drinks—a Cosmo for her and whiskey over rocks for him—on her couch. "He's not going for it." Adam hitched his chin in Oscar's direction. The little dog was lying beneath the arch separating the living room from the foyer and he never took his eyes off Adam.

"He's not used to strangers coming here."

"But he does recognize Kelly?"

Caitlyn sighed; second-guessed telling him about her twin. "Would you like to talk to her?"

"That would be a great idea."

"Hang on." She walked into the kitchen with Oscar tagging behind, found her purse and dug out her cell phone, which she carried back to the living area. Adam was seated in one corner of her floral couch, half sprawled over the cushions. A hint of beard shadow was darkening his jaw, his hair was mussed from their walk from the bistro to the house, his long legs stretched beneath the coffee table. Serious eyes watched her every move as she took her spot next to him, punched out Kelly's number and waited. "She might not be home."

"I'll bet."

"I'm serious . . ." Caitlyn listened to the phone ring and the answering machine pick up. At the tone she said, "Hey, Kelly, I'm home. Give me a call back, would you? I need to talk to you and no . . . don't worry, I'm not going to try and coerce you into going to Mom's funeral. Okay? Call me." She clicked off, glanced at Adam and saw the doubt in his eyes. "You still don't believe me, do you? Well . . ." She dialed Kelly's number again and handed the phone to Adam. "You listen to her voice, you leave a message. Tell her you want to talk to her, for crying out loud."

Adam's eyes never left her face. It was irritating that no one, not even her shrink, believed her. Even though the receiver was pressed against his ear, Caitlyn heard the phone ringing and Kelly's answering machine pick up. Adam didn't so much as flinch. "Yes, this is Adam Hunt. You probably know that I'm working with your sister Caitlyn. Would you give me a call back? I'd appreciate it." He left his number and pressed the end button on her cell, then sat holding the phone for a long time.

"You still don't believe me."

"I didn't say that." He handed her the phone.

"You didn't have to. I can read it in your eyes. Your name should be Thomas, you know. Doubting Thomas." She took a long sip of her drink, felt her anger rise. Why should it matter so much what he thought? Just because he was her shrink . . . no, it was more than that. She wanted him not as her psychologist, but as a man, her confidant, her friend, her . . . lover? to have some faith in her. Even if the reason she was with him was because she was mentally screwed up.

"You must see where I'm having trouble with this," he said slowly. "No one but you, that I know of, deals with Kelly."

"Wrong. Kelly's somewhat of a recluse, but she does

hold down a job. She does see clients. She does fly all around.''

''Has anyone else in your family talked to Kelly since the accident?''

''No, but . . . Oh, for the love of God, why would I create an imaginary sister? I mean, she's real. Look at the birth records.''

''It's not her birth that worries me,'' he said. ''It's her death.''

''Supposed death. *Supposed.* She's alive. You know, I'm going to insist that she meet with you. When she calls back, you can talk to her, and if that isn't convincing enough, we'll go see her at her house.''

''Which is where?''

''Out of town on Sorghum Road . . . I have the address somewhere in the den, I think, but she doesn't get her mail there, she picks it up at the post office—all part of her secret life, I guess—but her place is this little funky cabin right across the river from Oak Hill. Isn't that ironic? She never goes there but she can see what's going on from her spot on the river. I don't think my family is even aware the cabin is there.''

''Why not?''

''Well, maybe my father or his father knew about it, and my brothers probably have seen it as they used to fish around there, but it's pretty tucked away in the trees. No one suspects Kelly lives there.'' She finished her drink. ''And that's just the way she likes it.''

''Doesn't that strike you as odd?''

''A lot of things about my family strike me as odd,'' she said and felt a sadness for those she'd lost so recently, a sadness so cold that no amount of alcohol could warm her, an ache so deep she didn't know if she'd ever get over it. And behind all that was something else, the niggling fear that she was involved, that, as the police suspected, she might have caused pain and suffering for those she'd cared about. Had she gone to Josh's house that night? And what? Brought back buckets of blood? Had, as he'd accused, been negligent with their child? Mother of God, no . . . She shivered. Had she climbed the steps to her mother's bedroom on the evening she'd taken ill and, while no one was looking, replaced the nitroglycerin pills with placebos, and when that attempt on Berneda's life had failed, had she snuck into the hospital and finished the job? Images, faint, teasing and oh, so deadly, darted in front of her eyes, and though she didn't realize it, she began to shake. Had she, during those periods of her life she couldn't remember, have become a killer? Like Dr. Jekyll and Mr. Hyde? No . . . please . . . no . . .

"Caitlyn?"

Adam's voice brought her up short. Back to this room with its fading flowers and familiar wallpaper, to the cold grate of the marble fireplace and the piano with Jamie's picture upon its polished surface. To the man staring at her with concerned eyes.

"Are you all right?"

She nodded, but he must not have believed her for he pulled her into his arms and drew her near. They were half lying on the couch, she atop him, snuggling close. "Things will be better." He kissed her lightly on the forehead and she melted inside. His arms were strong. She let her head fall against his chest and heard the steady, comforting beat of his heart, smelled a faint scent of some aftershave.

"How do you know?"

"I know."

"Oh, yeah, right," she teased.

"Trust me." He kissed the top of her crown. "Some things have to be taken on faith."

She chuckled at the irony of it. "You're a good one to talk. You don't even believe me about my sister."

"I'm trying," he said and she wanted to believe him, turned to look into his eyes and couldn't help brushing a kiss against his lips. He tasted of whiskey and wine and all things male. Groaning, he kissed her hard, his hands coming up to tangle in her hair, his eyes closing.

Don't do this, Caitlyn, use your head.

But she disregarded the horrid little voice in her head and

gave in to the need for human touch, the yearning to be wanted. Her lips parted and his tongue slid into her, caressing the ridges of the roof of her mouth as he held her firmly against him. Her breasts tingled, her skin was on fire and through their clothes, pressed hard against the juncture of her legs, she felt his erection, harder as their kiss deepened. He found the zipper of her dress and she didn't object, let the fabric part until her bare back was exposed. His fingers moved lightly down her spine, tracing its ridge, sliding between her buttocks.

She felt her heart kick into double time, sensed the first dusky stirrings deep within, of want that yawned and begged for more.

"Caitlyn—" he said, his voice low and husky, sweat beading on his forehead. "We shouldn't."

"I know." But she didn't believe him, just kissed the side of his mouth.

"This could be trouble."

"Only if we let it," she whispered, kissing him again, feeling his heat, his need, so much like her own, pulsing in the thick air between them, throbbing in their blood. She moved against him, her long dress bunching, and he seemed to let go.

"God help me," he ground out as his hands grabbed the dress's hem and he pulled it upward, the tips of his fingers grazing her thighs, his need evident. She got lost in the smell and taste of him, kissing his lips, his eyes, his nose as he stripped them both, yanked her dress over her head, unhooked her bra and pulled off his shirt and slacks. There was no more talk of denial, no more worry about propriety. He kissed her as if he never intended to stop, stripping away her bra and panties as her heart pounded and her blood thundered in her ears. He pulled her atop him and lifted his hips, thrusting into her from below, claiming her while she was straddling him, caressing her breasts as she moved.

His eyes were closed as they kissed long and hard, the air between them dense, the heat palpable. Her pulse raced, lightning quick, moving her to that dark, dangerous beyond.

Faster and faster they moved and the room spun crazily . . . wildly. Her nipples hardened beneath his touch, and when he curled up to take one in his mouth, she cried out. Her breathing was rapid and shallow, her thoughts losing connection. Electricity seemed to crackle around them and she closed her eyes, feeling the need building within her, the great swelling that was as consuming as it was pleasurable. He knew just where to touch her, just how to . . . .

"Oh . . . oh . . . oh, God, Adam!" she cried as the first spasm hit. Jolting her. Catapulting her into another time and space. Her eyes closed and for the moment she was lost. Couldn't find herself, couldn't breathe.

Beneath her, every muscle in his body contracted.

He cried out, his voice raw, his fingers digging into her buttocks.

He lost himself in her and she opened her eyes, stared down at this stranger who was still inside her. Shivering, she blinked hard. Then Kelly realized what had happened.

Caitlyn, the fool, had made love to this man . . . her shrink. God, what a mess, Kelly thought, still straddling him. Oh, he was good enough looking, chiseled male and all. A damned Adonis with his square jaw, intelligent eyes and honed body. Just the kind of physical specimen Kelly liked. Caitlyn sure could pick 'em, that much was certain. She wiggled a bit and he groaned. Oh, she liked that. The ultimate power of sex over a man.

What a trip.

"Caitlyn?" he said, and she smiled naughtily.

If he only knew. Caitlyn was long gone . . . wouldn't be back for hours. Maybe days. "Ummm."

"Come here," he said, his voice low, as he motioned for her to lie against him, to cuddle in afterglow. Jesus, he was predictable. She hesitated, then lowered herself, tangling her fingers in his chest hair and getting off on the fact that he had no idea that she'd switched, that her personality had taken over wimpy, whining, always-the-victim Caitlyn's. She cooed against his skin and felt his fingers caressing her shoulders, holding her close, his breath whispering in her hair. So romantic. And so damned foolish. But she could play along and he'd never know.

She leaned over and kissed his nipple. His eyes flew open as if he was surprised that she could be flirty and aggressive so soon after. But then, he didn't know her at all. Didn't realize what kind of fire he was playing with. She stared straight into his eyes as the tip of her tongue rimmed his nipple and he sucked in his breath. "Tell me, Adam," she suggested throatily. "Was it good for you?"

Twenty-Nine

Reed checked his watch. It was after one in the morning, and Caitlyn's shrink had been inside her house for nearly three hours. *Doing what?*

Nothing good. He remembered his old man telling him that nothing good ever happened after midnight. Reed had been sixteen at the time and considered his father an idiot, but now, looking back, he decided the man was right. He tapped his fingers on the steering wheel and refused to drink one more swig of the coffee he'd picked up an hour ago at an all-night convenience store operated by a pimply-faced kid who looked pale and sick—like a heroin addict—under the flourescent lights. He'd nearly bought a pack of cigarettes from the kid, then thought better of it. Now, as he stared through the night, he would've killed for a smoke.

He'd relieved Morrisette hours ago and almost envied her the need to get back to her children, to her little family. Almost. He'd watched her juggle her duties as an ambitious cop along with her life as a single mother and wondered where she got the energy.

"Nicotine and caffeine," she'd replied when he'd asked her about it. "My drugs of choice and all perfectly legal."

Right now he could use a shot of both. He stifled a yawn and considered going home; nothing was happening here. The big news of the evening was that Lucille Vasquez had been tracked down at her sister's home in Florida. She was tired, scared, and had been planning to leave for years, but she wasn't running away from anything, she'd assured Reed when he'd returned her call and woken her up. In fact, she planned to return for the funeral. She'd just needed a break from all the bad omens, deaths, and hard work she'd put up with for most of her life.

"I'll be fine," she'd assured him, but when he'd asked about her daughter, remembering the call he'd gotten from Detective Montoya in New Orleans, she'd gotten quiet. "She and me, we weren't that close no more," Lucille had confided. "She told me she was comin' home last Christmas, gonna straighten some things out between us, but she never showed up and I figured she'd changed her mind. This isn't so strange. There was a time when she didn't speak to me for eighteen months. No birthday card, no call on Mother's Day, no Christmas present, no nothin'. But that's the way she is."

When he explained Detective Montoya's concern for Marta, Lucille had sighed. "There just ain't no tellin' about that girl. Maybe about no child. I dunno. She's been problems from the day she was born and I did my best to raise her, but what can you do? Kids these days, they do what they want." She went on a defensive litany about her skills at motherhood, and eventually Reed had hung up, knowing not a whole lot more about Marta Vasquez than he had before. She was missing, had been headed toward Savannah and hadn't shown up. Her mother wasn't concerned; maybe he shouldn't be either.

Something moved in the house. The front door opened. Backlit by the foyer lights, the shrink kissed the widow hard and then half jogged to his car. Reed watched and wondered what kind of fireworks they'd cooked up together. He wondered if he should follow Hunt, see what he was up to. Or stay here and watch the house.

One by one, the house lights were switched off. First downstairs and then up. Apparently Caitlyn Bandeaux had gone to bed. Alone. So if they were lovers, why hadn't Hunt stayed over?

Reed checked his watch and waited. Ten minutes. Twenty. He yawned. Thirty minutes into the total darkness, he decided to give it a rest and go home. The department wasn't paying him for this; only his curiosity and doggedness kept him awake and in the street. And he had a long day tomorrow. With one last glance at the darkened windows, he turned on the ignition and pulled away from the curb. As he passed by her house, he imagined he saw a movement of the curtains, but it was probably just his imagination. He drove straight home, walked into the house, and after stripping off his clothes turned on the timer on the bedroom TV and got into bed.

He was asleep within minutes, never knowing that Caitlyn Bandeaux had watched him from the window, waiting patiently; then, once she was certain he wouldn't return, had quietly slipped into the night.

The creeps were lined up at the stage of Pussies In Booties. Sitting at the low bar that surrounded her dance area, some with platters of food in front of them, all swilling drinks, they smoked and joked and drooled as Sugar danced her way through the set. She kicked a leg up high, nearly losing a five-inch heel, then snuggled up to the pole situated in the middle of the stage, sliding against it as if it were a lover, moving up and down, showing off what she knew was a great ass.

Ross had the bass cranked up on the sound system, and a couple of guys in jeans, work shirts and suspenders were standing behind the first row of patrons and gyrating to the pulsing beat, moving so that she might notice them. Like she'd give them the time of day. Or night. Perverts every one of them.

She twirled beneath the lights, back to the pole, and recognized some of the regulars. Guys whom she considered her bread and butter, though she never encouraged them, never gave them so much as the hint of a smile. Their money might pay the bills, but she didn't want to get into a situation where she would encounter someone who might want to get involved with her—or worse yet, become obsessed. She'd heard about dancers with their own private stalkers.

You drop dead.

The voice on the phone seemed to shimmy across the rafters of this old dive and echo through her brain. Maybe she had already picked one up . . . one of these sickos who stared at her and fantasized. How about the bald guy who always sat in the corner near the stage curtains? Or the man with the graying beard and mean eyes, who waited until she'd shed her skirt and blouse to put his money on the stage in front of her, all the while ogling her tits as she leaned over to retrieve the cash. One time she'd seen him crease the bills, licking the seam with his long, pointed tongue while his eyes held hers. He was a scary one. Then there was the flat-faced man who'd stood in the shadows one night and had pointed his finger at her, like a gun, taking aim right at her crotch.

She had to get out of this life and soon. Before it caught up with her.

She rolled her head around and ran her hands up her thighs.

The Montgomery money was her ticket to freedom and respectability. She swung around on the pole, letting her long hair billow behind her.

At that moment she saw him.

Deep in the shadows, from a corner table away from the bar, far from the stage. His gaze followed her every move. Lusting. Wanting. The man who she willingly let into her bed, though she'd tried vainly to close her heart to him.

He was respectable.

He had money.

A member of Savannah's elite.

And yet he yearned for her; she saw it in his eyes and in

the tightness near the corners of his mouth. He hated what she did for a living, but was tantalized by it. Teased and turned on. So she'd give him a special show, step out of her routine. Leaning up against the pole, making sure it was firmly against the split in her rump, she grabbed her breasts, teased her nipples, arched and licked her lips.

A roar of approval rippled through the crowd, but they didn't know that she was dancing for only one man, that while she'd take the money left on the linoleum at her feet, even wiggle her tits and ass in front of their slobbering faces, she was mentally fucking the big man in the back, the man who wore admiration as easily as his uniform.

He was married, but that didn't make her want him less. She flipped over, showing off her buttocks, pinching them tight as she licked the pole. She almost felt him tremble as he leaned against the back of his chair, a shot glass in one hand, the other discreetly hidden in his pocket.

The music faded and she blew a kiss, aimed directly at him, though every man in the place thought she had the hots for each of them. God, if they only knew how she despised them all. They disgusted her. Nothing would ever change that. Provocatively, she danced her way off the stage and through the curtain where she slipped into a robe and dabbed at her face with a cotton ball.

He didn't come here often. And never on the weekend when the crowd was heavier and there was more of a chance that he would be recognized. But the few times he had appeared had become a signal. She knew that within minutes he'd be behind the stage door, a bribe to the bouncer allowing him into the shoddy area loosely known as the dressing room and there, while another girl was on stage thrilling the crowd, he would corner Sugar against the makeup counter, slip his cock out of his trousers and spin her around so that she was forced to look into the mirror as he mounted her from behind.

Without any pretext, he would shove inside of her. He would be hard, excited from the teasing dance. The act would be quick. Without a hint of romance attached to it.

She would see his face, red and grunting, and she would pretend to get off on the same sense of excitement about being caught that he did.

But she didn't. How could she? With the makeup trays and the edge of the vanity pressed against her abdomen and the few remaining lit bulbs surrounding the mirror hot and showing off her degrading position, she would feel cheap. Dirty. Used. If anyone lifted the stage curtain, they would be caught; if a dancer waiting for her set came in early, they would be seen; or if the owner of the establishment wandered through, her lover would have to pay big-time hush money, and Sugar herself would become fair game to the owner, a lowlife named Buddy Hughs. In order to keep his mouth shut, Buddy would expect the same treatment she willingly gave her married lover.

And that thought stuck in her craw.

Sugar prided herself on being one of the few of ''Buddy's girls'' who hadn't done him. She'd like to keep it that way until she got her hands on some of Grandpa Benedict's money and could tell Buddy and any other lowlife who came on to her to piss off.

Over the pulsing throb of music, she heard the back door open and then her lover's quick tread. His hat brim was pulled low over his eyes as he saw her.

''I caught your little dance,'' he said and reached inside her robe to tweak her breast. A sharp little pain shot through her, and her nipple was instantly hard. He was rough, but not too rough.

''Did you?''

''It was just for me.''

''Was it? How do you know?'' she teased, looking up at him.

''You can be such a tease.''

''Mmmm.''

''And a bitch.'' Again a tweak.

''And I can handle you,'' she sassed, seeing the flame leap in his eyes. He was a tall man and athletic, strong enough that he could spin her around, lift her over his shoulder or up onto his thick cock, all honed muscle and keen mind.

"Let's see," he said and pulled her robe to the floor, leaving her in the thong and pasties. Spinning her around, he pushed her into the makeup table, bending her over, already unzipping and unbuckling, insistently sliding his moist dick around her thong and grunting as he pushed into her.

She bucked and he grabbed her tits, tearing at the tassels with his big, meaty hands, rutting hard, as if he'd held it in too long.

A little shock of pain sizzled through her, but she didn't dislike it. Not from him. Not even when he slapped her buttocks with his bare hands. "That's it, baby," he said, pressing her down hard and grunting in pleasure. She arched up, knowing he loved it when she threw her rump against him.

"Like that, do you?" With a growl, he leaned forward and placed his teeth over the back of her neck, not enough to pierce the skin, just enough to remind her who was boss. Moaning on cue, she felt his tempo increase, heard the pounding of the music on the other side of the thin partition, heard him roar loudly above the hoots and hollers of the crowd as he came, gasping, grunting, falling against her. She saw his red, sweat-slickened face in the mirror and felt a moment's revulsion.

She was beneath him, holding on to the edges of the table for support, her hair mussed, her face flushed, her eyes hollow. A whore, just as Dickie Ray had always insinuated. Not for the regular crowd, not for her boss, not for anyone except this one man who would never love her. Not because he didn't like her, but because she wasn't of his class. She was meant to screw. Not to show off. Never to marry. She was less than a dalliance or a fling, she was someone with whom he could explore his naughty side, someone he could spank or pour champagne on and lick it off. She'd do any-thing for him and he knew it. It made him feel powerful and that, above the sex, was what he craved. She knew it, but she doubted that he did.

As he zipped up his pants and straightened his shirt, she felt shame that showed itself in the wash of heat that climbed up the back of her neck, the neck he'd so recently sunk his teeth into.

She found her robe. Threw it over her shoulders. Didn't ask the demeaning question, "When will I see you again?"

"That was nice," he said with a little smile as he adjusted himself and buckled his belt. "Real nice."

"Yeah."

He placed a small box on the vanity, a tiny gift that she wouldn't open until he slipped through the back door and into the night. It wasn't money, never money, but some little feminine bauble, nothing expensive. Never anything lasting, but it was something. He patted her on her buttocks and left.

Only later, as she stared down at the silver navel ring, did she realize that he hadn't kissed her. Not once during their brief interlude. There had been no tenderness. No love. Just pure, raw sex, and while she'd been turned on at first by the knowledge that she was fucking one of the most powerful men in the city, she was now disgusted or at least disillusioned. He could easily have a dozen girlfriends, women who danced for him at the Silk Tassel or The Odd-S-C, or any of the places his work took him, places away from the prying eyes of his wife. She had no idea what he did with his time when he wasn't working. All she was really sure about was that he was always rock-hard and cheated on his wife without conscience.

What a legacy.

She needed to go home, pour herself some cold vodka and take a long shower. To wash away the sweat. To rinse off the dirt. To wipe away the feeling that she was wasting her life. To find Cricket.

Sugar was worrying more and more about her wayward sibling. It had been more than two days now since Cricket was last home, and Sugar hadn't heard word one from her sister. None. Cricket's disappearance, in and of itself, wasn't unusual, but coupled with the strange phone calls where no one responded when she answered, Sugar had gotten nervous. What if something had happened?

She'd even mentioned it to Dickie Ray, who had told her she worried too much. Like that was a news flash.

"Christ, Sugar, give the kid a break," he'd said while trying to install a new fan belt on his truck. He'd turned and looked at her from beneath the hood, wiped his blackened hands on a greasy rag and clucked his tongue. "You gotta let her live her life. She don't need you cluckin' after her like some mother hen. And them phone calls. Hell, they're probably from the perverts you dance for. It don't take a fuckin' brain surgeon to figure that one out!"

She'd let the subject drop. Dickie Ray was an idiot. Had been from the day he was born, like all of his nerves didn't quite touch. He was probably the one who'd been sired by Cameron and hence had enough incestuous Montgomery genes to make him stupid. She'd read about that. Worried about it. But then, in that respect, Dickie Ray was right. She worried about everything.

But she couldn't shake the feeling that something was wrong. Really wrong.

On her way out of the club, she hastened down a dark hallway, tripped over a mop bucket, caught herself, swore under her breath and made her way down the short flight of stairs to the back door, where a broken exit sign gave off only a bit of green light. Outside it wasn't much better. The night was clear but dark. And still. Almost eerie.

The parking lot was empty except for one lone car.

Cricket's old Chevy.

And her sister was at the wheel.

Thank God!

What the hell was her baby sister doing just sitting in her car in this part of town in the middle of the night?

Probably looking to score a hit or was already high.

Well, that was just plain crazy.

Sugar started for the car, intending to give Cricket a piece of her mind. She crossed the potholes of the parking lot, twisting her ankle in her haste. "Ouch! Shit. Damn it all to hell!" It just wasn't her night.

At the hatchback, she tapped on the glass of the driver's door with her finger, but Cricket didn't respond. Just sat there, doped up and asleep, no doubt. Her skin looked white in the dark interior, though there were splotches on it. Dark, reddish welts along with streaks of mud. Like Cricket had been strung out for days and had a bad reaction. At that thought, Sugar began to worry all over again. "Hey!" she called. No response. She tried the door. It was locked. "Damn it, Cricket, open up!"

She leaned down and saw something in the reflection of the glass, a glimpse of movement in the shadows behind her. A figure running toward her on silent footsteps. Shit! Probably one of the perverts lurking by the Dumpster hoping to catch a glimpse of her. Looking over her shoulder, she said, "Listen, you warped son of a bitch, I'm not interested."

She was slammed against the car.

"Ooof!" Her breath came out in a rush. Her head crashed against the door frame. Pain exploded behind her eyes. Her purse flew across the lot. "What the fuck?" She couldn't see her attacker; her face was smashed against the side of the Chevy. A foul-tasting rag was stuffed into her mouth before she had a chance to scream.

What the hell was happening? Cricket was in the car, and this jackass was going to—what? Rape her? Shit.

Fear fired her blood. She fought for all she was worth. Sugar was strong and athletic, the hours dancing making her firm, but she couldn't move. Her arm was twisted behind her so hard it nearly came out of its socket.

Panic ripped through her. This couldn't be happening!

Cricket! For Christ's sake, do *something!* Why wasn't she moving? Why the hell wasn't she moving? Why were her eyes so glassy, drugged out . . . and her skin was so pasty beneath the welts . . . dozens of them all over her face. *Oh, fuck! No! Oh, God, no, no, no!*

Finally Sugar understood. She clawed and tried to scream,

but it was too late. Another rag was held to her nose, and she wrenched away from the smell of ether. Already her body disobeyed the commands of her screaming mind. Her knees sagged. Her arms and legs were like lead. Even her brain was failing. The lights of the parking lot were spinning in slow motion over her head, moving pinpoints against the dark canopy of the sky.

The pressure behind her eased. Slowly Sugar slid down the side of Cricket's battered Chevrolet onto the pockmarked asphalt. She was vaguely aware that her attacker was swearing under his—no . . . her? . . . breath and scrabbling across the parking lot trying to retrieve the contents of Sugar's spilled purse.

Sugar didn't care . . . her entire body was numb . . . her thoughts floating . . . she wasn't even scared, though she was certain she should be.

There was little doubt in her mind that she was about to die.

Thirty

Reed pulled the autopsy report on Rebecca Wade from the fax machine and immediately got lost in it. Probable cause of death was asphyxiation, not drowning. She'd been killed first, her tongue sliced out of her mouth and probably tucked into her empty purse, then the body ditched in the water.

Who would go to so much trouble?

Someone who was making a point.

You didn't hack off a body part and wrap it in goddamned Saranwrap and tuck it into a designer leather bag unless you wanted to show off a little, taunt the police, say, "Hey, cops! Look over here. *I* did this, you idiots. I'm smarter than you."

He refilled his coffee cup in the lunch room, nodded to a couple of beat cops. Still studying the report, he jockeyed his way through the cubicles as he made his way to his office. The minute the details of Rebecca Wade's death leaked out, the press would be over this like crows on road-kill. There would be concern and talk about a serial killer, a murderer focused on people associated with the Montgomery family. It was probably task force time, and the FBI would be called in. Which might not be such a bad idea. There were always the jurisdiction squabbles, of course, a few power struggles, but for the most part he didn't mind the feds.

Reed had worked with Vita "Marilyn" Catalanotto, the local field representative, before. She was all right, if a little pushy. Well, maybe a lot pushy. Transplanted from the Bronx in New York. Which explained a lot. Christ, it seemed lately that he was surrounded by female cops. All that equal-opportunity crap.

Office machines hummed, and phones rang outside his door. Someone told a non-PC joke that he caught the end of, and there was a ripple of laughter in the cubicles near a bank of windows. He didn't pay much attention. Had too much on his mind. All surrounding the Montgomery killings.

Caitlyn Bandeaux's daughter, mother, father, husband and now shrink were dead—along with a sprinkling of siblings. The way it looked, it was just plain dangerous getting too close to the recently widowed Mrs. Bandeaux.

Hearing footsteps nearing his open door, Reed looked up. A tall, determined man was steamrolling straight for him. His features were even, his skin a hue that hinted at his Latino heritage, his chin, beneath a dark, neat goatee, set. "You Reed?" he asked, his dark eyes serious, a diamond stud winking in one ear. It was hot as hell outside, and yet the young buck wore all black and leather. From first glance, Reed would have pegged him as a tough, but there was something beyond his swagger, an earnestness in his expression that suggested otherwise.

"That's right." Reed straightened.

"Reuben Montoya. New Orleans P.D." Montoya flipped opened his wallet, and Reed took a cursory glance at the badge. It looked authentic. "I heard Lucille Vasquez left town." Montoya stuffed his badge into an inner pocket of the jacket.

"That's right," Reed said, waving the younger cop into a side chair. "But she turned up at her sister's place in Florida. You're looking for her daughter, right? Marta?"

Something flashed behind the dark eyes, and his lips drew white against his teeth. "She's been missing for six months."

"A friend of yours?"

"Yeah," Montoya admitted. "A good friend."

"She's not with her mother, and Lucille doesn't know where she is, nor, for the most part, does she care. She's got a bad case of wounded maternal ego. I talked to her last night. She's got no clue where her daughter is."

"You're certain."

"I'd bet my badge on it."

"Hell." Montoya's lips pursed and he fidgeted at the pocket of his jacket as if searching for a nonexistent pack of cigarettes. "I checked around with missing persons and heard there was a Jane Doe found down in the water near St. Simons Island."

"And you thought it might be Marta. How'd you hear that so fast?"

"I made it a point to." He was brash. Cocky. Reed couldn't help but like him. "I've got dental records with me."

"With you?" This was beginning to sound strange.

"Copies. But they'll do for a match."

"Are you a little too involved in this one?" Reed asked.

"Some people might think so. But they're wrong."

"Maybe you should back off. Put some perspective on the case. Besides, the Jane Doe isn't Marta Vasquez."

"No?" Relief slumped Montoya's broad shoulders. "You're sure?"

Reed tossed the report across the table. "Yep."

Montoya scanned the pages, his expression hardening as he read the autopsy report on Rebecca Wade. His face grew darker than before. "Sick bastard, isn't he?"

"Or she."

"A woman?"

"Quite possibly."

"Who cuts out her victims' tongues."

"Appears as such."

"Hell." Montoya finally took the proffered chair. "I've had experience with some really bad dudes. A couple of guys into really sick shit. One called himself Father John and the other one went by The Chosen One. Serial killers. Both had a weird religious/sadistic bent."

"Our killer tends to pick people close to a wealthy family in town," Reed said and decided Montoya might look at this case with fresh eyes. Experienced eyes. Reed had read of the serial killers who had haunted New Orleans last year. Serious psychos. Montoya had helped Detective Rick Bentz bring them down.

"I was going to drive down to St. Simons in an hour. Check this out." He motioned to the report Montoya was skimming.

"Mind if I ride along?" Montoya asked.

Usually Reed would have declined. But he figured he could use all the help he could get. Whoever was taking potshots at the Montgomerys was upping the ante. The deaths were coming at rapid-fire speed. "Might not be a bad idea," he said, then added, "Our latest victim isn't going to look so good, you know. She's been in the water a while."

"I got no problem with that."

Reed leveled a gaze at Montoya and the New Orleans cop didn't flinch. Didn't so much as bat an eye. He'd be okay. After all, he'd witnessed some pretty grisly crime scenes with the killers he'd chased down.

"You're on."

"How is Rebecca Wade connected with the Montgomery family?"

Reed filled him in, told him about the Caitlyn Montgomery Bandeaux connection just as the clip of fast-paced footsteps in the outer hallway heralded Morrisette's arrival. She flew into the room with a cat-who-ate-the-canary smile pasted on her lips. "Guess what I've got!"

"Besides a serious attitude problem?"

"Watch it, Reed, or I might not give you the legal document you've been waiting for. Signed by his holiness himself, the Honorable Ronald Gillette."

"You got a search warrant?" Reed was already reaching for his jacket.

"Signed, sealed and now"—she slapped the damned paper onto his desk—"officially delivered."

"Let's go." Reed was around the desk. He motioned to the visitor. "Detective Sylvie Morrisette, this is Detective Reuben Montoya of the New Orleans Police Department."

"On loan or permanent?" she asked, sizing up the younger cop. Jesus, what was the matter with her? She'd already had four husbands, and from the swift change in her demeanor, it was obvious that she was looking for number five. No matter how much she protested the fact. As a seriously confirmed bachelor, he didn't understand her need to waltz up the aisle with just about anyone she'd ever slept with.

"Montoya's looking for Marta Vasquez."

"As in Lucille, the Montgomery maid's daughter?" she asked.

"One and the same."

"Thought so." Sylvie nodded, agreeing with herself, her blond spikes immobile on her head. "So maybe you want to come along," she invited.

"Already invited," Reed said as they snaked their way downstairs. He was hoping Montoya could shed some light on Lucille's quick departure. It seemed suspicious, and yet his gut told him the old lady wasn't their killer.

"It's possible Marta's disappearance could be connected to your case," Montoya thought aloud.

"Maybe," Reed allowed. Didn't believe it. As far as he knew, Marta didn't have any connection to the Montgomery clan aside from her mother. "But I think she's not close enough to the family. Whoever is doing this seems to concentrate on people who are related."

"Except for Rebecca Wade—if that murder is a part of it," Morrisette said, her interest turned from the newcomer to the job at hand as Reed held the door open for her. Behind her shades, her expressive eyes rolled at his act of chivalry and he thought she uttered, "Oh, save me," under her breath as she and Montoya walked outside into the heat. She said to Montoya, "You can ride with us and Reed'll fill you in."

While you ogle the merchandise, Reed thought, but kept it to himself. It didn't matter. What did count was that finally, thanks to the search warrant, he'd get to look through Mrs. Bandeaux's closets and find out for himself what skeletons she'd hidden away.

". . . so I don't want you to talk to anyone without representation," Marvin Wilder said, escorting Caitlyn to the door of his office. He was a short man whose girth possibly exceeded his height, and his shock of white hair made a sharp contrast to his deep country-club tan. His golf trophies exceeded the legal diplomas hung on the richly paneled walls.

Caitlyn didn't feel much better than she had before the appointment, and any hopes she'd had of getting what she knew off her chest were quickly put aside by the attorney.

"Let's not give the police anything more to work with, not until your memory returns. In the meantime, don't say anything to anyone. Not the police, not the press, no one."

"What about my family?" she asked. "Or my psychiatrist?"

"Please, Caitlyn, just wait a few days. Give me some time to work things out. I know the D.A. Let me talk to Kathy Okano and see where we stand."

Caitlyn wasn't convinced she was doing the right thing, wasn't certain the police were the enemy, though when she remembered Detective Reed standing on her doorstep, she was tempted to change her mind. She'd even caught a glimpse of him another time, at a coffee shop around the corner from her house, just casually ordering a bagel. In her neighborhood. Oh, sure. He was the reason she felt she was being followed, she was certain of it.

But would he call you on the phone and not answer?

Or would he pretend to be your child?

No. She didn't believe that of him.

He was relentless, yes, and she imagined that he was capable of bending the law a bit, but she didn't think he'd stoop to psychological harassment.

She left the lawyer's office and drove by Adam's office—Rebecca's old office. The fact that Adam now used it as his office was odd. Kelly was right. At times she felt he wasn't being straight with her, was holding something about himself back, and other times she felt he was being absolutely honest. She didn't know which but found him more fascinating than she had imagined. There was something restless about him, an impatience hidden beneath his calm veneer and it touched her . . . called out to her.

You really are wacko, aren't you? Worse yet, a romantic wacko. What do you really know about him? Nothing. Other than what he's told you.

Bothered, she drove out of the city. She still hadn't heard from Hannah, and she was getting worried. Caitlyn had called Troy, and he'd reminded her that Hannah was like a wounded dog when she was troubled, that she liked to be left alone to lick her emotional wounds. But Caitlyn wasn't convinced, and Amanda was jittery.

"I don't like it, either," she'd said when Cailtyn called her. "I'd run out there this afternoon, but I'm buried at work. And I've got to meet with the minister and the funeral director for Mom—Dear God, can you believe it?" She sighed. "Maybe I can run out later—oh, damn, I'm supposed to pick up Ian from the airport. But then I'll stop by."

"Don't worry about it. If she doesn't call me back this morning, I'll go out after my appointment with Marvin Wilder."

"Then call me. I want to know what Marvin says one way or another. In the meantime let's hope that Hannah calls." Amanda sounded distraught. "I'd insist upon police protection, but they're all such dicks. We'd be better off with a private service—bodyguards all around. I'm going to suggest it to Troy, and if he won't loosen the estate's purse strings, then I'll pay for it myself. My God, Caitlyn, we can't just let ourselves be sitting ducks. But . . . I'm sure Hannah's all right," she added with more of her usual calm.

Caitlyn wasn't convinced and dialed Troy again. With no luck.

She was told by a snippy secretary that Troy was "in a meeting" and couldn't be disturbed. So Caitlyn was on her own. Driving to Oak Hill and hoping like hell that Hannah was there.

The mailbox was empty and covered in cobwebs. The gate to the lane was secured by a heavy rusting chain. But the lock looked new, and there were what appeared to be fresh tire tracks in the mud. Adam double-checked the address. This was the place. He was sure of it. He'd pushed Caitlyn into telling him where Kelly lived, and she'd reluctantly come up with a place—she couldn't remember the address, but her description had helped him narrow the possibilities. He'd checked with the county, done some digging and found that this house had been rented to one Kacie Griffin. According to the not-so-tight-lipped receptionist at the rental management company, the checks came in like clockwork.

Well, if this was the place, so be it. He had his picks and the imposing lock was spring loaded, not much of a challenge for someone who as a youth had learned the skills from street kids he hung out with. Lock picking, hot-wiring cars, slipping in and out of houses undetected, he'd perfected these skills and was on his way to major trouble when his grandmother had found out and hauled his ass to his older brother, who was then a military policeman. He'd suggested she turn Adam over to the local cops. Grandma had given him one more chance, but taken him to a state prison and had a friend walk him through the place. The catcalls and whistles, iron bars, barbed wire and eyes in watch towers had convinced him to give up his juvenile life of crime.

But the old rusty skills still came in handy.

He neatly picked the lock, but thought better of driving

his car through the gate. He didn't want to be trapped. If someone came, he could hide and sneak away fairly easily— but not with the car parked out front announcing he was inside.

With that in mind, he parked his car at an abandoned gravel pit half a mile away and jogged back to the old gate, slipped inside and continued down the gravel lane, which was little more than two ruts with weeds growing between them. Guarded by oak and pine, the lane was shaded and secluded, but not forgotten. The grass and weeds were bent in places, and he wondered if Kelly, or Kacie, was at home.

What then?

It was possible she was a murderess.

People were dying daily.

Whoever she was, she wouldn't want to be exposed, would want to protect the privacy she'd worked so hard to create. He felt a chill, as if he were walking a path evil had already taken, as he rounded a corner and saw the house. It wasn't much. Not by Montgomery standards. Set in the trees with a view of the river, it had to be a hundred years old. Maybe more. Painted green and brown—well, once anyway and a very long time ago—it was nestled in the forest at a bend in the river and looked like a little hunting or fishing cabin.

Hoping he wasn't met by a man with a shotgun, he rapped on the front door. He'd be straight with anyone who answered, say he was looking for Kacie, and hope that whoever was inside didn't take offense and blow him away. *She could be a murderer. Remember that. And don't be macho enough to think that you can overpower her because she's a woman. She's killed before.*

He knocked again. Waited. Strained to hear some movement inside.

But there was no noise over the wind in the trees, the lap of the river or the occasional call from some marsh bird.

Carefully, he circled the small home, trying to peer through the windows, though most of the blinds were shut, dead insects and cobwebs and dirt between the closed shutters and the dirty glass. If Kelly Montgomery lived here, she was a pig. The front door was bolted; a small door to a lean-to carport was also locked tight. At the back of the house, he noticed footprints in the mud and dirt near the back veranda, cigarette butts crushed in the sand. Someone had been here recently.

On quiet footsteps he walked up two steps to the deck. It creaked under his weight, protesting his intrusion. The French doors were locked as well, but he withdrew his picks and quickly sprung the mechanism.

Slowly he pushed open the door. Then, telling himself he wasn't a common burglar, that the only law he was breaking was that of trespassing, he stepped inside.

It took a minute for his eyes to adjust to the darkness. The place wasn't unused, that much was certain. Just uncared for. It smelled of dust and mildew and smoke, probably from the ashes left in the crumbling brick fireplace. The curtains were old and faded, and not one picture adorned the dingy walls.

He was supposed to believe that Kelly Montgomery, pampered and spoiled princess, was living here, driving to a job from here?

No way.

No damned way.

He walked to the desk, where a dusty phone/answering machine sat, red light blinking, next to a picture of Caitlyn's little girl, Jamie. Kelly's one nod to her family? Or something else? He sensed that there were more layers here than were first visible. Something he was missing. He'd had the feeling for sometime, but it had intensified during the past few days and then last night . . . Jesus, what had he been thinking?

You weren't. You let your dick do all your thinking last night.

Disgusted with himself, he pressed the play button on the answering machine and waited while the tape rewound, then heard Caitlyn's voice leaving a message, the message she'd left from her house last night. While he was there with her. Then he heard his own voice identifying himself and asking Kelly to return his call.

His jaw slid to one side.

Hearing his own voice seemed eerily out of sync. Warped.

In a second of paranoia, he swept his gaze over the walls and ceiling, half expecting to find some sort of tiny camera or bugging device, as if he'd been lured here and then was going to be photographed and studied. But why? What the hell was going on here?

Fleetingly, he remembered the night before and mentally kicked himself from one side of Georgia to the other. How had he let himself get so carried away; how had he ended up making love to her? He frowned at his duplicity. He'd risked everything. His profession. His honor. His beliefs. His damned marriage, such as it was. All for a quick roll in the hay. Absently, he rubbed the ring finger on his left hand and noticed the indentation, still visible though he hadn't worn his band for a long time. How had he allowed himself to get so carried away?

Because the woman got to you. Intrigued you. Face it, you're falling for her. She's an enigma, Hunt, and that's what you like, what you've always been attracted to. Think of Rebecca. Another flighty, fascinating woman who caused you a few hours of joy and years of grief. That's what had started it all, his need to find Rebecca, and he'd discovered another woman, one far more complicated, one perhaps more emotionally dangerous.

He didn't want to think he was so twisted around by a woman, any woman, but he couldn't shake the feeling that both Rebecca and Caitlyn were more than they first appeared and were, in that sense, perhaps like each other.

Eyeing the surroundings, he walked through the sparse rooms. Leather couch, coffee table, dusty television. A bedroom with an antique iron bed and an old quilt, the bathroom stocked with the bare essentials, a bar of soap, tube of toothpaste, near empty bottle of shampoo and small box of tampons. One set of towels. The kitchen wasn't much better. Three bottles of Diet Coke and a bottle of ketchup in the refrigerator, an unopened bag of corn chips, one can of tuna and a jar of peanut butter with one finger scoop removed.

A roll of paper towels and one set of mismatched dishes that would serve four if stretched. The flatware was odds and ends that looked as if they'd been picked up at garage sales or secondhand stores. Certainly not the kind of place one would expect an heir to a damned Southern fortune to call home.

No one called this place home.

Except for the rats, snakes and termites he figured slithered and crawled around the foundation or burrowed in the closets. The little house looked like a place teenagers would break into and claim as a secret gathering place—except there were no beer bottles or trash to be found. Not one speck of garbage.

He walked to the desk and opened the drawer. Not much inside, just a few pictures . . . all of members of the Montgomery family. So someone came here. Someone associated with Caitlyn. He looked around one last time and slipped out the way he'd come. He'd found nothing of consequence and certainly nothing to help him in his quest to find Rebecca.

If push came to shove, he'd go to the police. He'd have to. And endure their skeptical looks and disbelief when he explained about her.

In the meantime, there was Caitlyn. Beautiful, puzzling Caitlyn. What the hell was he going to do about her?

Sugar opened a bleary eye. It was dark and she was lying in a bed . . . but not her bed, not in her bedroom. Music was playing faintly. A song she should recall. What was it? Had she heard it in the club?

Lookin' like a tramp

Why couldn't she move? Couldn't think straight.

Like a video vamp.

Def Leppard. That was it and the song, ''Pour Some Sugar On Me,'' or something like that. What the hell was going on? She squinted, tried to think clearly. The only light came from moonlight filtering through the windows, lots of windows with lacy curtains. The bed was soft, and there was

the scent of honeysuckle drifting in through the lacy curtains
billowing at the windows. She was lying on her back, naked
. . . wait a minute . . . she couldn't move and her mind wasn't
working right; the images were blurry, as if she were on a
bad LSD trip. She tried to roll over but couldn't, finally
realizing that she'd been bound. She was tied to the bedposts,
her legs spread-eagled, her arms pulled tight to one post
over her head.

What the hell?

She shifted and realized with mind-numbing fear that she
wasn't alone. *Shit!* She turned her head and saw her sister.
Christ! Sugar jumped. Her bonds didn't move. Cricket, too,
was naked, lying on her back, her head twisted to one side
so she stared blankly at Sugar. All over Cricket's body were
little reddish pockmarks, stings or pimples or bites . . .

Sugar tried to let out a scream, but no sound came from
her throat. She tried to strain and buck, but she didn't move.
She'd been drugged for certain. She heard a movement,
looked down to the foot of her bed and recognized her
captor. All hope sank as she stared into the condemning
eyes.

"So you're awake. We, your slut of a sister and I, have
been waiting. Do you know who I am?"

Of course I do, you bitch!

"I'm Atropos. One of the three fates. Not that you would
understand, you cretin, but I wanted you to know. And I've
been watching you, seen what you've done . . . oh, yes."

Sugar felt cold fear. She knew. Oh, God, she knew about
Sugar's lover. Sugar didn't doubt for a second that this was
the person who had made the terrifying calls. This was the
person who'd been stalking her.

"You've wanted to be a Montgomery for so long and
now you can. Do you know where you are? Can you guess?"

What kind of sick game was this?

"Oak Hill. You've always wanted to see inside, haven't
you? Well, here you are, and now you can stay." Atropos
moved slowly out of the shadows. She walked to a table
and picked up a jar. "No more guessing games." As she

walked closer, Sugar, terrified, saw that she was wearing gloves. "This is honey, and it's just the start, to make sure the rest sticks."

The rest? The rest of what? Sugar was trying to buck away, terrified. Whatever this sick bitch had in mind, it would be awful. She'd already killed Cricket, that was for sure and now . . . and now . . . She didn't feel the sticky stuff being poured over her body, between her legs, over her breasts, on her lips, in her hair. Her attempts at trying to shrink away were fruitless and her mind was wandering. This couldn't be happening. This was nuts. A horrid dream.

"Sugar. Such a sweet name. And it has so many possibilities."

Go to hell!

Then she heard a ripping sound and saw Atropos standing over her with a huge sack. She began to pour, and white powder, sugar, came rolling out, covering Sugar's body. "Such a sweet name," Atropos said, then hummed along with the music that played over and over and over, that song . . .

Little miss innocence.

Sugar wanted to cry. To scream. To rail against this horrid, sick woman, but she could only watch.

Pour some sugar on me.

One bag wasn't enough. Atropos ripped open another, and the pouring continued, over the bed, over Cricket, over Sugar. She was saying something about insects and soft tissues, and Sugar being a whore, but she couldn't hear it over the roar of the sweet crystals falling over her body, in her hair, on her hands and finally, over her face. She gasped and sputtered, disbelieving. No, no, no!

Please stop.

Please, someone help me.

Thirty-One

The problem was, Reed couldn't be two places at once. With Montoya and Morrisette, he stopped by Caitlyn Bandeaux's house, found her not home and delegated the search to a couple of detectives he worked with. He trusted Landon and Metzger to do a thorough job and figured he could run down to St. Simons and be back within a few hours if he pushed the speed limit. He might miss Caitlyn's return, but he'd deal with her later. Once they knew what she'd hidden away. He was hoping for a murder weapon, but he'd take any bit of evidence that would link her to the crime.

The trip to St. Simons took over an hour, but they didn't have to stay long.

Viewing Rebecca Wade's body wasn't easy; nor, Reed thought, had it been necessary. He could have asked for pictures, though there was something compelling about actually seeing the victim rather than flipping through pictures, not that they wouldn't have been bad enough. They'd seen the remains and he'd wanted to heave, as he imagined had both Morrisette and Montoya, but they'd all managed to get through the ordeal without throwing up and had learned an interesting piece of information from the deputy in charge.

". . . The dentist we got the records from knew her pretty well. She'd gone to him for years and he was pretty upset to think that she might have been killed, let me tell you." Deputy Kroft, a fleshy man pushing the last loop of his belt buckle as he edged ever closer to retirement, nodded to himself as they walked out of the morgue to the intense sun of Georgia in June. Water was visible, sunlight skating off the surface, nearly blinding in its intensity. "And the kicker is that he said she was married. Didn't you say you didn't know if there were any next of kin?" Kroft asked, taking off his hat to smooth his hair, then squaring it onto his thinning patch of gray.

Reed nodded. "We don't have much information on her."

"Well, she'd grown up in Michigan, small town outside of Ann Arbor. The dentist, Paxton, his name is, Timothy Paxton, he knew her as a kid, knew the family, remembered her getting married to another student at the university. The folks passed on a few years back, but Paxton was sure she was married to a guy named Hunter or Hunt or Huntington or something like that. Never had any kids that he knew of, but he never heard much about a divorce, neither."

"Adam Hunt?" Reed asked, exchanging a look with Morrisette.

"That sounds like it. Yep. Could be."

There was no 'could be' about it. Reed was sure of it. Crap. How had they missed that? He took the information, and filling Montoya in, they drove north toward Savannah. Morrisette took the job of calling the dentist and verbally pushing her way past a receptionist who didn't want to put her through, some idiot who thought an impression for a new crown was more important than an ongoing murder investigation. Eventually she got through. She plugged one ear and listened as Reed drove ten miles faster than the speed limit.

She hung up and said, "Looks like Deputy Kroft's information is on the money. The dentist was an old family friend, choked up about Rebecca."

"What did he have to say about Hunt?"

"Not much more than we learned from Kroft. Rebecca met him in college where they were both psych majors, lived with him a while, married him after she'd graduated and then lost touch with Dr. Paxton. Her folks are dead, and apparently so was the marriage."

"Hunt has a lot of explaining to do. Did anyone ever talk to him?" They were driving through the swampy flatlands, the highway cutting close to the coast.

"I tried a couple of times. Should have pushed it," Morrisette admitted, frowning and reaching for her cigarettes. She and Montoya lit up, cracking the windows of the Crown Victoria. "I went to the office twice, figured I'd catch him there. Called just yesterday."

"But he never called back."

"Nope."

"Let's find him. Give him the news that his wife or ex-wife is dead."

Reed wondered how the guy was involved. If he was involved. The police would find out if a missing persons report had been filed, if Hunt and Wade had been married at the time of her death, if he'd been around before, if there was a will, insurance money or another man or woman involved. He remembered seeing Hunt on the doorstep of Caitlyn Bandeaux's house, kissing her as if they were lovers. He gave the Crown Vic a little more gas and discussed Adam Hunt and what they were going to do about him all the way back to the city.

He pulled up in front of Caitlyn's house, where the search was still going strong. Handing the keys to Morrisette, he said, "Check out Hunt. Tell him about Rebecca Wade. Find out what he knows. I'll catch a ride back with Metzger." To Montoya he said, "You can go with her if you like . . . make sure she doesn't get into any trouble."

"Blow it out your ass!" Morrisette said with a twinkle in her eye. "Make that your big, hairy, effin' ass."

One of Montoya's eyebrows arched.

"Don't ask. She can tell you all about her deal with her

kids on the way over to Hunt's. It has to do with a kitty-cat bank.''

"Hello Kitty," she said as Reed climbed out of the car and Morrisette took over the wheel.

"Wear your seat belt," he advised Montoya, then slapped the side of the car and hurried up the brick walk. From the corner of his eye, he caught sight of a news van rolling toward the house. *Great. Just what he needed.*

Before the reporter could clamber out of the van, Reed was inside the house, the door closed firmly behind him. The detectives had taken the liberty of putting the little dog in his kennel in the laundry room and, according to Landon, "The mutt hasn't shut up for a minute. Always with the yapping!"

"The owner hasn't returned?"

"Not yet," Landon said. He was big, black and beautiful, as they used to say. Tall enough to have played college basketball and smart enough that when the NBA didn't come knocking, he'd earned himself a B.S. in criminal justice. Landon was taking law classes at night and had his eye firmly on Katherine Okano's job. He shaved his head these days, sported a soul patch and had one of those sculpted bodies that only came from a military-like dedication to lifting weights. "Good thing we had a no-knock-and-search," he said now.

Reed agreed. It would have been a pain if they'd been restricted by having to ask for Caitlyn Bandeaux's permission. "You found anything?"

"No weapon, nothing like that, but come upstairs." Landon led Reed to the second story. "Take a look here . . ." He pointed to discolorations on the carpet. "And in here. Check out the shower." He nodded toward the bathroom, where the glass shower door had been cracked, the fissures radiating from a hole in its center. "We think the stain in the bedroom might be blood. We found a few flecks on the baseboard, so we've already called the crime scene team. They're going to go over the place with Luminal."

"Good. Check it out." The Luminal test would prove if

there had been blood on the carpet or anywhere else in the room. "And find out the type or types." He was getting a bad feeling about this.

"Looks like a lot of blood," Landon said. "But the victim was killed elsewhere, right—at his home? Could we have it wrong? Maybe he was killed here and transported."

"Unlikely from the way the body was found, rigor and the way the blood had settled in his body, but the kicker is that someone took the time to stage his suicide in a clumsy attempt to make everyone think he'd slit his wrists, but there wasn't enough blood at the scene or in his body to explain it."

Landon snorted. "You were missing blood?"

"Yep."

"My guess is you just found it."

"Hannah?" Caitlyn called, knocking loudly on the door of the old house she'd once called home. She was worried. Hannah hadn't returned her calls, and Caitlyn had spent most of the day trying to track her down. First in town at the few places she hung out, because she hadn't answered; then, finally running out of options, she'd left another message saying she was coming to the house and would wait for her baby sister. She didn't like the idea of Hannah living out here in the middle of nowhere in this old, empty, falling-down mansion. There were rust spots on the down spouts, shutters listing from the windows, mortar crumbling away from the bricks of the wide front porch. Where once this house had held a huge family, it now was nearly empty. Only Hannah remained, and that wasn't good. No one her age should be tucked away in this old dilapidated museum of a home. When her sister didn't answer, Caitlyn walked to the back of the house where the table and chairs were positioned on the wide back porch. It had been only days since she'd sat here, her mother in one chair, worried whether Caitlyn would be charged with murdering her husband.

Good Lord what had happened in those few days?

And what about last night? What had happened then? One minute you were kissing Adam, fairly throwing yourself at him, really getting it on, and the next you don't remember anything, you blacked out again, lost hours . . . hours. How?

She didn't want to think about the blackouts; they were coming too close together, too often, her life spinning out of control. It was stress, that was it. The police were breathing down her neck, she was guarding this incredible secret about all of the blood she'd found the morning after Josh was killed, her mother had been murdered and now . . . oh, God, now, she was worried about Hannah.

She had a key. One she'd never given back when she'd moved out. Finding it on her key ring, she decided to let herself inside. She pushed the door open and walked into the house. Her heart tightened as she glanced at the table where she'd eaten breakfast with her siblings before school, saw the hooks by the back door where their backpacks and jackets had hung.

The floorboards creaked beneath her feet, and though it was still light outside, the clouds had covered the sun and the broad porches flanking the first floor had cooled the house and shaded the windows, making it seem dark. "Hannah?" she called, but heard nothing. The house felt empty and yet . . . did she hear music or a television on? Playing from somewhere upstairs? "Hannah? Are you home?"

Her cell phone rang and she jumped, then chided herself for her case of nerves. This old manor had been her home; she'd grown up here. And bad things had happened here. Along with the good. *You remembered the nights you hid beneath the bed, the menacing footsteps in the hall outside your door, the frightening shadow that would pass, blocking the slice of light under the door as they moved on the other side . . . monster . . . brother . . . Charles with his hot breath and rough hands . . .*

She was breathing fast now, adrenalin pumping through her blood. The phone jangled sharply and she gasped, then dug through her purse and dragged it out. "Hello?" she said breathlessly as she hit the talk button. Silence. *Oh, no, not now.* ''Hello?'' Nothing. She clicked off quickly. Shut the damned thing off. Whoever had decided to terrorize her knew her cell phone number. How much more? What other intimate details of her private life did they know?

Hannah wasn't here. She should just leave now. But she started for the stairs and was certain she heard soft voices and thin music playing, coming from upstairs. Fear pounded in her heart. *Don't be a wuss. You've climbed these stairs a million times in your life. For God's sake, Caitlyn, you're being foolish. It's broad daylight. This was your mother's home. Yours.*

Taking in a deep breath, she climbed to the landing, and the sound of music grew louder. Maybe Hannah had dropped off while watching television. She walked up the stairs but stopped. Hannah's door was open. The light off. No radio or television playing.

But there was in Caitlyn's room. The door was closed, but the muted sounds were definitely emanating from the other side of her room at the far end of the hall. Music. Vaguely familiar. She hesitated, watched the shafts of sunlight pierce the colored glass of the skylight above the landing, and told herself it was now or never. She could leave and never open the door, she could call Kelly or Troy or Adam and wait for them to show up, or she could just goddamned show some guts and walk into the bedroom where only a few days before she'd slept in her old canopied bed.

Or . . . the door to Charles's old room was open as well. Swallowing back her fear, she eased into the room. It wasn't disturbed. Had been left the way he'd had it when, at nineteen, he'd been killed. Athletic trophies lined a shelf, his high school letter, faded now, was still pinned to a bulletin board, and beside his bed, in the nightstand, should be his pistol. She opened the drawer and there was the little gun . . . just as he'd left it.

No bullets were in the chamber and she had no idea where . . . Her eyes narrowed on one of his shooting trophies, one that was a cup. Years ago, before he'd died, she'd seen him empty this little pistol and place the bullets in the cup. "To be safe," he'd told her and winked when he'd caught her watching from outside the door. Could it be? Would she be so lucky? She took the cup from its resting place and sure enough, along with an unused and ancient condom, was a box of tiny bullets. Before she could think twice, she loaded the gun and slipped the rest of the box in her purse. Then, armed and dangerous, she eyed the only closed door on the second floor.

"Go for it," she muttered, disregarding the sweat prickling her scalp and the warning hairs rising on the back of her arms. Her running shoes were muffled against the hall runner as she forced herself down the hallway and twisted the doorknob.

The door opened, and she walked into the room.

She wasn't alone.

Two women, two naked women, were lying tied to her bed.

Caitlyn gasped. Stepped back. Terror gripped her as the television flickered. Tied to the headboard, Sugar Biscayne and her sister Cricket stared sightlessly at her. They were dead; their flesh, where it hadn't been bitten or eaten, white where it was covered by mounds and mounds of white crystals. Pounds of sugar that in turn was crawling with insects. Ants. Crickets. Flies. Hornets. Music pulsed through the room, was playing from a small CD player set up in the corner, the same song over and over . . . *Pour some sugar on me* . . . The television flickered with some muted cooking show.

Stumbling backward, Caitlyn half fell into the hallway. Her stomach heaved as she scrambled to her feet and fled down the stairs. She had to get out of here, to leave before whoever it was that did this, found her.

She flew out of the house, leaving the door open. Her heart was pounding wildly, fear pumping through her blood. She found her keys. Slid behind the wheel, could barely think, barely jab the key into the ignition. "Come on, come on," she muttered as her fingers trembled and fumbled. She twisted on the ignition.

Nothing happened.

What? Oh, God, no!

Frantically she pumped the gas and tried again. "Come on, come on!" she cried. Oh, this was no good. No good. Her heart was jackhammering, pounding crazily, her pulse leaping. She felt it then, that horrible feeling that she might lose consciousness, the blackness threatening to swallow her. She wouldn't let it. Couldn't. But the damned car wouldn't start.

Don't panic. You have a gun.

But what good would this tiny weapon be against an unseen enemy who had killed so many?

She found her cell phone and dialed Adam's number and left a panicked message.

Call the police.

The blackness was pulling at her mind. Trying to drag her under. She started to dial the phone again. A simple number. 911. But before she could punch the numbers, the phone rang in her hand. Relieved, trying to keep the world from spinning, she pressed the talk button. "Adam? I'm at Oak Hill and something terrible's happened. People are dead and my car won't start and . . . and . . ."

"Mommy?" a child's breathless voice whispered.

"Oh, God, no!" It couldn't be. It wasn't Jamie . . . or was it? Things were beginning to jumble. She was breathing so hard, so fast, her heartbeat racing out of control.

"Mommy . . . I can't find you . . ."

"Baby! Jamie? Mommy's right here . . ."

"Mommy, I'm scared . . ."

"I am too, baby, I am too," she said and suddenly she lost control, was slipping away, fading . . . oh, God . . . She shuddered, fought the overwhelming feeling and lost. She was no longer herself . . .

Jesus H. Christ, Kelly thought, slipping easily to the fore. Caitlyn had always been too mentally frail, a weakling, one of those simpering, feeble women that Kelly had always hated. A loser with a capital L.

Well, she wasn't here right now, was she? She'd disappeared. Maybe now she would be lost forever. Gone. Vanished. And that was good. It was time for Kelly to be in control.

In the sterile sanctuary, Atropos clicked off the recorder. Caitlyn's maternal instincts were so predictable. So easily evoked. A tape recording of her dead child's voice and she'd come running. Even though she knew the kid was dead.

But then, Caitlyn never had been all together, now had she?

And it had only worsened with time. As a child she'd had an imaginary friend in Griffin ... someone to play with when her siblings, especially Kelly, who tormented her sister, were busy. Griffin had emerged after the episode when Caitlyn had been locked away with dead Nana. Atropos smiled. Even Nana hadn't suspected that her tea was being doctored, that her frailty was manufactured.

After the trauma with Nana, Caitlyn had found solace in her little pretend friend. She'd gone on and on about Griffin to the point that Berneda had forbidden her to ever speak of him. Refused anyone's suggestion that Caitlyn needed help; she was just a child with an imaginary friend. What was the harm in that? And Berneda hadn't wanted to believe that any of her children could have been afflicted with the Montgomery curse, that they might be mentally unstable.

So Griffin, the invisible, had stayed with Caitlyn and was there when she'd discovered Charles's body buried deep in the snow. An imaginary friend or the first evidence of schizophrenia? What did it matter? Caitlyn was a fruitcake. Had really lost it after the boating accident.

As she thought of Caitlyn, Atropos snipped at the pictures of Cricket and Sugar. She'd gotten the snapshot of Cricket from her driver's license, a pretty ugly shot, but she didn't need much. Atropos cut off Cricket's head and attached it to a bug's body ... yes, that was a nice touch. And for Sugar, the cunt, she used the Polaroid she'd found in Sugar's lover's wallet ... a naked shot of Sugar spread-eagled on a bed. The picture was sickening, but would be perfect for the gnarled family tree with its broken, falling branch reserved for the Biscaynes.

With relish, Atropos mangled the damning photograph by snipping off Sugar's breasts and the juncture of her legs. She glued both pieces to the wrapper of a small packet of sugar Atropos had slipped into her purse when she'd visited the coffee bar a few days earlier. She slipped Sugar's head into the packet, so that only her eyes were visible. Perfect. So now they were ready to mount with their life cords. Little Cricket complete with antennae, wings and insect legs. Atropos pinned her to her branch as if she were a butterfly to be displayed upon a velvet background and ran the life cord to the main trunk of the tree. Next, she stuck the empty packet of sugar with a set of boobs and cunt attached, to the same twisted branch and added Sugar's life cord.

She admired her work, but only for a minute. She had so much more to do, and time was running out.

Thirty-Two

Adam didn't go straight back to his car. After slipping out of Kacie Griffin's house, he'd explored the grounds, found nothing significant other than a few fairly fresh oil stains in the carport, then taken a short path that cut through the trees to the river. The cabin sat up from the water, the deck having a view of the river and beyond, to the far shore where, as Caitlyn had told him, Oak Hill stood. There was no dock, but a small canoe had been pulled into the tall grass and weeds, oars and a flashlight tucked inside. The flashlight looked new, and when he switched it on it worked, its beam bright in the coming dusk. Insects buzzed and whirled around the light, and he clicked it off to gaze across the darkening, ever shifting river.

Something was wrong . . . evil. Something malicious lurked unseen in the gloom. Something that followed Caitlyn around as closely as her own shadow, something he didn't understand.

Something? Something? How about everything?

He'd lingered several hours at the cabin by the river, hoping someone might show up—Kacie? Kelly? Or someone else. He'd walked the shore, stepped in the stream by mistake and eventually sat on a flat boulder and tossed stones into the water, watching the ever-widening ripples as he thought and wondered about Caitlyn. He cared for her. Big time. More than he should have. She was the first woman since Rebecca whom he'd allowed to get so close to him.

And she was the most complicated.

You mean the most screwed up.

Caitlyn and Kelly. Twins. They spun and blended in his mind, so alike yet, according to Caitlyn, so different. And Kelly was dead. Or so everyone thought, everyone but Caitlyn. Even though Kelly's body had never been found. The family had buried her and buried her deep. In the cemetery where Josh Bandeaux, her father and brothers were buried, Kelly Griffin Montgomery had been interred, with or without a body. She had a grave with a headstone; he'd seen it himself, and the permanence of that etched marble pounded into the earth had caused his skin to prickle with goose bumps.

Caitlyn believed it was all a lie. That Kelly was just in hiding because of a big rift in the family. A major rift; one that couldn't be bridged.

The truth?

Or what she wanted to believe?

Was Kelly real?

Or a ghost?

Shit, now he was wearing out. No ghosts. Just overactive and wishful imagination. Caitlyn was troubled, made up imaginary friends, hadn't been able to suffer the loss of her sister in the boating accident and so had conjured her up, brought her back to life.

Standing, he dusted his hands and glanced across the river to Oak Hill. It stood on a bluff overlooking the river, about half a mile downstream. From here he could stare at the old manor and wondered how often Kacie, whoever she was, did.

He looked at the pictures he'd taken from the cabin and had slipped into his pocket, a group of odd photographs of Caitlyn and Kelly, Amanda, Hannah, Troy, and, he presumed, Charles. There was even a snapshot of a baby, probably Parker, the one who had died of SIDS.

Or been killed.

So many deaths. At Kelly's hand? Caitlyn's? Someone else's? He had to talk to Caitlyn and then go to the police with what he knew. First he'd advise Caitlyn to get a lawyer, tell her he would help her as best he could. *You can't tell the police anything; you're her counselor, her mental doctor.*

But he had to save her from whom?

More and more he felt he was trying to save her from herself.

If that was possible.

Disturbed at the turn of his thoughts, he jogged back to the car as twilight was descending. Out here, where he could see the sky, a million stars were winking, and the scent of the river was strong. Frogs began to croak, insects to sing. It could have been peaceful but for the underlying feeling of evil. Ever present and pervasive. Opening the hatchback of his little car, he searched for a rag to wipe off his shoe and spied the backpack Rebecca had kept hanging in her closet, the one he'd found in her office. He'd always thought the backpack had been out of place there, one of the few things she'd kept from their life together. It was worn and frayed and he'd used it to haul some things from her office. There had been nothing in it when he'd found it, and it was nearly empty now.

"So where the hell are you?" he wondered aloud as he located an old golf towel he'd stashed in a compartment with the spare tire. He swabbed his legs and shoes, wiping off any trace of river water. He was about to throw the used towel into his car and take off, but hesitated and, instead, picked up the backpack. Inside he found a few things from her office that he'd intended to return. He took them out. Files and computer disks, a couple of pictures and a notepad. Laying them on the back floor of the hatchback beneath the tiny bulb, he examined the bag more closely. It was a simple design, made of a canvaslike material and reinforced with leather on the bottom. One of the straps had frayed. The leather was scuffed and torn in places. All of the pockets and zippered closures were empty. The main zipper to the biggest compartment was jammed and wouldn't close. All in all, the old bag was a piece of crap. So why hadn't she gone out and gotten a new one? Why hang on to the thing? Nostalgia? For this? He doubted it. Get rid of the men in her life, but keep this old battered backpack when she had a leather briefcase he'd discovered in her home? Definitely not Rebecca's style. He held the bag aloft, turning it beneath the dim light on the roof of the car. As it slowly spun, he noticed something that wasn't right, a slit in the bottom where the leather had been reattached to the canvas.

Rebecca fixed the cut, but not the zipper?

He pulled; the thread was tight, the rudimentary hand stitches gone over several times. He didn't have a knife, but he used his keys, pulling at the stitches and shredding them there in the gravel pit, feeling like a fool because this was probably nothing but a hasty repair job, then finally opening the bottom of the bag enough to peer inside. Tucked deep inside was a compact disk.

His throat tightened. He knew in a heartbeat that it was the information he was looking for, the information on Caitlyn Montgomery Bandeaux.

Reed caught a ride with Metzger back to the station. The guy was fifty pounds overweight. When he wasn't smoking, he was chewing tobacco. He had a wife and five kids and a cholesterol count in the stratosphere. And he was one of the best cops Reed had ever worked with.

Reed left Diane Moses and her team at Caitlyn's house and gave her instructions to detain Caitlyn Bandeaux and call immediately if she returned. Reed had asked specifically for hair samples from the dog as well as from Caitlyn's brushes, for which he earned one of Diane's famous don't-tell-me-how-to-run-my-team looks. So he'd shut up. Diane wasn't the most fun at a party, but she knew her business.

As he and Metzger pulled into the station parking lot,

Morrisette and Montoya were just getting out of their unmarked Crown Vic.

"Any luck?" Reed asked, but could tell by Morrisette's sour expression that she'd come up empty-handed.

"Nada. Not at Hunt's place or his office, which we're sealing. Couldn't locate any of the Montgomery relatives either. Troy's quote 'out of the office' and the secretary won't say where, though she promises to try and call him on his cell. Translate that to 'on the golf course' or with some woman he's not supposed to be. Amanda's not in the office, out with a client somewhere, again, the secretary at the law firm will try to call. Sugar Biscayne seems to have joined her sister as I can't raise her either; no one's seen her since last night. Hannah's not answering out at the house, and I've got a county deputy going out to knock on the door. As for Lucille Vasquez, she's still in Florida, right?" Morrisette asked and Reed noted that the skin over Montoya's face tightened.

"As far as I know, though supposedly she was coming back for Berneda's funeral."

"Which is when—day after tomorrow?"

Reed lifted a shoulder. "Soon. The family's been demanding we release the body."

"Have we done that?" she asked as they walked toward the station.

"Yep. Autopsy's finished. Toxicology's back. No reason not to let her go."

"What about trace evidence? Anything found in the bed sheets or room or the scrapings under her nails?"

"Still checking."

"It's a bitch, you know?" Morrisette said as she flipped her sunglasses onto her head. "The whole effin' family being out of touch. Ain't that about as convenient as free hot dogs at a vegetarian convention? I've got All Points out on both Hunt and Bandeaux and their vehicles, but so far nothing.

"We'll find 'em."

For the first time since Reed had met him, Montoya grinned. "That's the attitude."

"Yeah," Sylvie agreed. "Sure beats cryin' in your beer. We get enough of that poor-me attitude from the jerk-offs we arrest. Is it the same in New Orleans—they couldn't help themselves, got caught up in a life of crime because, you know, they had it rough as kids? Bad stepdads, lousy teachers, mothers who had to work. Give me a fuck—effin' break. If you ask me, the whole world is filled with whiney-asses." Her cell phone rang suddenly, and she pulled it from her belt. "Morrisette," she growled into the phone, then immediately turned all of her attention to the conversation. "Yeah . . . you're sure? . . . Okay . . . got it. I don't like the sound of this. Call for backup and apprehend. We're on our way." She clicked off the phone, her face serious. "Let's go," she said, turning back to her vehicle. "Hunt's car has been spotted. Looks like he's on his way to the Montgomery family estate. I'll drive. And don't fuckin' argue with me."

Kelly felt the cold steel of the gun in her hand as she moved in the shadows of the shrubbery, the big old house looming behind her, only one window, that of her bedroom, glowing with the flickering blue light of the television set. The rest of the grounds were quiet. Eerily so. Seemingly deserted. Which, she figured, was a crock.

Someone was here. She sensed it in the prickle of apprehension running down her spine.

She'd learned to shoot years ago, at her father, Cameron's, insistence. The old bastard. Talk about someone who got what he deserved. Well, they all did, didn't they? Cameron dying on his way back from visiting his lover and losing control of his car as well as one of his balls? Crazy Aunt Alice letting herself be put in a mental institution, allowing the rest of the family to decide what would happen to her fortune? It was fitting somehow that she had died at that place where the life was sucked out of a person while she was being waited on hand and foot. Then there was Charles, killed by an arrow through his cold, useless heart. Charles the predator becoming the prey ... yes, the deaths were making sense. Even Josh ... When Kelly hadn't had the nerve to go through with poisoning him with the wine, someone else had come in and lent a hand, polishing him off with some debilitating drug and then slitting his wrists in order to make it look like a suicide. She remembered going to his home that night—Caitlyn had been drinking in a bar and wouldn't remember what happened. The timing had been perfect. Kelly had decided to end her twin's anguish. Forever.

Pretending to be Caitlyn, she'd driven to the bastard's house in her sister's white Lexus. It was time to take Josh out. He'd been tormenting Caitlyn for years, destroying any sense of self-worth his ex-wife had ever had and Kelly was sick to death of it. So she'd shown up on his doorstep with the doctored bottle of wine and pretended to be Caitlyn.

Her ruse had worked. But it had taken some manipulating. And she'd had to grit her teeth not to tell the bastard to go straight to hell when he'd opened the door and scowling down at her had demanded, "What the hell do you want?"

Christ, what had Caitlyn ever seen in the jerk? She'd wanted to kill him right then, but she hadn't, and played the meeker Caitlyn role to the hilt.

He'd stood on the porch, claiming he didn't want her there, but rather than raise a scene, he'd finally deigned to allow her inside, making the mistake of leading her into the den where the damning wrongful death lawsuit papers had been lying on his desk. Never had a man more deserved to die. What a money-grubbing prick. Kelly had been glad she'd brought the wine with its fake label. She pretended to be weak and worried, even wringing her hands like Caitlyn sometimes did and Josh had lost some of his arrogance.

God, he'd been such a lying, two-faced bastard.

But she'd been lucky that night. At least she'd thought so at the time. Josh had already been drinking, enough that his judgement was obviously impaired. He'd softened up a bit, even offered her a glass of the wine he'd been drinking before he'd opened the second bottle—her deadly bottle. The cork had popped loudly, echoing in Kelly's ears as she'd watched with fascination as Josh "The Bandit" Bandeaux had poured himself a glass. It might as well have been hemlock.

She'd drunk from her glass and stared at him as he swallowed the sulfite-laden chardonnay in one long swallow.

"Your coming here doesn't change anything," he'd assured her, slurring his words a bit. "I'm still going to file the suit and . . . and . . ." He'd shaken his head as if dazed, then poured himself another drink and refilled Kelly's glass with the wine she'd brought.

She'd begun to have second thoughts as he swallowed more of the wine that could kill him.

Suddenly, she realized she'd made a horrendous mistake. She wasn't a killer. No way. So she hadn't been able to go through with it. Panic had seized her.

"Don't drink any more," she'd ordered. "Josh, look, I made a mistake. A really bad one."

"You've made lots of 'em Cait." He'd leaned heavily against his desk and she'd noticed beads of sweat on his upper lip and forehead.

"I mean it, the wine isn't what you think," she'd admitted, looking him straight in the eye. "You'll need epinephrin."

"What?"

"Now, Josh."

He'd nearly dropped his glass as he swept up the bottle and read the label. "But I drink this all the time . . ."

"That's not what's in the bottle. Look, there's no time to explain. But the wine you drank has sulfites—"

"Shit! You poisoned me? You . . . you goddamned bitch! Caitlyn . . . or . . . Jesus Christ who the hell are you? Get out! Now!" He'd taken one wobbly step toward her before reeling quickly and, nearly stumbling, heading into the bathroom where, she knew, he kept his anti-allergy kit. Through the open doorway, in the reflection of the mirror over his sink, she'd seen him give himself a life-saving dose.

Her legs had felt weak. What had she been thinking,

she'd wondered. Dear God, had she really been going to kill Caitlyn's ex-husband? She wasn't a murderess and she was feeling dizzy . . . woozy. Was she as nuts as her sister, she'd asked herself, her vision blurring a bit.

Now, as she slunk through the shadows at Oak Hill, she couldn't remember much more of the night Josh had died. She'd felt odd, her mind clouded, her legs like rubber as she'd tried to leave. From the corner of her eyes, she'd seen Josh return to the den and half-fall into his desk chair, but before she could call out to him, before she realized what was happening, she'd stumbled and . . . hit her head as she'd swooned to the floor of the den . . . and then she had blacked out, remembering nothing more. Later she'd learned that Josh was dead.

Obviously killed by someone who was picking off the Montgomery family members.

Whoever was behind all this had enviable sense of irony, but was as deadly as sin. That person had tried once to kill the twins in the boating accident, then recently, had attempted to frame Caitlyn for her husband's murder.

Silently, her heart a drum, Kelly crept around the hole of a huge oak tree, the branches rattling slightly. Smelling the heavy scent of the river and dry grass, seeing the Spanish moss swaying eerily in the wind, light filmy wraiths shivering as they clung to the gnarled branches, she gritted her teeth against a dark fear that burrowed through her. She sensed she wasn't alone. That the killer was nearby. Armed with the pistol, her cell phone and a tiny flashlight she'd retrieved from the Lexus's glove box, she felt every hair on the back of her arms prickle in dread.

Tough.

She couldn't back down and crumble into wimpy Caitlyn now. No more. She wouldn't allow her weak-minded twin to fall victim any longer. Never again. It ended here. Tonight. No matter what. A gust of wind passed by, ruffling her hair, seeming to laugh at her bravado.

Lucille had said it all. "There's ghosts here on this plantation, don't ya know? You hear 'em too, now, don'tcha? They talk to me and they talk to you.''

In Kelly's opinion that was crazy talk, but now, listening to the whisper of the breeze, watching the moss dance and shimmy, she wasn't so sure. Her fingers tightened around the pistol. She wasn't going to cower in the car like a cornered mouse when who-knew-what was waiting, ready to pounce on her—oh, excuse me, on Caitlyn— at the drop of the hat. Charles's gun would take care of that.

The cell phone rang and she cursed herself for bringing it with her from the car. Whoever was out here waiting for her would hear it as well. She ducked behind the old pump house and quickly hit the talk button but didn't answer. The airwaves crackled, and no one said a word. Any noise would bring her hunter fast upon her. She raised a finger to disconnect and turn the damn thing off when the first faint sounds of a toddler's voice cried softly. Pathetic mewling whimpers . . . ''Mommy? Where are you?''

Kelly gasped. Her heart twisted.

So this was the game. Using the memory of Jamie and Caitlyn's guilt as bait.

Kelly flattened against the weathered boards of the pump house, the peeling paint scratching the back of her neck. ''I'm here, honey, and I'm coming to get you,'' she whispered.

''It's dark and I'm scared.''

Kelly's gaze swept the lawn, the outbuildings, the old garage, the fruit cellar . . . the stables and old slave quarters. ''I bet you're scared, honey. Just tell me where you are . . . Mommy will come,'' she said, trying to make her voice quiver, hoping that she could fool whoever was on the other end of the line into believing that she was as ragged and frayed as damned Caitlyn. She put a hitch in her voice; faked a sob. ''Jamie? Honey, can you tell me where you are?''

''I don't know . . . it's . . . dark . . . icky . . . there's . . . there's . . . dirt and glass and it smells bad . . .'' She began to sob and for a second Kelly almost bought into the lame, frightened-toddler charade. Almost. But not quite. "Mommy, please come," the frail little voice said, all quavery and lisping and desperate. *Oh, for the love of God!*

"I am," she whispered. "Mommy has to hang up now."

"No! Please ... I ... I ... love you, Mommy, and I'm so scared ..." *Click.*

Kelly froze. Never would she have expected the person on the other end of the line to hang up.

Not unless she'd been seen. Unless whoever was on the other end of the line—an assassin pretending to be a little girl—had been near enough to hear her and pinpointed Kelly's hiding spot.

Damn.

Panicked, it was all she could do to hold on, not to bolt and expose herself further. Noiselessly, she slid past the barn, crawling behind a watering trough. Where would a person hide ... here, on these grounds ... what had the clues been? What had the caller whispered in a baby voice?

It's dark.

Well, hell, the whole place is dark.

There's dirt and glass and it smells bad.

Underground.

But there were several basements that ...

And then she knew. Of course she knew.

She'd played there as a child.

Adam drove like a madman. His cell phone battery was shot, and he couldn't call, had barely been able to hear the message that Caitlyn was on her way to Oak Hill.

His fingers curled over the steering wheel in a death grip, and he tried to shove aside the worry that had been with him since he'd put the CD he'd found in the backpack into his laptop computer. While parked in the gravel pit, he'd read Rebecca's notes and felt a growing sense of alarm with each new discovery. How had he not seen what had been, in retrospect, so patently obvious? How, he wondered as he hit the bridge at seventy and saw the turnoff for Oak Hill, had he been so blind?

Rebecca had decided that Caitlyn not only suffered from Dissociative Identity Disorder, DID, often called a split or multiple personality, but that the disorder had gone undiagnosed all of her life. It had worsened with time, and when she'd almost died after the boating accident, she'd taken on her twin's persona. She'd lose track of time, and in those gaps she became Kelly, whose body was never located. Caitlyn had kept her sister alive, giving her a fake job and renting a cabin for her on the river. Whenever Caitlyn became stressed, when her heartbeat accelerated beyond the norm, when her adrenalin was pumping wildly through her veins, she became Kelly.

As she had when they'd made love.

That was the trigger.

This was new ground for DID.

Adam didn't know of another case where the host personality took on a second personality from another real person. Usually the splits were fragmented people, all parts of the whole. Nor did the host person speak with his counterparts. That condition was much more like schizophrenia where the patient actually would see people and converse with them, even though the people he "saw" didn't. Caitlyn's condition was unique and had caused Rebecca, ever ambitious, to believe she would shake up the academic world and get a "million-dollar deal" to write a book.

Christ, he'd been a fool.

Blind.

Because you made one helluva mistake. You fell in love with your patient; the very woman you were using to find Rebecca.

Guilt placed a stranglehold on his heart, but he set his jaw. There was no time for recriminations. Not when Caitlyn's life was at stake.

Cranking on the wheel, his tires screaming in protest, he glanced in the rearview mirror and saw the lights of a police vehicle strobing the night. Good. He'd need help. If Caitlyn was Kelly and she was somehow responsible for the murders of her husband, mother and other members of her family, she could be dangerous.

Not only to him.

But to herself as well.

Self-destructive.

Christ, no. He couldn't lose her now. Wouldn't. Not if he had a chance.

He hit the gas, watched the trees lining the drive flash by in a blur.

Siren wailing, bright lights flashing, the cop car screamed after him.

Adam only hoped they weren't too late.

The cellar beneath the slave quarters was Stygian dark and silent as death. It reeked of musty earth, and something else . . . something metallic. Kelly swallowed hard as she inched down the stairs. Her muscles were tense, the gun clenched in her sweaty fingers. Dear God, what would she find down here?

Each step creaked against her weight, announcing her arrival. Her nerves were frayed as she reached the earthen floor and then the darkness was broken by one flickering sliver of light that shone like a damned beacon beneath a back wall covered by a rack of dusty, forgotten wine bottles. From a dark corner behind her, she heard a rat scurry and she jumped, nearly dropping the gun.

Get a grip she told herself, but expected someone to pounce on her at any second. She didn't take her eyes off the crack of light and suddenly all the old rumors congealed in her head. The slave quarters, unused for generations, had been renovated once years ago, the basement converted to a wine cellar. There had been hushed gossip within the family that Cameron had even had a secret room installed, one where he could meet with his lover when Berneda had gotten suspicious of the carriage house. Was it possible? Was someone in there now?

Fear gripping her, Kelly took a chance. She flipped on the flashlight and expected a shot to ring out and burrow into her heart.

Nothing happened.

Quickly, she ran the beam of her flashlight over the empty cracks, piles of forgotten burlap sacks, broken bottles and debris . . . all the old, decaying . . .

Her heart glitched. There in the middle of the floor, among the shards of glass, leaves that had blown in over the years and dust, was the bunny—the droopy eared stuffed animal Jamie had adored—the one that should have been resting on Jamie's bed in Caitlyn's house.

Kelly's heart wrenched for her niece, the innocent baby. How could anyone take her most precious toy and leave it here to taunt and agonize Caitlyn?

Because whoever is behind this is one sick, warped bastard.

Gritting her teeth, Kelly shone the beam of her flashlight onto the wall above the crack of light on the floor. She nearly missed it as the beam tracked over the old bottles and then she saw it, a glint of metal, the hidden lever in the wall. So this was it.

She eased forward, around the bunny and pulled together all of her courage. Gun in hand, she flipped the switch and stepped back.

The wall swung open silently.

Quickly.

Instantly, Kelly was blinded by the flood of white light. Everywhere.

She blinked and caught glimpses of flourescent lamps, white walls, white furniture, gleaming stainless steel. The images came at her in a bright rush.

Her eyes couldn't focus quickly enough. She saw movement from the corner of her eye and there, from a hiding spot deep in the shadows of the old wine cellar, caught a glimpse of a figure erupting from beneath the old burlap bags. Sacks flew, dust clouded and the figure raised some kind of club high overhead.

Kelly spun. Aimed. Fired as the murderer—oh, God, a woman—ducked, then swung wildly. The club slammed into her head.

Crack!

Pain exploded behind her eyes in a terrifying flash.

Her legs wobbled.

The gun went flying.

The cell phone hit the dirt floor with a thud.

Kelly's knees buckled. She tried to hold on to her consciousness, but as she crumpled to the cold, damp earth she saw the glint of something in the darkness. A needle. Thin. Wicked. Deadly. She tried to get away but couldn't. As if from a distance, she witnessed the hypodermic plunge into her arm.

She thought she heard a siren wail far away and as her head hit the floor, she looked into the clinical room and caught a glimpse of a grotesque piece of art on the barren white walls—a tree with long strings of black and red pasted to it. Distorted bodies were pinned to each string . . . ugly pictures. Horrifying shots.

"I am Atropos, Caitlyn," a familiar voice intoned as the darkness seeped from the edges of her eyes, threatening to claim her.

Atropos?

"And now it is your turn. It's time to join the others." A face she recognized came close to hers and with terrorizing certain, she knew she was about to die. "That's right . . . it is time," Atropos said with a deadly smile. "You have finally met your fate."

Thirty-Three

''We have to go in,'' Adam ordered. He was antsy, ready to climb out of his skull and this dull-headed cop was holding a gun on him. ''Now! Don't you get it! There's a killer on the loose and—''

''Just turn around, sir, and lean against the car and no one will git hurt.'' A pair of handcuffs dangled from the cop's free hand.

''Listen. You have to understand.'' Adam was frantic. Afraid for Caitlyn's life. ''There's a woman in danger here. Serious danger. From herself or someone else. Caitlyn Bandeaux. She's the widow of Josh Bandeaux, who was killed.''

''I know who he is. Now, turn around.''

''You have to believe me! We don't have any time to waste!''

''Do it!'' the cop ordered, and when Adam considered lunging for the gun, he warned, ''Don't even think about it.''

''But we have to help her. We have to. It might save her life!''

The cop hesitated just a fraction. His scowl deepened. He'd heard it all a thousand times probably.

"Look, we've got to find her. Soon. Before it's too late. Let me go inside and—"

"No way."

"But—"

"Get over it! Turn around!"

Adam wasn't about to give up. "Call Detective Reed at the Savannah Police Department. Homicide. Tell him that Caitlyn Bandeaux's a split personality, that she's Kelly Montgomery."

"You're talking nonsense," the cop growled, his nostrils flaring. "No more lip."

"No! I'm her psychologist and she's here—look, her car is there. Run her plates. It's Caitlyn Bandeaux."

The cop glanced at the white Lexus and Adam saw him hesitate again. "Listen! There's not much time! Call Reed. Do it now!"

"First you put your hands on the hood."

"Then you'll call him."

"Then I'll think about it."

"Shit." Adam wanted to punch the guy in his bad-ass cop face, but knew it would only make the situation worse. Reluctantly he turned, did as he was asked and let the cop wrench his hands behind his back and cuff him. "I'm serious. Put in the call."

"After you're in the cage."

"There's no time—"

"Get the fuck inside!" The bruiser of a cop yanked the door open, put his hand over Adam's head and nearly shoved him into the back of the cruiser. Adam fell against a backseat that smelled suspiciously of urine and Lysol, then struggled to a sitting position to glare through the window. The cop slammed the door shut, then placed a call on his cell and started talking while Adam mentally climbed the walls of the meshed-in backseat. Seconds were ticking by. Precious minutes that might mean life or death for Caitlyn. Oh, God, what could he do? He should never have allowed himself to be locked in the car.

"Hey!" He started kicking the windows. "We've got to get inside. Now! She's here!"

"Shut up!" the cop growled, but he'd pulled his side arm. Acted as if he was going inside. Alone. Oh, Christ, the dumb shit didn't know what he was going to face.

Frantic, Adam kept kicking. He had to get out. He had to help.

In his mind's eye he saw Caitlyn's face—Kelly's face. And he imagined it streaked with blood, her lips pale, her eyes staring glazed and dead upward. No! No! NO! He beat against the glass wildly and heard sirens cutting through the night. Twisting, he stared out the back window and spotted two cop cars racing down the long drive, their headlights splashing on the trees and old siding of the aging manor, their overhead lights flashing blue and yellow.

The Cavalry. Or the enemy? Adam didn't know which.

Tires crunched to a stop and dust rose in front of the headlights.

Three detectives clambered out of their cruiser, their faces obscured in the night.

He couldn't stand it. Adam began kicking at the windows all over again, making as much noise as he could with his heels.

Suddenly, the door was thrown open and the cop who had cuffed him stuck his head inside. "Do that again and I'll have you in shackles so fast your head will swim."

"Let me talk to Reed."

"I said—"

"Let's hear what he has to say." Another male voice. "I'm Reed. Step out of the vehicle. And don't do anything stupid."

Adam half rolled out of the back seat and straightened as his feet hit the gravel. He found himself standing eye to eye with a no-nonsense cop.

"Okay, Hunt. What's your story?"

A woman in uniform stood next to Reed, one hip thrust out as she lit a cigarette and glared at him over the flame of a match. She passed the lit cigarette to a tall man with a dark goatee, black pants and leather jacket, then lit another.

"Caitlyn Bandeaux is Kelly Montgomery or at least she thinks she is, " he said, frantic. "She's suffering from DID and possibly schizophrenia."

"DID? What the hell's that?" the woman asked.

"Dissociative Identity Disorder." The younger cop with the goatee narrowed his eyes and drew hard on his cigarette.

"Bullshit," Reed said.

The young cop asked, "What the hell does DID have to do with anything?" He blew out a cloud of smoke.

"It could mean she's in danger. Or that she's dangerous. Either way, she's here. And I think the killer's here. We have to find her. Now!"

"This is all blue smoke and mirrors," Reed said.

"I don't think so," Adam insisted. "My ex-wife . . . is the one who diagnosed her."

"Your wife?" Reed's eyes narrowed and Adam's panic rose. They were losing time. Precious seconds were ticking away.

"Rebecca Wade. I came down here to find her. It's a long story. We don't have time for it now, but she'd run off before, I wasn't sure she was missing as we've been divorced for years but—" He caught the glances sent between the cops. "What? Oh, God."

"I'm afraid I have some bad news for you," Reed said, and the night seemed to thrum with malice.

Adam braced himself. Knew what was coming. Still, he couldn't prepare himself for the finality of Reed's words. "Your ex-wife's body has been found. Positively identified as Rebecca Wade."

"Where? How . . ." He couldn't breathe for a moment. Couldn't think. *Rebecca? Dead? Lively, live by the minute Rebecca? No . . . Oh, God . . .* He thought he might be sick.

"We pulled her out of the water off St. Simons Island. Been there a few weeks." Reed was solemn.

"She . . ." He shook his head to clear it. "Was she . . .?"

"Murdered?" Reed asked and nodded. "I'm sorry," he said and Adam felt a hand upon his shoulder.

The thought of Rebecca being killed made his skin crawl. They'd had their differences, and many a fight, but Rebecca had been passionate and vital. Adam squeezed his eyes shut, silently grieved, but knew that if he didn't move fast, the same fate could await Caitlyn.

"We . . . we have to find her," he said. "Caitlyn . . . we have to find her before it's too late."

"Agreed." Reed scanned the eyes of the small group of cops. "Let's get to it. Before we have another homicide on our hands. You get back in the car."

"But—"

"Don't argue. We're wasting time." He glanced at the bully of a cop who had cuffed Adam. "Stay with him and call for backup."

Then, before the damned psychologist could argue, he led Sylvie and Montoya inside the dark house. It felt empty and smelled like death. But there was music playing, some eerie song. Reed got a bad feeling that only worsened as he stepped from one dark room to the other. They followed the sound, up the stairs and through and open door to a bedroom where two naked women had met their doom.

"Son of a bitch. Son of a fuckin' bitch," Morrisette blurted as she gazed at the bed, illuminated by the flickering light of a television. Covered in white powder that looked like sugar and another substance that Reed guessed was honey, the bodies were crawling with vermin.

"Bastard." Montoya's mouth tightened to a hard, unforgiving line, as if he'd seen it all already.

Sylvie Morrisette gagged, then swore a blue streak that would put her into hock for the rest of her life if she paid into the damned kitty bank as she recognized Sugar and Cricket Biscayne. "What kind of sick fuck would do this?" she asked. "Sugar—because of her name and crickets and . . . oh, God, let's off the bastard."

"First we have to find him or her," Reed said, looking at the revolting display. "Call the crime scene team." He glanced through the windows to the night. "Let's go. We're not done here. There might be more bodies."

"Jesus," Morrisette muttered.

Montoya added, "Or the killer."

"Right. Now, let's go. Somewhere around here maybe we'll scare up Caitlyn Bandeaux."

"If we're not too late," Morrisette whispered, making the sign of the cross over her chest for the first time that Reed could remember.

"She could have done this," Reed reminded them soberly. Who the hell knew? Adam Hunt thought that Caitlyn was a split personality. That explained a lot of things, but Reed wasn't convinced. It sounded like psycho-babble-mumbo-jumbo. For all he knew, she could be the killer.

Or the split could be.

Or the split could make a convenient alibi.

Until he found Caitlyn Montgomery Bandeaux, he'd keep his options open.

She was floating, neither alive nor dead, one minute Cait-lyn, the next Kelly as she lay upon the desk in the white, bright room. Flourescent lights blazed and the tile floor was covered with a clear plastic tarp.

Caitlyn's eyes were open, but she could barely move, only drooled, her head turned, her cheek lying on the cold desktop . . . the way Josh had been when he'd died. The room spun, but she saw her attacker—Atropos—in her blurred vision, working deftly, measuring cords only to cut them with a pair of long-handled stainless steel scissors that winked under the harsh lights. Atropos, my ass, Caitlyn thought. The murderer who seemed to be talking to herself was Amanda, Caitlyn's sister and she was dressed in hospital scrubs, latex gloves and even slippers and a cap under which her hair had been tucked.

Caitlyn couldn't believe it. Didn't want to. Amanda whom she had turned to for comfort and wisdom.

Was Amanda the one who had killed everyone so cruelly?

Amanda? But that was impossible. Amanda herself had been attacked. *Yet not killed.* The tree she hit in her sports car was the only one for a long stretch. She could have staged the accident to make it appear as if she was a victim. But that was crazy. Wasn't it? Caitlyn's head thundered but she couldn't lift it, couldn't move. Could only wonder.

Amanda looked at her and for the first time Caitlyn realized that her older sister had been talking as she'd braided the red and black cords. ''. . . so you see, Caitlyn . . . or is it Kelly? Sometimes it's hard to tell. You were definitely Kelly when you came here.''

What? Kelly's here? Where?

Amanda's eyes narrowed pensively as she stared at Caitlyn. ''You must be Caitlyn because you don't seem to understand. You don't even remember that Kelly is really dead and that you took on her personality after she disappeared.''

Caitlyn's head was spinning; she couldn't think straight. Amanda was making no sense, and yet, a very small, chilling part of her acknowledged some truth in her older sister's words.

''That's right, *Caitie-Did*, you're a fruitcake. At least two people, God knows how many more, but part of the time you thought you were Kelly, you were damned convinced of it. Even lived out in that old cabin . . . Jesus, the one across the river and you had blackouts. You ended up with the Montgomery curse. Didn't you know?''

You're wrong, she wanted to say, *you're the one who's cursed. You're the one who's mad. You're the one with the split personality—sometimes Amanda, sometimes Atropos.*

''Well, anyway, all those who were fated to die, all the pretenders to the Montgomery fortune were not merely killed, but their deaths were planned . . . plotted carefully . . . and fitting. By me. Atropos.''

As if Atropos were somehow separate from her. Two entities. One body.

''It started with Parker. I killed him. He was my first and it was . . .'' Amanda's quick-moving fingers hesitated a moment as she thought. ''Well, it was almost by accident.''

Oh God, Amanda was confessing to killing Baby Parker. Caitlyn thought she would be sick. It was all so horrible. So bizarre.

". . . Smothering him while no one was looking was easy," Amanda said, her eyes narrowing at the memory. "And really, I did everyone a favor. He was always crying and colicky and . . . just such a pain in the butt. Such a noisy, rotten baby. I couldn't believe Mother was still having children even after . . . Well, you know Cameron, dear old Dad, was screwing around on her. But he still had time to keep knocking up his wife as well, creating more little Montgomerys to fight over his money."

Amanda looked directly at Caitlyn. "Can you imagine that? Having children with a man you knew was fucking his own half sister?" Amanda's face darkened. Her lips twisted in disgust. "And not just that. Copper was having kids, too. Cameron couldn't keep his dick in his pants, could he? And he didn't know diddly squat about birth control. Not our sick bastard of a father. He just kept spawning kids. With two women. What an amoral prick. He deserved to die."

She snipped off a bit of thread with her teeth and admired the cord she'd been braiding.

Caitlyn tried to concentrate, to keep hold of her wits as Amanda seemed obsessed with unburdening herself.

"It wasn't just with Copper, you know. Dad had other mistresses." Her jaw slid to the side as she glanced at Caitlyn. "Bet you didn't know that even ever-faithful Lucille couldn't resist him. I overheard her talking to him about it years later. Oh, she was crying and carrying on, promising to look after Mother, but the truth of the matter was she had a one-night stand with Cameron and bang-o, got herself pregnant."

Caitlyn was horrified. What was Amanda saying? God, could this twisted woman really be her sister, the girl and woman she'd grown up with? "That's right, Marta Vasquez, Lucille's daughter was really our half sister. But Lucille managed to pass her off as her ex-husband's. Why do you think Lucille took off so fast after Mom died? Because she figured it out. Knew that someone was killing off everyone close to the Montgomerys, including her daughter. I got lucky with that one. Marta was stupid enough to come to the office where I work, as the firm had handled Dad's will. She was going to contest it because she'd found out that she was a Montgomery. I guess Lucille must have finally told her the truth. Who knows? Rather than go to one of the partners, Marta started with me. Luckily no one knew that we met. And so . . . I had to improvise.'' Amanda's gaze moved to the hideous family tree with its broken branches. There was a picture of Marta as a child.

Caitlyn felt sick.

Amanda nodded, as if to convince herself. ''Oh, yeah, Marta had to go. Like the rest.'' She hesitated, then added, ''Including Dad.''

Caitlyn was still having trouble tracking the conversation, but Amanda helped her out.

''That's right, I killed him. Didn't know that, did you? No one did. But I did. I was with him in the car that day and I just grabbed hold of the damned steering wheel and forced him into the river. It helped that he was drunk but''— she smiled slyly—''the real trick of it all was that I'd already fiddled with his seat belt, made sure it wouldn't hold.'' She looked up at Caitlyn then, as if seeking approval for being so clever. ''The seat belt was the easy part, though. Cutting off his testicle, that took a little more stamina, let me tell you. I had to surface, then take a couple of dives. Good thing I can hold my breath for a long time.''

Amanda the athlete. Of course. She could swim, shoot, run, row . . . you name it. Always an overachiever. Caitlyn trembled. She remembered seeing Cricket and Sugar in her bed . . . lying beneath the crawling insects, their eyes and mouths and other areas of soft tissue already devoured. Amanda had killed them . . . she'd killed all of them.

And without a doubt she'd planned Caitlyn's fate as well.

It was only a matter of time before she'd kill her. Caitlyn retched at the thought.

Amanda sighed. "You were always such a wimp, Cait. Such a weakling. Once Kelly disappeared, you were never the same. I orchestrated that, too. Wanted you both dead, but though Kelly presumably drowned, you survived and took on part of her personality. I'm surprised I'm the only one who caught on, but then the rest of the family was in such shock. You cracking up actually helped things along. Now, I had a scapegoat—I made sure that you were always around before I knocked someone off. Clever, don't you think?"

You bitch!

The thought was foreign. As if it had come from some-where else—the Kelly personality? No . . . Kelly wasn't dead . . . *Yes, she is. You've known it for a long time, you just wouldn't face it.*

No. I'm Kelly.

What? No . . . you're Caitlyn. You've known it all along. Fight the blackouts, fight the urge to let Kelly take over, to hide from the pain. You have to stay clear. Fight. You have to save yourself. Caitlyn shivered inside, refused to close her eyes and as she did she noticed that her mind was clearing a bit. Her head throbbed but her vision was less blurred, her thoughts more connected.

She heard a noise and glanced to the floor. Oh God. Hannah, poor Hannah was tied and bound, her eyes as big as saucers, sweat rolling down her face.

Alive! She was alive! For a second Caitlyn felt a glimmer of hope, but it was short lived. Amanda wouldn't set them free. Already she was cutting lengths of red and black thread, another braid to be cut and trimmed and added to the macabre family tree. Hannah didn't appear drugged, just frightened out of her mind.

Think, Caitlyn, think! You have to save her. Save yourself. Somehow you've got to get out of here and soon. There isn't much time.

"Oh . . ." Amanda saw her sisters exchange glances. "I

guess you didn't know that Hannah was here, too. She's been waiting for you. I let her see the others—you know, the ones up in your room, Sugar and Cricket—damned interlopers, so she understands what's going to happen."

Behind her gag Hannah made mewling noises.

"Shut up!" Amanda shouted at Hannah, kicking at her, then looked at Caitlyn again. "She always was spoiled. Talked back. She goes, too. And Troy . . . I haven't quite decided. I won't be able to blame his death on you, so I'll have to make it look like he was involved in a horrible accident, kind of like the fire that took Copper Biscayne's life." Arching an eyebrow she said silently that she'd killed Copper.

Hannah was screaming behind her gag, trying to roll on the floor.

"I said, 'shut up!' Do you want me to give you a shot of what I gave Caitlyn? Christ, you've been a pain ever since I called you from Caitlyn's, pretended to be her and invited you 'out to dinner.' And," she added with a touch of sick humor, "uh-oh, you never made it to any restaurant. Instead you disappeared, didn't you? No one could find poor Hannah and even her older sister, Amanda, was frantic." Amanda laughed to herself. "Don't play the victim, okay. This isn't a B-horror flick."

Hannah was blinking hard now. Terrified. Tears welled in her eyes and Caitlyn, too, wanted to crumple. To hide. To pretend it was a dream and hope she'd wake up . . .

Stop it! For crying out loud, there's no one here to help you, Caitie-Did! This is no time to be a wuss. You have to save yourself. To save Hannah. To save me. Kelly's voice was loud as it pounded through Caitlyn's brain.

What could she do . . . *what?* Her mind was racing, searching for answers, her gaze traveling from Hannah's terrorized face to the deadly calm of Amanda . . . Atropos, who kept on braiding, weaving the hideous red and black cords.

"You know, I worked it all out," she was saying, as if letting Caitlyn in on a deep secret. "I made sure I killed all of them right after you'd seen them. Remember when you visited Aunt Alice Ann? Remember you told me about it? And then the attempts on Amanda's life, I made sure you'd been over and in the garage, that you'd touched the TR so that your fingerprints would be on it. Amanda had to appear a victim," she said and Caitlyn realized she was Atropos now, the murderess, a separate entity from her older sister.

Come on, Caitlyn, try to move. Try, damn it!

"I knew you were so fragile, that you wouldn't remember." Atropos looked up from her work for a second. "You should never have told me about your meetings with the shrink. That's what tipped me off. I knew something was happening, that you were changing, becoming stronger, but I didn't realize what it was all about until I witnessed the change myself after your hypnosis therapy. I saw the transformation once, when you were really upset and your adrenalin was pumping. It was weird the first time, seeing the Kelly personality emerge, but then I realized what the trigger was, how to get your heart rate up, how to bring out Kelly when I needed her. But I also figured Rebecca Wade had discovered that you were a split personality, so I broke into her office to make sure. Everything was in the computer files, and as I read and realized that she meant to write a book about you, make you some kind of landmark case, that she, too, had to bite the big one. It was interesting, using the GHB on her, slipping it into her coffee—oh, no, let's see, not coffee." She hesitated and placed a finger along side her jaw. "It was a tall non-fat single latte with light foam, I think." She laughed again, amused at herself. "Didn't you like my little mafia touch of cutting out her tongue to keep her from talking—even though she was already dead?"

Oh, God no. Not Rebecca, too!

Caitlyn felt something. A tingle. Was it her imagination, or could she move one thumb?

Don't listen to what she's saying. Move, for Christ's sake. Move. It's your only chance. Kelly's voice seemed to scream at her from inside her mind.

"But the shrink's notes did help me in one way," Atropos

continued. "They showed me how to bring out the Kelly personality when I needed her. Once I figured out how to make you hyperventilate, get your blood pressure up, I was able to bring Kelly out whenever I needed you to lose track of time and therefore not have an alibi."

Hannah let out a panicked squeak and Caitlyn stared at her, willing her to understand to be calm.

"Clever?" Amanda asked as she tied off the braid.

Not clever, you maniac. Psychotic. Sick. Horrible. Amanda had killed so many people, tortured them, used them and then set it up to blame Caitlyn. But she had feeling in her feet and arms though she didn't lift her head, didn't show any sign that she was recovering. If Amanda had the slightest inclination that she could move so much as one muscle, she'd drug her again. Better, for the moment, until she had her strength, to pretend to be incapacitated.

"So now you have to die, here in your lair . . . I'll claim the roles were reversed, that you captured me. See, look here." She lifted her arms, showed where there were bruises around her wrists. "Handcuffs," she explained, "because it's going to look like you handcuffed me to a post out in the wine cellar and I broke free, we struggled, the tables were turned and you ended up dead, not me."

She tied off another cord. Time was running out.

"It helped that you . . . or was it Kelly . . . made a pathetic attempt to kill Josh. You didn't know that I'd already arrived and caught him drinking. So while he was using the facilities I slipped in the GHB. I ducked outside to the patio to watch and guess what? That's when you showed up. Giving the police a perfect suspect. Josh didn't suspect his drink had been doctored, so he gave you a glass. Bingo, I got two birds with one stone."

She admired her work and slid one eye in Caitlyn's direction. It was all Caitlyn could do to remain still. Her limbs were beginning to tingle, feeling was coming back to her hands and feet.

"You know," Amanda said, "it was fitting, don't you think, the way Josh died? Josh, the bloodsucker, had his own lifeblood drained.'' She finished braiding and again looked over at Caitlyn. For a second Caitlyn's gaze cleared and she focused more clearly on her sister. The horrendous implications curdled her stomach. Amanda or Atropos, she was a murderer, a cold-blooded killer.

''. . . little Jamie was difficult.''

What? She'd killed Jamie?

No, oh, God . . . No! No! No! Agony ricocheted down her body, tore at her with angry claws, bit into any peace of mind she'd found. *Not the baby. Please, please, not my precious, precious baby.*

Caitlyn quaked from the inside out, felt her self begin to slide. No . . . not now, she couldn't step aside now. She couldn't, *wouldn't* let the Kelly personality take over. She had to fight. She had to win. But it was so hard. Caitlyn's personality had always been weaker, but now she wouldn't let go. Couldn't.

''She would have died anyway,'' Atropos insisted with a beatific smile. ''She was a wonderful child, but, we all know she was very, very sick, there really was no hope.''

Caitlyn's heart froze. *How could this monster talk of Jamie so coldly, so clinically?*

''I hated to do it. But I just helped her along, like I did Mother. She was an heir, you know. In the way. Just before I did it, I managed to tape Jamie. She was scared in the hospital. You'd just stepped downstairs for dinner; it was the only time she was alone and I had my little recorder in my pocket when I slipped in to 'visit' her. That's what you heard on the phone, that and my impersonation of her.'' She paused a second then said in a scared little voice, ''Mommy . . . Mommy . . . where are you?''

Caitlyn tried to scream, tried to move. Her baby! Her sister had killed her baby! Adrenalin pumped through her bloodstream. Anger and rage poured through her. Her fingers curled over the edge of the desk.

Hannah let out a muffled wail.

''You're all so pathetic. I find it incredible that we came from the same damned gene pool,'' she said, glowering

down at Hannah before pointing a finger at Caitlyn. "So
now you pose a problem. Are you Caitlyn? Or are you
Kelly? Twins. Two people in one body?" Amanda began
to pace. "I think the best thing to do is to cut you in half.
Right down the middle. One half put somewhere, another
half somewhere else. But it's so messy. So messy . . . I
already had to deal with one mess. Draining Josh's blood
from him and splashing it all around your room wasn't that
easy. You were so out of it, and I needed your handprint to
make the marks. Fortunately you hit your nose when you
fell at Josh's and spilled some blood. I bet the next morning
you freaked, didn't you, when you woke up? And you
thought you had too much to drink?" She laughed then, and
the sound was as evil as Satan's cackle. Caitlyn quivered,
but tried desperately to pull herself together. She could move.
Barely. Her vision was getting less blurred and she thought,
over the droning of Amanda's voice, that she could hear
footsteps. But maybe she was imagining the sound.

"Don't ever let anyone slip GHB into your drink again,
Caitlyn. You really do pass out and not remember." Then
she smiled and stood near the horrendous family tree. "I
guess you won't have to worry about that anymore. You
won't have to worry about anything." Hannah was slowly
inching her body close to Amanda's feet. She caught Caitlyn's eye, and Caitlyn blinked slowly, hoping her sister
would understand.

Amanda was prattling on, but Caitlyn barely heard her,
was concentrating on moving her fingers and listening. Was
someone outside this hideous lair getting closer? Was that
a creak of the stairs? She almost jumped . . . and felt a
measure of control return to her body. If she tried . . . With
all her concentration she attempted to lift the index finger
of her right hand.

Hannah saw the movement and froze.

Amanda was admiring her work. "Now let's see"—
She looked at Caitlyn—"the fun part. I'll cut the cord as
Atropos." With her pair of long-bladed surgical scissors,
she snipped the red and black braid cleanly.

Caitlyn managed to move one finger. Just barely.

"Perfect," Amanda announced, setting the scissors on the desk and turning to the image of the grotesque tree with its frightening pictures. "Pretty soon you'll join the others."

Not if I can help it! Kelly's voice reverberated through her head. *Move your fucking hand, Caitlyn! Grab the scissors!*

Caitlyn strained, inched her hand forward. Amanda's back was turned. Obviously she thought Caitlyn couldn't move, nor had she noticed Hannah slowly getting closer, inching her body near enough that Amanda, with one false step, could trip.

"What're you doing?" Amanda suddenly demanded, glaring at Hannah. "You never learn, do you? I guess I'm going to have to teach you a lesson." She reached for the scissors and swiped them off the table. "Maybe I should show you what happened to Josh?"

Hannah shook her head, began scooting frantically away.

"He bled to death, one little drop at a time." She advanced on Hannah who was cowering between the desk and the rest of the room, wedged and unable to move, just below Caitlyn.

Amanda leaned down, but instead of untying one of Hannah's hands and reaching for her wrist she grabbed a handful of Hannah's hair and pulled it back, exposing her sister's throat.

Oh, God.

The gun! Where is Charles's damned gun?

Caitlyn searched wildly, saw it on a corner of the tarp, seemingly miles away. She could never reach it in time. All too slowly, the drug in Caitlyn's bloodstream was wearing off. She could move. Her toes wiggled slightly. Bit by bit, her muscles were responding. But she didn't have time to wait and she couldn't reach the damned pistol. Amanda was drawing an imaginary line on Hannah's throat and Hannah was quivering in fear, trying to pull away, but tied in such a manner that she could do nothing but cry and whimper.

"Watch, Caitlyn. Can you see?" Amanda asked. "You're next. That's what the tarp is for, to catch the blood splatter. As soon as Hannah passes out, it'll be your turn. Now."

She opened the scissors. The blades glimmered wickedly. Ever so slowly, drawing the drama out, Amanda placed the open blade against Hannah's white throat as she struggled. A drop of blood showed against her skin.

It was now or never.

Do something. Do it now!

Caitlyn strained. Her hand moved with a jerk. In her peripheral vision, Amanda saw her and reacted. Sliced quickly. Just as Hannah squirmed away. Blood spurted as she lunged at Caitlyn, bloody scissors raised. "You little bitch. You thought you could get away?"

The blades swung down, straight at Caitlyn's face, but she shifted, threw all of her weight to one side and Amanda missed, the scissors hit the desk hard and Caitlyn kicked, one shoe jamming into Amanda's abdomen.

Startled, Amanda fell backward, tripping over Hannah. Caitlyn scrabbled for the scissors as they clattered across the desk. On the floor Hannah was gurgling and spitting blood. Oh, God, it was all over.

More noises. Amanda finally heard the sound of footsteps as she nearly fell onto the gun. "What the hell?"

"Police. Open up!" A man's voice rang through the underground rooms.

"Shit." Amanda grabbed Charles's pistol and her eyes were bright with anger. She glared down at Caitlyn. "This is your fault, isn't it? You led them to me." Her eyes narrowed.

"This is the police. Open the door. Now!"

"Go screw yourselves," Amanda muttered and leveled the gun at Caitlyn's head. "This isn't what I had in mind, Caitie-Did, but it'll have to do."

With a muted squeal, Hannah rolled under Amanda's feet. Blood smeared over the tarp.

Caitlyn swept the scissors into her hand and lunged, throwing all her weight at her sister.

The leap was clumsy, awkward.

Amanda stumbled. She fell backward over Hannah with Caitlyn atop her.

The gun blasted. Rocked the tiny room in a deafening roar.

Hot pain screeched through Caitlyn's abdomen. With all her strength she plunged the scissors deep into Amanda's neck and rolled away.

In a horrifying red plume blood spurted from Amanda's throat and she screamed hideously.

The door to the room crashed open.

Caitlyn was gasping, in agony, her skin on fire. *Hannah, oh, God, please don't let Hannah die!*

Weapons drawn police officers burst through the doorway. Guns pointed at her as the blackness came, pulling her under, a balm against the hot pain in her stomach.

"Get the EMTs," a man shouted. It was a familiar voice. Reed. That was it. Detective Pierce Reed.

"They're on their way," a woman said, but Caitlyn couldn't see her and the buzz in her head was louder than the voices, drowning out the noise.

"We need them now! Jesus Christ, they're all gonna bleed to death!"

The voices were far away, from a distance and she was fading away. Images floated behind her eyes, a kaleidoscope of pictures. Kelly laughing as a child, teasing her and running in the sun then the explosion, a burst of fire and light that lit up the night . . . Griffin sharing secrets in the woods . . . Nana with her cold eyes and colder touch . . . Charles lying bleeding in the forest, no longer able to come into the room at night and Jamie, sweet, sweet Jamie giggling as they built a sand castle on the beach one summer . . . then there was Adam. Handsome. Strong. Patient, dark hair and enigmatic smile . . . knowing eyes and firm lips . . . Her throat closed and over the far-off din of shoes scraping and the remote voices of people yelling, she imagined what she would say to him if only given the chance.

Oh, please . . . Adam . . . forgive me for not being stronger.

Thirty-Four

Adam stalked from one end of the hospital's waiting room to the other. He was alone, wearing a path in the blue carpet that stretched between a dying potted palm and a plate-glass window overlooking the parking lot.

It had been twelve hours since the shooting, four of which Caitlyn had been in surgery to remove the bullet that had torn through her spleen in her struggle with Amanda. Caitlyn had survived; Amanda had not. Which was just as well, Adam thought angrily. Amanda Montgomery had killed and tortured too many as it was.

Hannah was hanging on by a thread, transfusions not yet making enough difference to ensure her life. He sent up a quick prayer for her and Caitlyn as well.

Caitlyn worried him. Already mentally frail, how would she react when she came face-to-face with the fact that she'd killed her sister, the very sister who had murdered most of her family, including Caitlyn's daughter? How would she accept the news that she suffered from DID and possibly schizophrenia, that she was unique to the world of psychology by taking on her sister's personality? He rubbed his jaw and felt a day's worth of whiskers.

Guilt had been with him for hours. Gnawing at his brain. Tearing at his soul. He should have told her the truth from the get-go, should have risked telling the police about Rebecca. Maybe things would have been better. Maybe lives would have been saved. Maybe some of the carnage could have been avoided. Maybe Caitlyn would never have had to suffer.

Mother of God, he'd blown it. If only—

"Doctor Hunt?" A nurse was approaching him.

His head snapped up. "Yes."

"Mrs. Bandeaux's awake and the police are through interviewing her. She's asking for you."

"Let's go." Adam felt immense relief.

The nurse didn't move, but stared at him with knowing eyes. "Just so that you understand it's only for a few minutes. The doctor wants her to rest."

"No problem."

The nurse cracked a smile. "She's in three-oh-seven. The elevators are just down the hall, around the corner."

"Thanks." He half jogged to the bank of elevators, passing an aide pushing a wheelchair. Now that he was finally allowed to see Caitlyn, he couldn't put it off a second later. He needed to see that she'd survived the ordeal. That she was really Caitlyn, that she understood about her condition, that . . . oh, hell, so many things.

He'd been such a shortsighted fool. Rather than wait for an elevator car, he threw himself into the stairwell and took the stairs to the third floor two at a time. What would she say when she saw him again? How would she react? He'd have to tell her all of the truth. Everything.

Through the doors and around a corner he jogged, nearly plowing into Detective Reed who lingered near the door to Caitlyn's room. Reed was rumpled, his hair a mess, his tie loose, his jaw ragged with beard growth, his eyes bloodshot from lack of sleep. Probably a reflection of Adam himself.

"I thought you guys were finished."

"We are. But I wanted to ask you a few more questions, just to tie up some loose ends."

"Fine, but first—"

"Yeah, go in and see her. I'll go grab a cup of coffee in the cafeteria, if the media lets me. They're all over this one." He shook his head wearily. "Have been from the onset. You can meet me downstairs when you're done here."

"I will." Adam nodded, then strode into the sterile looking room.

Caitlyn was awake. Lying flat on her back, IVs running into one arm. Her hair was mussed and she looked as if she'd lost ten pounds in the last twenty-four hours, but as he walked closer to the bed, her eyes cleared. And they were angry as hell. "You knew," she charged before he could say a word. "You knew about the split personality—and don't worry, just for the record, I'm Caitlyn now, not Kelly."

"I didn't know. I guess I should have, but I only figured out the truth when I found Rebecca's disks. I was going to tell you as soon as—"

"You bastard!"

"I know how you feel—"

"How could you? Are you crazy?" She heard her own words and rolled her eyes. "You couldn't have any idea how I feel, what I've been through." He took a step closer and she leveled him with her gaze, silently warning him to keep his distance. "As to my sessions, were those even real? Were they? The way I understand it, you were married to Rebecca. You weren't interested in me. You were just trying to find your wife and—"

"Ex-wife."

"Enough of a wife that you cared for her, that you were willing to come down here and lie to me and . . . and—"

"And fall in love with you," he said flatly.

The room was suddenly silent. He realized that his hands had balled into fists, that his nerves were strung tight as piano wire, that he'd wanted to tell her the truth ever since realizing it himself.

"In love?" she whispered suspiciously.

"Yes."

She rolled her eyes. "Give me a break."

"Okay, it's not how it started, it's not what I intended, but I swear to you, Caitlyn, that's what happened."

"In between all the murders. And abductions. And damned lies. Get real, Adam." Her jaw was set, the flicker of happiness that he'd seen in her eyes only days ago, now extinguished. Probably forever. It was no use to try and tell her differently.

"I'm sorry." He stuffed his hands into the front pockets of his jeans.

"You should be. Not that I believe you."

"Listen, Caitlyn, I don't blame you for being upset. Really." His jaw worked with the effort not to rush to her and try and convince her how much he cared. "Look, I want you to know that I'm sending all of Rebecca's notes on you, her paper files and a computer disk, to you by registered mail. You can do what you want with them, take them to another psychiatrist, give them to the police, it doesn't matter. They're valuable. You were a unique case. That's what Rebecca was looking for. She had an agent and a publisher interested."

"So she thought of me as a lab specimen, too." Caitlyn blinked against an onslaught of tears. Her eyes filled but she didn't let any drops slide down her cheeks. "And it cost Rebecca her life."

"I don't think that's the way it started but go ahead and look through everything and judge for yourself." He considered touching the back of her hand, but the rage in her gaze convinced him it wasn't a good idea. "When you get out of here, if you want to discuss anything, I would be glad to—"

"I don't think so," she clipped out, and he didn't push it. She'd been through hell and back a dozen times.

"I'll be waiting."

"Really, don't bother."

One side of his mouth lifted. "No bother at all."

"Go back to Wisconsin or Ohio or wherever it is you're from and leave me alone."

"Is that what you really want?"

"Yes." She glared up at him. "Since you asked, you may as well know that what I really want is to put this nightmare behind me." She blinked hard and clenched her jaw. "I want my daughter back. I want my siblings and mother alive. I want to see Kelly, not be her, I . . . I want this damned thing never to have happened, but it did. And somehow I've got to put it all into some kind of perspective. So in order for me to be right, really right, I'm going to need time and lots of it."

"I can wait."

"Don't bother," she said. "No one can wait that long."

He touched her hand then, squeezed her fingers for the span of a heartbeat. "Just watch."

Reed didn't much like the shrink. But as they talked in the cafeteria, he started to revise his opinion. Either the guy was one hell of an actor or he really cared for Caitlyn Bandeaux. Well, someone should. The woman had lost about every bit of her family. Troy had survived and Hannah, who had been marked for death, might pull out of it, though the doctors were saying it was touch and go. She was young and strong, but she'd lost a lot of blood and the scar at the base of her throat would be a jagged reminder of the one inside. God, who could turn out normal after that? Not that any of the Montgomerys even brushed normal.

So even if physically she managed to survive, there was the psychological angle to consider . . . Hell, the remaining Montgomerys could keep all the shrinks in the area in BMWs for the rest of their lives. Morrisette had been right. Looney-effin'-tunes.

Right now the psychologist—and he was one legitimately, Morrisette had checked—was slumped in a plastic cafeteria chair while shredding his empty coffee cup. Reed was convinced that Hunt didn't have anything to do with the killings. But he did have information. "So you're not giving up the notes on Caitlyn Bandeaux."

"No. I told you, that's privileged information. You'll have to subpoena me."

"Which we will do."

"Fine." Adam's lips formed a thin line.

"We're trying to understand why your wife was killed."

"My ex-wife. We were divorced quiet a few years back."

"But you came down here to find out what happened to her."

"That's right."

"You should have come to the police."

Reed lifted a shoulder. "That's the beauty of retrospect. One sees so much more clearly."

The conversation wasn't over, but as many questions as Reed asked, he didn't find out much more information on Caitlyn or Kelly. Hunt wasn't going to give the police or anyone else the material on any of the Montgomerys, and he seemed determined to camp out here at the hospital until Caitlyn was officially released. Fine. He could help fend off some of the reporters who had gathered.

Reed tossed his empty coffee cup into the wastebasket, walked out a back door and saw Nikki Gillette lurking near his police car. "Detective Reed," she called, waving a hand. God, would she never give up?

"No comment."

"I haven't even asked a question."

"Good." He slid into his car.

"Look, Detective, the citizens of Savannah need to know the truth."

"The Public Information Officer is giving a statement."

"But you led the investigation. If I could have a few minutes, buy you a cup of coffee—"

"No, thanks." He slid behind the wheel of the Crown Vic. Obviously the woman didn't understand the word 'no.' But then she'd grown up privileged, the daughter of Judge Ron "Big Daddy" Gillette, a spoiled pretty girl not understanding that she couldn't have everything she wanted. Driving off, he glanced in his rearview mirror to see her standing, arms folded under her chest, hair glinting red-blond in the late afternoon sunlight.

At the station, things were buzzing. He ducked past another reporter, Max Whatever-His-Name, the square-jawed pushy son of a bitch who reported for WKAM, by hustling up the back stairs. Reed caught up with Morrisette at his office. "What have you got?" he asked.

"Plenty." She looked tired as hell. "They're dredging the river in a spot between that house Caitlyn Bandeaux rented for"—she made air quotes with her fingers—"Kelly AKA Kacie Griffin. Jesus, can you imagine paying for a place for your split personality? Makes you wonder how much she really knew about herself. Anyway, a fisherman saw something in the river and we sent down divers. It's a white Mazda with plates that match Marta Vasquez's."

"She inside?"

Morrisette looked him square in the eye. "Someone is."

"Montoya know?"

"He's already there."

"Shit. Let's go."

They drove just under the speed of sound. Morrisette was at the wheel, juggling a lit cigarette, her cell phone and traffic. By the time they arrived the car had been hoisted, dripping and dirty, from the bottom of the river. A woman, so decomposed it was hard to tell much about her, was positioned behind the wheel, no doubt another of Amanda Montgomery's victims. Hell, she'd been a sicko. Reed had seen the sterile lab with its macabre family tree. The lab had been sealed off, the crime scene team going over it for trace evidence.

Now, looking at the car, Reed figured Diane Moses's team would be racking up hours of overtime.

Montoya was there. Back ramrod stiff as he watched the car being lowered onto the riverbank. Morrisette and Reed approached him.

"You okay?" Morrisette asked, reaching into her purse for her smokes and offering one to Montoya.

He took the cigarette and lit up. "Yeah."

Reed wasn't buying it. "This her car?"

"Yep."

"I'm sorry," Morrisette said.

"Aren't we all?" Montoya's jaw was set, and when it was suggested that he might not want to see the badly decomposed body, he'd stood fast, his dark eyes going over what was left of his girlfriend. It would take a while to check the dental records, but they all knew that the remains behind the wheel were probably those of Marta Vasquez. A muscle worked in Montoya's jaw, but he calmed it by taking a long drag on his smoke.

There wasn't much more Reed or Morrisette could do.

There wasn't much anyone could.

Caitlyn was itching to get home. She hated lying around the hospital, fielding calls from reporters, seeing her picture on the front of the paper, being poked and prodded by doctors and looked at with curiosity by psychiatrists. Even some of the staff treated her differently and when she was supposed to have been sleeping, she overheard a couple of aides talking about her as if she were some kind of tabloid princess or lab specimen.

Not that home would be that much better.

But it had been five days, she was recovering and the doctors had agreed to release her. Like it or not, it was time to face her new life. As one person. No more of the split personality stuff . . . at least she hoped not. Adam had stayed at the hospital most of the time. She'd constantly told him to go home, but had never had the heart to have a nurse throw him out, though the thought had occurred to her. He'd even taken breaks and seen that Oscar had been fed and walked. He seemed genuinely concerned about her.

But Caitlyn didn't trust him. Not yet. Nor had she forgiven him.

Granted, she was thawing, and there was the nagging suspicion tucked far back in her mind that had circumstances been different she might have fallen in love with him.

However, things weren't different. Nor would she have met him if she hadn't been some bizarre head case.

She couldn't forget that Adam was an accomplished liar. A very accomplished liar. And she figured she was really little more to him than an interesting case, a unique case, a case that might be able to garner him some fame and fortune by means of a lucrative book contract and movie deal. If he wasn't interested in her because he was a greedy son of a bitch, then maybe he was hanging out because of guilt. If that was the situation, then it was his problem.

She struggled into her shorts and T-shirt. The bandage around her middle would be with her for a couple of weeks, but the drain had been removed and she was given a clean bill of health by her doctors, told to come back for a post-op checkup. Her mind was another matter, but she felt stronger mentally than she had in years and so far, the personality of Kelly hadn't manifested itself . . . except that Caitlyn had her own sharp tongue and new-found determination, remnants of her twin's stronger personality.

The good news was that Hannah was going to live. One of the few Montgomery children to have avoided Amanda or Atropos's deadly scheme.

A nurse with a wheelchair appeared in the doorway. She must've expected Caitlyn to protest. "Hospital policy," she insisted, dismissing any of Caitlyn's complaints before they were voiced. "Is someone coming to get you?"

"My brother said he'd be here at ten." Adam had offered to pick her up but Caitlyn had declined, insisting that Troy, less enthusiastic, could pick her up.

"Then we'd better get going." The nurse checked her watch. "It's five after now."

An aide with wild, curly hair clipped in springy clumps gathered up her personal items, the cards and flowers, and pushed them on a cart that rattled and jangled Caitlyn's nerves.

She was still on pain pills, and sleeping pills. She was still suffering from nightmares and her doctor had put her in touch with a new psychiatrist. Her first session was a week from Friday. She wondered if it would ever end, if she'd ever be completely normal.

Not likely, considering what you've been through . . . just take it one day at a time.

As the nurse pushed her down the hallway she thought of the past few days. Would it be possible to put all this behind her, she wondered as she was wheeled into the elevator car. God, it was hard to think of Amanda as Atropos, the murderess, that she'd killed everyone in the family including Josh and Jamie. There were so many things Caitlyn didn't want to believe . . . that Rebecca Wade had wanted to write a book about her, that Adam had been married to Rebecca, that Amanda had set her up, staged Josh's fake suicide to make it look like a bungled coverup on Caitlyn's part. Amanda had stolen her lipstick, tripped over the cord of the alarm clock, sneaked Jamie's bunny out of the house, had pretended to be her daughter on the telephone and tried to drive Caitlyn crazy—well, even more crazy than she really was. And to think that Adam had known some of the truth and held it back from her, at least for a little while. It still made her blood boil.

Don't dwell on the past. Move forward.

Give Adam a chance.

She snorted in disgust. Adam had lied to her. Used her. Just like every other man in her life.

But he's hung around for a while now. Isn't that something?

The voice nagging her was her own, no longer sounding like Kelly's. Now Caitlyn wondered if the voice had ever belonged to her twin. Kelly was dead. Though her body hadn't been found after the boating accident, everyone had accepted the fact that she'd died. Only Caitlyn had fought the notion and so her personality, already shattered, had split into a second entity. If the psychiatrists were to be believed. She'd been told that she had years of therapy ahead of her, that eventually she would be able to mold the Kelly personality into her own, to be one whole person rather than two distinct entities. It would take time but she would be complete, her own person, happy and secure, left with only memories of her twin.

The elevator doors opened on the first floor and Caitlyn froze. In the lobby of the hospital, camped out near the doors, were two reporters. Max O'Dell, square jawed and dressed in a sport coat, polo shirt and khakis was with a cameraman from WKAM and Nikki Gillette was flipping through a battle-scarred magazine in a lounge near the information desk.

Great.

Just what she needed.

Both reporters saw her within the same millisecond and pounced. "Mrs. Bandeaux, if I could have a word," Max said, striding closer and flashing his most charming smile.

"You know hospital policy," the nurse said.

"No comment." Caitlyn returned his aren't-we-the-best-of-buddies grin with a cold replication. She turned to Nikki who, backpack slung over one shoulder, was swiftly approaching. "The same goes for you."

The nurse pushed her wheelchair through the double sets of glass doors and the aide rolled the rattling cart of flowers behind them. Undaunted, Max and Nikki trailed like bloodhounds. It was all Caitlyn could do not to scream at them that she wanted to be left alone, that she didn't want to see her face or name splashed all over the evening news or the front page of the *Savannah Sentinel*, that she just wanted some peace in her life.

Outside Adam was waiting, one jean-clad hip resting against the fender of his double-parked rig. A beat-up leather jacket was stretched across his shoulders and one side of his mouth lifted at the sight of her. He opened the passenger-side door, as if he expected her to climb inside.

"Wait a minute, where's Troy?" Caitlyn demanded.

"Hung up at the bank."

"What? I just talked to him an hour ago."

Adam's eyes glinted with a bit of mischief. "It was last-minute."

"Bull."

"That's what he said."

"Maybe we should call him." Caitlyn didn't have any time for this nonsense.

"My cell's in the car."

"Good, maybe you could bring it to me," she said, then realized the nurse was becoming impatient, the aide had pushed the cart of flowers and gifts to the back of the SUV and Max O'Dell, Nikki Gillette and the cameraman were all hovering nearby, waiting for a story, watching the drama playing out between Caitlyn and Adam Hunt.

"Come on. I don't bite." His eyes actually sparked for an instant. "Well, not usually."

"Maybe I do."

"Oh, you definitely do."

She narrowed her eyes at him. "Very funny."

She glanced over her shoulder. Was the cameraman really filming this? Oh, for God's sake! "Isn't there something more newsworthy than me leaving the hospital?" she asked of Max O'Dell before turning back to Adam. "I've changed my mind. Let's go."

He helped her into the rig, and she wondered if she was making the worst mistake of her life.

That would be going some, considering your track record. Give the guy a chance. Just hear him out. What have you got to lose?

She didn't want to think about it. She watched him climb into the driver's seat and twist on the ignition. He smelled of leather and the faint scent of some masculine cologne. She remembered kissing him, the feel of his lips on hers and quickly killed the thought.

"Let's see if we can lose the press," he said as he gunned the accelerator, wheeled out of the parking lot and she relaxed against the tufted leather. She was just too tired to fight. Glancing out the window to the sunny day beyond she wondered again about falling in love with him. Would it be so wrong? Wouldn't he just break her heart?

Oh, get over it. Your heart's been broken before. If he turns out to be a loser, you can always throw him out on his ass. Come on, Caitie-Did. Go for it.

It was almost as if she could hear her sister's advice again and she figured that every once in a while it didn't hurt to imagine that she was listening to her twin. Every once in a while she needed to remember. Even now she could recall Kelly as a child, pushing her to climb a tree, or swim in a deeper part of the river, of laughing at her and teasing her, the girl who looked so much like her and was so different. As a teenager Kelly had been daring, nearly as accomplished as Amanda at sports and yet feminine and a tad naughty. She'd been so confident and free on the day of the boating accident . . . Yes, it was good for Caitlyn to remember. She just wouldn't let it go too far.

Hell, Caitie-Did, Kelly seemed to say now, *give Adam a break. You're an idiot if you can't see that he's in love with you.*

Caitlyn glanced over at him as he shoved a pair of sunglasses over the bridge of his nose and angled the Jeep through traffic. As if feeling the weight of her stare, his lips twitched and he placed his hand over hers to give it a quick squeeze before letting go.

Her heart stupidly skipped a beat.

"Just drive," she said.

"Your wish is my command."

"Yeah, right."

He laughed and so did she. Maybe he wasn't so bad after all.

Time would tell.

It always did.

* * *

"So that does it. The Bandeaux case is officially closed," Morrisette said a week later as she strode into Reed's office. She was waving a check and smiling broadly.

"What's that?" Reed looked up from his paperwork and leaned back in his chair.

"Money from Bart. Can you believe it? He's actually caught up with the child support. First time in years!" She plopped onto the corner of his desk and folded the check into her pocket.

"He win the lottery?"

"Close enough. An aunt died, left him a little and before he ran out and bought a new pickup—oh, yeah, he did that, too—his conscience got the better of him and he decided to pay me what he owed me before I sicced a bevy of lawyers onto his ass. What a prince. Did I say prince? I meant dickhead." She ran fingers through her spiked hair. "So—we're all clear on the Montgomery thing?"

"Think so. Paperwork has to be caught up, but yeah, we're done. The remains dragged out of the river did turn out to be Marta Vasquez's. Her mother's having a memorial for her. I talked to Lucille on the phone and she gave me the whole story. That she had a one-night stand with her boss."

At the lift of Morrisette's eyebrows he shrugged. "One-night stand, that's what she says and does it really matter? The point is who would have thought Marta Vasquez was another one of Cameron Montgomery's illegitimate kids? Man, did that guy ever keep his pants on?"

"Bad luck for her that she ran into Amanda, or Atropos or whoever she was, before anyone else."

"One more kid after the old man's money—she just got a late start. Didn't realize Cameron was her father until around last December when Lucille told her on the phone."

"And she didn't bother telling Montoya about it?"

"She didn't tell anyone. Except Amanda, as she was part of the law firm that handled Cameron's estate." Reed leaned back in his chair and rotated the muscles of his shoulders.

"So where is Montoya?" Morrisette asked as if the

thought had just jumped into her head, but Reed recognized the signs.

In the few short days Montoya had been in Savannah, tough-as-nails Detective Morrisette had taken an interest in the younger man. That was the trouble with Sylvie; she was always swearing off men, then falling for the next guy who caught her eye. Reed had to give her the bad news. "Montoya already took off."

If Morrisette was disappointed, she hid it as she scanned some of the reports littering his desk.

"He said something about taking a leave of absence from the New Orleans force. Seems to think his partner, Bentz, will understand. It's just a matter of convincing the higher-ups."

"Why doesn't he come back here?"

"Probably a lot of bad memories."

"Yeah, but *some* woman might make him forget Marta."

Reed leveled his gaze at her. "As long as *some* woman doesn't get too involved with a young buck ten or twelve years her junior."

"Or even seven?"

"Yeah, even seven."

Morrisette's eyes twinkled, but she changed the subject. "I hear Dickie Ray Biscayne is still after the Montgomerys for his share of their estate. He's kept Flynn Donahue on retainer. Now he wants Cricket and Sugar's share and maybe even Amanda's. It seems he learned something about wrongful death from Josh Bandeaux."

"Greedy son of a bitch."

"Aren't they all?" Morrisette asked. "Ian Drummond, Amanda's ex, is being courted for a tell-all book and he wants his wife's share of the estate, even though he was banging Sugar Biscayne. For a guy who just lost his two lovers, he sure has his hand out. Money must be able to heal a broken heart."

"That I wouldn't know about."

"Hannah's expected to recover. She's talking about moving away. Starting over. Putting this behind her. If that's possible.''

Reed nodded. ''I don't blame her. She was involved with Bandeaux, too. And then her sister tries to kill her by slitting her throat.'' He shook his head. Savannah had a reputation for scandalous stories, but this topped them all. ''Hell, Rebecca Wade sure stepped into it, didn't she?''

''And ended up one more victim.''

''In a long string.''

''No pun intended,'' Morrisette said and Reed was reminded of Atropos with her surgical scissors and braided cords. ''What a psychopath! And when it gets right down to it, Amanda killed for the Montgomery money.''

''Nah.'' Reed wasn't buying it. ''She killed for the killing's sake.'' He thought of all the victims, how they'd suffered, how much thought and effort Amanda, as Atropos, had put into the murders. ''It was a thrill for her, a way she could prove that she was smarter than the others, that she deserved to inherit the old man's wealth. She loved it—got off on it.''

Morrisette nodded. ''Point taken. What a shame. An effin' shame.'' Morrisette was religiously putting money into the damned Hello Kitty bank, but her language still suffered. At least her kids would end up with a decent education— hell, they could probably go effin' ivy league.

''I wouldn't be surprised if Adam Hunt wrote a book on it, you know, pick up where his ex-wife left off,'' Reed said. ''I hear that book publishers are sniffin' around him and Caitlyn Bandeaux. Even talk of a movie deal. How about that?''

''Someone will probably do it.'' She scratched an elbow. ''You know, if Amanda killed everyone to inherit the fortune, she sure took her damned time about it. First Baby Parker and then years later she escalates? Come on. That's not usual.''

''Nothing about this case was.'' Reed had thought about the time frame. ''Between you and me, I think she snapped, mean really snapped when she found out her husband was having a fling with Sugar Biscayne, but then, I don't really know. I'm not the shrink. It's damned ironic that she was setting up Caitlyn, using all the rumors about the mental illness running through the family when she was the one who thought she was other people, had delusions of power, a real head case. She seemed like a split personality with all that Atropos crap. Caitlyn Bandeaux did the taxpayers of the city a big favor by blowing her away." He glanced out his window to the bright day outside. Savannah was a grand old lady of a town, one he'd lived in twice, but she had her secrets. Dark, ever-present secrets.

"How would you like to have that on your conscience— killing your own sister?" Morrisette asked.

"It wouldn't bother me a bit. Remember this is a sister who had killed my kid, my mother, my father, my husband and everyone else she could murder. How would I feel about putting her out of her misery?" Reed flashed a grin. "I'd feel just fine about it. Guaranteed."

"Yeah, right."

"But I'm sure Caitlyn Bandeaux is going to have years of therapy. Maybe even a lifetime of it."

"At least she's alive. And I hear she's been seeing Adam Hunt."

"Romantically?"

Morrisette lifted a shoulder. "He *is* a hunk."

"You would know."

"Amen, brother. Amen!" She slapped his desk as her pager went off. "What now?" She glanced at the readout and hopped to the floor. "It's my sitter. I've got to run. I'm taking the rest of the day off to be with my kids. Takin' 'em swimming, now that they're both healthy again. We're going shopping on Bart's fuckin' money. And don't worry, I've got another bank on the shopping list. The first one's full up."

"You getting another one of those kitty things?"

"Is there any other kind? If you need anything, don' call." She was out the door in a heartbeat.

"Drive safely," he yelled after her. "Remember we have speed limits in this town and they're strictly enforced."

"Up yours, Reed!" But her laughter echoed back to him. Sylvie Morrisette was okay, once you got past the prickly I'm-as-good-as-any-man-cop attitude. He could do worse. Lots worse.

Epilogue

"You want to go for a ride?" Caitlyn asked Oscar as she hurried down the stairs. "Well, come on." The little dog bounded ahead of her through the door to the garage. The Lexus was already filled with small bouquets of holly boughs and bright poinsettias, Christmas bouquets for the cemetery.

While Oscar stuck his nose out of the open window, she drove through the town where grand old houses were festooned in lights and greenery and ribbons. It was nearly Christmas, and Caitlyn felt better than she had in a long, long while. She was going to a new therapist, one with whom she wasn't personally involved, and she was even considering allowing Adam to write her story. Not that he'd asked; he'd never mentioned it once in the past six months and he'd been with her nearly every day. He wanted her to move in with him and there was the hint of marriage, but she wasn't ready. She needed more time to find out who she was, Caitlyn Montgomery Bandeaux. Until she was certain that she was mentally whole again, she didn't want to become a part of someone else's life.

She parked near the family plot and snapped on Oscar's leash. The wind was brisk for Savannah, rustling through the dry leaves and billowing the Spanish moss. With Oscar tugging at the leash, she carried flowers to each grave, holding back tears when she saw her daughter's headstone.

Her throat thick, she kissed her fingertips and brushed them over the cold marble. "I love you," she whispered and sent up a prayer for Jamie's sweet little soul. Some pain would never completely go away, she knew, and she accepted it.

But the terror of the horrible ordeal with Amanda was fading, blurring into her past, very rarely keeping her awake at night.

From the corner of her eye, she saw him and smiled through her tears. Adam had said he'd meet her here, in this place where he'd first approached her. Her doubts about him had faded with time and she'd found him to be warm and gentle, a considerate lover who was patient or passionate. The first time they'd made love since she'd left the hospital, she'd been worried, concerned that it might spark the return of her Kelly personality. She needn't have been concerned. The entire night of kissing and touching and exploring, she'd been herself, feeling for the first time the joy of loving him.

They'd been outside for a walk with Oscar when the sky had opened up. Rain pelted them as they'd dashed back to the house and dripping, hurried into the kitchen. She'd nearly tripped over Oscar's leash and Adam had caught her. They'd both tumbled to the floor, she on top of him and Adam had pulled her close, pressed his face into the cleft of her breasts visible through her soaked blouse, then begun to kiss her. She'd responded eagerly and this time as they'd come together, slick, wet bodies joining, she'd experienced each emotion, every tingling sensation—his hands on her buttocks, his tongue on her nipples, his erection hard against her abdomen before he'd finally slid between her legs and made love to her as if he'd never stop.

Even now the memory was crystal clear. She hadn't lost herself in the Kelly personality. In fact as the weeks passed, that personality seemed to be fading. Caitlyn knew that someday she would be completely whole. And Adam would be at her side. She turned to him and fought the tears burning the back of her eyes.

"Hey," she said as he approached.

"Hey, back at you." He saw the tears in her eyes. "You okay?"

"You're the shrink. You tell me."

"My professional opinion? You're hopeless."

She socked him in the arm.

"My personal opinion?"

She arched an eyebrow.

"You are definitely okay." He wrapped his arms around her. "Maybe beyond 'okay.' Even perfect."

She laughed. "God, Adam, enough, okay. Perfect?" She thought about what she'd been through, what they'd shared, how well he knew her. "You need to get out more."

"Good point. How about dinner?"

"Mmm. Maybe."

"I'll cook."

She laughed again. "Then I think I'll pass."

He squeezed her. "You're bad."

"From perfect to bad in ten seconds. That must be some kind of record."

"Come on, let's go home. *You* can cook."

She rolled her eyes as Oscar ran around them, wrapping the leash around their legs. "No way. Let's go out."

"Whatever you want." He dropped a kiss on her lips and she felt warm inside. Safe. Complete. Which was silly.

"I think I just changed my mind," she said, knowing her eyes were glimmering with mischief. "Let's stay in. All night."

"So it's pizza and beer."

"To start with," she said, unwrapping Oscar's leash and trying not to trip. "After that, who knows? Maybe we could do some role playing."

A grin slid from one side of his mouth to the other. "That could be dangerous, don't you think?"

"Oh, I don't think," she said and kissed him again. Taking his hand, she pulled him to the car. "I know."

Dear Reader,

I didn't intend to write companion stories set in Savannah, but that's just how it worked out. The characters of Detective Pierce Reed and reporter Nikki Gillette grabbed me from the second I sat down and started writing THE NIGHT BEFORE, so it seemed a natural that they would also appear in THE MORNING AFTER.

Nikki is one of those characters I just can't forget and so I decided to catch up with her again and write another novel about her, Detective Reed and the intriguing city of Savannah, Georgia. That book, TELL ME, will be available in hardcover and as an e-book in July 2013. It's another twisted tale that I think you'll like.

As in THE MORNING AFTER, Nikki takes center stage again. It's a few years after the "Grave Robber" case and she's engaged to Pierce. Even so, and despite his pleas, she's not about to give up her career. Investigative journalism is in her blood and now one of the state's most celebrated and infamous murderesses, Blondell O'Henry, is getting out of prison. Because of a technicality, Blondell, a beautiful and secretive woman who was found guilty of murdering her own daughter and harming her other children in a blood-chilling act of violence, is about to be a free woman again. The town is in an uproar. Nikki, who's close to the story already as she was friends with the murdered girl, is determined to get an exclusive and ferret out the truth. What she doesn't realize is that she's about to step into a deadly, well-laid trap where she will become the ultimate victim . . .

A full list of all my books is available at www.lisajackson. com. If you want to contact me, you can reach me on the website where there are excerpts and contests and the latest breaking news. Or you can follow me on Facebook – become a fan and interact with me there. Join the conversation! Trust me, it gets interesting!

Keep Reading!

Lisa Jackson

Lisa Jackson

You Don't Want to Know

Two years ago, Ava Garrison's cherished two-year-old son Noah disappeared.

There was no ransom demand; his body was never found. Ava, wracked with grief, has been in and out of mental institutions since that night.

Back on the family estate now, though, Ava is having strangely lifelike visions – visions of Noah on the dock of her island estate, or in his nursery. Visions that seem to be urging her to risk her own life ...

Ava doesn't trust anyone now. Not her husband. Not her cousins. Not the servants her wealth is paying for.

They know more than they are saying. They appear to be anxious about her well-being. But the truth is more dangerous than Ava can imagine; and the price is higher than she ever thought to pay.

HODDER

Lisa Jackson

Devious

When a troubled novice is found garrotted in St Marguerite's cathedral, the first detectives called in are Bentz and Montoya. And Montoya knows who she is – Sister Camille was once his brother's girlfriend. He even knows the prime suspect: Father Frank O'Toole, rumoured to be the father of Camille's unborn child.

The deeper the investigation goes, the eerier it gets. More nuns are dying, brutally slaughtered by someone who seems to know their darkest secrets.

Bentz is sure Father O'Toole is their man. But arresting him is another matter. And there are other suspects, too, including a ruthless murderer who is supposed to have died years ago.

Has the monstrous killer known as Father John returned to New Orleans? Or is the truth even more twisted and terrifying?

HODDER

Lisa Jackson's books are number one bestsellers in America. She now has over twenty million copies of her books in print in nineteen languages. She lives with her family and a rambunctious pug in the Pacific Northwest. Readers can visit her website at www.lisajackson.com, become her friend on Facebook and check out her blog at lisajacksonauthor.blogspot.com.

The Night Before

'Adam,' Caitlyn said, and her voice sounded unnatural,
even to her own ears. 'There's something you should
know. I don't think I'm crazy – I mean,
I pray that I'm not, but . . .

The morning after Josh was killed, I woke up
and . . . and there was blood all over my bedroom.
I'm afraid that somehow I'm responsible for
my husband's death.'

You think you killed him?'

That's just it. I don't know. I don't remember.
But the police are saying that my blood type was
at the murder scene.'